STORM QUEST

STORM QUEST

Book 9 in the Quest Series

Lisa Wright DeGroodt

iUniverse, Inc.
New York   Bloomington

This is a work of fiction. All of the characters, names, incidents, organizations, and dialogue in this novel are either the products of the author's imagination or are used fictitiously.

iUniverse books may be ordered through booksellers or by contacting:

iUniverse
1663 Liberty Drive
Bloomington, IN 47403
www.iuniverse.com
1-800-Authors (1-800-288-4677)

Because of the dynamic nature of the Internet, any Web addresses or links contained in this book may have changed since publication and may no longer be valid. The views expressed in this work are solely those of the author and do not necessarily reflect the views of the publisher, and the publisher hereby disclaims any responsibility for them.

ISBN: 978-1-4401-8718-6 (sc)
ISBN: 978-1-4401-8719-3 (ebook)

Printed in the United States of America

iUniverse rev. date: 11/12/09

~ Prologue ~

▼

When the object lumbered out of the surf onto a warm stretch of the Beaches Region, no one took notice of its appearance. Even if they had, it would have appeared to most eyes to be a large sea turtle coming on shore to lay her bounty of eggs upon the warm sands that abounded in the southern Edges of the Beaches Region.

Yet the creature did not stop to deposit eggs in the sandy dunes of the beach. It continued in a straight line, heading directly toward the Meadows Region. Roughly four feet in diameter, a circular shell covered it completely, so that not an ounce of flesh was exposed. The shell was smooth as glass, unlike a turtle's ridged and rippled texture. It was a perfect half circle in shape, seemingly *too* perfect for nature to have formed. The color—as the sun dried the surface—turned to a mottled bronze that gave the impression of a textured exterior despite the glassy appearance.

If someone, anyone, curious at these anomalies would have taken a moment to flip the creature over, they would have seen that it possessed dozens of small legs that protruded from the hard cover in evenly spaced intervals. These legs propelled it at a slow and steady pace. The creature had no discernable head, nor olfactory devices that could be seen. But of course, no one looked closely at the creature. This stretch of the Beaches was largely uninhabited, and the creature was able to cross into the Meadows where it blended more with the landscape.

While people did not remark on its passing, other Land inhabitants certainly took notice. The local animals gave the creature a wide berth, scurrying out of its path with a twitch of whiskers and an animal's innate sense of wanting to avoid danger. The only animal brave enough to approach was the Black Stallion of the Prince's Herd, as he came across the creature one sunny day in the Meadows. The Black edged up to the creature, sniffing at it cautiously before backing away, pawing at the ground anxiously. Then the proud animal immediately moved his entire herd to the Forest Region, seeking distance from the strange animal.

The creature trundled on, seemingly oblivious to the curious horse's perusal or concern, its thick, stumpy legs working over the uneven ground.

The creature passed by several villages, which remained blissfully unaware of its journey. It even crawled right by a Barracks of the Prince's Guard. The guardsmen worked and slept and gossiped, completely unaware of the alien presence as it glided by them. One day, a group of people consisting of a woman and three male companions walked right by the creature, singing at the top of their voices. When the woman came within range of the creature, she lifted her head for a moment, as if sensing the creature's presence. For the first time since it crawled onto the shores of the Land, the creature stilled in response to her unprecedented observation. It hunkered down and stayed quiet, as if programmed to avoid the woman at all costs. Once the people were past, bound for a hidden fortress in the Meadows, the creature whirred back to life and continued its slow and steady progress.

A large red tailed hawk observed the creature's movement and followed it curiously for several days. The bird's eye view showed that the lumbering creature did not appear to stop to eat, drink, or sleep. The hawk circled about this creature; it seemed so foreign to the landscape, yet managed to blend in very well. The bird's sharp eyes kept track of the creature, even when it seemed to go so slowly it might have been simply a large boulder. Finally, the hawk flew to the opposite end of the Rivers Region, wanting—much as the Black Stallion had desired—as much distance between herself and the creature as possible.

It took almost a month for the creature to reach its final destination, an innocuous stretch of the Meadows, completely unremarkable in appearance.

The creature's legs ground to a halt, and it lowered to the grassy floor with a creak and groan. As time passed, grass grew around the base of the creature, and flowers bloomed beside it. Other animals became accustomed to its presence and ignored it, some even using its smooth shell as a momentary perch from which to look out over the area.

Around the creature, the Meadows Region continued to grow and prosper, completely unaware that in their midst was a time bomb waiting to explode.

▼

ECONOMIC FALLOUT

The inside of the shop *Arts Extraordinaire* gleamed brightly in the late autumn afternoon. The shelves were clean and free of dust and fingerprints; the arts and crafts were displayed in an eye-catching and vibrant manner. The offering of merchandise ranged from the unusual to the fantastical to every step in between. The very eclectic nature of the inventory was the store's best draw. Located along the main thoroughfare of a bustling town known for its music, arts, and antique shops, the store had done well for many years.

The proprietors, Emma and Harry Rupert, prided themselves on being modern day hippies. Harry was a ceramics artist, who had gained some local renown for his work while his wife puttered about the store, making enough money for them to live comfortably year after year. Their only son had moved abroad to study photography about a year earlier. When their child had left, many neighbors wondered how the couple would manage the store alone, but fortunately the owners had a part time sales clerk in the summer months to help them during the busy season.

The salesclerk, Claire Jones, was a steady fixture in the store as the summer edged toward fall. While not a stellar salesperson, her quick and efficient manner proved her more than competent to do the work. She was also able to master the computerized inventory control as well as handle the modest website purchases that helped keep the store afloat. The profitable summer faded into fall, and the storekeepers shifted and reorganized displays to reflect the harvest season. Loads of visitors came to this area of the Catskills Mountains to view the fall foliage, after all, and the Ruperts hoped they would be inspired to take some of the local art back to their homes in Westchester and New York City.

"Let's try these shelves a little further to the left," suggested Emma, tossing her long brown mane of hair over one shoulder. She wore one of her flowing dresses of organic cotton that nearly swept the floor, this one dyed in various shades of blue.

"Sure." Claire shoved the glass and metal piece over to where Emma pointed. Claire stood at an average height, with a slim build and a fall of dark brown hair cut to a bob just under her ears. Her face was angular and strong, her eyes a clear, intelligent mossy green.

She favored simple outfits of jeans paired with t-shirts in the summer, sweatshirts in the fall. The cut of her shirts was always a size or two larger than necessary, since Claire liked to do what she could to hide her bust line, a bone of contention to the teenager ever since she'd started to develop. Out of necessity, Claire had learned long ago the art of being as unremarkable as possible.

Emma tapped a heavily ringed finger against her chin. "That will work," she declared happily. "That new earthen pottery Harry just finished will look fantastic on this shelf. The pieces will be so happy here until they find a new home."

Claire worked to suppress a smile. She liked Emma and Harry. They were kind, even if rather goofy in her opinion. Yet they never failed to make her feel comfortable. It impressed her that during the winter months, the couple had made it a point to call and check up on her, to stop her in the local grocery store and chat with her, and otherwise make her feel appreciated. This summer, they had given her as many hours as they could, knowing she desperately needed the money. That brought to mind the question she needed to ask, but secretly dreaded. She needed to just get it over with, out on the table. Dealt with and done and…yeah. She was stalling. Big time.

"Um, I had a question for you." Claire shoved her hands into her back pockets, shoulders hunched slightly. It was a common defensive posture for her, one she was completely unaware of, but it seemed to clue Emma into the fact that this was an important question. Putting down her clipboard, Emma gave Claire her full attention.

"Sure, honey, what's up?"

"Do you think that you'll need part time hours consistently this winter?" Claire asked in a rush. "Like, a regular schedule every week and not just during the holidays?"

"We can give you some hours through the end of September," Emma said thoughtfully, "but after that, I'm afraid it just dies out until the holiday season. Then, after the holidays, well, you know we often close the store completely until spring. It just doesn't make sense for us to hire someone to sit in the store when we don't make a sale for days and days. Not to mention the heating costs."

"Yeah, that's what I figured." Claire worried her bottom lip with her teeth. "I have to be honest, I need to work solid hours throughout the winter. I was counting on a job over at the nursing home, but they just went union and now I don't meet the minimum age requirements. I'm getting desperate to find another job. If I do, it will probably conflict with my holiday hours here, so I don't know if I'll be able to pitch in during the holidays as much as I did last year."

"Whatever hours you can give us would be fine," Emma assured her easily.

"Thanks again." Claire turned back to stocking the shelves. She knew it had been a long shot, asking for more hours, but it had been worth a try.

Emma watched her as they worked, and after several long moments asked, "Are you still doing the overnight babysitting a few times a week?"

"Yes." Claire shrugged. "It's not really hard, I'm just there in case the kids need anything while their mom's at work. I actually get to sleep, so unless one of them has a nightmare or is sick, I really don't consider it a difficult gig."

"You're starting college, right? How could you expect to work full time, go to school full time and also manage two part time jobs, both here and with the babysitting?" Emma hastened to add, "If you don't mind me asking, that is."

"Well, I aged out of the foster care system as of my birthday last month," Claire replied evenly, keeping her eyes on the pottery she was arranging and her voice purposely light. "I have a full scholarship for college, but it doesn't pay room and board. So I'll need to earn enough money to rent a place. My old foster care parents, the Bassins, have been nice enough to let me stay with them, but they were just informed they're getting a new foster kid next week. So, I'll have to move out, and quickly."

"Rent around here isn't cheap."

"I know. I have a line on a room for rent in a local place, but the people are a little leery of renting to a teenager."

"Oh, you mean the Brewsters?" Emma asked with recognition. Claire nodded. "Well, I know Marlene Brewster. I can certainly vouch for you, if you'd like me to."

"That would be great," Claire replied gratefully. She really needed that room. All the other rentals had been exorbitant in cost. She didn't need much space, after all, just a place to sleep and study.

"I'll call her tonight," Emma promised. "I promise I will impress upon Marlene how mature and responsible you are, quite unlike most of the girls your age."

"Thanks." As always uncomfortable with praise, Claire turned back to the display, fiddling with the arrangement or pottery.

"The full scholarship must make you breathe a little easier. I know when Jay was going through school, it was always a relief to have that scholarship money come through each semester."

"Without it, there's no way I'd be able to go to college. Now, if I can just make enough money for rent and some food, I'll be set."

"If anyone can do it, you can," Emma said to her encouragingly. They were both distracted by the sound of the bell that adorned the shop door, which tinkled merrily, signaling that someone was entering the store.

A slender woman came into view. She had shoulder length, dark blond hair and light green eyes. Emma put down the pottery she was arranging, giving a happy little squeal of glee as she walked over to hug the woman.

"Sasha! How good to see you." Emma greeted the woman with delight, leaning back to look at her critically. "Marriage becomes you, honey. I haven't seen you in ages, it seems."

"Busy year," Sasha admitted with a laugh. "Did you get the wedding pictures we sent?"

"Yes, I did," Emma exclaimed, clapping her hands happily. "I just wish you and William could visit New York more often. Why, I've seen more of Liz this summer than you. But I guess it's hard, given that you and William are making North Carolina your main residence."

"It is," Sasha replied ruefully. "We've been really trying to settle ourselves into our careers and all, but now that the frenzy of the hectic summer months is over, we'll be up to visit more often."

"So how is Tracy doing? I was out at the Orchards a few weeks ago. My, my, my, how that girl has blossomed." Emma laughed gaily, holding her hands out as if to encompass a wide girth.

"She's hanging in there." Sasha rolled her eyes expressively. "Being pregnant is no picnic. For her, or for the rest of us."

"Ah, I well remember that," Emma replied somewhat wistfully, her eyes drifting to a picture of her son that was on the shelf behind the cash register.

"That reminds me—" Sasha dug into her purse, withdrawing a thick pack of papers and brandishing them. "The main reason I came by. We don't like making you wait to get these. Ben just came back and brought these letters from Jay." She held them out to the older woman, who clapped her plump hands with joy.

"Oh, thank you so much." Emma accepted the letters eagerly, her eyes filling with tears. "I so look forward to hearing from him. I just miss my son so much…"

"I know you do," Sasha said indulgently. "That's why I made it a point to drive them up to you today rather than making you wait. Which brings me to the last question I have from the gang. Are you still planning on heading out to the Orchards this weekend to be with us until the baby is born?"

"Definitely," Emma said stoutly. "I know that William is an excellent doctor and all, but I think Tracy will benefit from having a woman there who's trained as a midwife. Especially one with knowledge on drug free birthing."

"I know she's anxious." Sasha sighed, leaning against the counter. "Katie and William are so grateful for your coming out to help. We don't dare use any narcotics due to the, um, special circumstances," Sasha finished, casting a sideways glance in Claire's direction.

Claire was listening avidly to the conversation, even though her attention was on the display in front of her. She was decidedly curious about Emma and Harry's son, Jay. She remembered him well, a tall thin guy with a shock of dark hair who was always taking pictures of things around town. He had simply disappeared, and the couple's claim that he was overseas studying photography was pure bullshit in Claire's opinion. That boy was too close to his parents and was the mature one of the family. He wouldn't just up and leave them alone. Then there was this group of people who brought Emma and Harry letters from Jay, envelopes that had no postmark or stamps on them. Why the personal drop off, why would the mail come through them and not the regular post? Yet there was no denying the people who came by with the letters were always welcomed by Emma and Harry as if they were fast friends of the couple.

In addition, Emma and Harry had taken to visiting this "Orchards" place quite often in the past year. Claire was very suspicious about the whole thing, and whenever one of the Orchards group would stop by, she would do everything possible to glean more information.

Now, she wondered, what circumstances would prevent a woman from being able to use medication during birth? Huh. Yet another mystery.

"Well, Liz is planning on driving up to get you on Saturday morning, then," Sasha was saying, closing her purse. "I hate to drop off the letters and run, but I need to get on back."

"I'll walk you out," Emma said, still clutching the letters to her chest. "Claire, I'll be back in a few minutes."

"Sure." Claire gave a nod to Sasha, who responded similarly. "Nice to see you again."

"Same," Sasha replied cheerfully.

Outside the store, Sasha asked Emma about the quiet girl. She'd noticed Claire in the past, and had meant to ask Emma about her but had never had the chance before now.

Emma sighed. "Claire's a really good girl," she stated firmly. "Much better than her circumstances should allow, actually."

"I sense a sad story coming," Sasha said as they walked to her car.

"Very sad. Her mother had Claire at a young age, very young. I'm not sure Claire even knows who her father is, really. When Claire was five, her mother married a very nice man, and they lived as a family for a few years. Then her mother died. The stepfather remarried and started having children right away. I guess the new woman in his life wasn't too happy that Claire was still in the picture. She persuaded the stepfather to turn Claire over to the state's custody, since they weren't her blood relatives and Claire's stepfather had never formally adopted her. She's been in foster homes ever since."

"That's horrible," Sasha exclaimed, a surge of anger blasting through her like a blowtorch. "How could the stepfather do something like that? To a little kid who'd just lost her mom, no less." The sheer amount of abandonment issues the girl had faced was astronomical.

Emma nodded gravely. "I agree. Simply horrific. But Claire, while she certainly hasn't thrived emotionally, has managed to graduate with honors and is attending college on a full scholarship. Unfortunately, she's having some financial strain because she aged out of the foster care system. I don't know how she's going to manage going to school full time, scraping together the hours needed to earn enough for rent and still be able to sleep, not to mention study. But, she's very focused on getting a degree. I admire that in her. I just wish we had room above the store for her to stay with us."

Sasha jiggled her keys, looking back at the store. Through the window, she could see Claire working methodically, stocking the shelves, her oversized sweatshirt and cropped hair making her look like a tall boy at this distance. There was something familiar about that girl. Something that tugged at the edges of her brain like a whisper. She filed the feeling away to examine later, when she had more time.

Sighing, Sasha unlocked her car and tossed in her purse. Then she turned and gave Emma a huge hug. "Well, I'm off. I'll see you this weekend at the Orchards, alright?"

"I'm looking forward to a nice long visit. Please, tell Ben thanks again for bringing back the letters from Jay. I can't tell you how much Harry and I look forward to reading them. Such adventures he has in his new home." Emma's shoulders rose in a happy little shrug. "It's just such a delicious secret, the Land."

"Oh, I agree," Sasha replied with a grin. "I think you and Harry have been simply wonderful about his staying. I can't imagine many parents who would be so willing to have their only child in another dimension and take it in such stride."

"Well, we always suspected there were other places out there. The universe is just too big for us to be the only people in it." Emma spoke with her usual philosophical bent.

Sasha shook her head. "You're amazing. It's just so nice to know that you and Harry are still a very big part of his life."

"I miss him terribly," Emma admitted. "But we're so proud of what he's done. How many people can say their son is a full fledged wizard, after all?"

Sasha laughed and slid into the car. As she gave Emma one last wave, her eyes slid past the woman to see that Claire was watching her through the window. In that split second of eye contact, Sasha realized what it was about Claire that seemed so familiar.

Why, she's just like me, Sasha jolted with a frisson of surprise. *The me I used to be. Before I met the Protectors, before I visited the Land, before I met William. So dreadfully alone and feeling like it was me against the world.* Sasha's smile faded from her face as she realized that Claire was truly a kindred spirit.

Claire moved back from the window as Sasha stared continued to stare at her, fading from view behind the wavy glass of the old storefront. Sasha shook herself and forced a smile back on her face, waving to Emma and pulling away from the curb. The entire way back to the Orchards, Sasha thought about Claire and her situation. By the time she pulled into the courtyard formed by the old Victorian house, stables and outbuildings, she had the beginnings of a plan.

~ 2 ~

▼

LESSONS LEARNED
THE HARD WAY

When Emma came back inside the store, she was fingering the parchment envelopes longingly. Claire, back at the display stand, looked over at her.

"Why don't you go and read your letters? I'm fine here. It's a slow enough day." Emma looked sorely tempted by the chance to read the letters as soon as possible. Claire gave a sigh. "Seriously, go." She made a shooing gesture with her hands.

"Well, maybe I'll sit in the office and read them," Emma said slowly. "That way, if you need me, I'm close by."

"Whatever," Claire replied, finishing up with the shelves as Emma scurried toward the office like a child getting ready to open a birthday present. She moved on to the front of the store, continuing to straighten and position objects, trying to make an attractive arrangement out of the most butt ugly potholders she had ever seen in her life.

The soft music that played continuously in the shop, a mixture of new age and classical that most would consider soothing, cut off, leaving the store in silence. Not minding the absence of tinkling chimes and piano, Claire continued to work, her mind running over different payment scenarios and ideas to increase her monthly income.

A sound drifted through the shop. Claire paused, her ears straining. It came again. Walking softly, Claire approached the office. She peeked around the corner and then stopped short.

Emma was seated at the desk, the space in front of her littered with Jay's letters. She was sobbing quietly into her hands, her plump shoulders heaving.

Uneasy to be intruding on the woman's grief, Claire took a step backwards. Of course, she stepped squarely onto a section of the wooden floor that gave a huge, loud creak. Emma jumped as if shot and Claire winced in response to the noise.

"I'm sorry. I heard a noise and I thought you might be in trouble. I'll just leave…" She started to edge away.

Emma waved a hand. "No, no, I'm not crying because I'm upset. My son is just doing so well, and it makes me so proud that I just want to burst."

"Oh." Claire again shoved her hands in her jeans pockets, shoulders hunching.

She was decidedly unfamiliar with parental pride but supposed that crying with happiness over your child was a good thing, relatively speaking. "Uh, so his photography is going well, then?" she asked to cover the awkward moment.

Sniffling, Emma shuffled through the papers. "No, he can't do much photography where he is," she said absently, then froze as she realized what she had let slip.

Claire's eyes narrowed. "But I thought he was off in Europe, working on his photography."

"Well, not exactly…"

"Is he in prison or rehab or something?"

"No," Emma exclaimed horrified, then had to laugh ruefully. "Although I guess to an outsider it would appear that way, wouldn't it?"

"You have to admit, having people courier his letters to you, and you never have a current picture of him, no phone conversations at all, and to top it off he never visits you and you never visit him, well, it's just weird." The words came out in a rush.

Emma tapped the letters against one palm, watching Claire with those calm eyes of hers. "You've given this a great deal of thought, haven't you?"

Claire blushed and ducked her head. "Sorry," she mumbled, starting to back away. "I was just curious, that's all."

"No, really, it's ok." Claire paused and leaned against the doorjamb. "I'm sure people talk about it around town, right?" Claire shrugged and looked away, then sighed and nodded. "It's to be expected. Small town and all." Emma fell silent, rocking back and forth on the ancient office chair absently.

"Whenever someone asks me about Jay, I tell them it's none of their business," Claire said fiercely.

"My, aren't you the brave one, sticking up for me even though I'm not there and you having your own concerns about my boy." Emma paused again, then asked slowly, "Do you really want to see a recent picture of Jay?"

Claire hesitated, then nodded. Hell, yeah, she wanted to see. Emma reached into the bottom right hand drawer of her desk. Claire could see it was jammed full of letters like the one Emma had been reading. The woman withdrew a photo encased in a glass covered frame and dusted the image lightly before handing it over to Claire.

Claire took it and looked down at the picture. It showed a man who was clearly Jay, robed in a red gown embroidered with golden thread. He was leaning against a large boulder, his arm around a pretty girl who had a mop of honey colored corkscrew curls. Jay was smiling—at least Claire assumed he was, she couldn't really tell since the lower half of his face was covered with a dark growth of beard—and the girl appeared to have been caught mid laugh.

"They seem very happy," Claire said cautiously.

"It's a self portrait Jay took, using a timer on his digital camera. Before it stopped working, that is."

"Um, were they at some sort of medieval festival?" Claire looked at the strange outfits with confusion.

"No, why do you ask?"

"Emma, he's wearing a robe," Claire said with exasperation. "How can you be sure he isn't in some sort of cult?"

Emma looked startled, then laughed gaily. "You know, I'm so used to seeing Jay in his robes that it doesn't even register with me any longer. No, he isn't in some cult. They just do things differently where he lives, that's all."

"Uh-huh," Claire said, unconvinced. She handed the picture back to Emma and put her hands back in her pockets. "Well, I'm done with the stuff out front, so if you don't mind, I guess I'll head out."

"Thank you so much for your help today." Emma replaced the picture in the desk drawer. She folded the letter and tucked it in her pocket. Claire was sure it was for Harry to read later that evening. "I'll lock up after you leave, you go on ahead."

"I'll stop by tomorrow between classes, and help you put out the shipment that is due to arrive," Claire offered, picking up her keys from behind the counter.

"Thank you, dear," Emma said, her mind clearly anticipating discussing Jay's latest news with Harry.

Claire let herself out onto the darkening street. It was getting darker earlier as the autumn days grew shorter. The wind was colder as well. Claire had not brought her jacket with her to work, so she hunched over, wrapping her arms around her waist as she trudged toward a small house set on the outskirts of town.

Inside, the Bassins were sitting down to dinner in front of their television set. "Hullo, Claire." Mr. Bassin waved at her.

"Hi."

"There's some casserole for dinner if you'd like some," Mrs. Bassin added.

"No, thanks," Claire declined, although her stomach was rumbling from hunger. She felt funny eating their food, knowing that the state was no longer reimbursing them for her expenses. They refused to take any money from her for groceries, telling Claire she needed to save it for when she moved out. Claire had taken to buying food and storing it in her room so that she was eating her own stuff. It just made her feel better somehow. "Would you mind if I got on the computer tonight for about half an hour?"

"Sure, go ahead," Mr. Bassin said genially.

Mrs. Bassin gave her an assessing look. "Is it for school?" she asked primly. It wasn't that she didn't trust Claire. Rather, Mrs. Bassin didn't trust computers and liked the Internet even less.

"Yes." Claire squirmed, the lie not coming easily. Well, it was partially true, she conceded to herself. She wanted to run some numbers on a spreadsheet she'd developed to see what kind of salary she would need to make to be able to survive while attending school. She went down the hallway to the small room that was tucked under the staircase where the Bassins had put in their computer.

Claire absently booted up the computer, thinking about her conversation with Emma. She shook her head over Jay and his eccentric clothing. Some lifestyle. What did he think he was, some sort of magician or something?

Within moments, she was immersed in the spreadsheet, making notations and crunching numbers. Muttering to herself, she tried several different variations before sinking back in the chair with disgust.

Rubbing her hands over her face, she considered her options, which were few. First, she could go to school full time, and have it all be paid, but would be basically homeless since she could never find a job that would pay her enough money to live. Or she could go to school part time and work more hours. That would give her a place to live, but she'd lose her scholarship, which required her to have a full course load. So she'd be forced to pay all of the tuition and book fees, and that was not going to be feasible. Or, she could quit school completely and work in a minimum wage job the rest of her miserable life.

"You want fries with that?" she muttered with frustration, crossing her arms.

Tears pricked at her eyes. It wasn't fair; it just wasn't fair at all. She had a chance to make her life better, to get an education, and she was going to be denied that chance because of her limited options. She powered down the computer, her fingers hitting the keys sharply in her disappointment.

She gave serious thought to calling her stepfather. He'd been the beneficiary of her mother's life insurance policy when she had died. Claire wondered if she could convince him that he should give her some of the money to pay for her housing costs while in school.

It was worth a shot.

She stood up and went back to the living room where a sitcom was blaring from the television. The Bassins were watching it avidly, their mouths slack.

"Um, I need to use the phone," she said to them. God, she hated having to ask before she did every little thing, but the Bassins had been so nice about letting her stay an extra month that she didn't dare express that frustration.

"Who are you calling?" Mr. Bassin asked, his eyes glued to the screen.

"I need to speak with my stepfather." This statement earned her a sharp look from Mrs. Bassin.

"Your stepfather? Why on earth would you need to speak with him?" Mrs. Bassin's thin lips compressed even more tightly. She detested the way Claire's stepfather had behaved, and never made any bones about it to Claire.

"It's personal," Claire said rigidly. "But I promise I won't take long, and I'd be happy to pay you for the long distance charge." Her stepfather had moved several counties away a few years earlier, but had given Claire his phone number. Why, she had no idea, but she supposed he felt guilty. *Good. The bastard should feel guilty.*

"Well, if you feel you have to," Mrs. Bassin said begrudgingly.

Claire withdrew to the kitchen, where the only phone in the house was located. The Bassins were very nice people; in fact, Claire felt they were by far the best foster parents she had lived with in the ten years she'd been in the system. But they were older than most foster parents and very old fashioned when it came to their beliefs. The kitchen she entered hadn't been redecorated since the seventies and still boasted an avocado green décor that was, to say the least, hideous.

Claire picked up the receiver and dialed her stepfather's number. Her legs were surprisingly weak and wiggly, so she leaned against the counter for support. When a woman answered the phone breathlessly, Claire winced. It was the new wife, Linda. She steeled herself for the inevitable.

"Hello?" the wife asked.

"Hello, is Richard there?"

"Who is this, please?"

"Um, it's Claire Jones," she replied, rubbing one finger between her eyes.

There was dead silence on the other end of the line. Then the woman spoke again, all traces of cutsie pie gone from her breathless, little girl voice. "Why do you want to talk to Richard?"

"Is he there?" Claire asked, willing her voice to remain calm and even.

Linda sighed, a gusty breath of huffy air. "Hold on," she barked crossly, throwing the phone down with a clatter. Her voice came over the receiver distantly. "Richard. Richard! That Claire girl is on the phone for you."

Claire heard footsteps, then muffled voices. The receiver was finally picked up and she could hear her stepfather's voice. "Claire? Is everything all right?"

She closed her eyes. The sound of his voice brought back memories of her mother, Richard and her going out to dinner, playing games, chasing fireflies in the backyard. When they were a family, in every sense of the word. Resolutely, Claire swallowed the tears that threatened to choke her. "I'm fine, thank you."

"Oh that's good," he replied, then fell silent. "Um, is there a reason why you called?"

"Yes." Claire took a deep breath. "I'm in college now and I have a full scholarship that pays for all my school fees and books and stuff. But it doesn't pay for room and board. So I was wondering…" she was twisting the phone cord around one finger tightly. "When my mother died, she had a large life insurance policy. I was hoping that maybe you could give me a portion of it so that I could use it for rent."

There was dead silence on the other end of the line. Then Richard repeated slowly, "The life insurance money…"

In the background, Linda let loose a screech that Claire could clearly hear over the phone line. He covered the mouthpiece, but she could vaguely hear a furiously whispered argument occurring on the other end of the line. Finally, Richard came back on. "Well, Claire, it isn't as easy as all that. The money was put into investments, see, and I can't really go pulling collateral from it to just hand over to you."

"She was my mother," Claire said, feeling her stubborn nature kick in, "and she took out that policy long before you two got together. She only signed you on as beneficiary because she thought you'd look after me if she died. I think it's only fair that I get some of the money."

"Claire…"

"I'm not asking to buy a car, or clothes, or a vacation to the Bahamas or something trivial like that. I need money to pay rent so I can go to college. Do you understand that?" Claire's voice was rising and she knew the Bassins could probably hear her, but she was beyond caring.

"I understand, Claire," he said wearily, "but I just don't think I can help you."

"Maybe I should talk to a lawyer about this," Claire retorted recklessly, her head feeling hollow and buzzy, like she'd taken a shot of hard liquor.

"Are you threatening me with a lawsuit?" Richard asked, as if truly offended. Then the phone was yanked from him and Linda got on the line.

"Listen, Claire. Your mother made Richard the beneficiary of her life insurance policy. You have no legal rights over that money," she stated triumphantly. "Believe me, we've checked this thoroughly."

"My mother made him the beneficiary after Richard assured her he would take care of me should something happen to her," Claire shot back. "Well, we all know how seriously he took that promise, don't we?"

"Claire, you are nothing but trouble, and I won't have you disrupting our lives with these kind of phone calls on a continual basis," Linda screamed into the phone.

"Continual? This is the first goddamn time I've called you in three years! My mother bought that life insurance policy. My mother had me as the beneficiary until she married Richard, then he persuaded her to change it to him, promising he'd take care of me. Well, you tell Dick that I expect him to live up to his word!" She slammed the phone down and put her hands on the mustard colored countertop, taking deep breaths to calm herself.

"Claire? Is everything alright?" Mrs. Bassin asked tentatively from behind her.

Claire hastily wiped her eyes and pressed her cold hands to her cheeks, which felt like they were on fire. "I'm fine," she said in a strangled voice. "I'll be fine." With deliberate dignity, she walked from the room. Once clear of the doorway, she pelted up the stairs, taking them two at a time.

Her room was miniscule, a mere closet sized space crammed with a twin bed and a dresser. There certainly wasn't enough room to pace off her anger. Claire flung herself down on the bed and looked up at the ceiling.

On the planked ceiling directly above the bed was the one belonging that Claire displayed in the room. It was a picture she had done, not long after her mother died, of a tree. A golden tree. The leaves were touched with gold glitter to make them shimmer, the trunk painted a vibrant, deep red.

At various intervals in the branches, splotches of orange paint depicted some sort of fruit hidden in the leaves. Although childish in its execution, she'd never gotten rid of the painting, even after all these years.

Whenever Claire was moved from home to home, the tree picture always went with her. She'd had it framed so that it was protected, and it was by far her most prized possession. It was silly, really, but looking at the painting always made her feel better, no matter how tumultuous her existence was at the moment.

Tonight was no exception. Claire lay on her back, staring at the tree, tears spilling from her eyes. She concentrated on the tree, the bark and the leaves. As always, a sense of peace drifted over her, slowly but surely. One hand lifted up to rub the bead hanging from a chain around her neck, the only other item she had left of her mother's, and stared at the tree as the night marched on.

Claire let it take her away into slumber, gladly slipping into a deep sleep, free of dreams or strife.

~ 3 ~

▼

CLOSING RANKS

Unfortunately, the next day did not bring a new revelation or magical solution. Nor did it bring a winning ticket for the lottery or any other means of being independently wealthy. Claire figured she had enough money squirreled away to last the fall semester, if she was very, very careful. The spring semester, however, was a whole other story. One that did not look like it would have a happy ending. Well, she didn't believe in fairy tales anyway, so she shouldn't be too surprised.

Claire made it a point to be working on Saturday morning. She was curious to see who was going to pick Emma up for her visit to the Orchards. Since her talk with Emma about Jay, Claire was even more intensely interested in the mysterious group. Emma and Harry were incredibly sweet and trusting people; they could be taken in by a con fairly easily.

She kept busy in the front of the store cataloguing merchandise that was stored in a locked unit along one wall. Each time the doorbells jangled, she craned her neck to see the arrival.

Midmorning, the bells heralded a tall, lithe woman walking into the store. The woman looked vaguely familiar, and Claire realized she was one of the group from the Orchards. Picking up her clipboard, Claire sidled up a side aisle to see her more clearly.

A man had come in with her. A really tall man, with chestnut hair glinting with golden highlights. His profile was also familiar, but not from the Orchards people. When the stranger's identity sank in, Claire gasped audibly, causing the man and woman to swivel in her direction.

"You're Zach Neol," Claire exclaimed, clasping the clipboard to her chest tightly.

"So they tell me," he replied easily, grinning at her.

Emma bustled around the counter and soon enfolded first the woman, then the movie star, in her warm hug. Claire stood, dumbfounded, staring at them. How the hell did innocent, naïve Emma know the hunkified goodness of Zach Neol? Christ, the woman didn't even own a television set that worked.

"Well, Zach you know," Emma said to Claire in a brisk but amused voice, "but I don't think you have ever formally met Liz. Claire, this is Liz Keeper. Liz, this is our salesclerk, Claire."

"Oh, Sasha mentioned you," Liz said, then held out her hand for Claire to shake. "Nice to meet you."

Claire, automatically reached to shake Liz's hand, noticing Zach and Emma exchanging a surprised look. Before she could pull away, Liz had enfolded her hand in a brief shake, then released it. "Nice to meet you, too." Claire continued to fidget with her clipboard.

Harry came ambling out of the back of the store, where he was working on his pottery wheel. Covered in clay from head to toe, he graciously declined giving Liz a hug, settling for a kiss on the cheek that still managed to transfer a smudge of clay to her smooth skin.

"Are you ready to go?" Zach asked Emma courteously, his drawling voice noticeable in the realm of the Yankees.

"Yes. Oh, I have a bag, where is it…oh, here it is," Emma said, flustered. Zach took the bag from her, rolling his eyes over Emma's head at Liz, who gave him a warning look that clearly said he needed to behave. Claire watched it all, fascinated.

"Claire, now, you need to make sure that Harry helps you in the store." Emma bustled over to give her husband a hug and kiss. She clearly didn't care about the mess he transferred to her cotton shirt and skirt, simply brushing at the clay as she continued, "I don't want you having to work all the time by yourself, especially on Saturday."

"We'll do fine, mother," Harry said mischievously, patting his shirt pocket for his glasses. Claire reached up on top of his head and plucked them off, handing them to the man.

"I'd have to say that Claire will manage," Zach said with a laugh.

"Yes, I usually do." Claire forced her fingers to relax their death grip on the clipboard.

Claire watched the trio head for the large SUV parked in front of the store, more curious than ever about this strange group of people. She had no way of knowing that from inside the SUV, behind the tinted windows, Zach Neol watched her just as intently. He turned to the passenger seat, where Liz was busy buckling herself in.

"So what gives?" he asked Liz genially, but underlying there was an undeniable hardness to his voice. "Why'd you touch Claire like that? I happen to know your filtering shields weren't up."

"How on earth could you know that?" Liz asked absently as she pulled on sunglasses to ward off the midmorning glare.

"I just know." Zach reached over and ran a finger down her arm. "It worries me that you take chances like that, Liz. You were purposely trying to read that girl and I want to know why."

"I noticed that, too," Emma said, equally worried.

"I was making sure she isn't touched by Evil," Liz said complacently, staring out the front of the SUV.

"What? Claire?" Emma cried out. "Impossible! Claire is a good girl. I've known her for years."

Zach's eyes narrowed. "What did you get from her?"

"Nothing. She got nothing," Emma said staunchly, truly offended at the assumption that Claire could be in league with Evil.

Liz turned toward them, her expression mutinous behind the tinted glasses. "Listen. I'm not about to let anyone touched by Evil get near us. I love you and Harry, Emma, but you two are so sweet and so trusting, you'd believe anybody at face value and you have to admit that you two are a link to us. If Evil found out, he could use that link. He wouldn't hesitate. So yes, I purposely read that girl to see if there was any inkling, any whatsoever, that she could be a danger to us. And I'd do it again."

"But what did you discover?" Zach ground out the question through gritted teeth.

"She's clean. There are no mental shields that I could detect. She's had a difficult life, and what seeped through when I was checking her out jives with what Emma told Sasha about Claire. She's in desperate financial straits, probably more so than you even realized, Emma. She keeps it all beneath the surface because she has no one to share it with, no one she trusts." Liz swallowed heavily then reached for her cell phone. Putting it to her ear, she waited for the other line to be picked up.

"Sasha? It's Liz. Listen, go for it. Yeah. I think we need to get it done quickly. No, I would go and mail it today. Listen, send it priority, ok? Right. Thanks, Sasha." Liz clicked off the phone and slid it back into her purse.

Zach drummed his fingers on the steering wheel, his amber-flecked blue eyes watching Liz closely. "Any chance of my learning what that little phone call was about?"

Liz laid a hand on his cheek, smiling gently. "Later. We'll tell everyone later, when we're all together. Trust me, Zachary."

Turning his head, he kissed the palm that caressing his face. "Always, love," he replied before starting the SUV and pulling out into traffic. The conversation on the way to the Orchards was full of information from Jay and about the goings on with all the Protectors of the Land. Before long, they were turning into the small, rutted path that led to the Orchard House. Passing through the electrified gates, Zach halted the SUV in front of the large, rambling Victorian house where everyone congregated.

Emma never tired of going to the Orchards. Being around all the younger people was invigorating somehow, and there was an aura around this particular group. If she had to define it, that aura would best be labeled power.

First to greet her was Katie, the original Protector of the Land. An Oracle, whose powers were growing stronger in the World, she was a petite blond with wide, cornflower blue eyes, a quick wit and even quicker smile.

Behind her stood Ben Harm, an artist by trade, but even more spectacular to Emma was the fact that he was from a completely different dimension, where the people could breathe underwater. He was tall, with spiked blond hair, sea green eyes and dark rimmed glasses. He never seemed to lose his tan, no matter how long he stayed away from the beaches of the World or Land. Ben was also the one who, besides Tracy, was able to Travel to the Land at will. Because he was a direct conduit to her son, Emma felt a special affection for him.

Sasha was next in line for hugs, and Emma thanked her again for bringing out the letters earlier in the week. Sasha was quickly shoved to the side by the irrepressible Sarat.

Emma had to laugh at Sarat's enthusiasm. The woman, petite enough to be frequently mistaken for a teenager, was originally from the Land, but now lived in the World Dimension. She was bright, bubbly, and full of life. She had been a great joy to Emma, able to explain the intricacies of Jay's new environment and the details about his duties as a Wizard.

"Where is Tracy?" Emma asked, craning her neck to find the tall woman.

Sarat's nose wrinkled mischievously. "She can't get out of the chair unless we help her," she said, laughing. "We were all so excited to see you we kinda left her inside."

Emma shook her head. "Probably stewing, our Tracy."

Katie linked arms with Emma as they walked to the porch and into the large farmhouse. "Actually, Tracy has mellowed with the final stages of the pregnancy. I was rather expecting to have a stark raving lunatic on our hands, but she seems to have actually de-stressed about the whole thing."

"Really?" Emma's eyebrow arched up. "How fascinating."

They trooped into the kitchen, which was a large, welcoming space. There was obviously some sort of baking happening, as flour, sugar, and spices littered the large table set in the center of the room. To one side, comfortably ensconced in a plush chair with her feet propped up on an ottoman, sat Tracy.

"Don't even try," Emma warned Tracy, who was attempting to swing her legs off the ottoman to stand and give her a hug. Instead, Emma leaned over and brushed a kiss on the top of her dark blond hair, one hand automatically going to Tracy's stomach. Emma then knelt by the chair, holding her hand firmly against Tracy's fully rounded belly.

"The baby is moving strongly," Emma observed, then started moving her hand over Tracy's stomach, pressing gently here, stroking there. "The head is definitely down. Are you starting to feel pressure in your pelvis?"

"I'm feeling pressure everywhere," Tracy replied cheerfully. "You name it; it's swollen, distended, uncomfortable or downright painful."

Emma tilted her head to one side. "That does happen. I don't think you have much farther to go. You're about fully cooked in there."

"Thank goodness." Tracy sighed, then frowned painfully. "Guys, I gotta pee again. Sorry."

"Move aside," Ben commanded to Emma. Zach followed him over, rolling up his sleeves. After kicking the ottoman to one side, they positioned themselves and grasped Tracy's arms, heaving her to her feet.

"My gracious, you're huge," Emma exclaimed involuntarily. She was used to seeing Tracy as an extremely trim, taut, fit girl. Now, she was all belly, but the added pregnancy weight made her features more rounded and gentle. She was also giggling like mad at Emma's response to her changing body.

"I feel like the blob." Tracy waddled in the way only a very pregnant woman can manage.

As Tracy exited, Emma turned toward the people at the table, her eyebrow raised.

"I told you," Katie said, pointing a wooden spoon in Emma's direction. "Positively giddy, that girl is."

"Pre-birth hormones," Sasha predicted, measuring out some flour and dumping it into a bowl.

"I still say labor will bring out the inner Too'ki beyotch." Ben snagged some chocolate chips from the table, earning him a smack on the back of the head from Liz, who was passing behind him with a carton of eggs. "Ouch!"

"Serves you right," Liz replied calmly.

"Making cookies?" Emma guessed. "Is Tracy having cravings?"

"These are for us," Sarat said as she pulled out several cookie sheets. "We're going mad with waiting and had to do something."

"How much longer does William think Tracy has to go?" Emma asked, taking a seat. As a rule, she did not approve of white flour or refined sugar in her baking, so she decided not to participate in the event. She also vowed to herself to make some oatmeal raisin cookies—her own recipe—that the group had seemed to enjoy so much the last time she visited. Why, they had disappeared almost instantly!

"William thinks she could go at any moment," Sasha replied.

"I'm not a volcano," Tracy said mildly as she came back in. They watched with trepidation as she lowered herself gingerly back into the chair. Everyone breathed a sigh of relief when she was safe and secure, the ottoman back in place and her feet elevated.

"Where are the Sigots?" Emma used the Protector term for their spouses, an abbreviation for Significant Others. "I don't see Steven, William or Owen around."

"Steven is in New York City for a few days," Katie explained, rubbing some flour off her nose. "He has several board meetings and such. William is at the medical supply place, making sure we have what we need for a home birth."

"Owen is in Los Angeles for a series of meetings," Sarat chipped in. "They are discussing the full length Rosy movie."

"Tell me the news of the Land. How are Anja and Orli doing?" Emma rested her chin on her hand, referring to Ben's mermaid wife and Tracy's husband, both of whom lived in the Land.

"Anja is well," Ben said with a grin. "She's been incredibly busy this season, hauling merchandise to the outer islands, but she's happiest out to sea, so it's all good in the end."

"And Orli?" Emma cast a look in Tracy's direction. The pregnant woman was still smiling, but it was clearly more strained. She had not seen her husband since becoming pregnant, because no one was clear whether Traveling would harm the fetus. "How is he handling impending fatherhood?"

"With great impatience," Ben said, rolling his eyes. "I've taken to Traveling every other week just to keep him up to date with the events."

"Like that's a hardship," Tracy retorted, but it was without any real heat.

"Let's see, who else am I missing?" Emma looked around the table. "Oh yes, Amber. Where is she?"

"She's off and about," Katie said vaguely.

Katie had never told Jay's mother that Amber was really an Interdimensional fairy, a purely magical creature. Amber was currently visiting her life partner, the Interdimensional Grid Manager Daniel, who had become one of the Protector's greatest allies. Katie just hoped that Amber came home before Tracy went into labor. They might need to have a conduit to get advice from the Grid Manager should something unexpected happen.

Katie chewed her bottom lip, glancing in Tracy's direction. She was more worried than she cared to admit. The first concern was the Too'ki virus, which Tracy carried in her blood. She'd been infected by a Too'ki blade during her trip to the Land, and it still affected her blood screens. No one knew if it could be transmitted through the placenta to the baby. The other was the fact that the baby's father was a Land inhabitant. No one really understood what kind of impact that would have on the child, if any. William was unable to do sophisticated tests such as amniocentesis in a home environment, and they needed to avoid hospitals and birthing centers at all costs, as the blood tests alone would be unusual. Not to mention the fact that while a normal World pregnancy lasts for nine full months, Tracy's was accelerated. It looked like a full six months was going to bring her to term. The stress on Tracy's body and the resulting toll it could take had kept Katie awake many hours.

Yet they had done all they could do. Liz was keeping an eye on Tracy's aura, which was still glowing with the bright colors of health. Liz also kept a psychic eye on the pregnant woman, trying to ascertain any possible problems. Katie smiled as Emma walked back over to Tracy and plopped down by the ottoman, picking up a swollen foot and starting to massage it. Emma, with her holistic remedies, and William, with his medical ones, would do all they could to keep Tracy and her baby safe and healthy. But Katie knew that possibly the greatest threat to the baby was beyond their control.

Evil.

Katie had been in a personal fight with Evil for years now, and the entity continued to be relentless in his pursuit of dominating the Land. If their past cycles were any indication, it was about time for another assault on the Land, another Protector. Another risk to be taken, another soul she'd have to send into jeopardy.

Katie looked at Zach, who was quietly and steadily stealing chocolate chips, passing some to Ben. Zach had been on the most recent quest, and it had very nearly killed him. The actor was barely recovered physically, and Liz told her that he still woke up in the throes of nightmares about the experience on a regular basis. Katie worried about sending another Protector into the Land, knowing that she might be sending that person to their death. It was a sobering and troubling thought. What if Evil discovered that a baby, born of both Land and World genes, was alive and well? What kind of diabolical plot could Evil hatch to use the child? If the baby also had Too'ki influences, how would that factor into the mix?

Katie saw that Liz was watching her quizzically. She must have clued in to Katie's dour turn of mind. The Oracle gave Liz a small smile and shook her head, indicating she was fine. The Seer tilted her head to one side and returned the smile, then nodded as if to say that she understood and was feeling the same worries and frets.

Katie turned her attention back to the cookies. Sometimes, she thought, it was nice to have another person who really understood her.

- 4 -

▼

Changing Views

William walked in just as the first batch of cookies came out of the oven. He greeted Emma warmly and helped himself to a handful of cookies, setting down several large bags.

"Don't forget me," Tracy said plaintively from her chair, eagerly accepting her own special plate full of cookies. "'fanks," she said, her mouth full.

"So Liz, it occurs to me that you haven't spilled it about the phone call to Sasha," Zach commented as the Seer settled herself in his lap and snagged one of his cookies.

"Oh, that's right," Liz said, looking over at Sasha. "Did you get the letter out?"

"Yep," Sasha replied, chasing her cookie with a swig of milk. "I sent it priority, like you suggested."

"Oh, this is about that thing you asked me for," Katie exclaimed, hitting her head with her hand. "I'd forgotten about it. I'm glad someone remembered. It's a really good idea, and I think it'll be great if it all works out."

"I still think you should have asked Emma first," Tracy piped up from her seat. "After all, she knows the situation better than you guys do."

"Why? What's not to like about it?" Sarat asked as she tucked her legs up under her in the seat.

"Seems to me it'll be really well received," Sasha said reflectively.

Ben, Zach and William exchanged confused looks. They looked at Emma who shrugged, holding up her hands. "I'm with you, boys. I haven't a clue what they're talking about."

"Typical," Zach snorted.

"Why are we the last to know?" Ben demanded.

"Sounds like a girl plan," William commented.

"Sorry," Sasha said, reaching for another cookie. "The thing is, I was struck by what Emma told me about Claire. About her aging out of the foster care system and all, and how scholarships often won't cover non-educational expenses. So, I asked Katie if the Wrightstone Foundation would consider doing a scholarship that would cover those kinds of costs."

"So, I said, sure, why not?" Katie picked up the thread of the conversation. "We've never done it before, but it sounds like a good thing to branch out into. Since it is someone that Emma knows, it's a good case study to see if it works. If it succeeds, we can explore granting them on a regular basis."

"Then I overheard the conversation, and got worried about this girl," Liz continued. "I wanted a chance to read her and make sure she was a clean entity before we do anything that could bring her into the auspices of the Wrightstone Foundation. So, I convinced Zach that we should be the ones to go and pick up Emma so I could meet her in person. Then I called Sasha and said it was a go."

"I sent her a letter today indicating that she's been accepted into a pilot program with the Foundation, and all she needs to do is sign up," Sasha finished triumphantly.

"You did all that just because I happened to mention that Claire was a good girl?" Emma said weakly, hand at her throat.

"Coming from you, that is the highest of high praises," Sasha said lightly, then her pale green gaze shadowed slightly. "I know what it's like to face financial pressures at a young age. The fear of not knowing if you'll have enough to eat, or have a place to sleep. It's debilitating, emotionally and physically. The choices are never easy, and the pressure makes the school part very difficult. Claire has a full educational scholarship. That means she's smart. Why should her lousy economic status hinder her chances of getting a college education?" She looked at the men somewhat defensively, as if anticipating resistance.

Ben put up his hand. "Hey, I have no problems with it. Seems like a good idea. I'd like to partner with Wrightstone, in fact, and kick in some money for the project."

"Must be nice to be a ga-zillionaire," mumbled Sasha good-naturedly.

"The plan sounds great to me," Zach added, giving Liz's hip a squeeze. "I like saving damsels in distress." Liz rolled her eyes and elbowed him in the stomach.

"It's wonderful," William vowed, leaning over to give Sasha a kiss on the lips.

"What do you think, Emma?" Sarat asked eagerly.

Emma fiddled with a napkin, a worry frown wrinkling her forehead. "I don't know. I mean, the concept is wonderful and it makes me so proud I could burst. But with Claire…I can see one of two things happening, really. First, Claire is very stubborn, and full of pride. She might refuse the offer simply because she doesn't want to admit she can't do it on her own. Or, she might accept the offer, but if she connects the scholarship with the Orchards, she'll be suspicious. She's already concerned you guys are some sort of cult holding Jay hostage."

That drew all manner of chuckles. Sasha, however, looked truly offended, and, Katie knew, for good reason. Her father and sister belonged to a fanatical cult in the south, and she viewed those kinds of organizations with great disgust.

"That's ridiculous," she sputtered.

Emma spread her hands. "Hey, I'm just repeating her fears, not saying I believe them."

"Well when you think about it, we are rather cult-ish," Katie said, turning to Sasha when the woman gave an unladylike snort of disbelief, "Well we are! We have our own belief structure, keep to our little clique; we don't open up to strangers easily. Some people, viewing that, would be naturally leery."

"I think it was seeing a picture of Jay in his wizarding robes that got Claire most concerned," admitted Emma.

Sasha grumbled, clearly still uneasy with the comparison. They were forestalled from further discussion when Tracy suddenly yelled and grabbed her belly.

Emma dashed to her side in a flash. Ben tried to stand up quickly but ended up toppling over his chair, since his long feet had been wrapped around the legs. That sent him crashing into Sarat and Sasha, who immediately got tangled up in a heap. William solved this roadblock by hurtling over them like a horse jumping a fence while the rest of the Protectors hovered in the background.

"Chill out," Tracy laughed. "It's just another Braxton-Hicks contraction."

Emma and William ignored her, pulling up the maternity top and talking medical jargon as they assessed her.

Zach and Ben paled at the sight of so much tightly stretched skin, both taking an involuntary step backwards as the rounded moon of a belly was exposed.

"Men," Liz muttered, pushing past them, eying Tracy's aura critically. "There's no change in her aura," she announced confidently.

"I think that was just a Braxton-Hicks," William concluded, and Emma nodded, concurring.

"So glad you folks agree with me," Tracy grumbled, yanking down her shirt. "Now that we've terrified the men with my huge white belly and all."

"You're beautiful," Zach said staunchly, although there were beads of nervous sweat on his forehead and he was leaning against the table as if nauseous. He looked simply terrified a baby would pop out of Tracy at any second.

"Well, your belly is huge, but you aren't," Ben added, then frowned, "Wait, that sounded wrong, let me try again."

"Don't bother," William, Emma and Tracy all said at the same time.

~ ~ ~

On Monday, Claire went to classes in the morning and then worked at the store during the afternoon. She had just enough time to run home before her next job, which was the babysitting gig. As she was leaving the store, Harry called out that he would be by the next morning to help Claire move all her things to her new residence. True to her word, Emma had given Claire a glowing reference and now, Claire was ready to move into the extra room at the boarding house.

Claire turned toward Harry. "You know, you don't have to help me." She tried talking him out of helping for what seemed like the thirteenth time. "I don't have a lot of stuff, and it won't take me long to walk it over to the new place."

"Nonsense." Harry waved away her words with an absent, albeit grimy, hand. "I'm driving you over and that's final. Now get on home so you can eat before your next job."

Claire sighed and left, pushing her hand through her dark, straight hair. There was no use telling Harry that she was planning on eating a pop tart on her way to the babysitting job. He'd want to give her one of Emma's frozen organic tofu casseroles or something. God knew Claire was not going to be eating something that contained virgin goat cheese, or some such icky thing.

As she walked down the street, Claire had the vivid sensation she was being watched. It was something she was quite familiar with; this sensation of being followed and watched. Of course, no one was ever really after her but it was times like this that Claire felt as though she was prey being stalked. Sure enough, a careful look around showed she was alone on the road and Claire shook off the sensation, sure she was just being paranoid. Who would want to follow her, anyway?

When Claire walked into the Bassins, they were seated, as usual, on the sofa in front of the television set. Mr. Bassin, without even looking in her direction, called out. "Claire, a letter came today for you. Priority mail. I left it on the table."

Claire picked up the red, white and blue envelope curiously. The return address was unfamiliar. She opened the envelope and withdrew the paper inside. Scanning it, she sat down in the kitchen chair with a plop.

"This can't be real," she whispered, going back to the top and reading the letter more carefully. When she finished reading, Claire stared off into space, thinking, one hand toying with the cloisonné bead dangling on the chain around her neck. Mrs. Bassin shuffled in, heading for the fridge. Pulling out the milk, she asked Claire about the letter.

"It's from the Wrightstone Foundation," Claire replied, clearing her throat. "Have you ever heard of them?"

Mrs. Bassin tilted her head. "No, I haven't."

"Well, they're inviting me into a new program they have established. It's a kind of scholarship, but it pays for things that traditional educational scholarships usually don't cover, like rent and food and clothing and such." Claire stood, sliding the letter back into the envelope carefully.

"But that is wonderful!" Mrs. Bassin beamed. "How nice that you got such an invitation."

"Wonderful," Claire echoed, but her brow furrowed. She'd never applied for this kind of scholarship. All the ones that had paid for non-educational expenses were combined scholarships, and she hadn't gotten any of those. She'd remember sending out an inquiry for a non-educational expenses grant. So how had her name come to the Wrightstone Foundation? And why was that name so familiar to her?

Claire glanced at the clock and got another shock. It was later than she expected. She said a hasty goodnight to the Bassins after telling them that Harry was coming over the next morning to help her move out. They gave her an absent good night and sent her on her way. Obviously the emotional ties—if they'd ever formed any with her—had been cut.

Claire got to her job in the nick of time. The mother, Mrs. Wilson, had already gotten the little ones to bed, so Claire's time was pretty much her own after the woman left for her night job at a local resort. She pulled out the Wrightstone letter and read through it once again. Tapping the letter on her leg, she eyed the computer. This family never had a problem with her using the computer, so Claire booted it up and started to research the Wrightstone Foundation.

Within a few clicks, she had a gold mine of information. The Foundation was primarily interested in medical research—her major was going to be in education, which had no medical connotations at all—but they did have a strong reputation for granting scholarships. Yet, there again, most of the scholarships went to people interested in medical related fields. The grants given out by the Foundation were also medical in nature.

Odd.

Claire delved further. She read article after article about the Wrightstone Foundation; the galas they held, the fund raising events in the city, the philanthropic nature of their business. It was a well-run organization, by the looks of it. The Foundation was rated very high in the not for profit field and had extremely low overhead. They did not contribute to politicians, they stayed out of the limelight, and they quietly contributed hundreds of thousands of dollars a year.

She also stumbled onto information about the Wrightstones themselves. Descendents of baron robbers, they had made their money in the Golden Age, mainly in railroads and communications. The last of the Wrightstones had died the previous year after a long coma brought about by a car accident that had taken the lives of her parents over a decade before.

The current executors for the Wrightstone estate split their time between the North Carolina coast and the mid Hudson Valley estate that the Wrightstones had maintained for many years. It was located in the middle of an apple orchard, one of the largest private apple growing producers in the area.

Claire sat back in the computer chair, tapping her chin. Call her paranoid, but they lived in an *apple orchard*? That sounded familiar.

She typed in some more key words, refining her search and soon had the names of the executors. After running Steven and Katie Noble through the search engines, Claire finally hit pay dirt.

According to a small article in a local paper, there had been a party out at "The Orchards," attended by Steven and Katie Noble, as well as the renowned children's author Owen Montclaire and his wife Sarat.

Sarat. Now that was a familiar name. One that Claire had heard Emma say over and over. She was the petite woman with the dark brown hair.

After several more searches, Claire was absolutely convinced that the people behind the scholarship where the same people behind Jay's disappearance. Call her paranoid, but that was a coincidence that made her heart pound and her gut suspicious. One thing Claire had learned in her life was to trust her gut.

The amount of the grant was generous. More money than she needed to live on, that was for sure. If she took this money, what would she owe these people from the Foundation? According to the letter, nothing. But Claire was savvy enough to know that some debts were not put on paper, but rather expected as part of a favor being given.

After checking on the kids—Claire found she rarely slept when she was on this job for fear of not hearing one of the children if they needed her—she sat down on the sofa and brooded about what to do, dozing fitfully.

When the sun rose over the horizon, Claire was still sitting on the sofa, her feet curled beneath her. The youngest of the family woke up at six and came out to see Claire, crawling into her lap to watch the early show of Rosy the Pink Octopus, which was the little one's most favorite show in the entire world. When her mother came home from work, the child bounced off of Claire and bounded over to her mom.

Claire left soon after, promising Mrs. Wilson that she would be back the next night and ensuring that she had Claire's new address and phone number.

When Harry came to pick up Claire, she was standing at the end of the walkway of the Bassins' house, two suitcases, a small duffle bag and her framed picture by her feet. She had a mutinous look on her face. The Bassins were no where to be seen.

Harry unfolded his tall, lanky body from the ancient VW Bug he drove and surveyed the items. "Where's the rest?"

"This is it," Claire pulled the strap of the duffle over her shoulder. Harry tilted his head to the side, bewildered by the lack of teenage stuff. As he reached for one of the suitcases, Claire blurted, "I need to talk to Katie or Steven Noble."

Harry froze, bent partway over in a crouch. "What?"

"You heard me."

Harry straightened, running one hand through his black hair. "Why? Wait. The scholarship."

"You know." It was a statement and not a question. Anger began to pump through her system. "Well, I don't want it."

"What do you mean?" Now Harry was shocked. "But, it's the answer to all your worries. You won't have to work like a dog on more than three jobs just to live."

"I don't know anything about these people. Why me? Why me over anyone else in the world? Because I know you and Emma? Because I asked about Jay? Do they want my silence for something?"

"You have a very suspicious mind," Harry said, stroking his chin. "Why can't it just be that we know you, we told the foundation about you, and they want to branch out into this direction? Why does it have to be more complex than the fact that they want to help people?"

"Because Jay's disappearance is more complex than the story that he's in Europe studying photography."

Harry sighed. "Claire, I care about you. Emma cares about you. We are upstanding people. Do you honestly think we would get you involved in anything, *anything*, that would jeopardize your safety or well-being?"

Claire shook her head reluctantly. He was right about that, she had to admit. Emma and Harry would never knowingly put her at risk. It was what they didn't know that worried her, quite frankly.

"Just think about it," advised Harry, his thin frame all angles in his worn denim jeans and vintage t-shirt. "Don't make any rash or instant decisions about the grant. Can you do that for me?" Claire nodded, giving Harry cause to smile. "Good. Now, let's get you over to the Brewster's place." He picked up the framed picture and walked to the front of the bug where the trunk was located.

Claire picked up a suitcase and followed him. As she rounded the front of the car, she noticed that Harry stood stock still, staring at her picture. She blushed furiously.

"Oh, that's just my tree," she apologized, reaching for it. "I drew it when I was just a little kid but I like it a lot. Silly, isn't it?"

"You drew it." Harry refused to relinquish his hold on the frame. One finger lightly traced the red trunk. "And you held onto it for all these years?"

Claire shifted from one foot to the other, uncomfortable with Harry still looking at her picture. The tree was private. It was almost painful to see Harry holding the picture, staring at it, wondering about it.

When Harry looked her way, Claire was rather surprised to find that his face was full of concern and worry. "You need to come with me to the Orchards. Right away. Right now."

▼

VORTEX

In the Meadows Region, jeweled butterflies danced in the gentle breeze. The flowers swayed to the beat of Nature's unheard melody, and the pink-tinted clouds scuttled across the sky. The sun shone in the eternal spring that graced this part of the Land.

A figure appeared over the top of a rolling hill, a small dust cloud roiling up from his feet and flattening the grass.

The man paused, ratcheting his neck to one side, then the other, a loud crack resulting with the movement. He kicked at a tuft of grass in absolute distaste. In truth, he despised spending time in the Land. Especially when he was behind in his duties elsewhere. Time was quickly unraveling and he needed this final acquisition to make him the dominant player in the struggle between Good and Evil. His number one competitor was churning out product left and right—although his success was by no means a done deal. Convinced that he had the right approach to maximize the fight for Evil throughout the Grid system, the man was none-the-less cognizant that his time was running out. He had his eye on several prime choices, all in the World Dimension, all with the important connection to that pesky group of Protectors.

All he needed was a little time and a little luck, and his experiments would bear fruit that would forever change the race for Evil's penetration into all sectors of the Grid. The failures he'd had—and they had admittedly been legion—would be forgotten, and he would rule supreme at the side of his master.

But for now, he must endure the stench of the Land to see if his other pet project was bearing its own unique fruit.

He'd heard rumors, of course. His master's network of spies told of unusual storms in the Meadows Region. Not the result he'd expected, but perhaps it could prove useful. He'd had the foresight to bring to the Land several nutrients he thought would intensify his pet's production and if he'd timed it correctly, within the next few moments should see if this particular tree would bear the destructive fruit he so desired above all.

Carefully lifting his binoculars—it would not do for the bright sun to glint off the lenses and give his position away—the man focused on the area where he'd discovered his little pet had lay dormant. Until now. Focusing his attention to the area, he trained his eyes on the creature.

A bird lit upon the mottled colored rock, preening its wings in preparation for an early morning song. The bird took flight, as if startled by something.

The man smiled. Excellent.

A small hole appeared in the rock, a perfect circle, as if a hinged door had opened. A puff of air swirled from the hole, twirling about lazily. The hole closed behind the gust of air, sealing completely.

The puff of air drifted toward the sky, growing and darkening until a cloud had formed against the sky, tinged a peculiar greenish blue. Out of the cloud, a downward wind formed, twisting toward the ground, pulling the cloud's material along with it as it reached a questing finger in the direction of the earth. The wind grew in strength and veracity, a vortex that continued to grow as the air of the Meadows Region was sucked into the spinning mix. The wind fueled the cloud, which in turn directed its energy into the twisting and spinning funnel that continued to spiral down to the grass. When the tip of the cloud touched the ground, it churned up the soft earth, the moist ground startling against the brilliant green carpet.

The grass started to rustle, the trees sway, the flowers flatten; all in response to the growing reach and strength of the wind. Within minutes, a full-fledged funnel cloud raced across the Meadows Region, ripping up foliage and overturning trees as it wound its way in the general direction of the Beaches.

From his vantage point on the hill, the man watched, confident as the storm raced away from him, heading toward the verdant farmland that lay between the Marshes and Beaches Regions. Even now, through the lenses, he could see a group of farmers pausing to watch the storm as it headed directly toward their fields.

Stupid idiots didn't even realize they were watching their own death approach.

He watched with satisfaction as they were swept up into the maelstrom, their houses, barns and crops destroyed in one fell swoop. His binoculars—the best the Grid could produce at this time—allowed him to continue to watch as the tornado fed and grew, a monstrosity of terror. The spiraling cloud continued, unabated, wreaking a wide swath of havoc and destruction as it raced toward the ocean. When it hit against the invisible barrier between the Meadows and Beaches Region, the funnel cloud bounced back as if it had hit an impenetrable glass wall. Furious, the storm battered at the invisible barrier before finally dying out at the edge of the Meadows.

Grunting with satisfaction the man hooked his binoculars onto his belt. Hands on hips, he surveyed the countryside, wondering what other little wonders his pet would produce. It was a satisfactory day, indeed. He checked his wristwatch, which was in actuality a universal Grid device that managed to work within the confines of the Land. He needed to check on a few things in the Land, make sure panicked pigeons were being sent to the Capital. He wanted there to be havoc, confusion and mayhem. Those were the frosting on his cake, the results that made him—and his master—content.

Yes. A visit to a few of his minions, then a swing by the World Dimension to acquire his latest experimental vessel. He'd also pick up some of the food his pet in the Land so loved to consume, the nourishment that would allow it to continue to expel these marvelous, utterly destructive storms.

The man started down the hill toward the nearby village, hoping he'd get there after word of the tornado had spread. The fluster that would ensue would give him time to slip in unnoticed.

Life, the man mused as a hawk flew overhead, was truly wonderful.

~ 6 ~

▼

PROTECTOR ALLEY

Claire seethed with fury. In fact, the right word to describe her state of mind was pissed off.

She was pissed off at Harry, who had remained uncharacteristically quiet on the trip to the Orchards. He absolutely refused to answer any of her questions, preferring, as he kept saying, "To wait until more qualified folk looked at the painting."

She was pissed off at Emma for not being there to talk Harry out of this insane trip. She'd always considered Emma to be the more stable one of the two. This excursion proved Claire's point.

She was even more pissed off at herself for agreeing to get into the stupid car in the first place. She had better things to do with her time; she needed to study, for one. This trip was taking away from work time, and she was missing her afternoon class. All in all, this was by far one of the most stupid things she'd ever done. She was stuck in an ancient beetle heading toward the cuckoo's nest with all her worldly belongings in the trunk.

In all honesty, she had no one but herself to blame. Which meant she was pissed off at herself most of all.

Claire was so pissed off, in fact, that she let Harry buy her lunch at a fast food place, figuring that if he was going to drag her off into the wilds of the Mid Hudson Valley region, the least he could do was feed her. It wasn't until she finished the burger and fries that she realized she had been neatly and adroitly manipulated by the man. Emma would never let him eat fast food, and Claire figured Harry had used her as an excuse to get his grease fix.

Claire decided that to get even with Harry, she'd just ignore him, staring out the window of the bug. She had no idea where they were, as they had left the main roads a long time ago. When Harry turned down a long, narrow, wooded road, Claire watched the greenery pass by without a word.

At the end of the road, there was a clearing, like a turn around, and it was bordered by a large wooden fence, through which Claire could see several buildings. It looked like there was a house and a barn, and maybe a few other structures. Beyond the barn, Claire caught a glimpse of some apple trees. She sat up, interested again despite the burning annoyance deep in her gut.

So this must be the mysterious Orchards.

"You don't happen to have a cell phone, do you?" Harry asked her, tapping his fingers on the steering wheel.

"I can't afford a cell phone," she shot back with ill temper.

"If you took the grant, you'd be able to get one," Harry pointed out, and then sighed. "I don't know if anyone is actually home right now."

"Why don't you jump the fence?"

"Electrified." He gestured toward the fence. Claire squinted, noticing for the first time the wires and red light on the fence.

"Why would people need to electrify their fence?" She slanted Harry a suspicious look. "What are they trying to keep out? Or is it something they're trying to keep in?"

"You're entirely too cynical," Harry commented easily, unfolding himself from the car, then leaning back in and hitting the horn, causing it to bleat out several anemic blasts.

The door to the house opened and a small woman with dark hair falling past her waist stepped onto the porch, shading her eyes and looking in their direction. When she saw the VW Beetle, she waved frantically then raced back inside. Within seconds, the gate opened.

Harry got back into the car, and they chugged through the gate. He parked near the large farmhouse, popping the trunk of the bug as he turned off the engine. He opened the door, then turned to Claire, jiggling the keys in his hand.

"You can take off your seatbelt now." Amusement rang in his voice.

"I'm not getting out. You wanted me to come, I did. I never said I'd actively participate in your little drama."

Harry sighed. "All right, Claire. Have it your way. If you change your mind, just come inside."

"Tell the Nobles I do want to speak with them. They can come out to the car. I'm not going in that house."

Harry shook his head and climbed out. Claire heard him rummaging under the hood of the car. He was pulling out her picture, no doubt. Soon he was tromping up the stairs to be greeted by the same woman who had been on the porch earlier. Sarat, that was her name, Claire recalled. When the petite woman looked in the direction of the car, Claire ducked her head to avoid making eye contact. The next time she looked at the porch, it was empty.

Claire looked around the courtyard. Idly, she looked toward the apple orchard. From this angle, she could only see a few of the trees, whose leaves were already beginning to change colors.

The increased stuffiness inside the vehicle forced her to roll down the window for some fresh air. The courtyard was quiet, the only sound a gentle breeze rustling through the leaves of the orchard. The ambient noise was actually soothing, the dry crackle reminding Claire of autumns in her youth, back when things were easier, when life made sense. Touching the bead on the chain around her neck, Claire leaned her cheek against her arm, staring at the leaves as they tossed about.

Claire grew drowsy. Her lack of sleep the night before and the long car ride had combined to bring her to a state of undeniable exhaustion. She took a deep breath, her eyes starting to close.

Just before she could drift off to sleep, she caught the sound of whispering. Her eyes snapped open, expecting to find the whackos of the Orchard arrayed in front of the car staring at her.

The courtyard was empty. Claire's moss green eyes looked at the apple trees. The whispering sound continued, as if the trees themselves were calling out to her. Claire tilted her head, trying to capture what the whispered words were saying, but the meaning eluded her. All she knew was that she was supposed to follow the whispers to find the source.

It was as if someone had drugged her. All Claire wanted to do was to go into the woods, seeking the answers that the whispered voices were asking.

"What kind of place is this?" she whispered, trying to shake off the compelling need of wanting to, absolutely having to go into the woods.

Despite all her best intentions of staying inside the car, Claire found herself reaching for the door handle. Before she could open it, a face suddenly appeared in the window. Claire recoiled in shock.

"Sorry!" the woman said, smiling. "I didn't mean to startle you. Do you remember me from the other day? I stopped by the store. My name is Sasha."

"Uh, yeah. Hi." Claire stared past the woman's shoulder toward the trees. The breeze had stopped, the trees were no longer swaying, and the whispers had subsided.

"Look, I know you're confused about all this," Sasha said softly, "but at least come inside and have something to drink. There's no need for you to hang out in a hot car."

Claire rubbed her eyes. "I'm fine." She slouched into the seat and took a long pull on the soda from the fast food restaurant.

"My, aren't you the picture of teen-age angst," Sasha chuckled.

Claire glowered at the woman, who smiled back.

"I've seen all the looks, trust me. I can be quite the master of them, as a matter of fact. I know you're interested, or you wouldn't have gotten in the car. So come on inside and we'll talk. I promise, we won't require you to sign anything in blood." Sasha opened the car door and looked askance at the young girl inside. "Unless, of course, you're too scared. Then, by all means, hide out in the car. But of course, hiding in a Volkswagen beetle isn't really a safe bet, is it?"

Claire's eyes narrowed. "I'm not going to fall for reverse psychology," she said in a warning tone. "Just because you imply I'm chicken, I'm supposed to bolt from the car. It doesn't work on me."

"Ok, then." Sasha shrugged, as if she didn't care. "Then you won't mind if we do whatever we want to that picture of yours, because believe me, we find it very interesting. Ben wants to analyze what kind of paint was used, and Katie is planning on doing some sort of experiment as well. I thought you'd like to have a say in what happened, but if you don't want to leave the car, then fine." Turning, she strode away.

Claire chewed on her lip. She was ninety percent sure that Sasha was bluffing. It was the other ten percent that worried her. The thought of her beloved painting being harmed or even taken from the frame was enough to edge her toward hyperventilating. God, she hated to panic like this; despised that she was not in control of her most precious belonging. Then those hated whispers and breeze started up in the trees again, which was enough to make her want to scream in frustration.

"This is ridiculous." Claire made a decision and reached for the door handle. There was no way she was sitting out here slowly going mad. She was not used to sitting around when she could be taking action. Ok, taking control. But it was her stuff, and her life. She swung her legs from the beetle and stood up, squaring her shoulders as she headed for the porch.

Letting herself into the house as quietly as possible, grateful for a respite from the whispers from the orchard, Claire could hear voices coming from a back room. At least these were normal sounds of a gathering of people. A quick look around showed her that the main living room was empty, although it looked like a recent game of dominoes had been played on the hearth before the fireplace, and a computer was still on, a book with a beautiful greenish cover propped next to it.

Claire followed the voices into the back hall. She assumed she was headed toward the kitchen. As she poked her head around the corner, she had to swallow the gasp that automatically tried to burst out of her. The kitchen was massive, stretching across the entire back of the house. A large farm table dominated the room, around which clustered a group of people. They were all talking and gesturing but without any discernable heat or anger.

Propped against a chair at the end of the table was Claire's painting. She breathed a sigh of relief, ridiculously glad to see it was in one piece.

"She's too young," a tall man with spiked blond hair and black glasses was saying vehemently. "None of the people chosen for a quest has been under twenty one."

"She barely turned eighteen, you say?" The petite blond was looking at Emma.

"Yes, Katie, she is, but Claire, because of her circumstances, is incredibly mature," replied Emma. "I find her to be more grown up than most twenty somethings I've met in my lifetime. Certainly more grown up than I was at that age."

"Hey, you married me when we were both eighteen," Harry protested lovingly.

"And a wiser, older, more mature woman never would have done that," Emma retorted, but her soft smile belied the words. "And, yes, not marrying you would've been the worst mistake for me to make."

"Still," Zach said, his voice failing to hide his skepticism from the group, which made Claire want to squirm and protest, which was just stupid. "I wouldn't want an eighteen year old to face some of the things we've had to go against in our quests."

"I agree." This came from a very small woman, or perhaps a teenager like herself, with long brunette hair and an impish face, currently set in stubborn lines. "Based on what you've told us, it is entirely possible she's got a darker spirit. Send her against Evil and he'll try and capitalize on that, seduce her."

"Ok, that's just stupid, Sarat," said Sasha, her voice colored with exasperation. "I can guarantee my childhood was as dark, if not darker, than Claire's. In fact, I was actively stalked by Evil. So, I don't think that's a guarantee she's going to automatically fall to Evil. I didn't."

"Maybe she's been stalked as well," said Katie, tapping her finger against her chin. "Wouldn't hurt to ask her…"

"How do we know that she's going to Travel now?" This came from a woman who was either incredibly fat or incredibly pregnant. Claire was guessing the later since Emma had left to stay with these people 'until the baby was born.' "After all, Harry saw the Tree when he was young, but he never Traveled, right?"

"Well, Harry and Emma saw the Tree then conceived Jay," Liz pointed out to the pregnant woman. "I've always taken that to mean the sighting was a kind of symbol that Jay was coming, and he was going to be a Traveler."

"I wish Amber was here," Tracy complained. "We could really use her advice in this matter."

"We can't keep relying on Amber and Daniel to tell us what to do," Katie stated adamantly. "There are some things we are supposed to figure out on our own. And finding potential Travelers is one of them."

"But Katie, the age thing is still troubling me. Is this Claire ready to Travel? Emotionally? Physically?" the blond man was saying.

"Well, Ben, that's a good question. Why don't we ask Claire herself?" Katie replied lightly, nodding toward the hallway. "She's capable of making such an important decision on her own, once she knows all the pertinent facts of the matter."

Claire swallowed as all eyes turned toward her. Resolutely, she stepped into the room. "I just came for my picture," she said hotly. "I don't want you people messing with it." She crossed the room, scooped up her picture and held it tightly against her.

Her face was burning, and she knew that everyone was still watching her. Turning on her heel, she stalked back to the doorway. "I'll be waiting in the car," Claire tossed over her shoulder in Harry's direction.

"Claire, wait." It was the petite blond, the one with the amazing blue eyes. Claire paused, one foot in the hallway. Defiantly, she turned toward the woman.

"I'm Katie Gaber Noble. I know this all seems really weird to you," Katie said slowly, rising from the table. She walked toward Claire, slowly and cautiously, as if she were approaching a wild horse that could bolt at any moment. "But in all honesty, we could be placing you in serious danger if we didn't at least explain to you what we think that picture means. What it could entail for you. Either now or in your future."

"Does this have to do with what is calling me from the orchard?" Claire blurted out, then slapped her hand over mouth in horror at having disclosed that information.

The surprise on Katie's face was mirrored by all of the people around the table. "The orchard is calling to you?"

Claire shifted her grip on the painting, one hand running over the tree absently. It seemed to give her a measure of strength. "Yes," she replied in a tone that clearly said she expected to be mocked for her admission.

"Then we really do need to talk," Katie said, tilting her head to one side with a thoughtful looking smile. "Why don't you come and sit down at the table for a few moments. After you hear us out, I promise, you can go if you want to. Harry will take you back with no questions asked. Just know this, Claire. We'll always be here for you. No matter how, no matter when."

Ok. This was better. This Katie woman seemed sincere, and so, well, normal. Claire nodded and crossed to the table, careful to sit at the opposite end, far away from the others. Harry and Emma gave her an encouraging nod.

"Claire, I want you to know that there's nothing in our Orchard that will hurt you," Katie started, after settling back down at the table. "But there is something that is incredible, magical, and could completely change your life. It's changed all of ours."

"Spare me the infomercial," Claire said tightly. "Cut to the chase."

"All righty then," Katie said agreeably. "In our orchard is a Tree that can transport you to another dimension. We call it the Land. The people of the Land are fighting Evil, who is trying to take over their world. Many of us," she gestured around the table, "with the exception of Emma and Harry, have Traveled to the Land. Or, in Sarat's case, from the Land to here. The fact that you have this Tree painting, which resembles the Tree in our orchard, indicates to us that you're next to go."

Silence fell around the table. Claire looked at each one of them in turn. Then she stared at her hands, clenched tightly enough to stretch the skin white. Finally, she turned to Katie. "That's it, then?" Katie nodded, so Claire pushed back her chair and grabbed her painting again. "I'll be in the car, Harry."

"Well, that certainly went well," Tracy observed with some amusement after Claire had swept from the room, painting under one arm.

"She's not ready," Ben said stubbornly.

"She's smart to run like hell," Zach disagreed.

"She just needs time to process it all," Liz suggested.

"I agree." Katie turned toward Harry. "Take her home." She arched an eyebrow as the others protested vehemently. "Look, I promised her she could leave if she listened. She listened. So I have to uphold my end of the bargain. I have a funny feeling that girl has had too many promises broken in her life. I'm not going to add to the mix."

"She's right," Emma put in. "It will go a long way with Claire if you hold to your word and let her go without a fuss. She'll be more likely to come back if you do."

"You'll keep an eye on her?" Liz asked Harry urgently. "Call us if you feel there is anything, anything at all that could indicate she is on Evil's radar?"

"Of course I will," Harry replied, pushing up his glasses. Zach and Ben exchanged worried looks. Harry was, at best, absent minded. Entrusting Claire's well being to his inattentiveness could be courting disaster.

"I'll walk you out to the car," Katie said, standing.

"Here." Zach tossed Katie a small cell phone and charger. "Give Claire this phone. Our private numbers are all programmed in. All she has to do is call and we'll come get her. Anyplace, anytime."

"Good idea," Katie said, giving him a smile.

Harry climbed into the seat next to Claire as Katie rounded the front of the beetle. Claire was sitting still, staring out the windshield. Katie leaned down and put her face next to the open window.

"Have a safe trip home," she told Claire, "and just think about what we said. Harry can tell you about his son Jay, who is still living in the Land, if you're interested in hearing it. Also, here's a cell phone. It's programmed and all you need to do is call us. We'll answer any questions or come and get you if you need us."

"I'm not taking the grant," Claire said through gritted teeth, although she accepted the phone without complaint, Katie noticed.

"Yes, you will," Katie replied evenly. "You'll take it because you know it's a good deal and you know you can't go through school without it. You aren't a stupid girl. There are no ties on that grant, Claire. Take it." Katie glanced over at Harry, who was hunched over the steering wheel, clearly miserable. "Take care of yourself, Harry. Don't hesitate to call us if you need anything."

Claire glanced at Katie, and then did a classic double take. For a split second, it seemed like the woman was glowing with a subtle pink glow. But when she looked at her fully, the image disappeared. She looked back out the windshield again, closing her eyes until they were far away from the Orchard and its bizarre occupants.

▼

7

COMING TO GRIPS

Claire and Harry spent the trip home in silence. Once, Harry tried to start a conversation with Claire, but she gave him a single, stony look and he quickly subsided. At the Brewster's house, Harry quietly carried her bags up the steps to Claire's new room, a small space that rivaled the one she had at the Bassins.

Claire slung the bags onto the bed and turned toward Harry, her shoulders hunched, hands shoved into her pockets. It was an awkward moment.

"Claire…" Harry started, then paused, rubbing his chin with his hand. Taking a deep breath he tried again. "Claire, I know this all seems bizarre. But I can honestly say that it's all true. And Katie, she's very powerful. She has abilities that are beyond you or me. She's offered you protection. Don't turn your back on that. If anything seems out of the ordinary, anything at all, call them."

"Anything out of the ordinary, huh? What about a bunch of people who think they can go to another planet via a plant?" Claire tucked her chin and looked at Harry through slit eyes. "Who do I call then?"

Harry sighed, his blue eyes reflecting sadness and, she had to admit, wisdom. "Sometimes, we can close ourselves off from wonderful experiences because we dare not believe in things we cannot see, hear, taste and touch.

The Land, well, you *can* see, hear, taste and touch it. Just give yourself the option to try, Claire. That's all I'm asking. Try and be watchful."

Claire did not sleep well at all that night, or for the next few nights, for that matter. She felt like she was constantly hearing those damn whispers in her mind, telling her to come back to the orchards, to visit the apple trees. At times, she found herself longing to walk beneath the boughs of the trees, watching the sunlight dapple the brown earth below. She could literally smell the unique scent of tangy ripe apples and the autumn fires burning in the barrels.

The funny thing was that Claire felt she was perhaps the last person who would ever want to commune with nature.

On Friday, Claire was scheduled to work at *Arts Extraordinaire* from three until closing. She would be alone, as Harry was going to go to his friend's house for dinner and a long anticipated game of poker. Claire figured he went for the snack food, not the card game.

The night passed with excruciating slowness. It had turned colder, and with the high school football games having started in the three surrounding counties that weekend, there were few people in town proper, much less in their decidedly avant garde store. Claire found herself feeling rather nostalgic over the games. She'd been on the high school color guard for her junior and senior years, twirling the six- foot flag as part of the band. It had cost her many nights of work to pay for the uniform, boots and all, but she'd done it. Being in college, she couldn't afford to continue on the color guard for her university. The band required too many hours and too much money for her participate.

The sound of the band playing at halftime wafted over the town. Claire sat behind the counter, one foot swinging in the air. She was adrift, with nothing to do but work and school. No friends, no place to hang out with her band buddies. Just…nothing. Her life didn't seem to fit anymore. She might as well be an outsider, watching everything pass her by while she stayed, stagnant, treading water and trying to keep from drowning.

At the end of the night, Claire locked up the store, turning off the display and overhead lights. Her last stop before leaving was the office, where she locked up the deposit and daily sales listing in the small fireproof safe located under Emma's desk. As she closed the safe, Claire's eyes fell on the bottom drawer of the desk.

Almost in a dream, Claire pulled on the drawer, which opened easily. Emma must not have locked it very carefully after her last visit to the drawer. The space inside was taken up by letters from Jay and several pictures. With shaking hands, Claire pulled out the pictures, leafing through them.

She saw snapshots of an everyday life that was simple, yet enchanting. Jay seemed fond of landscapes, and the vistas varied dramatically. One picture was from what looked like a wedding. Claire recognized the woman from the photo—she was the pregnant one from the Orchards. She shuffled to the next one in the stack. There was the blond man, minus glasses, posed next to a petite woman with a cloud of dark hair. They were looking at one another with obvious affection and appeared to be standing on a dock, an old wooden ship behind them.

The woman most often in the photos was the one with the riot of honey colored curls, the one who was in the picture Emma had shown her previously. In most of the pictures, the woman was laughing and smiling, but one poignant one reflected her pixy face in serious repose, as if she were contemplating matters of great importance. She seemed like a nice person, Claire thought as she replaced the photos. She must be someone Jay was involved with, given the sheer number of pictures she was in.

Her fingers traced over the edges of the envelopes in the drawer, hesitating. Looking at photos was one thing, reading someone else's private mail was quite another. Yet her curiosity overwhelmed her, the damned whispers loud in her head. Claire pulled the first letter out of the drawer, withdrawing the thick vellum from the envelope. She promised herself that if it was too personal, too intimate, she would simply return the material to the desk drawer and forget she'd ever breached Emma's privacy.

Sitting cross-legged on the floor in the dusty back room, Claire read through the first letter. It was a lengthy explanation to his parents about his choice to stay in the Land and live his life among the people there. Jay detailed the history of the Land, the fight against Evil and his success in sending a race known as the Too'ki back to their dimension. It also told of his love for the Land woman, Tona. Claire figured she was the woman in the pictures with the corkscrew curls.

It was intriguing reading, and Claire learned a great deal about the other Protectors of the Land—what an odd yet appealing name—who had come to the Land before him. There was no mention of Liz or Zach, so Claire was left to assume that they had come to the Land after Jay.

But it was interesting to learn that Katie was an Oracle, some sort of all-powerful being. That Tracy had been infected by the Too'kis during a sword fight. Then there was Ben, who could swim underwater and wasn't even from the World Dimension at all. Added to that was Sasha who could speak to animals and Sarat, who was originally from the Land but now living in the World. It was simply amazing, and incredible.

After reading the first letter, there was no going back. Claire raced through the rest of the documents, reading about the Land, the people, the culture. She read how Jay was slowly but surely learning all about being a wizard, growing in his skills. It was also nice to read how much he loved Tona and how they were growing closer as a couple, despite some rather daunting cultural shocks along the way.

First, Liz, then Zach, was introduced to the Land; Claire learned that their quests had both been fraught with danger and personal discovery. It seemed like Zach's, in particular, was especially violent. Perhaps most startling was that Liz was a Seer, able to read the future and past through simple touch.

Touch. Emma and Zach had looked so confused when Liz had shaken hands with her. It must have been some sort of test. The fact that she'd been read against her will or knowledge made Claire's hands shake. It was then she realized, with no small astonishment, that she actually believed what was described in the letters. Somehow, in the course of the night, Claire had gone from cynical skeptic to cautious believer. The letters were too detailed and consistent to be anything but real. Even the paper they were written on was authentic to the story, thick vellum and the ink appeared to be applied with a quill, complete with ink dots and splotches.

The idea of fighting against pure Evil was at the same time scary and fascinating. How did one fight against a concept, anyway? Yet, these Protectors seemed to be rather good at it. Which, in Claire's opinion, further proved that she was not supposed to be a part of the program. She could not imagine anything she could do that would be able to deflect Evil.

Yet, the similarities between the Land Tree description and the picture she had drawn as a child were striking, even Claire had to admit that much. It was no wonder the Protectors thought that Claire was a potential Traveler.

Claire carefully folded the letters, placing them back into the drawer. Other than the information on the Land, which Claire was grateful to have without needing to stoop to asking any of the protectors for the details, Claire was struck by the genuine affection that existed between Jay and his parents. The familial love was obvious, and it gave Claire a pang in her heart. She'd never experience that kind of love, and envied Jay for it.

It was clear that the letters contained an ongoing dialogue between them, Jay regularly asked about the store, answered some question that had been asked of him and in general seemed to have a finger on the pulse of his parent's lives.

Claire was even more shocked to find that her name was sprinkled throughout the letters. Emma and Harry had obviously told Jay about their salesperson and her increased hours in the store. Claire didn't really appreciate it when Jay likened her to a new stray his parents had adopted, but she had to laugh when he admonished Emma and Harry for making Claire work in the store alone so that they could go see the Woodstock concert together.

Claire closed the drawer on the letters firmly, waiting to hear the latch of the lock. Dusting her hands off on her jeans, thinking about the content of the letters, she just stood in the silent, dark store. Something had changed within her, and Claire wasn't quite sure what to do about this fact. A look at the clock indicated that it was after midnight, so she'd been reading for several hours.

Claire grabbed her keys and turned off the office light, leaving the small lamp on the desk lit, as always. Shouldering the small backpack she used as a purse, Claire passed through the dark store and unlocked the front door with her key.

Outside the shop, the street was pretty much deserted. Down the road, tinny music could be heard from the restaurant and pub that was on the corner. All the shops were closed and locked up tightly for the night. A full moon hung over the street, casting enough light for Claire to be able to turn the lock in the door without having to move so the streetlight could hit the door.

Claire started down the sidewalk toward the Brewster's house. They lived farther from the center of town than the Bassins had, and it added to her evening walk/commute. But the night was still mild enough that it didn't bother Claire too much. In a few months, this walk would be a bitter journey, so she might as well enjoy the autumnal briskness. She just hugged her arms closer to her waist and kept moving.

About a block or two from the store, Claire passed by a wooded park area when she heard a peculiar rustling sound in the foliage lining the road. She ignored the sound, assuming it was just a neighborhood cat on the prowl for food or companionship.

When the bushes continued to move with increasing urgency, her steps faltered. It seemed like the disturbance was caused by something substantially larger than a cat. Claire took a cautious step backward.

The bushes parted and a huge, furry shape crashed through. Claire had a brief impression of gnashing teeth before turning on her heel and running back toward the center of town. Several paces down the road, she skidded to a halt just missing another creature standing in front of her, blocking her path.

Claire looked over her shoulder. Sure enough, there were two of them, one on either side of her, neatly boxing her in. They were ferrets, she realized with shock. Extremely large ferrets. Something about them struck a chord in her mind, even through her panic. A vision from dreams she'd had, something that was familiar yet terrifying.

Farther down the street, just out of range of the lamppost, lurked a tall figure. He appeared to be staring right at her. "Hey! A little help here?" Claire called out to him.

To her anger, the man simply turned and walked away, strolling down the street as if the appearance of large rodents was not his concern, a long blond ponytail rippling in the breeze.

"Asshole." Claire looked around frantically. Spying a large stout branch in the gutter, she picked it up, holding it in two fists like a baseball bat.

Now she just had to make a decision which rodent was going to be meeting the business end of her makeshift weapon. She had been walking toward the residential section of town, and it was late enough that most of the houses were already dark, their occupants fast asleep. The other way lay the center of town, equally deserted, but better lit. Plus, some bars were still open, and the chance of people being on the street was far greater in that direction.

Her mind made up, Claire started to step sideways toward the ferret between her and the business section of town. The ferrets were continuing to hiss and sway, their heads low to the ground as they stalked her. *Holy crap, are these things rabid? And when the hell did ferrets grow to the size of your average German Shepard?*

When she was within a few yards of the ferret standing its ground between her and the stores, Claire tightened her grip on the stick. With a sudden yell, she raised the stick high above her head and then swung down and away at the ferret, catching it along side its furry head with enough force to send the creature tumbling to the side.

As Claire took off running, the other ferret came racing down the street. It paused by its fallen comrade, which was staggering to its feet, shaking its head in a dazed fashion.

Claire skidded around the corner onto the main street, heading for the far end, where the pub and the police station were located. What she saw in front of her had her stopping dead in her tracks.

No less than three more ferrets trundled down the middle of the street toward her, their undulating bodies sinister in the lamppost light.

"Bite me." Claire ran across the street toward the store, fumbling for her keys as she went. She could hear a flurry of feet behind her, and the sound spurred her even faster.

She jammed the key into the lock, panting with panic and fear. When the door opened, Claire pushed her way through then shoved it closed behind her. One of the ferrets was right at her heels and actually got a paw caught between the door and frame.

Practically sobbing, Claire kicked at the furry paw until it jerked away, then she shot the security deadbolt on the door. Her breath sounded harsh in the quiet store. Through the glass, she could see the ferrets milling about in front of the store, one limping and another one sporting a bleeding gash over one eye.

"Good." Claire released her grip on her makeshift bat, shaking her tingling hand. Picking up her backpack, she dug through it, her hand closing around the slim cell phone. She'd shoved the cell Katie had given her into the bag, and pulling it out now she gave the ferrets a baleful glance.

"You said call if there was anything weird," she muttered, flipping it on and dialing the first number that came up on the memory.

"Hullo?" came a deep, sleepy male voice.

"Which one of you is this?" Claire demanded, adrenaline making her pace back and forth anxiously.

"This is Ben Harm, who the hell is this?"

"This is Claire. I have a bunch of ferrets outside of Emma and Harry's store. Big assed ferrets. At least five, no wait, make that six." The bastards were watching Claire avidly, like she was their choice of lobsters in a tank.

"Ferrets? What?"

"Oh, for God's sake, put one of the women on!"

"Wait. Claire? Claire? Emma and Harry's Claire?" Ben's voice cleared up quickly. "Ok, got it. Ferrets. Damn, you're at least an hour away from us. Shit! Sorry, I dropped the phone when I was pulling on my jeans. Ok. Do you have any weapons?"

"No. Well, I whomped one upside the head with a big stick, but I dropped it when I was running."

"Good job. When in doubt, whomping on the head is a good choice." Ben's approval glowed over the line. "Look around the store. See if there's anything you can use for a weapon. Stay inside. Whatever you do, don't go out. One of us will stay on the line with you the entire time."

"Ok." Claire sighed gratefully. She was poking around the store, looking for something that she could use as a weapon, but finding nothing. "This place is full of useless artsy fartsy crap," she wailed into the phone, earning a chuckle from Ben.

"I hear ya on that one." Through the earpiece, Claire could hear him pounding on doors and shouting to people. In a few moments, a female voice was on the line.

"Claire? This is Tracy. The others are getting dressed and ready to come to the rescue. I'll hang on the phone with you until they're going out the door."

"Thanks for not hanging up," Claire said fervently, picking up a large crystal rock and hefting it in one hand. It could be used as a weapon, she supposed, but not a very feasible one. She clunked it back down dejectedly.

"Honey, we won't hang up," Tracy assured her. "I just wish I could come too and kick some furry ass. Ben tells me you whomped one. Good show."

Claire laughed, but it was bitter and feeble, even to her own ears.

"Hang on; Emma wants to talk to you."

"Claire, are you alright?"

At the sound of Emma's worried voice, Claire doubled over, as if in pain. No one had sounded so concerned about her in a long, long time.

"I'm fine, really," wheezed Claire, half laughing, half crying. "But you and Harry have nothing that can be used as a freaking weapon in this place."

"Go into the office." Emma's firm voice helped Claire to focus on the task. "In the file cabinet, bottom drawer. You'll find something useful there. I'm giving the phone back to Tracy, but before I do…where's Harry?"

Claire froze. Harry. "He's playing poker at Jim's house," she said, her eyes flying to the clock on the back wall. "He might come home at any time."

"I'll try and call Jim's house from another line," Emma said immediately handing the phone off.

Seconds later, Tracy was back on the phone. "Emma's calling now. Did you find what Emma was talking about in the file cabinet?"

"Huh? Oh, let me go look." Claire shot one last glance at the front windows. Lined up along the sidewalk, the ferrets paced, teeth and eyes glittering. Creepy.

When she pulled open the bottom drawer, Claire's breath exhaled in a shocked gasp. "What the hell?" She pulled out a policeman's nightstick and a long, sharp hunting knife. Describing the useful finds to Tracy, she pulled the knife from the sheath. The blade gleamed, the serrated edge glinting with wicked intent in the florescent lights.

"Well, they might come in handy," Tracy observed. "Wonder what the pacifist twins were doing with those."

Claire eyed the handcuffs that were also in the drawer. "I don't think I want to know." Firmly shutting the drawer, she got to her feet, the fact that she was now armed made her more steady.

"Ok, I'm giving the phone to Sasha. She, Lizzie, Katie, Ben and Zach are coming for you. Take care of yourself, you hear me?"

"Righto." Amazing how the knowledge of some serious back up and a steel blade could cheer a girl up, despite the furry parade going on outside.

"Hey, Claire." Sasha greeted her genially, sounding like she was walking rapidly. "I'm going to be your cavalry guide tonight. We're going to be breaking some serious speed laws to get up to you as quickly as possible. Just hang tight and everything will be fine."

"Fantastic. So are we just going to listen to one another breathe for the next hour?" Claire stalked back into the main room of the store. She wanted those furry things to see their prey was no longer harmless and unprotected.

Only two ferrets remained at the front of the store.

"Shit!"

"What! What is it?" Sasha demanded.

"Four ferrets are missing," Claire replied, frantically looking around, half expecting them to come barreling at her from around a display case. Then she heard a familiar put-putting sound over the thud of her heart. "Oh, no...Harry!"

She dropped the phone and raced for the back door of the store. Just as Harry was opening the door to the beetle, Claire flung open the back door and bellowed at him to get inside quickly.

Harry paused, tilting his head to one side at the sight of Claire, holding the billy stick and hunting knife. Then four large ferrets came bounding around the side of the building, their sleek bodies undulating as they raced closer.

Claire had to give him credit. Harry caught on fast.

He threw the Tupperware container in his hand at the ferrets and sprinted for the open back door. One ferret nipped at Harry's heels and earned himself a swift blow to the snout from Claire's club. Howling, it wheeled away, shaking its head in pain. The other three pressed on, but Claire was already shutting the door behind Harry and hustling him into the main showroom, handing the knife to him as they went.

"Welcome home, Harry." Claire scooped the cell phone back up.

▼

8

RETURN OF THE FERRETS

"Hello, you've reached Ferret Central," Claire said into the phone.

Sasha, who had been repeatedly screaming Claire's name into the phone, growled deep in her throat. "What the hell was that, Claire?"

"Harry came home."

"Harry?" Sasha's voice faded as the phone was snatched from her.

"Claire, this is Zach. Listen, I've gone up against these ferrets before. They can be shape shifters, meaning they can take the form of anyone." His voice radiated concern.

All the blood drained from Claire's face, and she turned to face Harry with trepidation. "I just let Harry inside and gave him the knife," she whispered. Harry was staring at her, his head tilted to one side. He looked so familiar but suddenly, it was as if she had never seen him before.

"Ask him a question that only Harry could answer."

"Harry, what did Jay tell you he was going to do in his last letter, and what did he want you to send to him?"

"Huh? Well, he said he was going to ask Tona to marry him. And he wanted to know if we would send his grandmother's engagement ring with Ben on his next visit so he can give it to her." Harry frowned and pointed the knife at Claire. "Hey, how did you know about that?"

"It's Harry," Claire told Zach with relief.

Zach sighed. "Ok. Good. Listen, I don't care what you see, who you see, or how real what you are seeing seems, do not open those doors. Oh, Jesus, watch the road, will you Ben! I'm telling her, I swear I am. Do you hear me, Claire?"

"I hear you. But you better tell that to Harry, because he's looking pretty confused at the moment." Claire handed the phone to Harry and checked up on the status of the creatures. Three ferrets were injured now, the two she'd hit on the head and the one with the hurt paw. All six were staring at her with hungry eyes. With one ear, she listened to Harry on the phone.

"Ok, Zach. I understand. We'll stay put. But I worry about the people out in the town. Will these ferrets hurt them, do you think?" Harry walked up to stand next to Claire, but he didn't try to touch her. Which was a relief, since she was walking the edge of hysteria at the moment. Good old Harry. He knew she hated to be touched.

Claire could hear Zach's voice on the phone, saying they had no idea what the ferrets would or could do. Claire looked up at Harry, concerned. It would be just like Harry to race out into the middle of a ferret feeding frenzy if he felt someone was in danger.

Harry handed the phone back to Claire. "Katie wants to talk with you."

"This is Claire." Her gaze returned to the window. Claire eased away from Harry and noticed that the eyes of all the ferrets were glued to her and her alone. They were ignoring Harry. That made her feel better, somehow. She'd rather they be fixated on her and not him.

"Claire, I can't talk on the phone long or it will go all wonky. So listen carefully. You're doing really, really well," Katie said in a calm and collected voice. "But when we get there, you're going to see some things that may startle you. I want to prepare you for what's coming."

"You'll come blazing in with pink Oracle power, Zach and Ben will be flying in with swords swinging, Sasha too for that matter, but I think that she's along because you all feel she's bonding with me somehow. Or maybe because she might be able to talk to the beasties. I think Liz will be driving the getaway car, either that or she can blow these suckers up with her Seering power." Claire kept her eyes on the ferrets.

"Dang, girl, you do have it all figured out." Katie laughed merrily, as if they were chatting over cups of steaming hot chocolate and not the impending slaughter of a half dozen overgrown rodents in a quiet Catskill village road. "Except that Sasha will be driving the getaway vehicle, as Liz will be trying to read the area psychically. Not a good idea to mix forecasting and driving. But you may not know what I'm talking about."

"I read Jay's letters to Emma and Harry." Claire cast Harry an apologetic look. "I think I get the gist of what's happening."

"All righty then. You know what we'll be doing. Stay back, don't get in the way, and we'll get you out of there. I say that not because I don't think you can take care of yourself, Claire, but because we've been working as a team for many years now. We have a rhythm, a way of gelling together when we go into battle. You get in the middle and it could throw us and someone could get hurt. I can't risk that."

"I understand. I have no desire to go up against our furry friends, believe me." She turned toward the window, automatically counting the ferrets. "They're all still there."

"Keep counting them," Katie advised her. "Remember, these creatures are tricky. They could suddenly multiply or change shape to look like someone you know."

"And the joy of being connected with you guys just grows by leaps and bounds." Claire's snarky comment earned her another laugh from Katie.

"True, but you know what else? You're never alone when you're with us."

Inside the darkened SUV, Katie handed the cell phone over to Sasha. "Keep her talking. She's holding up really well, but it could all be a front."

Sasha nodded and took a deep breath, then got on the phone with Claire, moving to the third row seat of the large SUV, where it was quieter and she could concentrate on her conversation with Claire. Katie turned to face Liz.

"What are you getting?" she asked the Seer, who was staring out the window, her eyes slightly unfocused.

"Hard to say." Liz's reply came back clipped and distracted. "There's so much Evil in our World that it is hard to wade through it all and narrow down to one area. It's like trying to read through a mass of jello."

"Keep trying. I'd like to know if these ferrets are being directed by someone, like Zella did with her pets." Liz nodded and looked back out the window.

"What other option could there be?" Ben asked from the driver's seat as he continued to race up the thruway toward Claire and Harry.

"They could be some sort of hit squad." Zach's face was grim, highlighted from the sporadic lights they passed on the thruway, those famous eyes haunted.

"What worries me is this is the second time now Evil has attacked someone before they Traveled but after we'd connected with them." Katie hooked her arms around the front seats and stared out the windshield.

"That thought crossed my mind as well," Ben admitted.

"Evil seems to be getting better at finding us." Katie sighed. "And that, my friends, will make our job of targeting potential Travelers that much more difficult."

"Meaning that if we approach someone and they aren't meant to Travel, but Evil thinks they could," Zach spun out the thought process, "the person could still get hurt by Evil simply because we tagged them. Man that sucks."

"Agreed," Katie said grimly. "Regardless, Claire's now officially under our protection. Whether she is meant to Travel tomorrow or within the next five years, she's our responsibility."

"Somehow I think Claire will have an issue with that." Zach's voice wry. "She doesn't strike me as the complacent, go with the flow kind of girl."

"But we may have placed her in danger." A wave of guilt swamped Katie. "She'll just have to deal with the fact that, like it or not, she's with us."

"Hey…" Ben's greenish gaze meeting her blue one in the rearview mirror. "You can't control who's going to be tagged a Traveler, Katie. Get those thoughts out of your head right now."

"Watch the road, Ben." The oft-repeated phrase came automatically to Katie, who continued as the SUV veered back to the center of the road, "I know we have no control it, but I can't help but feel responsible for Claire."

Zach reached over his shoulder and grasped Katie's hand. "We're in it together. And together, we'll make Claire see that it's in her best interest to let us help her. Even if she's never meant to Travel, we'd be doing a good thing."

Katie swallowed and nodded. "You're right." Her tone more firm than before. "I need to clear my head of all these worries and negative thoughts."

"I'll take the worries," Ben told her with a grin.

"And I'll handle the negative thoughts," Zach offered.

Katie kissed them each on the cheek, grateful for their unswerving support. Then she leaned back in the seat next to Liz and started to clear her mind, to get ready for the fast approaching confrontation.

Claire and Harry were perched on two stools, facing the window. They watched the ferrets while the ferrets watched them. The two humans passed the cell phone back and forth between them always keeping their weapons in plain view.

A car, full of happy teenagers celebrating the football win by heading for the nearby lake with contraband beer and cigarettes, passed by the store.

With every light in the place on, Harry and Claire must have been clearly visible through the window, and certainly the steroidal ferrets should have been impossible to miss.

Yet the Jeep of kids just sailed right on by, without a single second glance from the occupants of the vehicle.

Harry and Claire exchanged a look at the surreal experience, the latter shrugging as the car turned the corner at the far end of the street. "Maybe they only see what they're meant to see."

"They're getting off the Thruway," Harry told Claire, as it was his turn on the phone. "They should be here in about fifteen minutes."

"Excellent." Claire turned to give the creatures a grin and froze. "Some of the ferrets are missing." She quickly counted again. "There are only four now."

Harry relayed the message to the Protectors. From overhead, they could hear the sound of items crashing from the apartment that Harry and Emma shared above the store.

"They're trashing your place." Claire gripped her baton and headed for the door that led to the upstairs apartment. Harry reached out and grabbed her by the arm.

"No, Claire. There's nothing up there that can't be replaced. All that I care about in this world is my family, and they aren't in that apartment. Let the ferrets rip it to shreds. As long as you, Jay and Emma are safe, I'm fine."

Claire was perplexed to be a part of the familial grouping, but nodded nonetheless. Then her eyes shot toward the door to the stairs. "There are no locks on that door."

At a dead run, she raced for the door, throwing herself against it just as the doorknob started to turn. "But ferrets don't have opposable thumbs," she yelled at Harry, who was shoving a heavy display case toward her, to block the door. "How the hell are they opening this door?"

The door was being pounded from the other side, as if the ferrets were repeatedly throwing their bodies against the door. It took everything Claire had to brace her feet against the floor, her back to the door, trying to keep it closed. She reached out as the display case slid closer to her, trying to help pull it in front of the doorway.

Together, Harry and Claire managed to maneuver the heavy object in front of the doorway, wedging it against the wood. Breathing heavily, they backed away from the door, clenching their weapons tightly.

The sound of the ferrets pounding on the door stopped abruptly. Then, to Claire's horror, a black tipped snout came poking through the amber tinted, old fashioned window transom over the door. The creatures must have formed some sort of living ladder to allow one to get that high.

Reaching up, Claire aimed her billy club squarely at the nose of the ferret, eliciting a shocked yelp from the creature as she connected with it. The ferret withdrew from the window, and it clanged shut.

Claire leapt to the top of the display case and fumbled with the transom lock. Just as she pulled the lock shut, a ferret's beady eyes appeared on the other side of the fuzzy, yellowish glass, giving it a monstrous appearance.

"Shit." Claire pushed away from the window. As she was perched on top of the display unit, the movement made her loose her balance, toppling her off the case. Harry caught her with one arm, righting her so her feet touched the ground.

"Thanks." Claire tugged down her shirt, self conscious.

"No, thank you," Harry said softly. "You're a much more fierce warrior than I could ever be."

"They'll try again." Claire's gaze roamed the store for possible weaknesses. "I bet they know that we have help coming. They can't afford to wait any longer."

"There isn't any other way to get into this store."

"Then they'll try to get us out," Claire replied instantly. "Now what could those furry beasts do to make us leave the store?"

As if in reply, a hissing sound could be heard coming through the doorway that led to the upstairs apartment. Blackish gray fog started to appear underneath the crack of the door. Claire could smell the noxious fumes and immediately backed away, coughing.

"What is that?" Harry's question muffled as he covered his mouth with his hand. He and Claire crouched behind a display case, just out of sight of the ferrets at the front window.

"I don't know," Claire replied, trying to breathe as shallow as possible. "But it's making me dizzy." She handed Harry a bandana from a display, wrapping one around her own mouth and nose. She pulled him down so they were closer to the floor where the fog was less prevalent.

"We'll have to make a break for it," Harry said grimly, his words muted by the material, "and hope that the Protectors get here quickly. Do you think we should go out the front or back?"

"I'd say back, and we head for your car," Claire thought frantically. "But we run the risk of the Protectors not finding us if they come to the front of the store."

"I think they'll figure it out," Harry replied. They crawled along the floor toward the door.

"I can see three ferrets out front." Claire coughed from the fumes, which were dancing through the store.

"Let's make a run for the car, then," Harry said, creeping back toward the rear entrance, Claire close behind him.

Harry reached out his hand, preparing to wrap it around the door handle. Claire thought of something and grabbed his arm. "Hang on!" Retrieving a ball of twine, she wrapped one end around the doorknob, careful not to let it move. She unclicked the lock as silently as possible, then, gesturing toward Harry, crawled back to the other room.

"Wait here." Shoving the ball of twine into his hands, she raced to the rear entrance, then came barreling back out toward Harry.

"Go out the front!" she bellowed, giving the twine a hefty yank. The ferrets galloped through the back door as Harry and Claire exited through the front, Claire shutting the door firmly behind them. Hopefully, that would confuse the ones inside the store and give them a reprieve before all six ferrets were at their heels. Plus, if the ones in the store were forced to breathe that horrible smoke, it might slow them down.

The three ferrets standing guard outside the store launched themselves at Harry and Claire, all teeth and claws.

Claire started swiping her club left and right, hitting fur-covered skin at every opportunity.

Harry jabbed ineffectually at the ferrets, his movements tentative. Claire spared a brief wish that she'd kept the freaking knife before whapping at one of the ferrets nipping at her. The other three ferrets, having figured out her ruse, were piling out of the store and heading for them as well. Within moments, they would be fighting all six creatures.

From around the corner, a black SUV came roaring down the street, screeching to a halt in front of the store. Ben and Zach jumped off the running boards of the vehicle, swords swinging. Sasha opened the driver's side door, yelling at Harry and Claire to get inside. Katie raced around the opposite side of the car, her hands glowing pink.

The ferrets turned toward the new menace, snarling. Zach and Ben waded in, blades slicing. Harry scrambled into the SUV, calling to Claire to hurry and follow. Sparing a moment to watch the guys in action–damn they were good with their swords–Claire aimed one last whack at the ferret closest to her and rushed for the SUV.

The ferrets that were still mobile, only two by now, were desperately trying to lunge past Zach and Ben to reach Claire. Sasha pulled the door shut after Claire, staring out the window at the guys.

"Go, Ben. Hurry, Zach," she muttered, her own sword gripped tightly.

"Where's Katie?" Claire strained her neck to see around the other woman, trying to spy the petite blond. Liz was missing as well, she noticed.

"She and Liz over by the store, trying to figure out what is behind the attack. Liz's doing a read and Katie is protecting her back."

"How can all this be going on in the middle of town and no one see it?" Claire wondered. Zach and Ben had taken care of the ferrets and were standing over the furry bodies, their stances watchful, as if anticipating the imminent arrival of more of the creatures. Claire waited a heartbeat then got out of the SUV, despite Sasha calling her back. Sasha growled and followed the girl.

"Nice job," Claire said to Zach, looking down at one of the ferrets.

"Thanks." Zach poked the ferret with the tip of his sword. Seeing the beast brought back all kinds of bad memories, which he firmly squelched, giving Claire a brilliant smile. "You did pretty good yourself, Claire."

"I did, didn't I?" Claire felt ridiculously proud of herself for her efforts against the ferrets.

Ben came over and put a hand on Claire's shoulder. "You all right?" Claire wanted to shrink away from the concern evident in his deep voice, not liking how his eyes raked her form. "Any wounds?"

Claire forced herself to not move away from his touch. She was unused to having people put their hands on her, but this Protector group seemed pretty touchy-feely. "I'm fine," she replied evenly, shoving her hands into her jeans pockets and rolling her shoulders forward slightly. Katie and Liz walked up to them, the former still glowing slightly around her hands.

"Anything?" Zach looked at Liz.

She nodded, then shook her head when he would have spoken again. Putting her fingers over his mouth, Liz whispered, "Shhh. Later." Zach caught her hand and squeezed it to his chest. Claire kept quiet. You didn't need to be a psychic to glean that Liz was saying it wasn't safe here, not yet. They had to leave, and quickly.

Turning toward Claire, Zach nodded to the SUV. "Get in. We're heading out."

"What about those?" Claire pointed at the ferrets, still littering the street.

Ben grabbed her wrist and dragged Claire after him. "Don't worry about it. I have a feeling they'll be taken care of by their master."

Katie was the last to get into the SUV. She turned toward the store and muttered something, then blew into her cupped hands. A pink ball zoomed from her palms and headed into the store. Giving a satisfied smile, Katie nodded and climbed into the SUV, settling next to Claire with Liz on the opposite side. Sasha had moved to the back seat with Harry. Zach got behind the wheel with Ben in the passenger seat. Their now-sheathed swords lay on the floorboard behind the front seats, the hilts gleaming in the darkened interior.

~ 9 ~

▼

AN EARLY FROST

In the streets of Convergence, people were getting ready to start their evening routines. Stores closed and pubs opened. Restaurants prepared for their evening rush and theaters readied the stages for the coming events. A few people looked to the night sky, frowning at the site of the clouds rolling in. Grumbles about the difficulty of walking in the rain could be heard, and a few people grabbed their umbrellas as they left for the night's festivities. A roll of cold air pressed through the town, also encouraging people to pull on a heavier coat than usual.

Jay Rupert, Protector of the Land and earth-based wizard, was among those strolling the streets. Visiting at the Prince and Master Wizard's request, he was attempting to ascertain how the wizarding community in this normally nonconformist town leaned in the growing schism between pro-Land and pro-wizard factions. One look at the night sky had him reaching into his bag for a collapsible Worlder umbrella, as well as the sheepskin lined gloves Tona had gifted him on their anniversary.

When the precipitation came, however, it wasn't the cold rain that the townspeople of Convergence expected. Amazed faces turned to the sky as white flakes came drifting down.

As Jay walked among them, he listened to their incredulous reaction.

"Snow?"

"But it never snows outside of the Mountains Region in this season!"

Yet, snow was indeed coming down in the Meadows and quickly accumulating on the ground. Soon, it was a veritable white-out. People, who had gone inside a pub to escape the blustery cold wind, came out to find the ground covered in several inches of white powder. Icicles formed over doors and on the windows, drifts started to pile up in recessed doorways and courtyard corners. Jay quickly returned to his lodging, eying the storm with growing concern.

There seemed to be no end to the blizzard, which continued throughout the night and into the next dawn. The people of Convergence, unused to such an event, quickly tired of playing in the snow. After an afternoon of snowballs and sledding, they realized that life in the middle of a snowstorm was no easy task. At Jay's urging, the Guards Barracks let loose a pigeon to the Capital City, warning of the strange, out-of-season snow. Whether the little bird would be able to navigate the storm was very much in question.

The town did not have the kind of equipment needed to remove such snow, and it was soon out of control. Snow piled up and the streets were becoming impassable. Wizards tried their best to melt the snow, but were unable to keep up with the accumulation.

Seated by the roaring fire in the Barrack's main lodge, Jay grew increasingly concerned with the news coming in from the city. Perishable goods were usually sold daily in an outdoor market, and since such an event was impossible to hold during a blizzard, the issue of keeping the population fed was getting increasingly dicey. More than one Guardsman reported back to the Barracks with a bloody face or news of having broken up a petty fight over wood to fuel fires. Several of the homeless in the city had already come to the Barracks, fearing death in the inclement weather, and were being quartered in some of the outbuildings.

Jay could not help but feel that Convergence was under attack. With no sign of the snow stopping, and knowing the way human nature could deteriorate in such conditions, the wizard could no longer continue to sit and wait. He had to find out what was happening outside the town proper. Despite the stringent pleas of the elder wizard in town, as well as the blustering of the guardsmen, Jay outfitted himself the best he could for a long winter's hike. Luckily his time spent in the Catskill Mountains during his youth made him a little more prepared for this kind of excursion. The ability to cast a few warming spells about his clothing helped as well.

Jay set out of Convergence, determined to hike through the storm. The logical way to go was to head deep into the Meadow's Region, along the region's end. If need be, he could slip into the Marshes Region to escape the storm, although a prolonged hike in the Quicksilver-infested waters was not high on his list of things-to-do. The storm had come from that direction, so he needed to follow the line of the storm to see if there was something other than a natural weather pattern causing the freak storm. The Barracks Leader pressed a pair of pigeons onto Jay in the hopes that he would be able to use them to either tell people his whereabouts or to get word to the Capital City of their plight.

Jay struck out of town at dawn, although the sky was still dark with clouds and falling snow. Pulling his cloak tighter around his head, he tucked his chin and kept walking, one foot in front of the other. Thanks to the warming spells, he wasn't miserable, but making his way through the snow made for slow and difficult progress.

Convergence slowly disappeared behind him, the smell of wood smoke and dense populations fading. Jay was surrounded by white, the blurring cascade disorienting to every sense. Worried he had gotten off track, he paused, squinting around him. There seemed to be a brighter spot in front of him, a sense of lightness. Stumbling toward it, Jay took two steps and was suddenly beyond the storm.

Similar to the break between Regions, one step had Jay in the blizzard, the next he was throwing an arm up to ward off the glint of sunlight on the snow left behind by the storm. The sudden lack of wind in his ears left a ringing silence. Turning, Jay could peer into the depths of the storm. Then he turned back to the direction it had come from. Already, along the horizon, the snow was melting, the green grass of the Meadows Region showing up in patches of brilliant color. He'd wandered farther inland than he'd wanted; the Marshes were a dim blur on the horizon to his left. Taking a moment, Jay scanned the sky seeking any sort of strange phenomena.

As he searched, Jay noticed a build up of clouds far ahead. The greenish black mass seemed to boil up, like a volcano, although no mountain created the dark plume. Tracking the storm as it grew and raced toward the Beaches— thankfully straight across the Region and not toward him—Jay knew at once that this was not a natural storm. His instincts were correct. This was no ordinary storm, nor was the one in Convergence. That could only mean one thing, at least to a Protector. There was Evil afoot in the Meadows.

One hand reached up to touch the gold and ruby necklace nestled in his robes. He was a Protector of the Land. He owed it to his adoptive home to try and figure out what was happening. After gaining the green grass of the Meadows, he stripped off the heavy traveling cloak, not needing it in the now-balmy air. Taking a moment, Jay scribed a message and sent it to the Capital City, sending the pigeon into flight with a swift upward toss. The bird circled once then arrowed toward the Marshes Region.

Jay settled his backpack, tightening the straps. He headed toward the heart of the Region. Hopefully, he would also find what, or who, was causing these abnormal storms. Given the primitive communication in the Land, he knew that solid intel was their best chance at beating whatever this new threat was to the delicate balance between Good and Evil.

Jay touched his Protector necklace once more, then headed toward the heart of the Land.

~ 10 ~

▼

MIDNIGHT DISCUSSIONS

There was very little discussion in the car on the way back to the Orchards. Liz refused to speak about what she had sensed back at the store, the rest of the Protectors worried about what she had to say, and Claire felt too shell shocked to put up much of a fight about going back to that place. a place she'd sworn she'd never see again. Harry simply put his head against the window of the SUV and fell asleep, his soft snores filling the quiet space.

Liz gave Katie a pointed look over Claire's head, nodding toward the young woman. Understanding, Katie put one hand behind Claire's head, a pink glow settling over the girl. Claire fell asleep between the Oracle and the Seer, never realizing that at that moment, she was safer and more protected than she would be for a long time to come.

When they pulled into the Orchards courtyard, Katie waited for Zach to open the door and then helped guide Claire out of the vehicle. The poor girl was still half asleep and swayed on her feet. Zach simply swung her up into his arms and carried her to the sofa in the living room as Sasha headed up the stairs calling for her husband. Setting Claire down on the nubby fabric, Zach smoothed the hair from the young woman's forehead. Even in her sleep, Claire moved away from his touch.

"She seems tired beyond her years," he said to Katie, who was following him closely. William hustled down the stairs, holding his medical bag. The doctor raked a shrewd gaze over them, grunting his approval that no one appeared injured.

Zach stepped aside as William knelt next to Claire, quietly and efficiently checking her vital signs, moving aside a red and gold colored bead on a necklace in order to listen to her heart.

"I may have hit her with too much Oracle power," Katie admitted to the doctor with a wry grin. "But she was on the verge of a breakdown, and I thought she could use some true rest."

"She seems fine," William assured Katie warmly, standing back up. "Just exhausted. I say we let her sleep as long as possible."

"I shouldn't have interfered." Katie fretted, chewing on a fingernail.

"I wouldn't worry about it." Liz covered Claire with a blanket from the hall closet. "Claire's going to need to be rested if what I gleaned tonight is true."

As one, they turned and headed for the kitchen. When they got there, Tracy was pouring milk for everyone, demanding to know all the blow-by-blow action. Sarat was also present, curled up in a chair next to Ben, listening avidly. To Katie's surprise, Amber was also present, handing out cookies with the milk. After hugging the Interdimensional fairy and welcoming her back home, Katie and Liz settled down at the table. Emma and Harry were sitting on the sofa that lay against one wall, Harry's arm around his wife. It was clear that while they were going to stay and listen to the discussion, they were going to be observers and not participants. It was a mark of their understanding that some things needed to be dealt with by the Protectors.

Once Tracy's bloodlust had been satisfied with the telling of each stroke of the blade, Katie turned toward their resident Seer, who was lightly massaging her temples, drinking ginger ale instead of milk.

"That's not a good sign," Katie said softly to Liz, instantly gaining the attention of all the other Protectors. "You only get nauseous and light headed when Evil is particularly strong in a reading."

"There was a definite, well-defined, extremely powerful Evil presence in that town," Liz smiled wanly at Zach, who had quickly come to stand behind her, massaging her shoulders as she spoke. "Those ferrets were acting on that presence's will and direction."

"So we killed the soldiers but not the general," Ben mused, raking his hand through his spiked hair.

"Why did you make us leave?" Zach asked Liz urgently. "Why didn't we stay and confront the real threat?"

Liz's amazing topaz eyes filled with tears. "Because we wouldn't have won."

The simple words left an empty silence over the table. Not win? They always won against Evil. Anything less was, well, inconceivable.

"We wouldn't win?" Katie echoed, her voice faint.

"It's too powerful. None of us possess the kind of strength to go against it. Not now, anyway. And definitely not here."

"Too powerful?" Tracy asked. "Like Kwade? God, just remembering that fight has me breaking out in goose bumps."

"No, this is not Evil personified." Liz paused, frowning, visibly trying to make sense of it all. "More like how Zella felt in the Land. Like a minion of Evil, not Evil itself, if that makes any sense at all. But this presence is not of the Land, or the World, for that matter."

"The Ferret Dimension, then?" asked the Oracle.

"No. Not like Zella. Despite the presence of the Ferrets, there was more. An overriding sense of something different than our furry pests."

"So a new dimensional player, from some other dimension we've never heard of?" mused Zach, but Liz was already shaking her head, automatically looking at one particular person at the table.

They all turned in that direction. Ben's face drained to white beneath his deep tan, his eyes taking on a stricken glaze. "Me?" The Seer nodded. "Wait. Really? The presence you felt was from the Sea Dimension? But that's impossible. Isn't it?"

"It was absolutely bizarre," Liz continued in a rush. "It was like looking at a negative and a positive image of the same thing. I could see Ben, fighting the ferrets, shining light and goodness pouring out of his very soul. Then there was this other presence that was like an Evil person from the Sea Dimension, full of hatred and bile."

"I don't understand," Sasha said flatly. "Ben isn't Evil. I could never believe that."

"I never said it was Ben," Liz shot back.

Amber spoke up, her voice quiet and intense. "We've always assumed that Ben was the only one from his world who was saved. But what if there were others? People who sided with Evil? Those who helped in the downfall of the dimension and were pulled out after the fall of the Sea?"

"We've seen that in the Land. People who have been seduced by the Evil forces," Sasha pointed out. William reached over and squeezed her hand as they all realized she was thinking about Lukus. "It's entirely possible that in each dimension, Evil seduces people to help him in taking over. We know he's done it in the Land."

Zach enfolded Liz's shoulders with his hands, pressing lightly. Here was another reminder, as Liz had learned that lesson in a particularly hard fashion. Liz smiled at him, grateful for his unswerving support. Ben was sitting at the table, still looked completely gob-smacked.

"Ben, there is no way this could be your fault." The Seer spoke firmly, her tone broking no dissention. "When I say I recognized the entity as being a negative image of you, I didn't mean you personally. It's more…" Her voice faded, then forged on with more resolve. "Ok. Let me get this right. Each dimension has its own distinct signature that it places upon its people, like tag of some sort that says 'Made in the World' or 'Made in the Land.' I can tell the difference between Sarat and Ben. And they are completely different in their feel than those of us from the World. There's just a subtle shift in the psyche that labels people. I could tell Amber wasn't human from the instant we met. Oh, it's just so hard to explain!" Her hands rose to her cheeks in frustration.

"No, I understand what you are saying," Ben said slowly, taking it all in. "I'm just rather shocked to hear that there are people from my dimension that are still alive. It's rather disconcerting. I'd always thought I was the last of my kind."

"There's something I don't understand," Tracy said slowly from her comfortable seat. "Ben is not invincible. Sure, it's hard for him to get sick like us, but he can be hurt physically. But you said that we couldn't win against this entity. That implies that this new Sea Dimension Evil dude has more power than Ben, but they are from the same dimension?"

Liz sighed deeply. "Again, this is really hard to explain. But I think this entity might be like an Oracle. There's a sense of power about it that is reminiscent of what I feel when I tap into Katie, or the Prince, or Scotty."

"Scotty? My son?" Katie blurted, clearly shocked. Liz looked at her, brows furrowing.

"You didn't know?" the Seer asked Katie, who stared at back, her cornflower blue eyes showing her consternation at the notion. Lizzie shook her head, chuckling. "That kid is strong, Katie. Strong, strong, strong."

Katie's mouth was hanging open. She looked around the table, then up at the ceiling toward the room where her son lay sleeping in his Star Wars pajamas. "An Oracle? Scotty?" Her voice was rather weak.

"He's of an age where in the Land he would be tested," Sarat pointed out

"It makes perfect sense," Amber said to Katie. "You're an Oracle. Steven is the counterpart of an Oracle. That means Steven had the genetic disposition to become an Oracle, but something was missing that made the final connection. But combine the two of you into a child and well…"

Katie put her fingers to her temples, shaking her head. "I cannot think about this right now." It was clear the thought of her son being an Oracle was a bit too much for her to contemplate with this latest crisis at their feet. "We need to concentrate on this situation. What does this Evil Entity want?"

"Claire," Liz replied promptly. "No question. It was after Claire. There was a single mindedness that was undeniable."

"So we are back to the fact that Evil seems to be finding people we tag as possible Travelers." Katie commented. "Why them and not us? We're the ones who are more a threat to Evil, I would think."

Zach touched the silver pendant around his neck. "I was thinking about that. I wonder if what Daniel said about the necklaces being important has anything to do with it."

"The necklaces are offering some sort of protection to us?" Katie paced, pondering the idea, then shrugged. "I could see that working."

"Then I'll give Claire mine," Ben said staunchly. He started to slide his necklace off, but Amber shook her head, stopping him with a gentle hand on his arm.

"It doesn't work that way," she said softly. "Believe me, you need that protection right now, if what Liz says about this other Sea Dimension entity is accurate. You may be the only person capable of fighting this new Evil, since you're from its dimension."

"But Liz said it was impossible to beat him," Ben replied hotly. "Damn, this is all so confusing!"

"I said that right now, we wouldn't win. Here we can't win. But later?" Liz shrugged and held up her hands as if weighing the options. "I think Amber is right. Someday, you'll have to go up against this entity, Ben."

"What does that mean? 'Go up against?' Is that a vision?" Sasha asked the Seer sharply, her pale green eyes narrowing at the idea of Ben being in any sort of danger.

"No, it's common sense. The thought of Ben having to fight this thing, or anything Evil, is absolutely terrifying. But we all have faced that demon before, and we will again. It's what we're all about, after all."

Silence fell around the table.

"Alright," Ben said, holding up his hand. "Let's put that aside for a moment. We have to concentrate on Claire right now. Obviously, she isn't safe in her hometown any longer."

"Somehow I doubt she'll want to leave school and just hunker down here in the Orchards for, oh, say the next decade or so." Sasha couldn't keep the frustration from seeping into her voice. "We don't know when she's supposed to Travel. Hell, we don't know if she is ever going to Travel, do we?"

"So, do we leave her with Harry and Emma? Basically unprotected? What if the next assassins that are sent are successful?" Sarat countered evenly.

"Ok, so that is not an option," Zach agreed.

"We could take turns guarding her," Ben supposed, then shook his head. "No, that would simply not be feasible in the long term, would it? I doubt Claire would allow us to be her bodyguards."

"I dunno, she might like have two guys at her beck and call," Zach joked, then turned serious. "Listen, this is not the way to make this decision. We're all exhausted and the person who has the most right to be a part of this discussion is asleep. I say we wait until morning and see what Claire wants."

"I want to go to the Land."

All eyes turned to the doorway where Claire stood. She knew her hair was disheveled, and she had to grip hard to keep the blanket wrapped around her body.

"Listening in the hallway again?" Katie said softly, rising and walking over to Claire.

"You never know what you'll hear, and I've heard enough. I want to go to the Land, Katie. I think it's the only way to face what is happening to me."

"We'll talk about it in the morning," Katie promised her. "We don't even know if you're supposed to Travel now or in the future. So let's discuss it in the morning when we're all more clear headed."

"That's what grownups say when they really mean that they hope by the morning the little kids will have forgotten all about it."

"I happen to think you're right about Traveling to the Land." Katie surprised Claire by divulging that juicy tidbit. "But I seriously think we're all too tired to think straight. Sasha, would you show Claire where she can bunk down for the night? Someplace more comfy than the sofa in the living room, that is." A chorus of goodnights followed Claire as Sasha joined her.

Sasha led Claire up the stairs to a nice sized room just off the hallway. "This is our last official guest room," she said, gesturing to the double bed, which was decked in clean blue and crisp white linens. "Sleep and we'll talk more in the morning."

Claire looked around. "I want my picture," she whispered forlornly, her fingers worrying the edge of the blanket. "I've never slept someplace without it."

Sasha put her hand on Claire's shoulder. "I tell you what. Tomorrow morning, I'll take you to see the real thing."

Claire glanced toward the darkened window. "It's really out there, isn't it?" Even to her own ears, her voice sounded flat.

"What? The Tree?"

"The Tree. And Evil." Claire shivered slightly. "They're both real."

"Yes, they are. I won't sugar coat this stuff, Claire. I think you're strong enough to take it. And you're strong enough to know that you'll need help to get through it."

"Did you like the Land, Sasha?"

The older woman rubbed her eyes, then looked up at the ceiling, one hand going up to briefly touch her Protector necklace. "I'm not the best one to ask. I had a difficult time, but mostly because I resisted the idea of the Land's existence. You're several steps ahead in your acceptance of the Land, so it falls to reason you'll have an easier transition."

"Meaning going to the Land is no cake walk."

"I can tell you that I wouldn't give up the experience of visiting the Land," Sasha said with absolute confidence. "It's the best thing that ever happened to me, hands down." As she spoke, Sasha was pulling down the comforter. "I have a purpose in my life that is beyond anything I could have ever dreamed of. I met the man who is my true soul mate. I have friends that would go to the end of the world for me, and I for them. The riches that the Land has given me far outweigh the hardships and difficulties of being a Protector."

Amber hustled in, holding a bundle of clothes. "Sasha and you are about the same size. Hope you don't mind, Sas, but I asked William to pull out a sleep shirt for Claire. Better than trying to sleep in jeans. And there are some things for the morning as well."

"Thanks," Claire mumbled, taking the clothes. She was not used to being the center of so much attention.

"I was just telling Claire that going to the Land was the best thing that ever happened to me," Sasha was saying to Amber, who smiled brilliantly.

"The Land. It's so many things to each of us, isn't it Sasha? Claire won't be able to fully understand it until she goes there and breathes the clear air of the Meadows, sees the lofty reaches of the Mountains, smells the woodland flowers of the Forests, hears the rush of water in the Rivers and sees the booming sea along the Beaches."

As Claire climbed into the soft, comfortable bed, she reflected on Amber and Sasha's words. The Land. Even the name evoked mysterious images of wooded glades and magnificent vistas.

Claire gave a delicious shiver. She was actually excited about the possibility of going, she realized with surprise. She would be disappointed if she was not meant to–what was the word? Oh yes–Travel to the Land.

After all, she reasoned as she snuggled down into the bed, what could be worse than facing a bunch of overgrown ferrets?

~ 11 ~

▼

TRANSITIONAL PERIOD

The next morning, Claire was up early when the sun barely peeked over the horizon. Despite only getting a few hours sleep, energy raced through her body. She made good use of the shower and pulled on her jeans from the previous day. Since she rarely wore things that were form fitting—Sasha's t-shirt was decidedly smaller than her own—Claire pulled on the black shirt, tugging at it to make it appear baggier on her body.

When she tromped down the stairs, Amber was in the kitchen, drinking tea. Without a word, she handed a mug to Claire, who took a cautious sip. It was delicious.

"You slept well?" Amber asked her.

"Yes, thank you. And you?" Claire asked politely.

"I don't sleep. I'm a fairy, you see. We don't need sleep."

Claire choked on her tea "Uh, right." She wiped her chin, self conscious. How did one act around a fairy? Should she clap her hands or something?

"Don't worry, we don't eat people." Amber gave Claire a wink.

"That's a relief to know," Claire said back with a grin, setting down her mug as Sasha skipped down the stairs, laughing. William was close behind her, and it was obvious the two of them were sharing some sort of inside joke as they entered the kitchen.

Seeing Claire, Sasha's face brightened. "You're up early, too. Excellent. We'll just wait for Katie and then head for the Tree." She poured herself a cup of tea, after ascertaining that William was going to pass on the beverage, preferring to brew a pot of coffee for himself.

"Katie is already in the orchard." Amber gestured with her mug out the door. "Bright and early. I think the Seer was giving her a jingle on the crystal necklace."

"Everything all right?" William asked, pulling down more mugs from the cupboard as the sound of feet and voices in the hallway above cascaded down the stairs.

Amber's eyebrows furrowed. "I don't know. It's not the normal time for a Land update. But we'll find out soon enough, I suppose."

"Can we go now?" Claire asked eagerly.

Sasha shrugged. "Sure," she agreed, putting down her mug. After giving William a brief, albeit passionate kiss that had Amber dramatically patting her heart, Sasha led Claire from the house.

The two walked in silence underneath the boughs of the apple trees, listening to the birds singing in the branches. The trees had been harvested of their fruit already, and some of the leaves were beginning to turn color, heralding autumn. Claire experienced a sensation of peace, oddly enough. There was a deep sense of homecoming, being in the Orchard. It felt right.

"It's just over the next hill," Sasha told Claire finally. They crested the hill and there it was, the Land Tree. Sasha hadn't seen it in its Land colors since she had Traveled to the Land, but she was watching Claire, expecting to see her face light up or change somehow. Yet, Claire still had the same expression on her face, reflecting an interest in what was going on, but certainly no wonder or amazement.

"I see Katie," Claire said, pointing. Sure enough, the petite blond was standing under the Tree, holding something in her hands and staring into the Tree intently.

"What else do you see?" Sasha asked her curiously.

Claire shrugged. "I see Katie standing beneath that huge oak tree. That's about it." Then, understanding dawned. "Oh. That's *the* Tree, isn't it?" She looked at it, frowning. "I thought it was supposed to be red and gold."

"Yeah, it usually shows up that way if someone is going to Travel soon."

"But it's not for me." Disappointment clouded Claire's voice.

"Apparently. Hey, maybe it's just not your time to go just yet, Claire. Give it some time."

They strode down the hill and approached the Tree. Katie was still concentrating on the necklace in her hand. Claire looked at it, frowning.

"It's a communication device," Sasha whispered to Claire. "We're able to get rudimentary information to and from the Land using them. Honestly, we rely more on Ben and Tracy going back and forth for our information these days. The necklaces aren't the most accurate means of communicating, and their power seems to be fading over time."

Claire nodded her understanding. Katie frowned, tapping on the crystals steadily. Beside her, Sasha stood still and quiet, as if instinctively knowing that whatever was coming over the necklace, it wasn't good. Finally, Katie's hand dropped to her side, and the Oracle stared out over the orchards to the strip of Hudson River just visible through the treeline.

"Let's go down and see what is happening," Sasha said. They made their way under the Tree. Katie was standing very still, her expression confused and concerned.

"Something is happening in the Meadows." Katie didn't even look their way, as if she had been expecting the pair. "They're having a series of weather anomalies, things the Land has never seen before."

"Like what?" Sasha asked, tilting her head to one side.

"Sounds like a tornado and a blizzard."

"Wow," Sasha chimed, and then her brows furrowed. "That's odd, I'd never really thought about the fact that the Land doesn't have those kind of things."

"They don't."

"Do they have seasons, like we do?" Claire asked, eager to learn more.

"Not that I'm aware of," Katie admitted. "I mean, there's always snow on the top of the Mountains, but I can't ever recall hearing of winter in any of the other Regions."

"Jay was in Convergence when a blizzard hit and then hiked out. He sent a pigeon to tell the Prince he was going to scout out and see if he could find anything out about the origin of the storms, but since then, they haven't heard anything from him."

"What does the Seer think is behind the storms?" Sasha asked, and then held up her hand. "Wait, stupid question. Evil."

"She wanted to know if anything strange had happened here, in our world, lately," Katie said. Both she and Sasha slid glances in Claire's direction.

"I'm guessing the attack of the steroid ferrets qualifies as something strange," Claire supposed, putting her hands in her back pockets and scuffing at the ground.

"It's the only thing out of the ordinary we've had lately," Katie admitted.

Sasha looked uncomfortable. "Katie...Claire doesn't see the Tree."

"I can too see it," Claire protested instinctively.

"Not in its Land colors."

"Really? Humph. That is strange." The trio stared at the Tree, then, as one, turned back toward the house. "That must mean you aren't meant to Travel now, Claire. I'm not surprised, really. After all, you're rather young and the responsibility of being a Protector is rather daunting."

"Damn it all!" Claire burst out. "I'm getting sick and tired of my age being thrown in my face. I may not be the same age as you guys, but I'm old enough to make a difference in the world. That's gotta matter for something, as far as I'm concerned." She kicked a stone on the ground and it flew up and hit the trunk of the Tree.

The stone glanced off the bark that covered the trunk, and a wave enveloped the Tree. As the image rippled, behind the wave the bark of the Tree changed to a brilliant, deep ruby. Her eyes round, Claire followed the changing color. When the leaves were all golden, the garnet berries swaying gently, she took an involuntary step back, trying to see the entire Tree.

"Wow!" she exclaimed, "It's beautiful!"

Katie and Sasha turned around at her words, only to find Claire reaching for a golden leaf above her head.

"Don't touch it!" they yelled out at the same time, racing back down to Claire.

"You can see it?" Sasha said, her face wreathed in smiles.

"Just like it's been described," Claire agreed, her eyes still glued to the Tree.

"Then let's do this the right way," Katie maintained. "We'll go back to the house, get you ready and send you over to the Land."

When they got back to the house, it was to discover that Zach and Liz had taken Harry back to the store. Zach wanted to make sure that everything was safe for the man, and would not leave Harry there unless he was convinced that Jay's father would be safe from harm. Liz was going to try and get a stronger read on their unexpected visitor from the Sea Dimension, and see if she could figure out where he was and what he was planning next.

Removing themselves the upstairs guest room, Sasha helped Claire pack a bag to take with her to the Land. "We don't have any Land gear your size," the woman told Claire, "but I'm sure that once you are there, the Seer will get you outfitted quickly."

"Ben will accompany you," Katie added, "get you settled and make sure that the Seer or one of our friends is with you. I imagine they'll want you to head for the Meadows to see about these weird weather patterns."

"I don't know anything about meteorology," Claire admitted, adding a toothbrush to the bag. Now that she was going for certain, she found that she was a little hesitant about the whole concept.

"Well, none of us really knew much about our quest topic," Katie pointed out. "It's a kind of learn as you go thing. On the job training, as it were." She held up a small stack of bound paper. "Now. These are accounts of our quests. Not the full accounts, because after eight of them that would be like asking you to schlep a library to the Land. These are more…"

"The Cliff Notes version," supplied Sasha.

"Exactly."

Emma bustled into the room, holding a rubber container in her hands. "I know that you're going to the Land, so I brought you some of my special oatmeal raisin cookies to take with you." She thrust them into Claire's hands then enfolded the young woman into her arms. "Oh, you'll take care of yourself, won't you?"

"I will," Claire said, awkwardly patting Emma on the back, a difficult task given that her arms were pinned by the older woman's embrace.

Emma's eyes shone bright with tears. "I'll worry about you the entire time," she vowed. "I wish you didn't have to go so soon…"

"I'll be fine," Claire asserted firmly, rolling her eyes in Sasha's direction while putting the cookies in her bag, even though she knew that she would probably never eat the contents. She'd had enough experience with Emma's baking to know that the cookies would likely taste like pressed cardboard.

Ben strode into the room, wearing a loose light blue shirt that laced up the front—the laces still untied—over darker blue breeches tucked into tall black leather boots. He was pulling on an ivory vest over the shirt, cursing as it caught on the sword he'd belted around his waist. He looked very blond, very tanned and just plain hot.

"Well hell's bells," Claire breathed, her eyes wide as she stared at him. Having only seen him in jeans and t-shirts, usually paint spattered, this was quite the transformation.

"He does clean up well, doesn't he?" Sasha said affectionately, helping Ben untangle the vest from the sword hilt. Ben gave her a grin and turned to Claire, completely oblivious to her approving gaze.

"Ready to go?" he asked her, briskly rubbing his hands together.

"Uh-huh," she managed, still rather amazed at his transformation. Sasha nudged the girl with her shoulder, grinning. Claire shrugged back. "Well, he's a hottie. Who'd have figured that?"

Katie reached over and tucked the silver pendant around Ben's neck into the shirt, smoothing the vest over his shoulders fondly. "Now you tell Anja that I need you back soon, you hear me? This is an unscheduled trip and with Tracy ready to go into labor at any time, I may need you to get word to Orli."

"I know, I know." Ben grinned, cricking his neck to one side, then the other, a loud pop resounding through the room. "I probably won't even see Anja. She's out to sea at the moment, unless she's making an unscheduled visit to the port. And who knows if that's where we'll end up. I really don't expect to see Anja at all this trip."

"How do you know where the Tree sends you?" Claire asked as she zipped up her bag and slung it over her shoulder. Sasha held the list of phone numbers to call the next day, to let the school know about Claire's absence, as well as the boarding house. A fictitious family illness had been invented to explain her departure from school. Which was a flimsy excuse as Claire had no family, but who cared enough to check up on that fact?

Ben frowned. "Well, where we end up is entirely up to you, actually. At least, that's been our experience. The Tree sends you where you're needed."

"Is the Land a sentient being?" Claire asked suddenly.

Katie looked startled. "No."

"Then how does it know what to do and when?"

Katie and Ben exchanged a glance. "We've never really thought about that," the Oracle finally admitted. "We just know that the Land calls people. How that process is started, we never really considered."

"Maybe it's like an animal instinct," Sasha supposed. "A reaction to the stimulus of Evil trying to endanger it."

"Makes sense," Ben shrugged then grabbed Claire's bag. "Let's rock and roll, Claire."

"Is he always this happy?" Claire asked as Ben tromped down the stairs, whistling.

"That's Ben. Pretty much the most easy-going dude you'll ever meet, unless someone he loves is in danger or harm's way. Then he's our resident worrier," Katie replied as they followed the Sea Dimension man down the stairs. "But don't let that demeanor fool you. Ben takes Traveling very seriously, and I know he's worried to death over this new Sea Dimension entity. But he'll never admit it to us, not yet anyway."

In the kitchen, Emma was sitting with Tracy, mugs of tea in their hands. As Claire came in, Emma rose, a strained smile on her face.

"Leaving so soon?" she asked brightly, but her blue eyes shone with tears.

"Yep."

Emma set the mug down. "Then you'll forgive me if I get a little sentimental," she told Claire before hugging her warmly. "It seems like I just wished Jay farewell, and now here I'm sending another loved one away to the Land. You better come back to us, you hear? I won't lose another loved one to the Land. She can't have you all."

"I'll be back," Claire promised, patting the plump woman on the back and feeling, rather inexplicitly, tears in her own eyes. "I promise. I need to finish school, right?"

Emma eased back, swiping at the tears on her cheeks. Tracy was also wiping her eyes, muttering about being a freaking waterworks while pregnant. Katie took Claire's hands in hers, pulling the young woman away from the table.

"You'll do fine. Ben will be with you for a day, and by then, hopefully the Seer or Prince will have you under their wing."

"What if I fail?" Claire whispered.

"We all thought that we'd fail at one point or another," Ben said quietly. "But somehow, we pulled through. Just be true to yourself and do the best you can. That's all that anyone can logically ask for, right?"

"But you guys have said it yourselves, I'm younger than the rest of you," Claire said, worrying her lip with her teeth, hating the doubts that were welling up inside of me. "What if there's some minimum age or something?"

Katie shook her head. "Listen to me, Claire. The Land is calling you. That means you're ready to go. So, head over and see what is what. Just try not to get too frustrated or let your temper—which is rather formidable by the way—get the better of you."

With that, Katie sent Claire, Ben and Sasha to the Tree. When they were standing under the boughs of the Tree, Sasha squeezed Claire's hand and stepped back, leaving the way clear for Ben and Claire.

Ben reached over and grasped Claire's wrist, instructing her to latch onto his the same way, so that they were tightly tethered.

Then Claire reached over and put her hand on the Tree. It was cool to the touch, and smooth as glass. A peculiar vibration seemed to come from deep within the Tree and then suddenly Claire felt like she was falling into a vortex, pulled forward by an unseen force. Ben tightened his grip on her arm, which reassured her as she fell forward into a kaleidoscope of color and texture.

~ 1 2 ~

▼

ENCAMPMENT

Claire stumbled as her feet hit uneven yet soft ground. Her nose was assaulted with the smell of pine trees and flowers, her eyes squinting at the sun shining brightly into her eyes. Sneezing, she didn't have time to right herself before Ben slammed into her from behind. They tumbled to the ground in a heap, the man already apologizing profusely as they fell.

Rolling, Claire found herself flat on her back, breathing in air that was so pure, so fresh, so *everything* that she could only suck it in breath after breath, waiting for that vitality to sing through her blood as she stared up at a bright blue sky that seemed to have flowed from a child's painting set, so vivid was the color. She couldn't help but smile. Suddenly, a small cherub face, complete with bright blue eyes and a riot of tight light blond curls, came into view, looking down at her.

"Pretty," the child said, sticking her finger in her mouth, showing a row of pearl white teeth.

"Well, thank you," Claire replied automatically, then sat up to see the child more clearly. She appeared to be young, but Claire had never gotten the knack of figuring out young children's ages. The little girl wore a pair of green leggings and a brown tunic-like top. Frankly, the only reason Claire assumed that the child was a girl was because of the long golden curls framing her round face.

Beside her, Ben groaned and pushed up onto his arms. "Sweetie," he exclaimed, staring at the child, then looking around them with a rather bemused expression. "Where are we, anyway?" He slipped off his dark framed glasses and gave a grunt of satisfaction now that he could see clearly again. "Forest Region." Next, he gave the child a grin. "And what are you doing here all alone?"

"Ben-men!" The little girl squealed with rapture, launching herself at Ben, who barely had time to catch her. "Ben-men bring Sweetie a pretty!"

Ben laughed as his arms closed around the little girl. "Yes, I did, Sweetie. This is Claire. She's from the World Dimension. Claire, this is Sweetie, a Seer in training. She was part of Zach's quest."

"Zach-ree," Sweetie chimed happily in her musical voice, settling into Ben's lap and happily playing with his Protector necklace, now flashing a deep ruby and gold in the sun drenched forest light. "Pretty, pretty Zach-ree."

From the trees came the sound of a deep male voice calling out the child's name. Ben brightened at the sound. "That's Maxt," he said with some relief. "He must be here with the Seer. She doesn't leave Sweetie alone anywhere. Did you wander off from Maxt, Sweetie?"

The little girl put her finger to her lips, as if asking for him to be quiet. Then she crept off his lap and hid behind a nearby tree.

Through the forest, Claire could see a large man walking toward them. He was dressed similarly to the child, but had a red slash of material across his chest. That, and there was the addition of several weapons about his person. When he spied Ben, who was getting to his feet, the man's stance changed from relaxed to warrior in a millisecond. The sword sang from the scabbard and was pointed at them in a mere heartbeat.

"Hey, Maxt," Ben said easily, not at all perturbed to be at the business end of a sword.

Maxt squinted as he came out of the shadows into the clearing where Claire and Ben were standing. "Ben?" His voice was like a shallow stream bouncing over sun drenched rocks, gravely and warm. "Ben!" he repeated with obvious pleasure. With a ringing of steel, the sword was sheathed and the two men grasped forearms in some sort of formalized greeting. It was both quaint and poignant, given how the men were grinning at one another.

A small hand slid into Claire's, startling her. "You are not 'apposed to be here yet," the child said solemnly at her side, her voice sounding much more grown up than it had a second before.

"I'm not?"

"No, but that not a bad thing," Sweetie replied easily. Claire stared at her, bemused by her words. "You gots chased so it all right you came now."

"Sweetie," Maxt rounded on the two girls, his face set in grave lines. "I was looking everywhere for you."

"Hiding." Sweetie dragged her foot in the leaves and slanted Maxt a shy and enchanting smile.

"Well, the Seer is frantic with worry since you blocked her from sensing you," Maxt replied, his hands on his hips as he towered over the small child with a grim expression on his face. "You know you are not supposed to run away from us like that. It is too dangerous for you to be roaming the woods. What are we going to do with you now? You simply will not obey our wishes, Sweetie, and it is getting to the point where we are going to have to take action if you keep misbehaving."

Claire pushed the child behind her back and narrowed her eyes at Maxt, who had a good foot on the smaller woman. "Back off, Robin Hood," she snarled. "If she's so important, maybe you should've been watching her better! She's just a little kid, after all. They wander if not looked after properly."

"Yeah!" Sweetie chimed gleefully from behind Claire. "Little kid!"

Maxt gave a growl and advanced, intending to duck around Claire to get to Sweetie. Instinctively, without thought to the consequences or even appropriateness of her actions, Claire brought the heel of her hand against Maxt's nose, using the force of her entire body in the gesture, just like she'd been taught in self-defense class. The warrior yelped and fell backwards, holding his nose tightly, his green eyes wide with astonishment.

"Claire," Ben yelled, as shocked as Maxt by the woman's actions.

"I'm not about to let him hurt her." Claire's heart raced. Man, she'd only been in the Land a few minutes and she'd already assaulted someone. Great way to kick off the World-Land interrelationship.

"I was not going to hurt her," Maxt said thickly, glowering at Claire over his rapidly swelling nose, dabbing at the blood that was starting to flow from one nostril. "I may hurt you, but I was not going to hurt Sweetie."

Claire bristled and stood her ground. Sweetie, realizing that her protector might be in harm's way, marched out from behind Claire and delivered a swift kick to Maxt's shin before darting back behind the older girl's form.

"*Ouch*," Maxt bellowed, clutching at his leg and hopping on one foot, the other hand still holding his nose.

"Nicely done," Claire told Sweetie, who grinned back at her. "But you should aim a little higher, at the knee. It's more vulnerable than the shin." The little girl stuck her finger in her mouth and nodded, listening carefully.

"Claire, stop it," Ben ordered firmly, but he was having a hard time not laughing at the situation.

Maxt was still rubbing his shin, glaring at Claire balefully. "Who are you?"

"Maxt, this is Claire Jones. Claire, please meet Maxt, Captain of the Prince's Guard," The formal introduction seemed a lost cause, but Ben gave it his all. Anything to try and bring some sort of normalcy back to this particular interaction.

"From the World Dimension?" Maxt guessed, taking in Claire's jeans and t-shirt.

"Yes," Ben replied. Maxt's eyes widened suddenly.

"She is not a potential Protector, is she?" he asked incredulously, giving Claire another look over, this one filled with barely contained astonishment. "She is barely out of her childhood."

"*She* is standing right in front of you," Claire said rather sarcastically. "And I'm well aware of my age, thank you very much."

Sweetie tugged on Claire's hand, trying to lead her away. Maxt looked at the little girl, his face softening slightly. The sight of his expression made Claire unfreeze somewhat, it was clear the gruff man truly cared for the little girl. "Sweetie, are you taking Claire to the Seer?"

"Yep," came the lisped reply. "She needs to see hers right away. Needs to know."

"Go ahead with Sweetie," Maxt instructed Claire, pointing through the woods. "The Seer is in the encampment over the next rise. I will follow with Ben."

"You just want Ben to fill you in on who I am and what's going on," Claire said over her shoulder as she allowed Sweetie to lead her away. "Away from the little kids and all. Won't work. Ben'll tell me everything, won't you Ben?" The last was called out as Claire and Sweetie disappeared into the wooded forest.

Claire put her finger to her lip and Sweetie nodded. They could clearly hear the men talking behind them.

"Sarcastic little bit of a girl, is she not?"

"Maxt, I will admit Claire is different, and young, as you pointed out. But when the Land calls, we listen. We figure there's a reason, even if we don't always understand it. Claire could see the Tree, and obviously was able to Travel. Plus there was some trouble in the World, with definite Evil influences, that made her coming here the most viable option. Therefore, we're here. But tell me, what's happening in Meadows Region?"

Their voices faded until Claire could no longer hear what the men were saying. As if on cue, Sweetie started to chatter constantly while she pulled Claire along behind her. Claire looked around eagerly, finding the environment was strangely familiar yet different at the same time. It was almost like someone had set the colors on a television set a shade too bright. The smell of honeysuckle was prevalent and the sound of the birds singing in the trees a constant backdrop. And the fresh air! Claire couldn't suck it in fast enough.

As they came over the rise of the hill, a veritable tent city spread before them. Brightly colored tents dotted the forest's floor. People milled around, working over campfires or sitting in small groups talking. Large wagons, now empty, waited beside a road that wound through the Forest. Oxen, obviously used to pull the carts, were tethered in a row several yards away from the main camp area. Several men strolled around the perimeter of the clearing, all wearing similar outfits to Maxt, minus the red sash.

Sweetie skirted around the outside of the encampment, never faltering in her direction. She halted in front of a rather large yellow and red striped tent, and then pushed Claire toward the doorway.

Claire ducked through doorway into the cool interior of the tent. Inside, a low bed was positioned along one side of the tent, and two collapsible chairs sat next to a table that also folded up for easy traveling.

Seated in one of the chairs was a woman about forty years of age. She had short reddish brown hair, the ends of which curled up slightly. She dressed much like Ben Harm in his Land gear; only her outfit was in various shades of yellow. The neckline of the shirt was also embroidered with brightly colored thread, another difference between her and Ben.

"Sweetie, did you run off again?" the woman asked, still perusing the book before her. "Maxt is going to be very irritated with you. How he can keep track of all his men but still manage to lose one little girl…oh, hello there!" she finished as she looked up to see Claire standing just inside the doorway. Rising, the woman held out her hand in the World fashion. "Welcome. I'm the Seer of the Land. And you are?"

"My name is Claire," she replied, shaking the woman's hand. "I've heard a lot about you."

"Really? Are you from a nearby village? Wait." The auburn head tilted to one side. "You're from the World Dimension."

"Yes. I just arrived here. With Ben Harm."

"Ben's here as well?" The Seer peered around Claire, as if seeking the man.

"He's out with Maxt. Gossiping like old women. Probably about me."

"Gossiping? I think they'd take offense to that characterization."

"I call 'em like I see 'em."

"Of course you do. Well, I suppose a new quest is about to commence. Makes sense, given what is happening in our fair Land. So, Claire, tell me about yourself."

Before Claire could figure out where to start, Ben ducked under the tent door, Maxt at his heels. Claire looked at the floor guiltily, at the sight of the latter's bruised nose.

"Ben, it is always good to see you, even during trying times. Come, sit. Why, Maxt, whatever happened to your nose? Did Ben fall on you when he came through the Tree?"

Maxt glowered at Claire but said nothing, swinging Sweetie into his arms, where she snuggled against his broad chest with an ease and trust that had Claire's throat clenching.

"Tell her about the other Sea Dimension person," Maxt said to Ben.

The Seer's hand flew to her throat. "Another Sea Dimension person? Ben, how wonderful! We thought you were the last of your people."

"Don't get your hopes up for a grand reunion," replied Ben grimly. He hurriedly filled the Seer in on the strange news about a possible Evil one from the Sea Dimension, as well as the attacks on Claire and her subsequent calling to the Land when the Tree had blossomed into its true colors.

"Another Sea Dimension soul?" the Seer breathed, pacing back and forth in the confines of the tent. "I never thought…but it does make sense in a sad, tragic way. Oh, Ben."

"Liz said she could sense that we were from other Dimensions," Claire said. "Can you tell if there are people in the Land, other than Ben and I of course, who are from another Dimension?"

The Seer gave her that curious head tilt. "I could try. Let me cast about and see what can be sensed," she said, closing her eyes.

You could have heard a pin drop in the tent as all eyes focused on the Seer, who was standing stock still, her hands slightly outstretched.

But it was Sweetie who spoke up first. "Good man," she said, pointing at Ben. "Bad man was der, but he gone now," she said with a pouty frown, pointing to the side of the tent.

"I concur," the Seer said, reaching out to ruffle the girl's blond curls. "There is a signature trail, very faint. But I could be reading it wrong. With the two of you here, it clogs things slightly."

"Where was he?" Ben asked eagerly, fingering the hilt of his sword.

"Hard to say," the Seer said thoughtfully. "Near the Meadows Region, I believe." She looked at Sweetie, who nodded her agreement.

"Bad man far away now. He likes pretties."

"Significant that he was where the storms are located." Maxt stared at the wall of the tent, toward the Meadows Region.

"If the storms are over there, why are you here, in the Forest Region?" Ben asked her, waving his hand around to encompass the tent and the encampment.

"We are heading toward the Meadows, to see what is happening for ourselves." This came from a man who just walked into the tent.

Ben turned and smiled. "I never thought you'd be here!" he cried, gripping forearms with the man. Ben turned to Claire, motioning her forward. "Claire, this is the Prince of the Land. Sir, this is Claire Jones, of the World Dimension."

Claire shook hands with the tall man, who had remarkable blue eyes, the color of the turquoise jewelry Emma and Harry sold in their store. His dark hair was long, just brushing his shoulders, and slightly wavy. He had a nice smile, and an undeniable sense of power lay about his shoulders like a cloak.

"Welcome to the Land, Claire," the Prince said formally, dropping a kiss on her cheek. "What happened to your nose, Maxt?"

"Pow!" Sweetie mimed, aiming her hand at Maxt's nose, then patted his cheek and chided, "Silly Maxt."

"Silly Maxt indeed," the warrior replied, putting the little girl on the floor and giving her a gentle push toward the entrance. "Go play outside, Sweetie. And I mean just outside the tent, not in the woods, do you hear me?"

"Yep, yep, yep," Sweetie chanted. She darted over and hugged Claire. "Careful for the turtle and no playing with da flames," she warned, raising one little finger at the young woman, and then she turned and darted outside.

"Why are you plodding along by land when you could go by sea?" asked Ben.

"Currents, my friend," replied the Prince. "The currents run in the opposite direction of where we want to go. Unless we want to take the long way around, by way of the Mountains Region and bulk of the Meadows, we needed to go this way."

"I'll never understand the Land," said Ben with a shake of his head. "What about across the Desert and Marshes?"

"Um, no," said the Prince, sounding remarkably Worlder in the expression. Claire wondered if he'd picked it up from Tracy or Ben. "Trust us, Ben, this is the best way."

"Sweetie, didn't I tell you to go?"

"Yep, but…she's not apposed to be here yet."

"That's what the Tree thought too," said Claire with a roll of her eyes. Noticing the Seer, Maxt and Prince were watching her with questions burning in their eyes, she explained that the Tree had at first declined to recognize her as a Traveler, but then morphed in front of her eyes. "I guess something changed, and I was meant to come over after all."

"Something changed…" the Seer trailed off, exchanging a single, searching look with the Prince. "I would say it has changed, Ben. We need to talk."

~ 1 3 ~

▼

METAMORPHOSIS

The Prince called for more chairs and soon they were all sitting down, Claire feeling extremely out of place as Ben chatted easily with the others. He told them how Tracy was doing in her pregnancy, gave the Seer and Prince various messages from Protectors and passed a small bag of mail to Maxt, who would make sure the contents were distributed. It was a well-known routine for the group and spoke of their closeness and true affection for one another.

Claire waited, her foot bouncing impatiently. She was here, and she was ready to get going. Sitting around talking was dullsville, in her opinion. For all the ominous foreshadowing from the Seer, they were taking their own sweet time to get to the meat of things. Finally, Ben explained about the ferrets, and how Liz had ascertained that an Evil entity from the Sea Dimension was stalking Claire.

The Seer looked at Claire thoughtfully. "I don't know…"

"Yeah, I know, I'm awfully young," Claire muttered irritably, crossing her arms.

The Seer smiled. "Age is meaningless in the long run. Look at Sweetie. She may be a child yet has the wisdom of the ages in that formidable brain of hers. No, I was thinking that you still might be in danger from this Sea Dimension person."

"True," Ben said, leaning back in his chair and rubbing his finger over his chin. "She saw someone with the ferrets who has my coloring and height. If you've sensed a Sea Dimension entity in the Land, then he could be looking for Claire. Waiting for her to show up. If he's ascertained she is a Protector, then he would do anything he could to take her out of the mix."

"Kill me, you mean," Claire stated baldly.

"Kill, or who knows what else? Evil has so many tricks that we can't possibly know what it has planned." The Seer gave a philosophical shrug, as if they were discussing whether or not Claire should take an elective class during the spring semester.

"This other entity knows what she looks like and who she would likely be traveling with," the Prince pointed out, giving Ben a significant glance. The Sea Dimension man grimaced and shifted in his seat.

"Meaning that hanging with you guys is about the worst thing I could do at this point in time," Claire finished for them. "To be safe, I shouldn't be with you. But I do need to go to the Meadows Region, right? That makes the most sense. If there are wacky things happening in the Meadows, and that's where this dude is hanging out, that's where I should go. But on my terms, not his."

"There is more," said the Seer. "Ben, did Katie get our message that Jay was heading into the Meadows Region to try and track the origin of the storms?"

"Yes." Ben morphed to high alert, leaning toward the Seer. "Is he all right?"

"We don't know."

"What do you mean, you don't know?"

"Just that, Ben," said Maxt, then started ticking off items on one hand as he spoke. "We know he left Convergence with a pair of messenger pigeons. We know he loosed one of the pigeons to tell us he was heading into the heart of the Region. Then nothing for days."

"Nothing but more storms," corrected the Prince.

"True. After the first pigeon, the Prince and I ascertained it would be necessary for us to go to the Meadows, to see if we could lend aid or help figure out this latest attack. Yes, Ben, we believe it is an attack. We have never seen this kind of weather in the history of the Land. It is too coincidental to be anything other than some sort of Evil plot." Maxt leaned back in his chair.

"What does this have to do with Jay?" Claire wanted to know. She could see Emma and Harry's faces clearly in front of her, worried about their son.

"He's disappeared."

Ben turned to look at the Seer. "How do you know he's disappeared? He could still be in the Region, just out of communication with us."

"The second pigeon came to the Forest Barracks. It was injured, and failed to go to the right location because it was disoriented."

"Ok...so what was the message the bird carried?"

"Nothing. Ben, there was no message."

"But that proves nothing! Jay could have let the bird go with a message that got lost, the bird could have escaped, anything!"

"There's more," said Claire, staring at the Seer, who was in turn watching Ben with compassion.

"Yes, there is. Day before yesterday there was a disturbance in the Meadows Region, one that was felt by almost every fifth level wizard in the Land." The Seer stood up and paced, the words coming paced and measured. "The consensus on those in the Wizarding University is that it pertained to a great battle, and that an earth-based wizard was involved."

Claire swallowed thickly. "What happened? Can they tell?"

"The battle was suddenly cut off, as if it were halted mid-spell. Then, nothing." The Prince spread his hands wide. "That is all we know, my friends."

"Not exactly."

They turned to the Seer. "As near as we can tell, at the exactly moment when the wizards sensed the cessation of a battle the likes of which hasn't been recorded since Katie and the Prince took on Catzil, every Land Tree in the Grid flared and came to life. It only lasted a few moments, but...it happened. The entire Tree system activated, as if seeking a Traveler, but not knowing where the person was located."

They all turned to look at Claire, who held up her hands.

"Could have been me...could have been anyone. It's possible I just happened to get caught in the flare up."

"Well, you are here now. And you have ties to Jay's parents. Emotional ties, which are strong." The Seer continued, ignoring Claire's instinctive protest about the relationship with the Ruperts. "I don't think that is something we should ignore. Claire is here, and we need to get her to the Meadows Region. But traveling with us will bring the attention of the one who hunts you. So where do we hide you? And how do we get you to the Meadows Region as quickly as possible?"

Sweetie ran in at that moment and handed Claire a handful of brightly colored wildflowers, the roots still attached and full of moist dirt. Claire plucked an earthworm off her lap and tossed it to the side.

"Thank you, Sweetie," she told the little girl, who frowned at Claire.

"Me not Sweetie," she said with a growly voice. "Me Maxt! Big, big man!" The little girl beat on her chest and strutted about, clearly mimicking the large guardsman's swagger.

Maxt laughed at the little girl's antics, but the Seer tilted her head to one side, as if a thought had struck her.

"What is it?" Ben asked, used to that look and realizing that the Seer had an idea. And usually, the Seer's ideas were simply brilliant, so it bore asking.

"What if we hide Claire as someone else?" she mused, tapping her fingers on the arm of the chair. "Her hair is rather short, and she has slim hips. She could pass for a boy…"

Claire snorted and gestured at her chest. "Obviously you haven't taken a good look. I don't think these will be hidden easily."

Ben squinted at her chest, and then gave a grudging nod. "She has a point there. Those are pretty…well, I mean, gosh, Claire!" Ben turned beet red and rubbed his nose sheepishly. Maxt just shrugged and the Prince shook his head.

"Any ideas?" The Prince asked the Seer. "Clearly you would have the most experience knowing what to do in this kind of case…"

"We could strap 'em down and see what happens. But I still think that even hiding Claire as a boy within our entourage will attract attention. She wasn't with us when we left the Capital City, after all. It would be too coincidental for Ben to show up and then suddenly we have a strange new person traveling with us. Evil may be inconsistent, but it isn't stupid."

"Who saw you coming into the encampment?" the Prince asked Claire sharply.

Claire thought back. "I don't know that anyone saw me, really. Sweetie took me around the outside of the camp. I saw people, but I didn't see anyone looking at me or anything."

"What do you think, Maxt?" the Prince said, nodding significantly toward the child who was now seated in his lap. Maxt frowned and looked down at Sweetie, clearly not understanding. Then comprehension dawned across the man's face.

"You mean as a guard?" he said, his eyebrows arching high into his hairline. "Have Claire dress up as a guardsman?"

"Well, we are near the Forest Barracks," the Seer pointed out reasonably, "and Claire could pass as teenaged boy."

"Yeah, those kids who I've seen at the Barracks…what do they call them?" Ben rubbed his chin.

"A page?" Maxt turned his gaze toward Claire, obviously dubious. She narrowed her gaze at the man in response, causing Ben to smother a grin behind his hand. Claire was clearly feeling the unspoken challenge. Despite his short experience with her, Ben knew that she would rise to that challenge with all her impressive innate determination.

"She's a natural warrior." Ben was compelled to stick up for his Worlder companion. "She fought the ferrets with just a nightstick and was more than holding her own. I think she can pretend to be a guy."

"It would only be until the guardsmen reach the Meadows Region. They are traveling ahead, as they can go faster than we can. We can ask to rendezvous with the guards outside the Meadows, and if Claire joins us there, it won't seem so strange." The Seer was clearly satisfied with her line of reasoning.

"But how do we get her to the Barracks?" the Prince wondered aloud.

"Point me in the right direction and I'll get her there," Ben promised. "We'll move much more quickly alone than you guys with all this gear."

"Ganth is in charge of the Barracks," Maxt reminded the Prince. "He will question a page coming into his ranks on such short notice, and especially coming from a Worlder liaison."

"Ganth…isn't he the one who imprisoned Sasha when she was in the Land?" Ben's aqua eyes narrowed and flashed with temper, a sight the others were obviously unused to seeing in Ben.

"Do not get upset," the Prince admonished, "Ganth did the right thing with Sasha. You cannot blame him for being judicious in his actions."

"I would trust Ganth with my life." Coming from Maxt it was high praise. "He is most trustworthy and steadfastly protects the Land with all his heart."

Ben's lips thinned. "No offense, but we've heard that before."

"Ganth." The Seer's eyes turned cloudy and she frowned as if trying to remember something. Then her eyes cleared and she sighed once, turning her gaze toward Ben. "Yes…oh yes. I remember. Yes. Ganth would do fine. I know your worries, Ben, and your concerns. And your fears. Put them aside. Ganth is a good choice in this matter."

Ben finally nodded brusquely.

"How do pages normally get assigned to a Barracks?" Claire asked, intrigued despite the fact that she would have to hide as a boy for several days. That whole strapping down business? Ye-ouch.

"Usually from a recommendation of another guardsman," Maxt said, "Someone who has been with the corps for a long time."

"Meet your long lost cousin, Maxt," the Prince declared with an easy laugh, waving a hand in Claire's direction.

"Still doesn't explain why she–he," Maxt corrected himself wryly, "is showing up with Ben several days before we do."

The Seer pondered the situation. "Well, really, Maxt, if you send Ganth a personal letter, saying you want Claire—we'll have to think of a different name—to be a page at the Barracks and expect him to be installed by the time we get there…honestly, will he complain? Argue? Try and fight it?"

Maxt quirked his mouth to one side. "No. He would do what I asked. Without question."

"Oh, boy," Claire intoned. "Literally, I mean."

"I think that it would be better if Maxt took Claire to the Barracks himself," the Prince decided. "Ben can stay with us. After all, his entrance to the camp was rather noticeable, and he has become a familiar face. If someone is giving information to Evil about our activities, it would be suspicious if a Protector were to suddenly disappear after coming to the camp."

"Maxt will take me?" Claire squeaked, glancing at the man's swollen nose. To his credit, Maxt didn't look any more thrilled by the prospect of spending more time with Claire, but he ultimately nodded.

"I agree. Along the way, I can instruct Claire on what to expect, as well as some rudimentary skills she will need to blend in at the Barracks. Ganth would definitely not give me any grief about her joining if I take her there personally. Nor would it seem strange if I leave the encampment and ride ahead to the Barracks. I can say to several people that I am going to a distant cousin's house and collecting Claire, who I wish to be assigned to a Barracks to learn a trade." Maxt was clearly warming to the scheme.

"Great. Then you go and get her some gear while Claire and I work on the chest issues," the Seer suggested, clapping her hands.

"Boobies!" Sweetie said with the absolute clarity of a child.

The Seer looked shocked and the Prince and Ben tried to hide their laughter. Maxt stared at Sweetie, clearly at a loss. Claire sighed and leaned forward. "No, Sweetie. Don't call them boobies. It's not nice."

"Oh," Sweetie replied with a shrug, obviously not phased by the gentle reprimand.

Once the men had left the tent, Claire balked at having the Seer help her strap down her breasts. She took the bandage from the woman and turned around, wrapping it around her chest tightly. When she was done, Claire turned toward the Seer with disgust.

"I look fat now," she complained. "I used to have a waist, but now? I'm shapeless!"

"You look like a boy." The Seer handed Claire a set of boy's clothes. "Now, put these on and then we'll discuss how you are going to pull this particular stunt off."

"Can you teach me how to pee standing up?" Claire's voice was muffled as she pulled the shirt over her head. "Cuz that's a trick I think will go over well with the college crowd."

The Seer laughed merrily as she pulled out a pair of thick socks, tossing them in Claire's direction where they landed next to the tall, laced up boots. "I'm not a miracle worker, Claire. Oh, and we need to come up with a better name for you."

"My last name is Jones. Would that work? I'd remember that, since most of my foster families just called me by the last name until they got to know me better."

The Seer paused and looked over at Claire, her brownish green eyes reflecting her silent concern. It reminded Claire of the fact that the Seer knew nothing about her, really. Yet, the Seer was perfectly content to do everything possible to help her. Such unconditional acceptance surpassed anything she'd ever experienced in her life.

"Jones would be fine." The Seer laid a hand on Claire's forearm. It seemed she wanted to say more, but Claire turned away before they could get deeper into some asinine Hallmark moment.

Claire finished dressing. The soft cotton shirt with the leather vest over the top helped to hide any of her curves that may have remained after the tight wrapping. She tucked her necklace under the shirt so that it wasn't as noticeable, and the Seer assured her that men in the Land wore necklaces, even if her red and gold enameled bead was unusual. The Seer even laughingly noted the colors were that of a Land Tree.

"Proof that you were destined to be a Traveler, perhaps?"

Claire snorted and peered down at herself. The long leggings were tucked into knee-high boots that laced up, molding to her calves. The long vest drew away from her hips, which were slim enough to pass as a boy's anyway. The Seer brushed Claire's hair straight back from her face and cut another inch off the length, so that the ends barely teased her jaw line.

"I wish your eyebrows weren't so clearly defined," the Seer mused. "I can tell they are plucked and shaped."

"I'm rather OCD about my eyebrows. I have to have them perfectly shaped or I get antsy."

"I could never get mine so well shaped when I lived in the World, that's for sure. I'm just worried that they might tag you as a female."

"Would your average warrior dude realize my eyebrows are plucked?" Claire tilted her head to one side, considering the woman with serious brown eyes.

"Ah, yes. This is true." The Seer nodded her agreement. "Most men don't want to think about tweezers, much less look for how they are utilized by a woman. In fact, I would be willing to bet that most men don't even know what women do to their eyebrows, so it is probably not an issue. Just stay away from women, ok? So, now your disguise is complete. But let's work on some male mannerisms so that you will blend in perfectly with the boys."

When Maxt and Ben ducked back into the tent, carrying a bundle, Claire felt she'd mastered a swagger that was worthy of any high school jock. The Seer was nearly delirious with laughter, holding her sides as Claire continued to walk the length of the tent, thumbing her nose and pretending to adjust her nonexistent groin package.

"Oh, my, goodness," the Seer wiped her eyes, wheezing as she fanned herself. "I haven't laughed this hard in a long, long time!"

"You look—well, not necessarily great, but you do look like a boy," Ben admitted, dumping some swords and scabbards on the table.

"Needs to be dirty," Maxt grunted critically. He stooped down and scooped up some dirt, rubbing it between his hands. Wiping the palms of his hands on Claire's cheeks lightly, he stepped back and looked at her critically. "That's better."

"Let's try some swords." Ben was at the table by the weapons, pulling out one and eyeing it critically. "Too long," he declared, tossing it back and selecting another. "This might be too heavy, but give it a try."

Claire took the sword, her arm dropping to the floor under the weight of it. Ben shook his head and took it back immediately, switching it for another one. They passed through several swords until Claire held one that felt right in her hand. It was dull silver in color, almost like a pewter finish, the hilt simple in its design, with an art deco feel to it. When she withdrew the sword, she could see that the blade was razor sharp and etched with a geometric pattern that appealed to Claire. The sword was perfectly balanced in her hand, and she took several experimental swipes with it.

"Wow," she said under her breath. "Now this I could definitely work with."

"It was my first sword, given to me by my father."

Maxt spoke softly from behind her. Claire wheeled about and looked at him. "Then I can't take it. Such a possession is much too important." Claire held the sword out to him.

"I would be honored if you took the sword and offended if you did not." Maxt's reply was forthright, his arms crossed but his demeanor anything but threatening. "It is far more important that it be used by someone in the defense of the Land rather than sitting at the bottom of a trunk gathering dust."

Claire bit her lip, glancing first at the sword, and then at Maxt. Finally, she nodded, sheathing the sword in the scabbard and belting it around her waist. Maxt reached out, brushing her hands aside, and adjusted the belt so that it rode low on her hips.

"You know, this may just work," the Seer mused as she watched them together. "There is even a kind of resemblance between the two of you. You really could be family. You have the same reddish highlights in your hair that Maxt does, Claire, and the way you set you jaws when getting stubborn is almost identical."

"You're right," Ben agreed, and then laughed as they both scowled. "Even that expression is exactly the same!"

"It is getting dark," Maxt announced, clearly needing the distraction. "After night has fallen, I will come back and get you, Claire. By then, I will have told Joaren about my side trip. I shall make it sound like it was something I planned all along, which the Prince and Seer can help me out with."

"I'll be waiting," Claire promised.

Ben waited until the Seer and Maxt had left, and then faced Claire. "I have to stay with the Seer and Maxt for a day or two. We're going to make it look like the Protectors are clueless about what is happening here, try and deflect attention from you. But I'll leave before the Prince's camp hooks up with the guards, just to be on the safe side. Plus, I need to get back in case Tracy goes into labor."

"Ok." Claire unconsciously fiddled with the sword hilt, her stoic and upright carriage very reminiscent of how Maxt stood, Ben realized with a smile.

"I'm leaving you in very good hands," Ben promised Claire, knowing the girl must feel adrift in this strange place and with these strange people.

"I know." Claire straightened her shoulders purposely. "I'll be fine, Ben. The Land chose me. If nothing else, Emma and Harry deserve to know what happened to Jay, and if I can find him, I will. I'm not going to let them, or the Land, down after that kind of faith has been shown to me."

"That, my friend, is the perfect attitude," Ben declared heartily, hesitating only slightly before reaching out and enfolding her in a hug. For the first time, Claire melted into his arms and really hugged him back tightly. " Progress."

"What?" Claire pulled back from him, looking up at those aqua eyes. Realizing she was still within his sheltering arms, she pulled back, jerking down on the hem of her tunic.

"Good to know you are still in there." Ben tweaked her nose before walking out of the tent.

Claire stood there, alone in the tent, adrift. It was a sensation she was used to, unfortunately, having experienced the dread of being dropped off at a strange house time and again during her foster care days.

"Ok. I can do this. I've done it in the past. Go to the Barracks, be a boy, get to the Meadows, find Jay. Easy. No sweat." Claire rubbed the top of the sword with one hand. "I just gotta take one step at a time."

~ 14 ~

▼

GIFTS DISCOVERED

As promised, when Maxt came to get Claire, it was fully dark outside. Claire, who had eaten earlier when the Seer brought her food, lay on one of the cots, staring at the canvas ceiling of the tent. She'd tried to get some sleep, anticipating a night-long hike, but had been unable to relax enough to fall into slumber. So, she had listened to the sounds of the camp through the material walls, getting used to the quaint accent of the Land people, scarcely believing that she was really here, that her quest was finally going to start.

When the tall warrior ducked into the tent, Claire swung her legs off the cot and stood up, looking at him evenly.

"Good," Maxt grunted with approval. "You don't smile when a man enters the room like most females tend to do."

Claire grimaced and rubbed her hands on her leggings. "Won't it look funny that I'm carrying a Worlder bag?" she asked Maxt, pointing to her duffle. The black backpack with white skulls adorning with a pink bow did seem out of place in the candy-colors of the Land.

The guardsman nodded, "Good catch." He picked up a leather pack and helped Claire transfer her belongings. Maxt paused over the Tupperware of cookies, looking at Claire with a question clearly in his forest green eyes.

"Really bad cookies," Claire grimaced as she took them from the man, "from Jay's mom. Trust me, you want to stay far, far away from those." Yet she could not bear to leave them behind, so she shoved the tub into her bag, pushing it down to the bottom. She added an extra shirt and leggings that the Seer had procured, and figured that would hide the decidedly non-Lander Tupperware container.

Maxt handed Claire a long, deep red cloak. "It belongs to my lady Seer. When we leave the tent, it will look like my lady is seeing me off on my journey."

Claire nodded and tossed the cloak around her shoulders, unconsciously fingering the velvety material. Maxt brushed her hands aside and fastened the cloak at her throat, pinning it with a gold brooch. Pulling up the hood, he made sure that all of Claire's brown hair was hidden.

"That should do," he told her with a smile.

"Can I do this?" Claire asked Maxt suddenly, as she stared up at him. "Can I pull this trick off, do you think?" She almost bit her lip, horrified at having blurted her darkest fears to this fierce man.

Maxt regarded her steadily. "I think, of all the Protectors I have had the pleasure of meeting, that you are the one that will be able to pull this off."

"Thank you, Maxt," Claire replied, realizing with some amazement that his sure and steady opinion meant a great deal to her.

They left the tent and walked toward the edge of the camp, Maxt with all his gear in plain view and Claire hiding her pack under her cloak. As anticipated, their departure did not warrant any special notice. A few people called out a farewell to Maxt, but no one remarked on their leaving the encampment. Once under the enveloping canopy of the Forest, Maxt led Claire to a small clearing about a half-mile away from the camp. There, the Seer and Ben were waiting.

The Sea Dimension man smiled as Claire came into view. He helped her take off the cloak and handed her a shorter, nondescript, greenish brown one in its place. Claire slung it over her arm, already warm from the walk. She'd put it on later if she needed it. Draping the red cloak over the Seer's shoulders, Ben spoke in Claire's direction.

"I'll tell Katie and the others that you're making good progress," he said to her.

"Progress? I'm dressed as a boy. That's hardly progress," Claire said with deprecating humor. "I also don't have a clue what my quest is supposed to be at this point."

"I'd advise finding out as much as possible about these weird weather condition. That's clearly something out of the ordinary and they coincided with your appearing on the radar, so to speak, in the World. Your quest may not have anything to do with this other Sea Dimension person. That could be coincidence."

"Oh, and what does one do to stop the weather?" she said in a biting tone.

Ben glanced toward the Seer with amusement. "I've come to realize that when she is unsure of herself or her surroundings, Claire tends to get argumentative and sarcastic," he observed to the woman in a mild voice.

"Grrrr," Claire growled, deep in her voice.

"And she sounds more and more like Maxt when she does that, which is a good thing for her disguise," the Seer replied just as easily.

Claire and Maxt glowered at the two, then, realizing at the same time that they were increasing their resemblance to one another, wiped their faces clean of any expression. Ben just laughed. "Take care of yourself, Claire," he said to her, hugging her tightly.

"I will," she replied, then gave him a mischievous grin, which transformed her face into that of a bright, happy teenager. "I'll take care of Maxt, too."

Ben tweaked her nose. "I think you will at that."

The Seer pushed him out of the way gently, and then took Claire's hands in hers.

"It's time to begin your journey as Jones," she told Claire. "I have faith in you. We all do. When it seems to be most dark in your world, remember those who care for you and how they express that love. Something tells me that will be important."

Claire felt a lump form in her throat. How could she tell this woman, this great and wise Seer, that nobody had loved her in a long, long time? Not since her mother, who had died so long ago that Claire found it difficult to remember her face any longer. Uncertain once again, she simply nodded at the Seer then moved away, ready to follow Maxt.

The guardsman set a brisk pace, heading deep into the Forest Region. He eschewed the main road, he explained to Claire as he moved, to avoid meeting anyone who could later pinpoint her as being near the encampment. The way through the forest was not arduous, but with the uneven ground and scant light offered by the waning moon, it took all her attention to keep from tripping.

Maxt rarely looked back to see how Claire was doing, which irritated her to no end. She was a guest, for all intents and purposes, and was hardly a seasoned warrior used to tromping through the wilds. The least the man could do was give her a glance now and then to make sure she was all right. The asshole was totally ignoring her and the longer the night went, the more pissed off Claire became.

It also made her that much more determined not to ask Maxt to slow down or even stop for a break. She took frequent sips of water and kept his large back squarely in her eyesight. She started to pretend she was shooting a dagger or a blow dart or some other sharp instrument into the man's flesh, imprinting a large imaginary target on his back. That helped pass the time and alleviated some of her frustration at Maxt's complete lack of courtesy.

In the wee hours of the night, Maxt stopped suddenly. Claire had to skid to a halt to avoid plowing into the man's broad back.

"We will rest here until dawn," Maxt said, tossing down his pack. Adjusting it next to a tree, he dropped to his knees and then sat, his back against the pack. He draped his hands over his midsection and closed his eyes.

"Well, nighty-night to you too," Claire muttered. She put her pack against a neighboring tree and sat down after wiping the area clean of any twigs or rocks.

Settling onto the hard ground, she grimaced. Damn but this was uncomfortable, she thought, wiggling against her pack to get into a better position. She closed her eyes with a sigh, missing the grin that spread across Maxt's face.

It was surprisingly easy for her to fall asleep. Claire drifted along, dreaming about running in a bright green pasture with butterflies dancing on the breeze, when Maxt's hand gripped her shoulder, shaking her awake.

Claire's feet lashed out, taking Maxt's legs from underneath him. The warrior fell on his hip with a grunt, his astonished face looking up at Claire, whose heavy breathing and clenched fists denoted her fear despite her automatic defensive stance.

"Sorry." Claire winced as she straightened, stretching cramped muscles, working out the soreness from the previous night's hike. "I don't like people sneaking up on me."

"I can see that." Shaking off the leaves and twigs like a big dog, Maxt gained his feet. "Why are you so tense?"

Claire shrugged, bending down to pick up her pack. How would Maxt understand about the foster care system, too many kids in need of a good home, and not enough homes for them to go to? While many of the foster parents were wonderful, it was a sheer fact that many of them were in it for the money, and abuse was rampant.

"Ben told me about your upbringing."

"What, are you reading my mind or something?"

"I am not my lady Seer, but I know that having someone your age so worried about a simple touch is worrisome."

"It's no big deal." Out of habit, Claire slouched, not meeting his eyes.

Maxt reached out and grabbed Claire's arm, gently but firmly. She looked down at his hand, the skin beside her nose white with tension, then glanced up at him, wary. His words surprised her, however.

"Has anyone ever done *anything* to you against your will?" he asked her with an intensity that had Claire biting down her usual tart retort.

"No," she replied, not even trying to pretend she didn't understand exactly what Maxt was asking her. "But not for lack of trying. I learned quickly and early on how to defend myself." Claire yanked her arm away from Maxt and acted like she needed something from inside her pack. "I don't want to talk about it." Blinking rapidly to avoid him seeing the tears that threatened, she waited for him to walk away.

"I wish," he said with low intensity, "that I was capable of traveling through the Grid System. If I were, I would go to the World Dimension and demand that someone be held accountable for the fact that you cannot enjoy the realms of sleep without fear of being harmed."

Claire froze, her fingertips brushing over the hard plastic side of the cookie Tupperware. Other than Emma and Harry, she'd not had an adult want to help her in…ages. She had no idea how to respond.

"Here." A strip of jerky appeared over her shoulder. "Eat this."

Claire accepted the makeshift meal and turned around, sitting on a root. Gnawing on the jerky, she tried to get her rampaging emotions under control. For long moments, all that could be heard was the sound of their breakfast being eaten and the early birdsong.

"We got much farther last night than I expected," Maxt admitted, surprising Claire. "I would like to get a few more miles between us and the others, then I will give you a quick lesson in some of the weapons you would be expected to know."

"When will we get to the Barracks?" A coil of nervousness tightening in her belly had Claire regretting the jerky consumption.

"By nightfall, if we are able to keep the same pace we did last night. Now if you need to take a few minutes to, uh, well, you know, then get to it. We need to get moving."

After a brief trip into the bushes, which had her blushing wildly, Claire was ready to continue the trek. Maxt set an even more brutal pace than the night before.

Claire was hard pressed to keep up with him. Yet, like the night before, she was bound and determined not to cause any delays to their arrival at the Barracks.

The sun filtered down through the trees, causing foggy rays to slant toward the ground. The air was fragrant with honeysuckle and pine trees, birds chirping and insects singing. Periodically, the two of them forded a stream or brook, jumping over the water or walking across a fallen log. The mossy boulders sheltered small sprigs of flowers and chipmunks cavorted through the bushes, seeking nuts. It was like a master movie director had designed a living forest, complete with cute animals and designer flowers. All it needed was a soundtrack to make the picture complete. Claire found herself enchanted.

Maxt paused in a large clearing, turning around in a circle to see if the space would be suitable for their practice bout. "This will work," he said, shucking off his backpack. Claire followed suit then stood still, staring at him.

"What now?"

His sword sang from the scabbard, flashing in the sunlight. "Draw!" he roared, swinging the blade up over his head.

"Shit." Startled, the movement had her yanking out the blade out of the scabbard awkwardly. She brought the sword up to meet Maxt's blade, the impact sending a ringing jolt through her arm.

"Good. Instincts work well, but you will need to work on your technique."

"Technique?" Claire shot back, gripping the sword double fisted, low and in front of her.

"Yes. For example, you are in a perfect defensive stance at the moment. You have good instincts for this kind of work."

Claire's mouth hung open. "I was just trying to keep you from decapitating me!"

Maxt flung the sword in the air, so that it arched around in a perfect circle before he caught it again. "Now, do what I say, when I say," he instructed Claire as he came to stand by her side. Walking her through each parry and thrust, Maxt gave Claire a brief but thorough sword lesson. Her years on the flag corps had graced her with pretty impressive upper body strength, which helped tremendously. Finally, Maxt sheathed the sword, nodding encouragingly.

"You are not bad at all," Maxt said with a thoughtful quirk of his mouth. "I think you are on par with any lad your age."

"Land gift?" Claire guessed, sliding the blade back home. "I know each Protector had something that was unique or special about them in the Land. Maybe mine is weapons."

Maxt looked at her consideringly. "I do not think so. It is more that you have a natural balance and an extremely good eye. You have learned to anticipate people's movements before they do them. I think that is more a factor of your childhood than anything else."

"Really?" Claire was careful to answer with exaggerated nonchalance, trying to put her hands in her back pockets, except, there weren't any in leggings. She just ended up rubbing hands along the sides of her hips. "Well,

I guess as long as I can fake enough skill to fool the guards, that's all that matters."

"Let us try knives next," Maxt suggested. He fashioned a target against a tree and showed Claire the basics of balancing then tossing the blades. Claire followed suit, but it quickly became clear she was not as adept at the blades as she had been with the sword. Still, after an hour of practice, Maxt declared her knowledge to be close enough.

"Most guardsmen come to the corps with knowledge of archery, but it is not required until after induction. Now, the final skill is jousting poles." Maxt scouted around the floor of the forest, kicking sticks aside, searching. He plucked up a fallen sapling, about five feet long and as thick as Claire's wrist. Using his large hunting knife, Maxt stripped it off its branches. He handed it to Claire and moved off to find another stick. "Jousting poles are an old sport, one that really is no longer used in battle. Yet the guards keep the tradition as it is one they are most enthusiastic about. The goal is to either disarm the opponent or push them out of the defined jousting space, if on level ground. The other variation of the joust is to knock the opponent off a beam if you are jousting above ground. We use the skill to improve our balance, discover how to read weaknesses in our opponents… it is a very useful ability, and I find it the cornerstone of all our tactics practice."

"Boys do like to whack each other with sticks," mused Claire, earning a snort from Maxt. She absently spun the pole, getting used to the dimensions and weight of the thing. It was remarkably like the old flagpole she had used back home, without the large swath of material on one end. Having it in her hand brought a familiar and comfortable feeling that had her grinning and upping the revolution of the pole.

Claire whirled about at the sound of Maxt's shout, thrusting her pole up and knocking Maxt's aside with mere inches to spare. She flipped the pole and spun, clashing the wood of his pole with enough force that her arms trembled.

Claire felt the blood singing in her veins. The poles met with lighting speed, and she found, just as she had with the swordplay, that she could predict Maxt's movements through the subtle shifts in his body posture, footing and pole direction. She flipped the end of her pole underneath his, knocking it straight up, nearly clipping his chin with his own jousting stick. Claire laughed merrily, spinning the pole and twirling around behind Maxt, her feet fairly dancing over the earth. Bringing the pole around her body in an arching motion, Claire smacked at the pole in Maxt's hand, neatly knocking it out of his grasp.

As the pole skid across the clearing, Claire pushed her hair out of her face, leaning against the pole with a grin. "Damn, that was fun," she crowed. Then she noticed that Maxt was staring at her with something akin to amazement. "What?"

"I think," Maxt said very slowly, "that we have found your Land gift, Claire Jones of the World Dimension."

~ 15 ~

▼

BEDDING DOWN AT THE FOREST BARRACKS

After quickly ascertaining that Claire was hopeless in archery, but could probably master the techniques with some practice, Maxt called a halt to their practice session.

"It is time we got going. We will need to make it to the road, as I want to approach the Barracks in as normal a fashion as possible."

As they picked their way through the forest toward the road, Claire asked Maxt about the Land gifts that the Protectors possessed. She'd read some of the outlines Katie had given her, but was by no means finished. Hopefully, Maxt would be able help fill in some of her gaps. By the time they reached the smooth expanse of dirt-packed road, Claire had a good idea of who could do what in the Protector group.

After gaining the road, they were able to march at a much faster rate, and without having to worry about tripping over a root or rock, Claire had a lot of time to think, which led to pondering the jousting poles. It seemed a rather, well, unglamorous gift to have acquired. At least Sasha got to talk to animals, and Zach could slay huge beasties with a sword. There were Oracles and Seers and Wizards. She, apparently, could whomp ass with a big stick. *Great.*

Yet time and again during the afternoon, Maxt continued to impress upon Claire that her skill with the poles was nothing short of miraculous, and her sword work wasn't half bad either. As for knives and archery—well, not every lad came to the Guards with all their skills in line.

"I cannot wait to see what you can do with a regulation pole."

Claire rolled her eyes. "Yes, so you have said. Several times."

Maxt also filled her in on the ways of a Barracks, giving her insight and valuable information so that Claire would not make an idiot of herself.

"You will need to watch the Worlder tendency to contract words."

"Huh?"

"Words like 'isn't' or 'can't'. We do not use those vernaculars…well, my lady does. I suppose I do on occasion as well. And a few others…" Maxt's eyebrows lowered as he pondered that fact.

"Contractions must be making their way into the Land vocabulary with your increased exposure to Worlders."

"I suppose they are. But keep them to a minimum. Ah, we are here."

Ahead, Claire could see that a cluster of low, long buildings was just off the side of the road. The light was failing as twilight spread over the Land, but the buildings were clearly visible due to the torches that were lit in the courtyard. She perked up, figuring they had finally reached the Barracks. Maxt veered off the road in the direction of the buildings, confirming her suspicions.

As they stepped off the road, a man came out of the shadows, an arrow notched in his bow. "Who travels to us by the night?"

"It is Maxt, Captain of the Prince's Guard."

"Hold, please," came the clipped reply. A warbling whistle rent the air and the door to the main lodge opened, several more men spilling out.

A tall man led the way. He had unruly red hair that spilled almost to his shoulders and high cheekbones, over which a piercing blue gaze raked over the two of them. He paused several yards away, his hands on his hips. Then a smile spread over his handsome face.

"Maxt," he exclaimed, bowing with one hand over his heart. "Welcome, sir, to the Forest Barracks. We did not expect you for another two days. What happened to your nose?"

"Nothing, just a little mishap," Maxt muttered, one finger tracing the bruise while Claire made it a point to study the trees along the side of the road. "I made a side trip, Ganth, and got here a little early because of it," Maxt said, stepping forward to grip forearms with the man.

Criminy, Claire thought, *that dude is tall!* Maxt was no slouch in the height department, but Ganth was easily several inches taller, and had incredibly broad shoulders underneath his guardsman uniform. Man, they sure grew them handsome in the Land. Despite the fact that the man was easily a decade older than her, Claire couldn't help but be impressed.

The brunt of the man's blue gaze fell on her with intensity. Claire automatically allowed her body to slump into a slouch so that her chest was not so apparent.

"Who is this?" Ganth asked, one eyebrow winging up.

"This is a cousin of mine. His name is Jones. I would like him to be assigned to your Barracks to learn the ways of the guards." Maxt reached back and pulled Claire into the light that spilled off the torches. "He is shaky in his arrow and knife usage, passable with the sword, but his main skill lies in jousting."

Claire, realizing that all the men gathered behind Ganth were staring at her, felt extremely uncomfortable. She reached to put her hands in her pockets, then realized that she didn't have pockets in her leggings, so ended up wiping her hands along the sides of her thighs restlessly.

"Well," Ganth watched Claire carefully. "We do not have a lad in our company at the moment. Octavia left us to be assigned to the Mountains Barracks a few weeks ago. You, boy!" Ganth turned to face Claire, crowding in close.

"Yes, sir?" Claire said quickly and clearly, standing her ground. She knew what game she needed to play here, and she would play it well. Being polite to new foster parents was the quickest way for them to leave you alone. Stood to reason the same would be true here.

Apparently, it was the right demeanor, as Ganth grunted his approval. "You wish to become a guardsman?"

"If that is the road my life takes me on, I will go," Claire answered. She figured it wasn't really a lie, after all. Her road was leading toward the Meadows, and if the guardsmen were the way to get on that road, so was she.

"Your cousin's name will not stand you above the others here," Ganth warned lightly.

"I stand on my own," Claire flared back, not liking his insinuation.

"Desire to do the job and a bit of a temper," Ganth observed, then grinned, holding out his hand toward Claire. "Welcome to the Barracks, Jones."

Claire almost shook his hand before catching herself and gripping Ganth's forearm as she had seen the other men in the Land do. It was rather like grabbing a steel beam, and Claire was hard pressed not to wince at the amount of force the man exerted on her arm.

Maxt and Claire followed Ganth into the main lodge, where the men were having their dinner and gathering for their night's routine of weapons cleaning and talking. Gossip, Claire thought with a mental snort, but she didn't dare say it aloud.

After showing them a seat, Ganth called for food and drink to be served to Maxt and Claire. "Enjoy the service well, Jones," Ganth suggested as he sat near them to speak with Maxt while they supped, "for on the morrow, it will be you serving us." A laugh rose from the men in the room.

Claire knew from her conversations with Maxt that there were anywhere from fifteen to twenty five guardsmen assigned to a Barracks, but usually only ten stayed at the Barracks themselves. The rest would be out traveling their assigned areas, seeking to assist the populace or settle petty disputes. The full company appeared to be at the Barracks at the moment, she realized as she counted them up quickly.

When Claire was done eating, Ganth had one of his men show her where to put her dishes and then take her over to the fire area, where the rest of the men were sitting. Claire crossed the wooden plank floor with a backwards glance at Maxt, who nodded at her reassuringly.

~   ~   ~

Ganth watched Jones cross the floor with narrowed eyes, taking in the look between Maxt and his new page. He scooted down the bench to sit closer to Maxt, their elbows almost touching. "Tell me, Maxt, why do you bring a female disguised as a boy into my Barracks? Is this some sort of test?" He spoke softly to avoid being overheard.

Maxt's lips quirked. "I should have known you would see right through it. What gave her away?"

"She eats like a girl," Ganth waved his hand dismissingly. "But more than that, you treat her like a girl. You watch over her, you have concern for her, beyond what a cousin would show for a healthy male relative."

Maxt rubbed his chin with one hand, looking at Ganth. "Have I compromised her disguise?"

"No. I know you well, Maxt. The others took what you said at face value. But I have never known you to willingly leave the Seer when she is traveling. And when I looked closely at this Jones, I began to perceive what was really beneath the surface. But the others? They will not think to look, quite frankly."

"Her name is Claire Jones. She is of the World Dimension," Maxt informed Ganth, who was taking a long pull of ale. "We believe she is to be a Protector."

Ganth set the mug back down on the table, his hands fiddling with the pewter handle. "She is quite young. And she is untried in the ways of our Land. That will make this transition very difficult for her."

"I was not jesting about her skills," Maxt assured him. "When you see her joust, pray remember that before today, she had no knowledge of the weapon. As for adjusting, I do not fear that. Jones is well versed at keeping her wits about her. Do not ever sneak up on her if you value your man parts."

"Am I to tell her I know of this deception?" Ganth wondered aloud, watching Claire as she sat gingerly on the ground near the fireplace, listening avidly to the men. He hoped they weren't telling a ribald tale that was too raunchy for her young ears, then shook his head. After lecturing Maxt about how his actions gave away his new page's identity, the last thing Ganth needed to do was fall into the same trap.

Maxt thought about it for a while, and then shook his head. "No, if she is aware of your knowledge, she might become lax in your presence, which could lead to the other men learning about her true sex."

"What is it you wish me to do with her, then? There must be a reason for bringing her here."

Maxt filled Ganth in on the fact that in the World, Evil had tried to harm Claire, and that it was the consensus of all involved that her true identity be hidden. Ganth nodded when Maxt mentioned the Meadows Region and the strange weather reported from the area.

"The bulk of us are going to head for the Meadows Region tomorrow," Ganth admitted with a grin. "To lend our assistance to the guardsmen and people of the Region."

"So, Claire can go with you and none will be the wiser." Maxt nodded and smiled. "That is good. It is also good to know that you are going to help the Region. Too many are sitting on their hands, waiting for someone else to do the work or give help." Maxt put down his cup, the ale inside sloshing with the force of the motion.

"I agree. Each Region looks to their own and are becoming increasingly less willing to reach out," Ganth said with a sigh.

"I wish that more of our Barracks Leaders had your kind of vision."

"On trips, the page usually attends the Barracks Leader, so I will be able to keep a close eye on our Jones," Ganth pointed out.

"I will head back to meet the Prince's caravan. They should reach the Beaches outside the Meadows Region in five day's time. My lady's foresight tells her to arrive by then, and not a day before. We trust her judgment, even if I chaff at the delay. By then, your team should already be there, in place. Make whatever reconnaissance into the Meadows Region that you can. Find out as much as possible about these storms, where they are coming from, how long they take to build up, how long they last, that kind of information."

"Understood." Ganth gave a firm nod, then hesitated slightly. "Do you want Jones to actually go into the Meadows Region?"

"I would take Jones into the Meadows," Maxt said immediately. "If she is a Protector, then we have to provide all the tools needed to figure out how to defeat the storms."

"As always, Maxt, I serve the Land," Ganth replied, giving the time-honored line that guardsmen used to swear their allegiance, one hand over his heart.

Maxt clamped his hand on the redhead's shoulder. "That, my friend, I never doubted. I must admit, I am relieved that you know about Jones. I have confidence that you will keep her safe and sound during her time with us."

"Why are you frowning, then, old friend?"

Maxt glanced over at Claire, then back to the Barracks Leader. Ganth held himself still. Whatever it was, Maxt was hesitant to share it with him, so instinct told Ganth it was going to be about Jones, and likely highly personal in nature. He continued to hold very still while Maxt told him that Claire may have been abused in the World Dimension, or at the very least threatened by the males around her. "She seems to have it under control, however, if a situation arises where it comes out, I want you to be aware of her past."

Ganth's lips thinned with distaste. "To hurt someone who is weaker than you, more vulnerable, is an abomination. It is Evil at its worst." Maxt nodded, agreeing wholeheartedly. They both turned to look over at Claire.

Claire listened to the men talk, her arms wrapped around her knees. It was clear that she was not used to being around so many men, and their closeness affected her. Every time one of them moved, they could see she jumped the slightest bit, jostling to keep an even distance between herself and the men. She suddenly yawned mightily as though the previous twenty four hours had just crashed down upon her.

Maxt stood and stretched. "We traveled far last night," he told Ganth. "Tell us where we can take our rest, and we will speak in the morning before I take my leave."

Ganth nodded. "You will stay in the visitor's lodge, but I think it is best if Jones sleeps in here. Our old page, Octavia, used to sleep in the room off the lodge, so it is empty."

When Ganth came to her side, Claire looked up at him and blinked several times. Ganth saw the weariness settling upon the lines of her face.

"You should take your rest, Jones. Come with me."

Claire stood up, slightly weaving as she did so. Without being reminded, she grabbed her bag and followed Ganth, giving a small wave in acknowledgement to the men who called out their good nights to her. Ganth opened the door to a small room—more like a closet, really—and gestured for Claire to step inside.

"It is not much," Ganth said to Claire, "but you will really only sleep here."

"It's more room than I am used to," Claire admitted, then winced as if realizing that sharing that kind of information was not appropriate. "This is fine."

Ganth didn't remark on the comment but simply handed Claire a small lamp. He waited in the doorway, leaning against the jam, watching as she put the lamp on the table, dropped the bag on the floor and yawned.

"Do not forget to unbuckle that sword before you fall asleep."

The girl jerked, as if already asleep while sitting. Unbuckling the belt she started to drop it to the floor then reconsidered, placing it carefully on the table. Ganth hid a smile behind one hand. Tired as she was, Claire was taking care of her weapons. It boded well for her. He waited until she blew out the lamp and fell sideways on the bed before easing out of the room, shutting the door.

He would have wagered a month's pay that the girl was asleep before her head hit the pillow.

The door to her room opened with a jarring thud. Claire sat up straight, clutching the blanket to her chest. "Wake up," came Ganth's voice, which was roughly the equivalent of a dragon's roar. "No time for sleeping when we have to ready ourselves for a march." Then he banged out the doorway again.

Claire groaned. Another hike? The joys just kept coming. Well, hopefully it would get her closer to the Meadows Region, she swung her legs over the side of the cot. Damn, it felt like she had just fallen asleep. She rubbed at her eyes wearily. Standing, she bit her lip to suppress a groan as her muscles protested the movement bitterly.

Out in the main lodge, the men were seated around the table, having breakfast. Claire, mindful of what Maxt had told her about her duties at the Barracks, headed for the kitchen area. Inside the large space, several women from the nearby town were busy cooking food to last the men the entire day. They generally left around midday, once they had finished with the lunch and dinner for the men.

"I am the new Barracks page," Claire announced to the women. One, a tall, buxom woman, separated herself from the others, wiping her hands on her apron. She looked Claire up and down.

"You are, are you?" she said, noncommittally.

"What do you need me to do?" There was no way was she going to piss off the people who made the food, she decided, her stomach growling mightily.

The woman smiled, showing a gap in her teeth. "I am Krono, the lead cook for this crew. You seem to know your place, not demanding to have food first like some boys do. Here, take this out to the men. Be sure to serve our esteemed visitor and Ganth first, you hear me?"

Claire accepted the heavy platter of meat, staggering slightly. "Got it." Juggling the plate to get a better grip, she headed back to the main room.

Damn, but the meat smelled good, Claire approached the table. Maxt and Ganth sat together at one end of the table, separated from the other men by several empty seats. They were deep in discussion. Claire waddled up to them, presenting the platter.

Maxt gave Claire a grin, then speared some meat from the plate. Ganth didn't even glance her way, but also helped himself to the meat. After they had been served, Claire made her way down to the men at the other end of the table, who greeted her with good-natured cheer.

Claire spent the next half hour trotting to and from the kitchen area, carrying food, taking away dirty plates, pouring something that smelled like a cross between tea and coffee. Finally, Krono waved her to a small table in the kitchen. "Your turn." Setting down a heaping plate in front of Claire, the woman nodded as she wiped her hands on a towel tucked into her apron. "You did very well. Most boys manage to spill at least one platter on their first day."

Claire shrugged, figuring her summer part time job waitressing had been a cakewalk compared to this morning's hard labor. Then she tucked into the food like a madman. "Dis is good," she mumbled around the food, washing it down with some of the tea.

"Thank you." Krono blushed brightly at the praise. Claire had a feeling the woman rarely was given positive feedback from the men, who most likely took the good fare for granted.

"Who cooks when the Barracks travels?" Claire asked suddenly, visions of trying to prepare a meal over a campfire looming in her mind.

"Normally, the men would go on rations. But this looks to be a long term project, so two of us are traveling along with them," Krono replied easily as she wiped down the workspace while the other women busily prepared the vegetables for the stew that would be served at dinnertime. "And you will help out, of course."

Finally feeling full, Claire stood up and crossed to the sink area. She cleaned off her plate and quickly washed it, leaving it on the drying rack with the others. When she turned around, Krono was watching her with a furrowed brow.

"What?" Claire glanced down at her top. Had she spilled something on herself?

"Someone trained you well," the woman replied thoughtfully. "To be so neat and clean. A lad your age? Remarkable."

Claire bit her lip mentally berating herself. She had to be more careful about not being too girlish. The men had emptied out of the main lodge, so Claire quickly grabbed her belt and pack and headed for the door. She didn't want to be left behind.

A wagon stood nearby, filled with items needed for the temporary Barracks. Maxt strode over and took Claire's pack from her hands, tossing it onto the cart.

"Ganth wants to make all haste for the Meadows Region," he told Claire as they stood in the shadows of the wagon. "Instead of a hike with your pack on your back, he is sending a wagon with those items. Take on your person only what you need to get through the day, and keep your water skein full."

"You're going now, aren't you?" Claire's small voice surprised her.

Maxt gave her arm a squeeze and when he spoke, his voice was low so that only she could hear his words. "You are doing well, Claire. Your behavior during breakfast was impeccable. No one can find fault with your willingness to pitch in and help. Keep that up and the men will be falling over each other to help you out. And no contractions when you speak!"

"So if I become a stark raving bitch, they'll—I mean they will—treat me like dirt. Fighting my natural instincts won't be easy, but I'll give it my best shot. I mean, I will give it my best shot." At Maxt's horrified look, she grinned. "Gotcha." She waggled her eyebrows.

Maxt glowered at her but was unable to keep the amusement from gleaming in his forest green eyes. "I will see you when the Prince's caravan rendezvous at the Meadows Region. Stay near Ganth. He is a good man and will watch over you well."

"Thanks, Maxt," Claire whispered. "For everything." She paused, scuffing her toe in the dirt. "I am really, really sorry about your nose," she blurted before rushing away from him.

~ 16 ~

▼

REGIONS OF INTEREST

Claire soon found that traveling with a group of guardsmen was very different than the clandestine dash through the woods with Maxt. The only similarity was the fast pace that Ganth demanded of his men.

The guardsmen were a happy group, laughing and joking with one another during their trek. Claire started out walking by the wagon, but was quickly assimilated into the main group as the men continued to chat with her. She had to lie quickly at some points when the men asked her specific questions about her childhood but overall felt like she was holding her own in the group. Unfortunately, the need to lie about her younger years was a long ingrained defensive mechanism. That, combined with the fact that the people of the Land seemed so trusting made it easy to gloss over the fact that she knew little to nothing about growing up in the Forest Region.

Being among men who had no idea of her sex was proving to be a liberating experience. There were no clandestine—or blatant—examinations of her chestal region. No one accidentally brushed up against her. The men joked around with her, sure, but it wasn't the kind of frat-boy bullshit she'd expected to experience. An aura of respect clung to these men like a second skin, and instead of it seeming fake or goody-two-shoes, it was comfortable and real.

When the men stopped for a break, without asking Claire went around to each man and collected his water skein, replenishing them from the stream that bubbled nearby. She handed the skeins back to the men, Ganth's last. As the Barracks Leader took his skin from her, his fingers brushed hers. A fission of awareness raced through her skin at the touch, making Claire frown. She rubbed her hand on her pant leg.

"Sit," Ganth ordered, seemingly oblivious to the affect the touch had on Claire. She folded her legs underneath her body and relaxed, taking a long pull from her own water bottle.

"You are doing well," Ganth observed, his eyes scanning the crowd of men. "The men respect the fact that you are jumping in to help out."

"Isn't that my job?" Claire watched a brilliant blue ant scuttle across the ground. "I mean, you are feeding me and giving me a place to stay, so I should work for my keep."

Ganth grunted, one massive shoulder rising casually. "You would be surprised at the entitlement issues some come to the guards with. I usually spend the first few months of a new recruit's tenure unlearning all the bad behavior they carry with them in their kit bags."

"Maxt told me what to expect and how I should behave," Claire told him, plucking a blade of grass and twirling it in her fingers. "I learned a long time ago that it is easier to simply do what is required rather than to fight it tooth and nail. Fighting really does not help matters, because you will end up doing what is expected anyway, and at a higher personal cost."

His blue eyes were wide with astonishment. "You have a wisdom that is beyond your tender years," he told her, then added with a wicked grin, "now if only your voice would deepen into manhood, you would be well on your way to becoming a guardsman."

Claire dropped the blade of grass with a grimace. She needed to make sure she keep her voice lowered, she realized with a mental sigh. There was just so much to remember.

They made good progress that afternoon, according to Ganth's assessment. "We will reach the Region's end first thing in the morning," he informed them as they set up camp, Claire struggling under large armloads of packs, which she passed out to their owners. "Then, we will take the Beaches route past the Desert and Marshes Regions."

Claire was anxious to see the famous Region's end, where there was an abrupt end to one region while another started immediately afterwards. It was one of the most fascinating things she had ever heard of, and frankly, she wondered if such razor sharp definitions were even possible.

That night, Ganth instructed Claire to stretch out her pallet in the back of the wagon, while the rest of the men bunked down by the fire. She wondered why she was so close to his bed, but assumed that since she was the new guy in town, the Barrack's Leader was just trying to make sure she didn't cause any trouble. When Ganth drew his sword, leaving it within easy reach, Claire frowned, trying to recall what kind of animals might be in the area that would cause Ganth to take such a precaution. Then Claire watched the unfamiliar night sky until she fell asleep.

True to Ganth's prediction, shortly after they broke camp, they passed through a strand of thick forest pines and were suddenly, almost inexplicitly, standing on the Beaches. Claire stared, amazed, then twisted to look behind her. Sure enough, a thick mass of vegetation was at her back, and then, with a precision that she was not accustomed to seeing in nature, pristine white sand started, stretching to the ocean.

Whereas a moment before, Claire had heard the chirping of birds and the rustle of leaves overhead, now the roar of the surf as the waves pounded against the shore occupied her senses. It was all part of the transition. The birds and forest sounds were soft in the background, the beach noises taking precedence.

"Now that is cool," she whispered with appreciation, her hands on her hips.

"Have you never seen the Beaches?" one of the guardsmen asked Claire curiously.

Claire shook her head. "I've never left the Forest Region before," she said truthfully.

"Ah, then wait until we get to the Desert and Marshes," he told her as they walked farther out onto the sand. "But nothing compares to the Meadows Region." He sighed deeply.

"Tell me about the Meadows," she asked the man, interested in the region that was under attack.

The man started to wax poetic about the Meadows. Claire envisioned rolling green grass dotted with flowers, butterflies and insects dancing in the breeze. Farmland and small villages nestled beside gently rising hills and trees that swayed in the sweet breezes.

"It sounds wonderful," Claire said as the man finished his description. "I cannot wait to see it."

"If there is any of it left," the man said in an undertone. "Word has it that the weather is just ripping it apart. I cannot help but feel such pity for all those poor farmers and villagers."

"Well, won't guardsmen from the other Regions come in, help out, rebuild?"

She'd been very impressed as, during their trek, the guardsmen had stopped more than once to help a farmer, or a traveler. She'd seen a strapping man help lift pigs back into an enclosure and another guard assist with a stubborn ox. The best was when more than half the team had helped fix a broken wheel on a stranded wagon, as it involved a lot of stripped off shirts and gleaming muscles. Her heart had skipped a beat or two at the site, that was for sure. The guardsmen eagerly performed such tasks without asking, purely to help their fellow Landers. Claire assumed that such courtesies would extend to other Regions. Or perhaps Ganth's troop was an exception to the rule.

The man shrugged. "Guardsmen will assist wherever they are needed. Others however, will not be as quick to help. Regional differences run deep, I am afraid." He shook his head sorrowfully over the sad fact. "It is not just our vegetation that stops at Region's end, it is our willingness to help, it seems."

"Well that is just stupid, given that Evil will have learned that fact and will use it against you all," Claire said without thinking, then bit her lip. "I mean, it stands to reason that Evil would do that, right?"

The guardsman nodded thoughtfully. Claire looked ahead and saw that Ganth was waving at her, motioning her to the front of the line. Claire jogged ahead of the other men, panting because it was more difficult to run in the sand, coming to stand next to Ganth, sucking in another lungful of salt-laden air.

"Yes, sir?"

"Look," he pointed to a blur on the horizon. "I assume you have never seen them, so I wanted you to be up front where you will have a good view."

"Of what?" Claire shaded her eyes with one hand. "Oh! Horses!"

Sure enough, a large herd headed their way along the beach, led by a huge black stallion.

"The Prince's Herd," Ganth proclaimed proudly. "Watch. They will race right by us, ignoring that we are even here." He shook his red head. "I never tire of the sight. Such proud and intelligent animals."

The black stallion raced by and then, suddenly and inexplicably, paused, his hooves cleaving he air as he wheeled to face the humans clustered at the Edge of the Beaches Region. His ears pricked forward, his stance curious.

"What is this…" Ganth's voice trailed off as the stallion pranced toward them. He took an instinctive, protective step toward Claire.

The rest of the horses milled about on the beach near the ocean's edge, clearly as confused as the humans were at this unexpected action from their leader. The black continued to approach the guardsmen, his black hooves digging up small tufts of sand as it drew ever nearer.

"Everyone hold still," Ganth ordered as some of the men moved restlessly. Claire contributed it to his abilities as a leader when the men obeyed him, instantly becoming motionless.

The stallion halted in front of Ganth and Claire. Up close, the horse was simply enormous. He was also gorgeous, with a glistening coat and intelligent brown eyes watching the two humans as they stared at the stallion. The huge black snout reached out and wufted along Claire's arm, the horse's breath warm and moist. Then the lips opened, nibbling at her shirtsleeve. Horsey teeth closed around the fabric with an almost delicate movement, pulling her forward.

With a helpless look at Ganth, Claire allowed the horse to pull her forward. The Barracks Leader started to follow but immediately, the stallion lifted his head and flattened his black ears against his head. It was a clear and unmistakable gesture to the man to back off. Ganth held up his hands and stepped back slowly.

Claire walked next to the horse, drawing closer and closer to the herd. Her heart pounding as the horses stepped around her, blocking her from the view of the guardsmen. In the center of the herd stood the foals that had been born that spring. Gangly, but with their own beauty, the foals were playful little creatures, bumping up against Claire with knobby heads.

"Aren't you guys precious?" Claire laughed, rubbing her hands over their short, bristly manes. "Ben would love to have spikes like yours," she told one, a palomino with bushy blond mane and tail.

The black watched over Claire's interaction with the foals like the indulgent father he was. Claire finally turned toward him. "They are beautiful." The horse tossed his head regally as if to agree. Then the stallion nudged Claire again, pushing her back toward the men who waited anxiously.

Ganth watched as Claire walked in their direction, the massive black still at her side. He breathed a sigh of relief, having known intense panic when Jones had been hidden from his view by the various colored hides.

The black paused several yards away from Ganth. Claire stopped, not sure if she was to continue or not. The black leaned over and with his muzzle gently pushed Claire forward. Reaching up with one hand, she gently rubbed his chin before stepping away.

When she reached Ganth, Claire was surprised to feel her knees shaking. She gave the guardsman a thin smile, then turned to look at the herd.

Surprisingly, the black had not retreated. He tossed his head, letting loose a thundering trumpet. The herd responded in kind, rearing and clicking their hooves.

The black kicked up his heels, then reared up impossibly high before wheeling and taking off at a dead run, the rest of the horses streaming after him like velvet ribbons.

Claire barely breathed as the herd disappeared over the horizon. She knew that the men were all staring at her, Ganth included. She wasn't sure what to say or do to alleviate their confusion.

"I have heard that the herd responds to the purity in people," Ganth finally said into the silence. "I guess that means our Jones here is about the purest lad we have ever met, eh, men?"

A round of raucous laughter followed that assessment, and, just like that, Claire was once again one of the boys. Ganth continued on the path along the Edge of the Beaches Region. They moved more carefully now, the shifting sand at their feet slowing them down considerably.

Up ahead, Claire could see a strip of bright yellow gold sand, a contrast to the powdery white of the beaches. With an abruptness that still astonished Claire, the Forest Region to her right stopped, and the Desert began. She knelt next to the place where the three Regions met, marveling at the precise border.

"Can I cross into the Desert Region?" She eyed Ganth curiously over her shoulder. He shrugged and nodded. Claire stepped over the region border and immediately felt all the moisture rip from her pores. The air was hot and arid; the wind whipping her face carried small specks of sand in it. The sun beat down on her with brutal intensity.

Claire stepped back over the border into the moist, cool air of the Beaches. "This is much better," she said with relief. Ganth laughed, his even teeth flashing. He clapped her on the shoulder with enough force to practically knock her over.

The troop continued to march along as fast as possible. Sweat pooled in the small of her back, the bandages wrapping her chest chafed uncomfortably. She tried to surreptitiously adjust the wraps, but soon gave up, resigning herself to the agony.

When the sun set over the Desert Region, sparking a spectacular sky washed in shades of gold, red and orange, Ganth did not stop as Claire had expected. Torches flared and they pressed onward, the Barracks Leader was bound and determined to make up some of the ground they'd lost when the herd had intercepted them, as well as to compensate for the slowing caused by the sandy terrain.

The men kept the pace steady, an accomplishment borne of repetition, no doubt. Claire concentrated on plodding along, determined not to cause any more delays, despite her aching muscles and wavering legs. At the dinner break, she rooted through her pack to see if the Seer had thought to give her extra wraps, wondering if she could sneak away to change her chest disguise. Her fingertips brushed the Tupperware container of cookies and she withdrew them with a smile. Sweet Emma was really such a nice woman. Sending her off on a quest with snacks. Only a mom would do that, she thought fondly.

"What are those?" Ganth asked, tapping the top of the container.

"Cookies," Claire replied, cracking open the tub. Surprisingly, the aroma that wafted up was actually appetizing. The deep smell of warm cinnamon and sweet sugar brought forth memories of the holidays, of home and belonging, the scent tingling in her nose in an appealing way. Ok. This was quite unlike how Emma's usual tofu concoctions smelled.

"What an unusual container."

"Oh. Maxt gave it to me," said Claire, realizing now that the Tupperware was probably not a smart idea. "I think the Seer gave it to him?"

She need not have worried. Ganth hovered around the open container like a boy itching to get his finger into the cookie jar.

"May I try one?" Ganth asked eagerly, rubbing his hands together. "I must confess that I love sweets."

"Knock yourself out, but I have to warn you, they are probably terrible."

"I have no wish to knock myself out." Ganth frowned at her in confusion.

"I mean, go ahead. But they may not taste very good."

Ganth scooped up a cookie and took a healthy bite of the cookie he held in his massive hand. His eyes widened and his mouth stopped chewing.

Claire grimaced. "I tried to warn ya…"

"Gimme those," Ganth ordered. Claire surrendered the Tupperware, expecting him to toss the contents into the sea. Instead, Ganth started passing the cookies out to all his men.

"These are the best cookies I have ever tasted," the Barracks Leader declared, helping himself to another one. His face displayed his sheer rapture. All around, the men nodded their agreement of his culinary assessment.

Claire frowned then picked up a cookie. Taking a cautious bite, her face flooded with surprise. "Hey! These *are* good." Claire couldn't help staring at the rest of the cookie in her hand. *Huh.* Maybe, like the Protector necklaces or other things, Emma's cookies had been transformed by their travel to the Land. Or maybe she'd finally broken down and used a conventional recipe. Either way, the cookie was damn good. She put the empty container back in her pack to give to Emma when she got home. It didn't seem right to just discard it in the Land.

After the snack, the men seemed to be in better spirits. Their steps were quicker, their jokes causing more laughter. Claire found herself grinning as well. The moon was high in the sky when Ganth finally called a halt.

Claire snuggled down in her blankets, looking at the stars above and listening to the lulling sound of the ocean a few yards away. Ganth was again at the foot of the wagon, his sword gleaming in the moonlight as his snores vied with the sound of the surf. She smiled. This was the best adventure she'd ever had.

~ 17 ~

▼

MARSHES

When Claire woke up the next morning, she sat up in the wagon and stretched, arching her sore back. Wooden planks were simply not fun to sleep on. Ganth stood next to the wagon, watching her with an inscrutable look in his blue eyes. Claire immediately dropped her arms, scratching at her shoulder absently.

"Morning," Ganth yawned.

"Morning."

"The men are washing up in the ocean, if you would like to join them," Ganth said, tongue in cheek. He was curious what Jones would do. Knowing she was a girl, she'd likely do all she could to avoid that situation.

"I'll go help the women get breakfast going," Claire sidestepped the idea immediately, resolutely trying not to look in the direction of the ocean. A shout came up from the surf and her gaze slid that way for a split second, and then quickly moved away after a glimpse of naked male butts wading into the ocean. Firm, naked, highly toned guy butts. Claire shook herself and crawled from the blankets. As she tried to get out of the wagon, her foot got tangled in the material, and she lost her balance, falling off the end of the wagon.

Ganth reacted quickly, snaking an arm around her waist and yanking her upright before she fell flat on her face. He carefully set her on her feet, his hand splayed over her belly as he levered her upright.

"Easy there, kid," Ganth chuckled.

"I'm fine," Claire muttered, her arms spread. She waited a moment, then added, "You can let go of me now, sir."

"Huh? Oh, yes. Of course." Ganth withdrew his arm slowly. Claire refused to look at him, and straightened her shirt with several rough jerks.

"I will just go help…" Claire's words uncertain. Ganth seemed frozen in place, staring at his hands.

"Yes, that is a good idea," the Leader finally said, then turned on his heel and headed for the ocean, stripping off his shirt as he walked.

Claire paused a moment, goggling at the rather spectacular display of muscles flexing and moving across his back like poetry before giving herself a mental shake and turning to head for the cook fires.

When they had set up camp in the dark of night before, Claire had assumed they were still next to the Desert Region. Apparently, the guardsmen moved quickly indeed, for stretching out into the distance was the Marshes Region. The view had her halting so quickly that she almost lost her footing in the soft sand of the Beaches. Staring, she drank her fill of what lay in front of her.

A sickly greenish gray fog lay over the vista, where slimy green pools of water interconnected to form the region. Here and there, a taller tree or other vegetation was visible, but mostly there were weeds and rushes and moss-covered rocks. A bird took flight from one of the trees, winging its way over the waters, but even its movements seeming sluggish and lazy. It was a desolate view but oddly compelling.

Claire could see how some people would reject this Region out of hand, especially given the beauty of the Regions she had seen. The majestic Forests, the beauty of the Desert, the abandon of the Beaches. They were sparkly, bright and demanded attention. The Marshes…slid under your defenses. You might not think it the most gorgeous place in the Land, but you'd never forget it, either. She couldn't look away. She understood the Marshes unlike any other place she'd seen, and to her, it was a siren call.

A lady in waiting. A world unseen. A place misunderstood. A Region disliked simply because of what it was, rather than what it could be if given a chance. There was more to this place than met the eye.

Yeah. Claire could totally dig the Marshes Region. She knew exactly what it felt like to be overlooked and forgotten in favor of things shiny, new, and pretty.

Enthralled by the place, Claire kept one eye on the Marshes the whole time she was helping the women with breakfast. When the men started straggling back in to camp, Claire wandered over to the Edge of the region, staring into the murky water.

"Careful," came a voice from behind her, startling Claire. She pin wheeled her arms to keep her balance. Ganth's hand closed around her wrist and pulled her farther into the Beaches. "Sorry, Jones. But your toes were awfully close to the Region's Edge. I did not want to attract Quicksilver."

"Quicksilver," Claire repeated, her heart beating triple time.

"Have you never heard of it?" Ganth knew she was from the World, but it would do the girl some good to remember that she was pretending to be a Land lad.

"Well, I have never left the Forest Region," Claire retorted quickly. "We do not know of much beyond our borders, after all. I have heard rumors of this Quicksilver, but I have never been one to listen to idle gossip." Ganth smothered a smile at her quick thinking.

"Here, let me show you." He walked over to the Marsh's Edge and scanned the area slowly. "There." He pointed, "Do you see that silvery object?"

Claire followed his finger and could see a small silver shape tangled in the low reaching branches of a bush. "It looks almost like a bug."

"Probably was at one time," Ganth replied. He put his hand in the water and waited. A gleam of silver streamed toward him, gleaming in the murky water and dull sunshine of the Marshes Region.

"That is Quicksilver." Ganth's voice echoed his distaste as he pulled his hand out of the water before the silver stuff could come in contact with his fingers. "It seeks anything made of living flesh. Wraps around it and eats it, but in doing so, dies to form a shell of what it has preyed upon." Ganth shook his head. "We avoid the area, as you can well imagine. Few cross its expanse unless absolutely necessary, for to pause, even a moment, will bring the creatures."

"They crave life," Claire breathed, watching the Quicksilver fade away into the marsh. It moved like a ghost through the water, streams of long silvery threads. "They want to live so much they die in the action of trying to become."

"I suppose it could be seen that way. I have never thought of Quicksilver in that way. To me, it is a parasite, a deadly creation with no real worth."

"All creation, simply by being, has worth," said Claire, her mossy eyes darting over the Region, seeking more of the elusive stuff.

"True." Ganth watched her carefully. "Breakfast is ready, and we will need to leave soon after."

"I ate earlier." Claire swung around to look at him. "While the men have their breakfast, I would like to go and wash up, if I may." Her expression challenged him to make fun of her for wanting privacy, but Ganth simply grunted.

"Just do not dally, and watch for jellyfish," he told her before walking over to the campfires.

Claire raced to the ocean's edge. A grouping of rocks was nearby A jumble of rocks loomed nearby, rising taller than her head. She shucked her clothes behind their sheltering embrace. Slipping into the ocean, she sucked in her breath as the salt water stung the abrasions where the wraps had rubbed her skin almost raw. Washing up quickly in the water, which wasn't as salty as the oceans back home, Claire hurriedly dried off and dressed again, grimacing as she wrapped the material back around her breasts.

"Poor boobies," she said to herself as she tucked the end of the wrap in, then pulled her shirt over her head. "I promise you, no bra for an entire week when we get back home."

Slicking her wet hair back, Claire jogged back to the camp. At least the wrapping made running a more pleasant task than conventional Worlder lingerie.

Breaking down camp was quick but brutal work. Claire kept busy, running back and forth to the wagon. She made sure that everyone had full water skeins, stacked packs, helped put out the camp fires, lugged kettles and pots to the wagons, virtually everything she could think of doing to make the process as smooth as possible. She did not want Ganth or any of the others to be able to say she was shirking her duties or not pulling her weight. She even helped yoke the oxen to the wagon, narrowly avoiding getting her foot stepped on by one of the nasty, heavy beasts.

The trek continued much as the day before, with the men continuing across the region. They were pretty jolly and happy for a group of competitive guys. Yet Claire noticed that the men's countenances grew more serious and grim as they approached the Meadows Region.

They ate lunch on the march, chewing their bread and cheese while continuing to stride over the shifting sand. Claire hugged close to the side of the wagon, her calves singing with pain. Racing over sand was bloody difficult.

The sun was beginning its final descent into the west when the Meadows Region came into view. As had been described, the grass was a brilliant green and Claire could almost smell the flowers. Yet once again, her eyes were drawn to the more drab countenance of the Marshes. For some reason, that Region just called to her in a way the others didn't. Their caravan ground to a stop. The men halted, milling about as Ganth strode toward the Region's Edge. He stopped just shy of the Edge, his hands on his hips.

"What's he looking for?" Claire whispered to one of the guardsmen, who shrugged and shifted his feet impatiently.

"Maybe he is seeking a place to set up camp, having our base in the Meadows will be much more comfortable than here on the Beaches."

Suddenly Ganth wheeled, and even across the distance, Claire could see the panic in his blue eyes. "Get down," he roared, running full blast in their direction. The guardsmen hit the sand immediately, the man next to Claire pulling her down as she hesitated a fraction of a second too long.

Her hesitation due to the huge funnel cloud racing over the Meadows Region, right behind Ganth, so that he was highlighted in front of the monstrous storm. She'd only seen such storms on the Weather Channel back home, and being this close to one literally stopped her in her tracks. As the tornado came closer, Claire could see the swath of devastation it left in its wake. Grass and trees were uprooted as the tornado ate up the ground.

It headed directly for them.

She lay on her belly behind a small sand dune, a slight swell in the natural topography of the Region. She looked around her at the guardsmen, their gear, the wagon and oxen. They all seemed so terribly exposed.

Ganth dropped to the sand next to Claire, his eyes glued to the Meadows Region. Claire rose up on her elbows, looking all around them. There was absolutely no place to hide. Not even a trench. *This was not good.* She didn't know much about tornados, but what little she did know; hugging sand was not going to be sufficient cover for the funnel cloud that was on a collision course with the guardsman on the beach. Ganth's large hand planted itself on her back and forced her face first into the sand.

Spitting out a mouthful of the beach, Claire glared at him balefully.

"Here it comes…" Ganth called out to the group.

With a kind of fascinated horror, Claire watched the tornado approach. There was a dull roar, like the sound of a freight train that had been somehow muted. "Wait a minute," she muttered, narrowing her eyes. "I wonder…"

"What?" Ganth's eyes remained glued to the approaching storm.

"What will happen when the storm reaches the Region's Edge?"

"What do you mean…oh." Ganth tilted his head, considering. "Well, we shall see in but a few moments."

"Yep," Claire clutched at the sand, fisting the grains between her fingers, heart in her throat.

The tornado was all she could see, the whirling debris and wind like a living force. Claire watched as pieces of wood, trees, even what looked like a wagon swirled about in the dark center of the storm. The funnel cloud hit the Region's Edge and, amazingly, bounced back into the Meadows several yards. It was as if the tornado had hit an immobile force and had been flung back from where it came.

As if in frustration, the tornado hit against the Edge of the Meadows Region time and time again. It seemed to give a scream of frustration each time its passage across into the Beaches was thwarted.

Finally, the tornado peeled away and dissipated into nothing. Chunks of debris fell to the ground, small boulders rolling and wood settling down as lightly as a feather in the wake of the ferocious storm's disappearance.

Ganth stood, brushing sand from his clothes. The other guardsmen did the same, muttering amongst themselves about what they had seen. Claire walked over to the Meadows Region, pausing just at the Edge. Ganth paused right behind her.

"I am crossing over. You stay here, you hear me?"

Claire nodded. "I am not deaf, you know," she snapped, then bit her lip. "Sorry, sir. I mean I heard you." *But I might not listen*, she added to herself.

Ganth stepped over into the Meadows. Claire could see his hair blowing back and forth by the winds in the region. He bent over and brushed at the ground, examining where the funnel cloud had etched a wide swath of freshly turned earth in its wake. He kicked at the wagon that had fallen on its side, as if trying to read the writing along the body of the vehicle.

Ganth strode purposefully to the top of a small hill, scanning the vista beyond. His hands were on his hips. He kicked at the ground, the toe of his boot pushing displaced sod back into place. Finally he turned around and came back into the Beaches Region.

"We will camp on the beach side," he informed the men in his barracks. "Set up for the long haul, boys. There is work to be done in the Meadows Region, and it will be up to us to do it."

"What did you see over the hill?" one of the men asked, his voice low and hesitant.

"You will see soon enough," Ganth replied tightly. "Set up camp and let us keep an eye out for the Prince's caravan."

Claire busied herself with the others, setting up tents and fetching tools and materials for the men. More than one paused to ruffle her hair, jostling her with their shoulder or telling her a ribald joke. Claire was amazed to find she didn't mind their touches, since there was nothing remotely sexual about them. There was such freedom in being a boy!

As she unloaded the last of the wagon, one of the oxen tethered nearby was spooked by a passing flock of quarreling seagulls. The ox pulled on the rope, uprooting its stake from the soft sand. Bellowing, it started to lumber toward the camp, slowly picking up speed. No one in the camp noticed the beast as they were busy talking and shouting to one another as they finished up the last tent.

Claire could see the ox was going to blunder right through the center of the camp. People were bound to get hurt. As the ox passed by the wagon, Claire hesitated only a second, then jumped on its back, reaching around the animal's neck to grab its halter. The ox, now enraged as well as confused, let loose a bellow and started to move faster.

Claire yanked on the halter, trying to turn the animal to miss the camp. Directly in front of the panicked ox was the cooking area, and she could see that Krono had finally gleaned what was happening. The woman started yelling for the men, who turned toward Claire and the runaway ox.

"Turn, you mother, turn!" Claire yanked with all her might. Slowly the ox started to turn. The guardsmen raced toward her, waving their arms to help ward off the beast.

Ganth appeared alongside the ox, helping to pull on the halter with Claire. His bulk and strength were certainly more effective than Claire's at turning the ox, and when he dug his heels into the sand, the beast actually slowed to a halt. Claire breathed a sigh of relief and slid from the beast's back, her legs wobbly.

"Thank you," she said to Ganth, smiling at him and rubbing her sore arm, shaking out the tremors caused by the exertion. "I was afraid he'd take down the camp."

Ganth's face was livid, his blue eyes thunderous. His huge hands were fisted on his hips as he struggled to maintain his composure. Emotions crossed his countenance at such a fast rate that Claire was unable to sort them out. He waited until one of the other men had taken the halter and was leading the ox away before rounding on Claire.

"What in the name of the Land did you think you were doing?" he roared at her. Claire actually took a step back from him, the veracity of his tone was so harsh.

"I was trying to turn the ox." She gestured at the animal.

"You could have been trampled! Thrown off the ox's back! Killed!" He gripped her arms giving her a good, hard shake.

Claire's teeth clicked together audibly, and she stared at him, horrified. "I do not like to be touched," she gritted through her teeth, twisting out of his grasp.

Ganth's mouth opened, then closed, then he sighed and turned on his heel, stalking off in the direction of the ocean, muttering under his breath.

"Hey, Jones." One of the other men stepped closer and, lowering his voice slightly, rested one hand coming on Claire's shoulder. "Do not mind Ganth. He takes his role very seriously and does not like it when one of his men is hurt. You did a great job with that ox." The other men who were gathered around nodded in agreement.

"Thanks." Claire smiled wanly, then trudged back to the camp. The other men closed around her, and she realized with some astonishment that they were silently offering her their support in the wake of her getting dressed down by the Leader of the Barracks. That cheered her up greatly.

This male bonding stuff was really rather amazing, Claire decided as the men continued to make sure they spoke with her during the rest of the night, including her as much as possible in their conversations. One of the guardsmen was always with her, encouraging her or just being a stoic presence. It was rather...comforting.

Darkness had fallen when Ganth came over to her again. His face unreadable, and Claire mentally braced herself for another tongue lashing from the Leader. He gestured for Claire to follow him, and she trudged behind him until they were enveloped in the darkness outside the main camp.

~ 18 ~

▼

ADMISSIONS

"I would like to apologize," came the unexpected comment from the red-haired man. The fact that someone was actually apologizing to her made flutters tumble in her stomach, at once welcome and unsettling.

"Oh," was all she could think to say.

"How old are you, Jones? And I mean the true age, not what Maxt told you to tell me."

Claire hesitated. "I am eighteen," she finally admitted, hoping that it was old enough to be in the guard. Maxt hadn't told her of any age requirement, but who knew, there could very well be one.

Ganth grunted. He continued to walk along the beach, Claire at his side.

"I know."

"Know what?" Claire's voice hesitant and confused.

"I know you are a girl."

"Shit."

They walked along in silence for several yards. The sounds of the camp receded behind them. "So how did you guess? What gave me away?"

"I knew from the instant I saw you," Ganth replied honestly. "Maxt knows I am aware, just in case you were wondering."

"He never said a word to me." Oddly, a lump formed in her throat. Claire realized that she'd never expected Maxt to keep something from her, and was even more surprised to find that she was hurt by his concealing Ganth's knowledge. It was silly, really. She hardly knew Maxt, after all. But that he would be deceitful and not tell her something like this hurt.

"Well, I asked him if I should tell you, and Maxt said no, because he did not want you to act differently around me, for your own protection," Ganth admitted, one hand raking through his red hair.

"Oh, I see." Claire did understand, yet strangely the hurt of Maxt's betrayal remained. She had no idea why it bothered her so much when it was no different than all the other lies she'd been told over her life. Claire pushed the hurt aside. It didn't matter. It couldn't.

"What he did not realize was that I would act differently around you knowing that you are a woman. I over reacted when I saw you on that ox. I saw you up there and instantly lost control of my own emotions for a moment. I could not imagine how I would handle it if you were hurt. You were given into my charge, and I cannot allow you to take such risks."

"I can handle making my own decisions about risks," Claire replied stiffly. "Where I come from, I have reached the age of maturity, and I don't have to stand for people telling me what to do or when to do it. I am respectful of my position within the Barracks, and I'm pulling more than my own weight. But beyond that, you cannot tell me how to live my life."

"Where you come from…" Ganth stopped. Claire faced him, her face set in mutinous lines. "That is yet an additional worry. You are from the World Dimension."

"Did Maxt tell you every freaking thing about me?" Claire's anger boiled over, her voice rising with each sentence. "I bet he and Ben had a hoot and a holler going over the history of Claire Jones…let's see. Don't forget to tell everyone about her mother dying early, step dad deserting her, oh, and don't forget the lovely fact that he embezzled all her mother's inheritance from her so that poor pitiful Claire has to work three fucking jobs to get through school. Man, am I glad I didn't tell the precious Protectors about how I was humiliated in the eighth grade because my foster parents didn't want to spend money on clothes so I went to school in sandals in the middle of the winter. Or how my foster brothers would corner me during my freshman year in high school and take turns feeling my chest to see how much I'd grown. Or, boy, this is a great one, how one of my foster fathers told me that if I was willing and able, we could make a fortune pimping me out to foreigners who came to New York City. Yeah, right tootin' old gab fest that would have caused."

Ganth was staring at her, horror in those bright blue eyes. Overwhelmed, her head buzzed as she gasped for air, leaning over to try and catch her breath. The wraps around her chest made it impossible to take a deep breath. Her vision blurred from the lack of oxygen, and she started to see sparks in front of her eyes. When Ganth took a step forward, wanting to assist, she waved him away.

"Back off," she ordered hoarsely. "Just get away from me, Ganth, I mean it." Lack of air had driven her to her knees, but she was still angry enough to see red.

"You are making yourself ill." Ganth moved forward resolutely. He knelt next to her and reached under her shirt. Claire was completely still for one shocked moment and then exploded with movement, arms and legs swinging.

Despite Claire fighting him tooth and nail, Ganth managed to find the end of the wraps and loosen them, then step away from her quickly.

Claire took a deep gulping breath while she crab walked away from Ganth. "Stay away from me, you hear?" Her mother's necklace banged against her pulsing heart as she put several feet between the two of them, gauging the length of his arms to determine if he could still reach her.

"I will stay right here," Ganth promised, hunkering down, his arms on his thighs as he watched her closely.

Claire felt the roar in her ears subside. She refused to look at Ganth, rather aghast at having disclosed so much to him. Things no one knew. It was downright embarrassing.

"Maxt told me nothing about you other than you do not like to be startled." Ganth spoke so softly that Claire had to strain to hear his words over the pounding of the surf. "I know nothing of your childhood, nothing of your past. All I really know about you is that you are from the World Dimension, are eighteen years old, your name is Claire Jones and you work yourself to the bone to prove your worth. That is all." He held his hands out as if helpless to conjure up anything else.

"It's enough," Her mouth was full of sandpaper, rough and crumbling. Yet she was oddly relieved that Ben had not breeched more of her confidences than she had expected and equally relieved that Maxt had not spilled everything to Ganth about her and her past.

"I just thought I should tell you that I know you are a female," Ganth said wearily, rubbing his eyes and standing up. He walked over to her and held out his hand to her.

Claire eyed the hand warily. He cocked an eyebrow at her and leaned in a little closer. "The Jones I know would not be intimidated by some help up from the sand."

Claire shook her head. "If you think you can taunt me into accepting your help, you're wrong. But I will accept your help because I think it is honestly given." So saying, she placed her hand in his and allowed him to pull her to her feet. "I don't understand something. Why tell me you know I'm a girl? You could have hidden the fact from me pretty easily." As she spoke Claire absently brushed the sand off her clothes.

"Because I find myself oddly attracted to you and thought you should know it, otherwise you might think I was the kind of man who was attracted to other men."

Of anything she'd been expecting, this was the farthest from her mind. Claire stopped mid brush. "You are *what?*" Her eyes wide as she took several steps away from him.

Ganth gestured at her movement. "You heard me. I am not going to say it again. I want to make it clear that I will not do anything about this attraction. It is clear you feel uncomfortable with such things. I would not want to impose on you in such a fashion given your experiences in the past."

"Uh-huh." Claire simply stared at him, her mind skipping around like an old arcade game until it settled onto one thought, which popped out before she could censor herself. "But why are you attracted to me?"

"I do not know." Ganth's face settled into a portrait of bemused frustration. "I just am."

"Well, knock it off," Claire demanded, stamping her foot. "I don't have time for this kind of thing. I'm too damned young to find my soul mate or whatever it is the Protectors seem to pick up here in the Land."

"Well, that settles that, then. I am not going to be your soul mate. I can live with that. It is just an attraction. I am a grown man and I can handle it." To her disgust, the man looked amused by the situation.

"Are you going to tell the others?" Claire gestured back toward the camp. "About me being a girl, I mean, not that you have the hots for me."

"Hots? What in the name of the Land is that? You Worlders are so strange." Ganth shook his head. "I do not think the troop needs to know. I say we keep this between ourselves for the moment. How does that strike you, Jones?"

"Strikes me fine," Claire replied with a grin.

After Ganth politely turned his back so that Claire could fix the wraps again, the two walked back to camp, keeping a careful distance from one another. Claire was actually rather relieved that Ganth did not want to tell the other men. She had come to enjoy being treated as one of the Barracks crew. If they found out she was a girl, all that would change, Claire knew.

When she got back to camp, Claire started toward the wagon, intending on turning in early. Ganth stopped her with a hand on her arm. Shaking his head, he said, "It is tradition for the Barracks page to sleep in the Leader's tent." Ganth grinned wryly.

"Oh, nice of you to say that once we are back in camp," Claire hissed at him with some anger. "No way am I staying in your tent, Ganth. Not after what you just told me."

He shrugged. "Suit yourself. Just be prepared for the men to question why you are breaking with long held traditions." Ganth laughed at her mulish expression, lowering his voice to add, "You are safe with me, Claire. I promise you that." Again, his voice was so genuinely sincere that it made Claire immediately angry for some odd reason.

"My name is Jones."

"Jones, then," Ganth agreed, waggling his eyebrows. "But I like Claire better."

Claire growled deep in her throat and stalked past him. Someone—Ganth probably, damn his huge red haired hide—had moved her gear from the wagon to his tent. Ducking under the flap, she found the inside of the tent to be surprisingly roomy. A large cot occupied one side, and a smaller pallet lay on the opposite. Claire kicked off her boots and crawled into the smaller bed, grumbling the entire time.

When Ganth came in much later, Claire was still awake, facing the outside of the tent, her eyes screwed tightly shut. She could barely breathe, fear flaming through her system like wildfire. She kept telling herself it was foolish, Ganth promised and from what she could tell, he was a man of his word. But he'd also admitted he was attracted to her. That made him a dangerous animal. One hand reached up to grab the bead around her neck, as if it could ward off any unwanted advances.

She could hear Ganth moving around the tent. When the unmistakable sound of clothes being removed came to her ears, Claire felt her stomach sinking. Then there was a creak of the cot and the lamplight was extinguished. Claire continued to breathe shallowly, her ears straining to hear.

It wasn't until Ganth's breathing evened out and deepened into a sleeping pattern that Claire relaxed and allowed herself to fall asleep. But every time Ganth moved during the night, Claire bolted awake for a moment then drifted off again when she sensed no threat. It did not make for a restful evening.

The next morning Claire withdrew from the tent as the sun rose, casting one quick look in Ganth's direction. She quickly averted her eyes as the brief look showcased a man with the covers pooled low around his hips. Ganth apparently liked to sleep in the nude. Great. She rolled her eyes and left the tent as quickly as possible. If she stumbled slightly, or there was a hitch in her breath, it surely wasn't from the memory of all that tan skin stretched over muscles taut from years of working out. Oh, no. Not at all. Nope.

Claire busied herself helping to make breakfast. Everyone kept an eye out on the Meadows Region, wondering if they would see another storm heading their way.

Listening to the men, Claire learned that during the morning, part of the troop was going to go into the Meadows Region on a scouting mission. The rest of the men would wait at the camp. Claire hoped she was going to the Meadows Region. She was eager to find out more about the damage and the storms.

Yet when Ganth called out the assignments, Claire was disappointed to find that she was to stay behind. Ten men were assigned to go on a three-day excursion to the far end of the Meadows Region, seeking out information and trying to ascertain what was needed most by the people in the region. Ganth explained that the remaining troops would go on shorter treks of less than a day to scout the areas closer to the Beaches.

While the men who were going on the longer trip packed up, the others set about making an area in which to practice their swords, archery, knives and jousting poles. Soon the men were busy honing their skills, the clash of steel and shouts of men ringing in the air.

Ganth saw the excursion group off, giving last minute instructions to the one he put in charge. Then he walked over to where Claire stood watching the men work, unsure of what she should be doing.

"You wanted to go into the Meadows Region with the men today."

"Of course I did. This is my…quest," Claire replied, keeping her voice down. "I can't very well do anything about the weather anomalies when I am stuck on a beach building sand castles."

"You are not going anywhere until I can assess your skill level. You cannot go into the Meadows unarmed."

"Oh. Yeah. Well. Can I get a can of mace or something?"

"Come." Ganth clamped his arm on Claire's shoulder, shoving her several inches into the sand. "Let us see what you can do with the weapons of the Guard."

"I suck at archery," Claire stammered as they headed that way.

"Then let us get it over with first," came the even-keeled reply.

Claire soon showed him how miserably wretched she was at archery. Having the other men in the area staring at her did nothing to improve her skills. She moved on to the knives next, and did marginally better. Ganth was a stoic presence, his arms crossed over his broad chest, saying nothing to her, merely grunting before moving to the next area. Claire followed, her head hanging low in disgust at herself for her poor performance. Swords were next, and there, at least, Claire felt she had managed a good showing. Ganth paired her with a guardsman who was a few years older than her and about the same height and weight. He was clearly better at swordplay than she was, but Claire felt that she redeemed herself slightly for the abysmal failure at archery and knives.

Finally, Ganth led her to the jousting arena. Again, he paired with the same guardsman she had faced over swords, whom Claire remembered was called Newmar. Claire accepted the jousting pole, which was only a fraction longer than the makeshift one Maxt had fashioned for their wood time practice. The ends were slightly blunted and flat, almost like an oar.

Claire faced the other guardsman and they both bowed. Guardsmen were big on etiquette. A word from Ganth and the two stepped forward, ready to spar.

Claire blocked Newmar's opening parry easily. His body language was a snap to read, and she could tell instantly if he was going to go left or right, to push or pull at her pole. Claire let him back her around the circle while she figured out all his moves, then suddenly and unexpectedly went on the offensive.

Within seconds, Newmar's pole flew outside the circle and the man sprawled on his ass in the dirt, his expression clearly astonished.

Claire flipped the pole around, spinning it easily. "Sorry about that," she said genially, stopping the pole and holding out a hand to him.

"Not at all," Newmar pushed up and gained his feet. He walked away, head shaking.

Claire started to leave the ring but a brusque hand gesture from Ganth had her staying put. "Telcor!" A tall, lanky man working on knife tossing jerked his head around and loped over in response to Ganth's beckoning wave. "Work the joust with Jones."

Telcor gave Claire a dubious look. "I am taller by at least a foot."

The Leader's brow arched. "And are we so lucky that we are able to pick and choose our battle opponents based on their height?" Telcor blushed and picked up a jousting pole, stepping into the ring.

Telcor was a trickier opponent, Claire soon discovered. He was brutally fast and had a longer reach. He was also very clumsy with his footwork. When Claire felt confident she had him down cold, she launched a counterattack, battling him back across the circle with ease. A flick under the ankle with the tip of her pole and the man was flat on his back, looking at the blue sky over the Beaches.

"Well done," Telcor bubbled, standing up. Leaning against his pole, he asked Claire, "Who taught you the skill of jousting?"

"No one." Claire flipped the pole into the sky in an arch before neatly catching it. "I guess it just comes naturally to me."

"Telcor, you may return to the knives," Ganth said softly. Then he picked up a jousting pole and stepped into the ring. Claire watched him, instantly wary. "I warn you, Jones, I will not hold back because of who you are, or what you are. I intend to be as vicious with you as I am with any of my men. Do you understand?"

"You want to test me to my limits," Claire stated, earning a nod from Ganth. She gripped her pole tightly and bared her teeth at him. "Now I can get back at you for the snoring last night. Bring it on."

"I have more strength and experience in these matters."

"I have youth and cunning on my side," Claire countered with a grin. "I'll take my chances."

~ 19 ~

▼

EXCURSIONS

As Ganth stalked Claire around the circle, she backed away from him cautiously. He'd had a chance to watch her battle two other men, not to mention his life's work in the Guard, and thus had a distinct advantage. She had no clue about his technique or skill level but had to assume one did not reach the level of Barracks Leader without expertise.

Around them, other men were stopping to watch the two in the jousting circle, nudging one another and nodding in their direction. Claire and Ganth ignored them. Ganth moved in and flipped the pole under Claire's, just a testing snap to see how hard she was gripping the apparatus. Claire pushed her weight under the pole, forcing his pole off with enough force to have Ganth grinning at her.

They continued to circle, taking pot shots at one another occasionally. Claire knew she was outclassed in the strength department. Ganth could squash her like a fly. She needed to go at it from another angle. Her mind worked quickly to come up with a feasible strategy.

She went on the offensive, smacking her pole as close as she dared to his fingers where they lay on the wood. He had pretty good footwork and parried her moves easily. With a few quick thrusts, he had Claire backing up as he pressed forward, his hands and feet moving with lightening speed for a guy so big.

The poles were clacking, the sound echoing over the Beaches as they continued to dance around the circle. Claire was getting tired and knew she was going to have to do something quick to get the upper hand before all her strength was gone. She tilted the paddle to the sand and with a quick flip, tossed some directly into Ganth's face.

He gave a startled bellow and spit out a mouthful of sand, his eyes blinking quickly to rid them of the grit. Claire moved in and pushed against his pole with hers, using all her might. He pushed back, not giving an inch. Claire snaked out a foot and hooked it behind Ganth's, pushing again. This time, he started to lose his balance and encouraged, Claire gave one last might shove, simultaneously flipping her pole under his, knocking it cleanly from one hand.

Ganth's arms pin wheeled and he managed to keep his balance, one hand still on the pole. He planted one end of the pole into the ground and skidded around it, then brought the length of wood up quickly to parry against Claire's with enough force to send a jaw-thumping jar through her entire body.

Her hands numbed instantly and the pole fell to the ground. Claire bent over, her hands on her thighs, sucking in air. It was entirely silent around her, the only sound the ocean's waves.

Then a scattering of applause sprinkled through the watching crowd. Ganth tossed aside the jousting pole and another guard member caught it easily. "You are good," he admitted with wonder in his voice. "Very good. Possibly the best I have seen in all my time in the Guard. I daresay we could train you to be a champion."

Claire actually felt a blush creeping up her neck at the praise. "Thank you. But I failed in my efforts. How can you praise me for that?"

"You were beaten by an opponent who has a decade more experience, almost a foot taller, and about fifty pounds more muscle than you. And I had to work hard to get the win," Ganth corrected as a murmur of agreement rose from the men behind him. "You did more than passable with the jousting pole for only having worked with it a few times. Trust me on this, Jones. You are a natural with the jousting poles."

"Ok." Claire grinned. "I can live with that, I guess."

Ganth returned her a grin and with a shake of his head, walked off. Claire found herself surrounded by guardsmen, all congratulating her and clapping her on the back with varying degrees of enthusiasm, meaning Claire alternated between staggering under their blows or wincing at the slaps on her back.

After lunch, Ganth called Claire over to him. "We are going to go into the Meadows Region," he told her in an undertone. "I am taking five men and you with me. Keep your eyes and mind open to see what can be seen and learn what can be learned."

Claire nodded and raced to get her gear. Strapping on her sword belt and canteen, excitement surged through her body. Finally, she was going to go into the Meadows. Even if it was destined to be just a brief outing, at least she'd get a chance to see the damage up close and maybe, just maybe, start to understand her purpose in the Land. Her journey. Her quest.

Within minutes the group assembled at the edge of camp. Claire pushed her way to the front, to stand behind Ganth. The men allowed her to do that with good nature. When she stepped over the Region's Edge, Claire left the moist ocean wind behind. The Meadows breeze was cooler, more fragrant somehow. Here, the sound of birds singing was the most prevalent noise. If Claire strained her ears, she could hear the ocean in the distance, and even see it if she looked over her shoulder. But it should be louder, given how close they were to the Beaches. The region's end must really have some sort of dampening affect on the sound waves.

Ganth took off at his normal fast pace, following the path of the most recent storm. The guardsmen walked in the center of the swath of churned up earth, talking quietly among themselves.

"Have all the storms in the Meadows Region been tornados?" Claire eyed the horizon, half expecting to see a funnel cloud at any second.

"Actually, no. I have heard word of tornados." He stumbled over the unfamiliar word. "As well as snow storms and winds that flatten trees, thunderstorms full of devastating lightening and rains that bring flood like conditions."

"Wow, the whole bag of tricks." Claire marveled, tripping over a clump of rocks that had been unburied by the force of the wind. "I take it those are unusual for the region to experience?"

"Weather that violently destructive is unusual for anywhere in the Land." Ganth stopped and squatted to examine the earth more closely. "Humph," he said thoughtfully, then shifted to look off in the direction of the Mountains. "Convergence is that way. The snow storm that incapacitated them came out of the east. This storm came out of the west."

"Which implies that the storms are originating somewhere in the center of the Meadows Region," Claire finished. "Has anyone tracked the paths of the storms on a map, see if they point to an origin of some sort?"

"Not that I know of. From what I understand, Jay was attempting to trace the origin of the storms, but I do not know what method or hypotheses he was utilizing before he disappeared."

Claire swallowed hard. Jay. Yet another reason she needed to get to the bottom of the storms and their origin. Perhaps when they discovered the source, they'd find Jay. She owed it to Emma and Harry to try her best to make sure their son was safe. She turned her attention back to Ganth.

"I asked the group that left this morning to chart the storms, and we can compile it when they get back, adding in what we know of the other storms that are seen."

"There is something strange about this path." Claire squinted, turning and looking back toward the Beaches. "Look back toward the region's end. The path of the storm is almost an exact straight line. There is a little variation to the left and right but mostly it is heading in the same direction, and only veers from its path by a few feet at most."

"You are right," Ganth said with some excitement in his voice. "I wonder if all the other storms passed in such a straight line."

"Nature usually doesn't like straight lines, but in the Land it does. You have sharp lines delineating between the regions. This may have something to do with the way it works in the Land and is not significant at all."

Ganth shook his head. "No, I think we are on to something. Our normal storms do not move in such a way. They always come from east to west, and they are never on such a straight line. They can drift from north to south or south to north, depending upon the season."

"Then we really need those guys to get back so we can try and chart it out."

"Agreed," Ganth stated. He rose and they continued over a small rise in the hill. Ahead of them lay a small farm, which had obviously been in the direct path of the storm. The only thing left of the barn was ragged boards and a pile of rubble. The livestock was scattered about the perimeter, worn looking and bedraggled. The farmer and his wife were trying to make repairs while their children ran amuck in the mess.

"We shall pitch in," Ganth instructed his men, who immediately headed for the farm, Claire along with them.

They spent the next few hours helping the grateful farmer get his place back in order. Again, Claire was impressed with the guardsmen, who waved off any thanks or offers of payment from the couple. A few of the men even paused to give the small children a piggyback ride. She also noticed that the children always seemed to be near her as well. She played hide and seek with them while helping to clear the area outside the barn, and thoroughly enjoyed herself. It was just a wonderful feeling to help out without the expectation of anything in return.

At one point, Claire noticed Ganth standing still, hands on his hips, staring intently into the west. Following his gaze, Claire barely suppressed a gasp of dismay. Huge black clouds boiled up on the horizon, ominous and oozing. Flashes of light sparked the sky, vicious and deadly. Watching with morbid fascination, she could see the clouds sprinting off in the direction of the Marshes.

"No chance of it coming our way, if it follows the other patterns," Claire commented to Ganth.

"No," he said shortly but not unkindly.

Claire realized he was concentrating on the storm, trying to glean whatever he could from the clouds and their race across the sky. She kept her mouth shut and did the same. Lightening forked from the sky to touch the ground, and thunder rolled over the landscape. It was fascinating and terrible to watch, all at the same time. The storm was like a monster, tearing over the plains in a vicious rampage.

Like Godzilla. The storms really didn't know what they were doing, the havoc they were bringing. They were just doing what they did, like Godzilla when the monster trampled the small Japanese village on the way to the final confrontation in the movie. The people blamed the storms, when they should blame whatever was causing them. Get rid of the originating mechanism and the storms would stop.

But how?

That, Claire decided as the storm raced out of site, was the one million dollar question.

When the farm was in some semblance of order, Ganth eyed the setting sun and declared it time to return to their camp. He accepted a warm loaf of bread from the farmer's wife. He also picked up the kids and tossed them high in the air, much to their delight. After speaking a few serious words with the farmer, Ganth and the troop took their leave. Bowing in a courtly fashion to the farmers, the guardsmen headed back to the Beaches.

As he handed Claire the loaf of bread to carry back to the camp, Ganth sighed and looked over her shoulder. "There is a Barracks not far from here, yet no guardsmen have been this way." It was clear he was troubled by the absence of his fellow guardsmen.

"Maybe they are helping other people in the region," Claire suggested.

"Perhaps." Ganth still sounded skeptical. He cast a look at the sky. "I wish it were earlier in the day, I would risk going to the Barracks. But those back on the beach will worry if we are late, and I dare not split such a small troop up to send a messenger."

"Tomorrow, then?"

"Tomorrow," Ganth agreed.

"Are there only one Barracks per Region?" Claire kept her voice low so that the other men did not hear her question and wonder why she didn't know more about the Guard system. They were several paces ahead of the others, but these guardsmen had excellent senses and could hear very well.

"Each Region has what is needed, based on the population," Ganth replied in an undertone. "Mountain has one, Forest and Rivers have three, Meadows, due to the population, has four. Marshes has none, while the Deserts have one. Each interior Region watches over the Beaches that are outside their area."

"That makes sense."

They continued to trudge along in silence, both eager to get back to camp.

They were greeted with high spirits and an even better meal at the camp. Claire was brusquely told by Krono to leave the kitchen area.

"You have had a hard enough day," the woman told Claire, who gratefully accepted a plate of hot food and escaped to scarf it down. She was starving after the hard work on the farm.

Claire made sure that she was in bed before Ganth entered the tent again that night. She was more comfortable being in his presence, but still kept her back to him as he undressed and slipped beneath the sheets. Only after he was lightly snoring did Claire reach under her shirt and loosen the wraps with a heartfelt sigh of relief.

She rolled on her back and looked up at the canvas ceiling of the tent. The storms were troubling her. They seemed to be freaks of nature, with a sense that they were not natural. So that implied they were man-made, which brought about a new slew of questions. What could harness natural elements to form a storm? Was it some sort of machine that Evil had made? But from what she could recall of the Protectors, machines did not work in the Land. It was all very confusing and very strange. Her biggest worry of all was what the hell to do about it. She knew nothing about machines or weather or anything of that sort. An overwhelming wave of inadequacy nearly swamped her will. Maybe she should just give up. There was no way she'd be able to figure this out, much less fix it. Surely someone could figure out how to get her back to the World Dimension. Hell, half the people here were convinced she wasn't supposed to Travel now anyway. As if she, a normal teenager, could change the weather? It wasn't like she was a wizard or something.

Wizard.

Jay.

He was still out there, still lost. And just like that, Claire knew that giving up was simply not an option. The thought of Emma and Harry, of telling them she'd bailed in the middle of her quest because she was terrified of failure. That she'd left the Land with their son still missing. Yeah. That was not going to happen. Emma and Harry had been more kind to her than her own stepfather during the past few years. She wasn't about to let them down.

Claire sighed and willed herself to sleep. She wanted to be in top form the next day so that Ganth would allow her to accompany the troop to the Barracks in the Meadows.

The next morning, it was clear she was not alone in that desire. Virtually everyone in the group wanted the chance to go to the Meadows Barracks. Ganth made the assignments and glared at those who would have voiced dissent when told they were to remain behind. Claire was just glad to be included in the group that was going.

They headed in a slightly northern direction, leaving the swath of the tornado to their right as they penetrated deeper into the Meadows Region. The troop moved at a quick pace, even faster than the one they had set the day before, and the men were prepared today with shovels, tools, and materials that might be needed to help region residents along the way. Everyone was loaded down with supplies, and they even had a small hand wagon they used to carry more supplies.

As they crested the hill near the Barrack's location, it became evident why the Barracks had not been out in the community.

~ 2 0 ~

▼

TENDENCIES OF
DESTRUCTION

The Barracks looked like it had taken a direct hit from a mortar shell, almost as if it were in the center of some sort of war zone. Smoking craters littered the courtyard and the main lodge smoldered, blackened logs of wood protruding from the ruins. Animals wandered in and among the destruction. There was absolutely no sign of human activity.

"Looks like lightening strikes," Ganth murmured. "They hit all around the site."

"But like no lightening strike I have ever seen," another guardsman added softly. A rustle of agreement rippled through the group.

Ganth turned and met the looks of his men dead-on. His face set in harsh lines. "We know what we will likely find," he said quietly. "You know what is expected of you in return."

The men nodded, tightening their grips on the weapons and tools in their hands. "Go on then, and be careful."

Claire started to follow the men, but Ganth called her back. His hands on his hips, he faced her. "I do not want you to go with us."

Claire's eyes narrowed. "Why not?"

"Because I have a feeling we are going to find a bunch of dead men down there," he shot back, his own bright blue gaze narrowed, "and I do not want you in the middle of it."

Claire swallowed hard. He was giving her an out, and while a part of her appreciated it, the other part—the more vocal one—was outraged. "If I were a boy, would you keep me from going down there?"

"I do not know."

"Yes you do," she replied with heat. "If I were any other Barracks page, you'd have me down there, knee deep. Because you'd want to make a man out of me and make sure I had what it takes to be a guardsman. Don't you dare treat me differently. The men will wonder, and they'll figure it out."

"Griffin's balls, Claire." Ganth rubbed the back of his neck. "You do not need to see this."

"Neither do they." Claire gestured at the men who were approaching the Barracks even as they spoke. "But they're doing it. And so am I."

"What if I order you to stay up here?" Ganth countered with frustration.

"Then I would remind you that I'm of the World Dimension and technically I'm not under your auspices," Claire bluffed wildly and recklessly. "I would go anyway, under the guise of my being a Protector and therefore operating under my own rules."

Ganth's gaze narrowed and they stared at each other for several long seconds.

Then he grunted, backing down. "Go then. But know that you can leave whenever you feel it is too much to handle. All guardsmen have that courtesy, I swear to that fact. No one will think less of you."

"All right." Claire marched down the hill, hoping her legs weren't looking too unsteady. Truth be told, she was terrified at what she might have to face in the middle of the ruins below. Yet, she knew she would never forgive herself if she sat out on the hill above while the other men did all the hard, messy, dirty, depressing work. She pulled on her gloves as she walked, grateful to have them.

Claire walked up to the group that included Newmar, the young man she had sparred with on the previous day. He was wrapping a piece of material around his mouth, his eyes sober. Claire pulled out her own bandana and did the same. Then they gave each other a resigned look and started to shift through the gutted building.

The troop worked in almost complete silence, the only sound that of the tools digging into the debris at a steady pace. Claire glanced around periodically to see that Ganth was moving from group to group, giving quiet directions and support.

From time to time she would hear a sharp whistle resonate through the camp. It was the signal that a body had been found, Newmar explained to her early on.

In the center clearing, there were an increasing number of blanket-shrouded corpses laid out in even rows. Claire turned back to the pile in front of her and lifted another shovel of ash and burned wood, then stared at what she had uncovered, horrified.

It was an arm. Or rather, the burned bone of an arm. Claire swallowed hard. Newmar looked over her shoulder, then raised his arm and whistled. Immediately, Ganth was at Claire's elbow, tugging on her arm gently. "Let someone else finish the excavation," he urged her in an undertone, not liking the way her face had drained of all color. Her mossy green eyes looked like bruises in her pale face.

Claire took a shallow breath and shook her head. "No," she whispered. "He's mine. I will finish it out."

"I will assist," Newmar offered, and Claire shot him a grateful look. The man nodded and then glanced at Ganth. "We will be fine, sir. I am with Jones, and will help him learn the way this sort of task should be done."

It was perhaps the most difficult thing Claire had ever done in her entire life. Working methodically, she and Newmar uncovered the body from the material that had fallen on it during the storm. Whether the mounds of debris or fire or smoke inhalation killed the man, Claire did not know. All she knew for sure was that the man had died a horrible death.

When the corpse was uncovered, lying on its back, one hand outstretched to one side, Claire sat back on her heels and looked at Newmar.

"Now what?" Her voice hoarse from unshed tears and the overwhelming stench of work.

"Get a blanket from the pile over there and we then have to move the body onto it," Newmar replied, his brown eyes steady as he looked at Claire. "Jones, you are doing well."

Claire fetched the blanket. They laid it out as close to the body as possible, then gently, Claire at the feet and Newmar at the shoulders, lifted the body and moved it to the make shift litter. The sound the body made as it was released from the grip of the debris below had Claire closing her eyes in horror. Once the body was transferred, Newmar and Claire picked up the edges of the blanket and carried it over to the growing pile of bodies. When they laid the body down, Claire let loose with a wavering sigh, fighting hard to maintain her composure.

"We will take a break," Newmar suggested, his own voice none to steady. "We need some water, at the very least." Claire nodded and they plodded halfway up the hill, sinking into the fragrant grass with weary hearts and bodies.

Claire took a mouthful from her water skein and rinsed out her mouth, leaning over to spit it out into the grass. Then she took a long drink. When she recapped the skein, she could see her hands were shaking, and she frowned. Then she noticed that Newmar's hands were likewise trembling and felt marginally better for the sign of weakness.

They did not speak but merely watched the scene below them for several moments. Absently, Claire counted twenty-one bodies. That was almost the entire troop, she realized with shock. Had no one survived? Another whistle rent the air, signaling another find. Claire shook her head. It was a devastating day for the guardsmen. With a sigh, Claire got to her feet and looked down at Newmar.

"We better get back down there." The man took one last swallow from his skein and stood.

"It looks like most of the bodies have been uncovered," Newmar said with relief. "We can start with the section that has been sifted through. We can pile up the debris and start clearing the site."

"That sounds good."

Soon they were busy sorting the debris into piles; that which needed to be carted away, that which could be burned, and ash, which needed to be disposed of. Another group tried to demolish the half standing main lodge, which had been deemed unsalvageable. Still another group was involved in the serious task of preparing the fallen for their burials.

"If a guardsman falls in the interior, we bury. If near the Beaches or water, we do a funeral pyre," explained Newmar as they stacked debris.

Claire nodded, it made sense. A lot of what the Guard did was practical, but seemed grounded in tradition. It was a solid kind of life, the appeal of it clear; here was camaraderie and companionship. Here was tradition and compassion. Here was fighting for the way of life that the Land was slowly loosing to the encroachment of Evil.

Bottom line…these were good men. The best. Her gaze strayed to find the flame of red hair in the group. Ganth was with that group, applying himself to digging graves with a forbidding countenance. He seemed to carry the loss at a visceral level, his broad shoulders slumped, the look on his face formidable.

The group labored far into the afternoon, taking small breaks along the way to rest and drink. No one felt much like eating. As the sun started to sink in the west, they all paused to bury their fallen comrades. Ganth said a few words over the graves. By then, Claire was encompassed in a numbness that felt as thick as the polar ice cap. Even lowering the bodies into their holes did not seem to impact her much.

Finally, Ganth stopped the men. "The area is cleared enough for a new Barracks to be built. Such an endeavor will be done by the new guardsmen assigned to the area. Maxt is coming to our camp within the next day or so. He will inform the families of the men who died here and start the recruitment process for replacements." The Leader paused and tilted his head to one side, his expression sorrowful. "We lost good friends here. We lost comrades in the Guard. Yet, I am most proud of the way in which you all handled yourselves today. I will not forget it, and neither will they." He gestured toward the fresh mounds of dirt covering the graves.

It was a weary, down-hearted group of guardsmen who trod back to camp that night. They did not arrive until well after dark. One look told those who remained behind all they needed to know about the fate of their comrades.

The entire troop, except Claire, headed for the ocean to wash away the day's dirt and grime and filth. She washed up her hands and helped set out dinner, then, as the men ate, took a solitary dip to clean away the ills of the day.

After bathing, Claire went immediately to the tent she shared with Ganth, not bothering to re-wrap her chest. She was just too exhausted, and had cleaned off the wrap as best she could. No way was she going to wrap a cold, wet strip of material around herself, only to take it off again after Ganth fell asleep. She gave a half hearted thought about going to get some food, but her stomach rebelled at the idea of eating. Her nose was still clogged with the stench of fire and death. Eating seemed as foreign an idea as walking on the moon. Plus she'd have to face all the other guardsmen out at the kitchen area, plus the cooks. They'd ask questions that Claire was not sure she was capable of answering. Not now, or possibly ever. How could one explain the utter devastation, the sights, smells, and feel of a day best forgotten? All she wanted was to be alone.

When she pushed her way into the tent, Claire could see that Ganth had already been inside. Her sword and water skein were by her cot, and a warm brazier of coals was set in the center of the tent to ward off the chill of the night. Claire hesitated a moment, then draped her wrapping material over the chair in the corner of the tent, hopeful it would dry by morning.

Swallowing, Claire's throat was strangely tight, as if her insides were stretched as thin as her heart at the moment. Her eyes burned, but whether that was from the acrid smoke at the Barracks site, the salt water, or exhaustion, she simply did not know. She shucked off her breeches and changed her shirt for the night. The cool cotton material felt good against her skin. It was an absolute relief to not have those bloody wraps around her chest, restricting her breathing and chafing her at every step.

Just as she was crossing to her cot, the tent flap opened behind her as Ganth came into the tent. Claire flinched at the sound but did not pause in the folding of her pants. So what if Ganth saw her legs? The shirt she was wearing reached mid thigh. It was no more indecent than the miniskirts the college girls wore everyday to school. And she was just too tired to care, frankly.

"I am sorry, I thought you would be in your bed by now," Ganth said, his voice low in the tent.

"Just about." Claire's voice sounded rather thin and high to her own ears. She tossed the pants on top of her pack and turned to look at him, her stance softening somewhat as she took in his expression.

Ganth looked as exhausted as she felt. His face was lined with fatigue and worry. His usually straight and proud shoulders slumped as he stood by the brazier, his hand rubbing the back of his neck. Claire didn't know what to say to him, but felt she had to try to break the silence.

"I was impressed with how you handled everything today," she said finally.

He gave a half laugh. "I was just trying to come up with a way to tell you that you shocked, amazed, and impressed me today as well. I never expected you to pitch in like you did, and you never once complained."

Claire shrugged one shoulder. "It needed to be done." The lump in her throat that threatened to choke all the air out of her system.

"Believe me, there are a lot of men who would have looked at that situation and walked away, unable to help. You waded in and performed, well, like a guardsman." He raised his hands helplessly. "I can give no higher compliment than that, in all honesty."

"It is a huge compliment." A second later the tears started to stream down her face. "It was horrible!" she said brokenly, covering her face with her hands and turning to face away from him, not wanting him to see her break so completely.

Ganth strode across the room and spun her about, then pulled her into his arms, one hand holding the back of her head gently. "Cry it out," he advised her in a whisper. "Do not try and hold it in."

Claire nodded against his shirt and just let the dam break. The front of his shirt was soaked before the pent up fear, terror, and sadness of the day had been purged from her system, funneling down the drain with her tears.

"I'm sorry," she whispered against his shoulder.

"No need to be," he replied into her hair. Claire was suddenly aware of the fact that she wore only her shirt, under which she was not wearing her wraps and that her legs were bare. She pulled away from Ganth self consciously, one hand swiping at the tears on her cheeks.

"It just kind of got to me."

Reaching for a blanket as casually as possible, she snuffled against her free hand. Ganth turned away to put his sword at the foot of his bed, and she seized that moment to wrap her body in the heavy blanket. Feeling more protected, she sank to her bed, staring at the coals in the brazier.

Claire drifted, her mind and body strangely disconnected. It took several moments for her to realize that Ganth was quite matter of factly disrobing in front of her. She squeaked and dove under the covers of her bed. Ganth chuckled and leaned over to turn off the lamp.

"Sorry. I forgot that you are squeamish about such things."

"Squeamish?" A spurt of hot emotion surprised her, since Claire had been certain she'd never experience normal emotions again after the grueling day. The sensation had her gaining some even ground mentally, even if her body was still exhausted. "It's nothing to do with being squeamish, it has to do with good manners. You don't go around shucking off your clothes in front of a woman you barely know."

"How else are you supposed to get ready to take your rest?"

Claire growled deep in her throat and rolled to face the tent. Ganth's answering chuckle followed her into sleep, the sound of it making her realize that he had tried—and succeeded—in snapping her out of her memories of the day.

~ 21 ~

▼

UNVEILING THE TRUTH

When Claire woke up the next morning, Ganth was already gone from the tent. She dressed quickly—the wrap thankfully dry—and headed outside. There, she stopped suddenly in surprise. Apparently, she had slept half the morning away. The sun was already starting its ascent to the center of the sky. Breakfast was clearly over, and many of the men were in the practice area that had been set up.

"Damn," Claire muttered, heading for the camp fires. Krono and her helper were busy peeling a potato like vegetable for the luncheon stew.

"I am terribly sorry," Claire exclaimed when she got within earshot of the women. "I must have overslept."

Krono waved the hand with the paring knife. "Do not worry yourself. Ganth said anyone with the party that went into the Meadows Region yesterday was excused from any chores today. You are not the only one who slept in, either."

Claire frowned, still feeling badly for not helping the women at the mealtime. She knew how hectic it was trying to feed over twenty hungry men, not to mention clean up and clear everything away. Speaking of hunger… her stomach growled audibly, reminding Claire she'd skipped the previous evening's meal. Well, she wasn't about to have the women stop their lunch prep to feed her.

Krono, however, had heard the tell-tale rumble and reached for a covered plate on the table behind her. "I saved you some food," she told Claire with a nice smile, handing her the plate. "Eat up, then go practice with the other men."

Claire thanked her profusely then sank onto a log near the campfire, devoting her entire attention to the food. When she was done, she washed up her plate and then dusted off her hands. Practice sounded good, she decided, looking over at the practice rings. Then she noticed something. Or rather, the lack of someone. Frowning, she scanned the camp but did not see what she was looking for among the men.

"Where is Ganth?" she asked Krono.

"He is out with a hunting party." The cook tossed another peeled vegetable into a bucket by her feet. "Fishing, actually. They should be back in an hour or so. We are expecting the Prince's party today and want to have enough food to offer them. The waters off this beach are just teeming with bounty."

"Oh." Claire was absurdly happy that she would not have to talk to Ganth right away. Some time apart would ease the awkwardness of her having blubbered all over him the previous night. She walked over to the jousting circle, whistling a jaunty tune.

The other men greeted her with hearty waves and calls of welcome. She grinned. It was good to belong. She sat on the sand outside the ring, watching the men joust. It would do her some good to observe the techniques. Telcor joined her and soon Claire was plying the man with a thousand questions about the sport, which the guardsman answered with indulgence at her enthusiasm.

Most of the men had taken off their shirts, due to the hot mid morning sun beating down on them. Claire found she didn't mind the display of male flesh, in fact, she was rather enjoying it. Telcor pointed out different jousting movements, explaining their origin, meticulously taking apart even the smallest of footsteps.

Finally, Telcor stood up and gave Claire a jousting pole. They took their places in the ring. Unlike the previous day, Claire and Telcor did not participate in a mock joust. Instead, they worked side by side, Telcor showing Claire a movement, which she mimicked and practiced until he declared her competent. He took her through more and more complicated movements, combining them until she was doing a kind of routine with the jousting pole. She pivoted, thrust, twirled the pole, spun in place and arched the pole with greater and greater accuracy each pass.

It was fun, but extremely hard work. She was sweating like a fool and kept having to wipe her forehead with her hand so her vision stayed clear.

"You are doing things I would expect a veteran to demonstrate," Telcor admitted as she completed yet another complicated, involved series to his satisfaction. "Most are unable to get the concept of the joust as anything other than a poking stick."

Claire shrugged, figuring it was her years of working on the flag corps that had given her a natural feel for the pole. She felt extremely comfortable with it in her hands and twirling it was just second nature to her. She remembered a particularly brutal routine from her last year in school, which people had told them rivaled what the most elite drum corps was doing on the national circuit.

"There is just one thing that would make you better," Telcor said with a grin.

"What is that?" Claire asked absently, tossing the pole in a quick circle as she spoke.

"You are sweating like a beast. We need to get you cooled off."

His words penetrated Claire's memories of being on the football field during halftime and she froze, raising horrified green eyes in his direction. "What did you say?" She automatically and unconsciously brought the jousting pole into a defensive stance.

"We have a tradition," Telcor told her, still grinning. The other men in the Barracks gathered around as well. Claire felt the brief stirrings of panic deep in her belly. "When we bring a Barracks page into our troop as a full fledged member, it is the decision of the troop, not the Barracks Leader. We decide when a lad has shown that he has the intelligence, drive, ambition, skill and work ethic of our troop."

"We have decided you meet those criteria," Newmar said from the sideline of the group. Claire's eyes slid his way, still feeling wary, despite the rather innocuous words. Something else was going on here. Her instincts were screaming at her to get away. Now. But these guys had shown her nothing but respect…

"But we cannot allow such a sweaty, smelly boy become a guardsman," Telcor continued, advancing again. "So it is off to the ocean with you!"

With a yell, the Barracks moved in on Claire. Panicking, she swung the jousting pole but it was quickly wrested from her hands by the laughing, jostling group of men. They hoisted her high over their heads, heading for the water.

Claire was silently kicking and twisting, trying to get out of their grasp. *This was not happening,* was her only horrified thought. A sane part of her mind tried to remind her that the men truly thought she was a boy and did not understand how terrifying their actions were to her, but that sane part was not heard as pure instinct kicked in.

The men, not realizing that it was abject horror fueling her fight, manhandled Claire to the front of the group, passing her hand over hand high above their heads. Claire had tears streaming down her face, still kicking and clawing to get away. Groping hands heaved her back and forth as they prepared to toss her into the water.

Chanting, counting down to when they would throw her into the shallows of the ocean, the men did not see Ganth tearing down the beach toward them, having seen what was happening from afar. He yelled at the men to stop, but they could not hear him over their jovial shouts and laughter. He was just too far away to stop the inevitable.

Claire felt herself flying through the air. She hit the water with a smack, and immediately swallowed what seemed like half the ocean in one gulp. She surfaced sputtering and retching, gasping for air. She flipped her dripping hair back out of her eyes and tried to turn around to stagger back for the beach. She felt oddly numb and betrayed by the men's actions; even though a part of her acknowledged that they were just treating her like one of the guys.

There was dead silence on the Beaches. The absolute stillness finally penetrated her dull mind. She looked up to see the entire group of men staring at her, shock on their faces. She followed their gazes, looking down, then groaned.

During the struggle, the wraps that bound down her chest must have come loose. And now her wet, nearly transparent shirt was plastered to her like a second skin. It was abundantly, and some would say gloriously, clear that she was not a boy. Claire reflexively brought her arms up over her chest and sank deeper into the water, hiding from their view, unable to meet their scandalized faces.

Then Ganth was there, splashing through the surf to Claire's side. He pulled her out of the water, shielding her from the men with his body.

"Are you all right?" he asked her roughly, checking her body, running his hands over her to make sure nothing was broken.

"I'm fine," she said shakily, slapping at his hands until he dropped them to his sides. "Just completely humiliated, that's all."

"I will get you back to the tent." Ganth swung her up into his arms. Claire, who seconds before had not wanted him touching her, burrowed deeper in his arms as he turned to face the men, who were still standing silent and uncertain.

As Ganth waded out of the water, Telcor stepped forward, his face etched with consternation. "We did not know," he told Ganth miserably. "We had no idea…"

Ganth silenced him with a single look. Telcor stepped back to join the men. The men parted, allowing Ganth to carry Claire back to their tent. Once inside, he set her on her feet. His hands stayed on her arms until he was sure she was steady. Then he stepped back courteously.

"I will leave you to some privacy."

She nodded but didn't respond, her arms still crossed over her chest.

Ganth started to say something, and then stopped, turning to leave. At the door he paused again, speaking to the tent wall instead of her. "They are going to be horrified at what they did to a lady, Claire. If they had known, they would not have treated you so."

"I know," Claire whispered miserably, "but now it will all change, won't it? I was finally accepted into the group and now I'm the outsider again."

"They respected you when they thought you were a lad. Knowing you are a female and still met all their expectations of a warrior; that will impress them to no end. It just may take some time to get to that point." Ganth gave her a little nod before ducking under the tent flap to leave.

Claire stood silently until her body started to shake from the chill of her wet clothes. She sighed, pulling out her comfortable jeans and a clean t-shirt from her pack. *In for a penny, in for a pound.* Let them know she was a girl *and* from the World Dimension. It was inevitable, and she might as well be completely honest with them about her true identity.

Claire finger combed her damp hair back from her face after getting dressed. It was rather nice to be wearing a simple bra, rather than the uncomfortable wrapping. She dallied inside the tent as long as she could, and then finally decided it was time to face the music, so to speak.

The sunshine gleamed brightly in her eyes after the dimness of the tent's interior. The practice rings were empty, and Claire realized with a start that the men were all eating their lunch. Was it that late already? Claire stuck her hands in her jeans pocket and shuffled over to the eating area.

As she approached, Telcor saw her coming. He elbowed the man next to him and nodded his head in her direction. They rose from their seats on the logs around the fire. The other men followed suit.

So it has already started. They are acting as if a woman had entered the room, standing politely to acknowledge her entrance. She wasn't sure what to do. Then Ganth appeared at her shoulder, a solid presence at her side.

"Would you like me to explain it all to the men?" he asked her softly.

"No." Claire straightened her shoulders and repeated more forcibly, "No, I'll explain. Sit down, please." She waited until the men were seated again, noting that they were watching her with curiosity, but not an ounce of anger or resentment, as she had expected. She took a deep breath.

"My name is Claire Jones. I'm from the World Dimension. The Seer believes I've been sent here to do something about the strange weather in the Meadows, but exactly what I'm to do is still a mystery." She paused a moment, rubbing one foot over the sand. "You should know that someone from another dimension, who is working with Evil, may be after me. He tried to hurt me when I was still in the World, and they think he's followed me here to the Land. In fact, that's why I was disguised as a boy. It was hoped that I would be able to keep hidden from him. I'm sorry. I never meant to deceive you or hurt your feelings. They were just doing what they thought was right to protect me and give me a chance to try and help."

Ganth put a hand on Claire's shoulder, squeezing it gently. She bit her lip and looked away, concentrating on the ocean's horizon, not wanting to meet the guardsmen's eyes. "The question that remains before us is should Claire continue to disguise herself as a boy once the Prince and his party arrive?" Ganth looked out over the men.

Newmar stood up. "We felt that Jones—er, Claire—was a member of our Guard before we knew she was a female. She passed all our criteria. She works hard, is talented in the joust, and did as much as any seasoned veteran over in the Meadows Region. I say she is still a member of our Barracks."

"But she is a girl!" came an incredulous snort from the back of the group. Claire winced.

"I do not care." Telcor unfolded his lanky body. "Should we deny someone who so clearly meets our criteria because of her sex? That is not an honorable thing to do. And a guardsman is always honorable. To give that kind of invitation then take it back because she is a woman does not strike me as being right."

"But traditionally, there have always been male guardsmen," another one pointed out dubiously.

"Claire is a Worlder. She will go home soon. I say she is in the Guard until she does," Telcor replied. There was a murmur of agreement from the rest of the troop.

"For her safety, I would prefer Claire to remain Jones for now," Ganth said into the rustling group, who quieted down. "I trust each and every one of you with my life, and with hers. But we do not know all who travel with the Prince. I do not want to risk Claire if one of them is a conduit to Evil."

"I agree," came the shout from the back of the group. "She stays Jones and she stays a guardsman. Those people from the Capital City don't need to know her true identity. We will protect her."

A chorus of "here-here's" rose from the Barracks. A smile blossomed on her face as she realized what was happening. Warmth suffused her body; she did belong with them. They accepted her, boobs and all. For the first time in a long, long, long time, Claire belonged somewhere. It was enough to make a girl giddy.

Ganth buffeted her arm with a loosely clenched fist. "Looks like you're going to stay Jones for awhile longer." Turning his head to the east end of the Beaches, he added, "I suggest you go change back into some non-Worlder clothes. The Prince's party approaches."

~ 2 2 ~

▼

CAN YA TAKE A HINT?

When Claire finally came out of the tent, dressed in her old uniform of ivory shirt, brown breeches and knee high boots—the latter still damp—the Prince's party had already arrived and were setting up their camp near the Forest Barracks troop. The entire area was a flurry of activity, the melding of the two camps creating a symphony of sounds. People shouting to one another, greeting old friends, gesturing and posturing. After the controlled chaos of the guardsmen, the Capital City folk were definitely less organized, but seemed to have a lot to discuss as they struck camp.

Her fellow guardsmen helped erect the tents, joking with the other guards traveling with the Prince and his entourage. Claire hesitated, not sure what she should do next; help with the tents or go and see if the women cooking needed assistance. At that moment, Maxt and Ganth appeared, heading toward the tent, their heads bent together as they walked.

Claire sucked in her breath and ducked between the tents, getting out of sight. She wasn't ready to face either Maxt or Ganth at the moment. Crouching down, she watched as the men walked by, deep in discussion. Neither one looked very happy to her. Claire waited until they entered Ganth's tent, then crept closer, sneaking around the back side of the tent. By leaning in close to one of the seams, she found she could hear everything that was being said inside the tent.

They were talking about the Meadows Barracks. Claire breathed a sigh of relief, and then silently berated herself. Being happy that they were discussing the death of all those poor men was horrible. She should be ashamed of herself. All that happened to her was that the men found out she wasn't a boy. That was a pretty good dose of perspective.

Then Claire heard Maxt ask, "How is our young Claire faring?"

"You mean Jones," Ganth replied evenly, to which Maxt gave an appreciative laugh. "She is doing well. Actually, there are some things you should know…"

Claire listened while Ganth filled Maxt in on her activities over the past few days. How she had integrated herself into the troop, the men respecting her willingness to help and learn. Claire gave a mental scoff at being considered obedient in any way, shape or form but had to admit she had toed the line when it came to listening to the other men in the Barracks.

Ganth also told Maxt of the trips into the Meadows, the insight regarding the directions of the storms as well as Claire assisting at the demolished site of the Meadows Barracks. He also filled the Captain in on her jousting prowess and the great strides she was making in learning the skills of being a guardsman.

She felt her cheeks burn when Ganth described her as being the epitome of all that the Guard held sacred, loyal, hardworking, diligent, compassionate and strong. He made her sound like the model guardsman trainee, actually.

It was when Ganth started explaining about her "de-masking" that Claire began to fidget slightly, shifting her weight from one foot to the other uncomfortably. Ganth admitted that he was too late to forestall the guardsmen learning about her true sex. After the Barracks Leader was done telling the Captain of the Guard that the men in his troop were going to continue the masquerade to protect Claire from this mysterious Sea Dimension man, Maxt was silent for a long time. When he did speak, Claire had to lean in to hear what he said.

"Are you telling me that you had an eighteen year old girl digging through rubbish to find decomposing bodies? Then you let the rest of your men handle her in an inappropriate manner, and discover that she is a woman? I leave her in your charge, Ganth, and this is how you protect her?" Maxt's voice was low but thunderous, if that was possible.

Claire's eyes narrowed as all the air in her body seemed to collapse, then expand exponentially. It wasn't Ganth's fault. She had wanted to help at the Barracks. As far as yesterday was concerned, the men in the Barracks were acting like they would with any other lad they felt was ready to be initiated. How dare Maxt blame Ganth for those actions!

"I failed to protect her," Ganth admitted stonily, his voice even and strong. "I failed you, Maxt, and for that, I am disgraced in your eyes."

Claire had heard quite enough and marched around to the front of the tent.

Striding in, she halted in front of Maxt, her hands clenched into fists at her sides. "You cannot blame Ganth for what happened. I wanted to help at the Meadows Region. I frankly didn't give him a choice unless he wanted to declare right then and there who and what I was. As for yesterday, the men didn't treat me any differently than they would have treated a boy page. That in and of itself proves that Ganth did a good job. In fact, you should be thanking him for protecting me so well!"

Maxt was eying her with a glint of amusement in his forest eyes, which made Claire's blood boil even more. "And another thing…"

Her thought was cut off by Ganth's hand efficiently and effectively clamping down over her mouth. She found herself unceremoniously hauled up against his solid form, his other hand firmly clamped around her upper arm. When she started to squirm, he gave her arm a warning squeeze.

"What I was about to say," Maxt said with amused sarcasm after a moment of absolute silence, "is that Ganth's feeling of disgrace is misplaced and unwarranted. I am, quite frankly, astonished you were able to keep the secret for as long as you did. Amazed at Ganth for not allowing his natural chivalry to shine through and amazed at Claire for willing to do what many men would simply refuse."

Claire relaxed somewhat in Ganth's grip, the tension easing out of her bones. Ganth leaned over and whispered in her ear, "Can I trust you to keep your mouth shut for a few moments?" Claire slanted him a baleful look, to which Ganth chuckled. "No? Then we stay like this."

She stamped her heel down on his booted toe as hard as she could. The man didn't even flinch, damn his tough hide, and merely tightened his grip on her even more. Claire gave a muffled growl behind the hand still wrapped around her mouth.

Maxt watched the byplay with a bland expression, although a smile flitted around the corners of his mouth. He had his hands behind his back and was rolling back and forth on the balls of his feet. It was clear he was enjoying himself immensely.

To Claire's intense mortification, the tent flap opened and the Prince, Seer, and Sweetie clambered inside. With so many people, the tent was quickly becoming full. Claire squirmed in Ganth's grip but the man merely hissed at her to respect her elders and be still.

"Maxt, is it true about the Meadows Barracks?" The Prince demanded, his turquoise gaze full of concern, but also surprise as it raked over the portrait that Ganth and Claire displayed. "We heard it was destroyed by one of the storms, and that all men were killed."

Maxt nodded, then gestured toward Ganth. "The Forest Barracks has cleared the spot and buried the dead, honoring them appropriately for their sacrifices. It appears that all were lost in the storm."

"I will send word to their families," the Prince sighed, rubbing a hand through his dark hair. "Personal messengers. Then we will call for those who wish to replace the fallen. I am sure that each Barracks will send men." Ganth and Maxt nodded their agreement to that assessment. "Maxt, I will need your counsel on who to appoint as Barracks Leader, of course."

The Seer looked over at Claire, who unsuccessfully tried to worm her way out of Ganth's hold. The woman smiled and tilted her head to one side. "So, Claire, how are the guardsmen treating you?" She knew that Ganth would have no choice but to allow the girl to answer on her own. To do otherwise would be highly discourteous to the Seer of the Land. Few were ever discourteous to her. At least not more than once, that was.

Reluctantly, Ganth removed his hand. Claire sent him a triumphant look. "The guardsmen are treating me well," she replied to the Seer, absently picking up Sweetie when the little girl tried to climb her leg to get her attention. "But I am no closer to figuring out what to do about these storms than I was a few days ago."

"Storms, bad turtle, you not supposed to be here!" Sweetie intoned, pulling on the laces of Claire's shirt so she could see the bead Claire wore more clearly.

"Yes, yes," Claire told Sweetie. "Storms are bad for turtles, but their shells help protect them." Sweetie sighed, a very adult sound, then went back to her playing with the bead with the diligence only a child could display.

"We sent a scouting party out. They should return at some point today," Ganth explained the thought process behind pin pointing the origins of the storms and seeing if there was anything unusual in the area.

"That certainly makes sense." The Seer stroked Sweetie's back with one hand. "As soon as we have the area ascertained, we'll have go there."

"Correction. We will go there, you and Sweetie will stay here," the Prince said, Maxt nodding his agreement. The Seer's gaze narrowed, much like Claire's had before.

"I think you will find that I am not some biddable lap dog." Her pleasant voice under laid with pure steel. "Content to sit in the camp while the big strong men do all the work."

"We cannot risk the Seer of the Land going into the middle of what is essentially a combat zone," Maxt maintained stubbornly, no longer rocking back and forth comfortably.

"Are you going?" The Seer turned to consider the Prince, who, to his credit, didn't flinch or squirm under her gaze.

"I am," he replied, crossing his arms. "I am the Prince of the Land, it is my prerogative to go where I choose."

"Same goes here, buckaroo," the Seer replied, then clapped her hands briskly. "If the Oracle of the Land is going, so will the Seer of the Land. End of discussion. Now that we have settled that little sticky situation, why don't we go outside and enjoy some of the sunshine while it still remains? I do so love being at the Beaches."

Maxt growled something at the Seer. In response, the woman laid a gentle hand on his cheek, shaking her head in a loving fashion. "Give it up, my heart," she told him in a soft voice. "I am going, and I trust in you to protect me."

Maxt sighed deeply and nodded reluctantly. Sweetie clapped her hands in glee. "Turtle!"

Claire winced as the word was yelled full force into her ear. She set the small child back onto the ground and watched as she scampered out the tent, the other two following, leaving Ganth and Claire behind.

Ganth turned to Claire, his face set in harsh lines. He opened his mouth to berate her but she surprised both of them by flinging herself in his arms, wrapping her own around his neck tightly.

"You said the nicest things about me." Claire spoke into his vest. Her head barely reached his shoulder. Ganth's hands came around her slowly, rather uncertainly, his hands finally coming to rest on her waist. "No one has ever said such wonderful things about me. Ever. Thank you."

"They were true," Ganth whispered over her hair. "But I did not tell him why I told you I knew about your secret. I should have told him that, in all honesty."

"That's none of his business. Maxt doesn't need to know that."

"I feel dishonorable for not telling him I have the hots for you."

The use of the familiar phrase coming from the Lander made Claire smile as a warm spurt of glee spread through her body like a sparkler lit in the summer night.

Claire angled her head up to look at his blue eyes square on. "It's none of his business."

They stared at one another, then, for the first time in her life, she took the initiative. Because she wanted to, and knew it was the right thing to do, Claire stood up on her tip toes and brushed her lips firmly across his. "This is between you and me, Ganth. No one else." Then Claire pulled away from his embrace, enjoying the rather stunned look on his face before she turned and left the tent, leaving Ganth standing there, the rapid pulse in his neck clearly indicating he was as affected by the kiss as Claire had been.

Claire spent the rest of the afternoon helping set up tents, fetch water and run errands for the Barracks. She was relieved that the men treated her no differently than they had the day before. If anything, they kept a closer eye on her, and often forestalled any awkward questions posed to her by the other guardsmen, who were curious about her. She was grateful for their intervention and vowed to let them know how much she appreciated their help.

At dinner, Claire made sure she ate with the men of her Barracks, far away from the Prince and Seer. She did not want to appear to be on speaking terms with the two, that would seem rather odd for a humble lad from the Forest Region.

But Sweetie could have cared less for the subterfuge. She wandered over soon after dinner and unceremoniously plopped herself down in Claire's lap. She nattered about storms and fish and turtles and the sky for the better part of the evening.

"Sweetie has taken a liking to you."

The rest of the men around her stood immediately as the Seer materialized behind Claire. Cursing under her breath, Claire tried to pick up Sweetie and stand at the same time. The Seer reached out and easily swung the child to her hip. Sweetie set up a howl of protest immediately.

"Sweetie, behave!" Sweetie scowled at the woman but subsided, her little chubby cheeks streaked with tears.

"Why doesn't she have a normal name?" Claire blurted out before realizing how forward her words must seem to those around her.

"Sweetie is a Seer. Her real name is not used. Sweetie knows what it is, and will make use of it when necessary," the Seer replied easily, apparently unperturbed by the comment. "She adopted Sweetie as her everyday name after Zach called her that when he was rescuing her from the fortress."

"Wan' Zach-ree," Sweetie said stubbornly.

"You and half the planet." The utterly sarcastic come back slipped out before Claire could stop herself. She winced, feeling she was fast loosing her grip on the masquerade.

"Zach is in the World Dimension," the Seer reminded Sweetie gently, pushing a blond ringlet from her face. "I don't think he'll be able to visit again any time soon."

Sweetie's bottom lip trembled and everyone tensed, waiting for the inevitable.

"Sweetie, want to go to the edge of the water and dip our toes in it?" Claire rushed. Sweetie immediately gave her an appraising look, but the diversion seemed to work as the little girl nodded regally. Like the Seer, Claire thought with an inner laugh.

The Seer set Sweetie down, and the little girl and Claire headed for the ocean's edge, the older woman trailing behind.

"That was a great diversion, and also gives me a chance to get you away from the others without seeming to be singling you out." The Seer and Claire stood side by side, their backs to the camp, watching Sweetie play in the shallows.

"I didn't expect you to follow. I just didn't want Sweetie to cry."

"Fair enough. So, how are you doing, Claire? I mean *really* doing, not the guardsman stoic facade you seem to have adopted."

"I'm—I am fine," Claire answered truthfully. "More than fine, if I'm going to be completely honest. The men of the Barracks are really good people. I liked helping the Meadows and learning the skills. I fit in here. In the Land, I mean."

"You say that like you do not feel like you belong in the World Dimension."

Claire blinked back unexpected tears. "Not that, just, oh, I don't know how to explain. It's more a feeling of completeness that I have here."

"Well, you'll take that with you," the Seer predicted. "All the other Protectors have that same sense of belonging and comfort in the Land. You'll never be alone again, you know that, don't you? The Protectors will always be there for you."

Claire was quiet a long, long time. Her entire past was laid out before her, with its myriad of deaths, betrayals and the sense of being shuffled off to a half existence. Then she had a glimpse into her future, full of people and love and laughter. "Yeah…they'll always be there for me. That is a totally weird thing to admit. It's even more weird that I'm ok with it."

The Seer reached out and put her hand on Claire's shoulder. "You've grown more than you realize, Claire. You are already willing to let the Protectors help you. That is a huge step."

Claire scratched her nose self consciously. "I know. I just hope they aren't going to try and impose a curfew or something. Because that could get ugly."

They were both laughing over the idea when they heard Maxt calling out to them. Turning, they could see that the man gesturing them over.

"I guess the excursion inland has returned," the Seer said, calling for Sweetie. "Let's go see what they have discovered."

Not only had the excursion come back from the Meadows, but a huge creature had landed squarely in the middle of the encampment. It was the Griffin, come to fetch the Seer. The woman said a hurried goodbye to Claire, kissed Maxt soundly and, with Sweetie, climbed onboard the large beast, taking off into the darkening night sky.

~ 2 3 ~

▼

AWAITED MEETING

The sound of metal clashing against metal rang over the courtyard, along with shouts from the midst of the battle. From the relative coolness of the porch, Katie sat, watching her friends engage in a mock battle. In the courtyard below Zach and Ben were moving with their usual fluid grace, feet and swords a blur. Farther down the porch, Tracy sat in a comfortable chair, her hands resting lightly on her extended belly, watching the men with hunger in her eyes. Sasha and Sarat sat on the grass near the barn, also watching while they polished their swords to a gleaming surface.

Suddenly Ben tossed his sword down with shout of alarm.

"Zach! Are you all right?" he said, as his sparring partner clutched his wrist tightly.

"I'm fine." Zach's words were terse. "Just a scratch."

Zach headed for the porch, Sarat and Sasha abandoning their work to follow.

"Let's see it," Katie demanded Zach as they climbed up the porch.

"It's not bad," Zach replied, but obediently he stripped off the rag he'd slapped on it. A shallow scratch was etched along his wrist, oozing blood.

Katie clucked over it, twisting it one way then the other. "You were sloppy out there," she admonished Zach, who ducked his head. Sasha headed inside to get William's kit, since her husband was off in town getting more ice cream for Tracy. When she came back out, Liz trailed behind her, eyeing Zach anxiously. But she didn't rush over like she normally would, Katie observed. As Katie bandaged up his cut, she noticed that Zach seemed to be a thousand miles away, his blue eyes clouded with what seemed to be anger and pain. But it did not seem to be a physical kind of pain.

"So, how did your big date in the city go last night?" The question was asked innocently enough, but it didn't stop Zach from jerking on his wrist when he gave a start of surprise. His amber flecked blue gaze rose up and met Liz's briefly before sliding away.

"Zach was recognized," Liz said softly. Katie nodded. That was an unfortunate side effect of Zach's fame, despite the fact that he hadn't made a movie in years.

"It was a shitty date," Zach stated baldly, making Katie's eyebrows rise. Zach rarely cursed in front of women, he generally considered it rude.

"Why?" Tracy asked point blank. Katie had to hide a smile. Tracy's Too'ki bluntness appeared to be making a return.

"I asked Liz to marry me," Zach replied, his eyes firmly on the bandage. Liz heaved a heavy sigh while the others gave exclamations of delight.

"So why the boosey face? I'm sure she said yes." Sasha narrowed her eyes at Liz. "You *did* say yes, didn't you Lizzie?"

"No, she didn't. She said she'd—and I quote—'think about it'." Zach gave a snort of disgust. "I know what that means in girl speak."

"No, you don't," Liz replied with not a small amount of heat. "I told you, give me a little time. That's all I asked for Zach. Time."

"Time. Riiiiiight. Got it." Zach pressed down a corner of the taped bandage and turned to stalk away. "Take all the time you want, Liz."

"Zachary Neol, get your ass back over here now," Liz bellowed as she stamped her foot, which caused all action in the courtyard to cease. Katie was at a loss to explain the dynamics swirling. Zach cursing was one thing, Liz yelling was quite another.

"Why, Liz?" Zach rounded, his arms held out. The fact that he had a sword clenched tightly in one fist didn't seem to register with him. "So you can tell me that you need more time to know if you love me or not?"

"I never said anything about not knowing if I love you," Liz shot back from her place at the top of the stairs. "I love you with all my heart and soul. I have from almost the moment you fell on top of me from the back deck of your beach house. Probably before that if I was totally honest with myself. All I asked for was some time."

"Why? Why do you need more time, Liz? Give me one good reason and maybe, just maybe I'll understand why you are tossing my proposal back in my face."

"*The Land*," she said succinctly. "I can't marry you when I don't know if I'll be called back to the Land at any second, to take over for the Seer until Sweetie is of age. I can't ask you to put your life on hold. I see how hard it is for Ben and Tracy, and they get to Travel to the Land. You wouldn't be able to if I had to go back. It's not fair to ask you to wait for me to return should that happen." Liz looked at him, misery etched on her cameo face.

"So we're *both* going to put our lives on hold?" Zach said, still angry. "Wait for something that may never happen? How many years, Liz? Are we going to wait a lifetime on the off chance that you'll be called?"

"It might not be an off chance, Zach. But I need to know. I need to know…"

"Uh, guys?" Tracy spoke in a surprisingly quiet and tentative voice from the porch. The weakness in her tone had everyone swinging her way, the heated voices dying off as they took in her terrified expression.

"What?" Zach's voice was barking, but lacked the harshness of his earlier words.

"My water just broke."

There was a moment of absolute silence, then everyone rushed around and talked at once.

"Enough," Tracy finally bellowed as she was being pushed and pulled in several directions at once. "Amber, go get the bedroom ready. Sasha, call William on his cell. We'll need him. I'll need him," she corrected with a laugh. "Katie, get the linens and Sarat, go lay out everything the baby will need once it gets here. The rest of you, well, do whatever you want but keep the hell away from me."

"Right," Katie took a deep breath, then looked around. "Well, you heard the woman. Go!"

Soon enough, they had Tracy upstairs, wearing a fresh nightshirt. She refused to get in the bed, preferring to walk up and down the long hallway. "Walking accelerates the labor," she said over and over again.

Katie kept close, hardly leaving the woman's side. Whenever a contraction hit, Tracy would lean against the wall or whichever Protector was nearby, biting her lip and concentrating on her breathing. It seemed that the usually highly emotional Tracy was withdrawing into herself, saving her strength for the coming ordeal. Her quiet demeanor and utter concentration both awed and worried Katie.

Since no one knew how she would react to medications, given her Too'ki infection, not to mention the fact that the baby was half from the Land, Tracy was forced to go through the labor without any kind of medication to take the edge off the pain. She tended to remain calm as long as Katie was with her, as the Oracle subtly used some of her Oracle powers to help ease the tense muscles in the laboring woman. Everyone else took turns being with Tracy, even Zach, who, despite his white face and sweating brow, was remarkably strong for his friend.

"Where the hell did Ben go?" Sasha hissed at Amber as she watched Zach try and comfort Tracy during a particularly bad contraction. It was late morning and Tracy had been in labor for almost six hours. "Tracy and Ben are close, and he's not taken a turn with her at all."

"I sent him to town to pick up some food for the next few days," the fairy replied easily. "It didn't make sense for us to be worried about cooking for this huge crowd during a time like this. I sent Liz with him. I thought she and Zach could use the time apart." Sasha nodded and blew her bangs out of her face.

"This is just so much harder than I expected it to be," she admitted to Amber.

Zach staggered from the bedroom. "I can't take it!" he gasped, leaning against the wall, his hands shaking. "How can women go through this torture?"

Katie rolled her eyes at him. "Spare me the male dramatics," she said, giving him a shove. Owen hung back in the shadows, grumbling his agreement with Zach's assessment and trying to stay out of the way. Sarat stared at her husband with a woeful look on her pixie face.

"Somehow I think my sex life just went into the toilet," she complained with a pout, earning a snort of laughter from Katie as she passed through on her way back to stay with the expectant mom.

The day crept by, full of starts and stops and a whole lot of waiting around. Tracy withdrew more and more, her entire concentration turning inward. More than once, Katie could hear Tracy whisper her husband's name, and knew her friend missed the companionship of her soul mate during this difficult time.

Mid afternoon, William asked everyone but Emma to leave the bedroom so he could check Tracy's progress, as he had periodically during the day. The rest of the Protectors hung out in the kitchen, anxiously awaiting the results.

Emma came out of the bedroom after William examined Tracy. "Six centimeters," she announced cheerfully to the group waiting. "Almost there."

It actually took several more hours for Tracy to reach the full ten centimeters. Right before midnight William announced that it was time to get ready to deliver the baby. Emma bustled about the room, getting everything ready for the final hours of their vigil while Katie stayed close to Tracy's side, whispering encouragement. When Tracy indicated she was ready to push, Katie sat next to her, Amber on the other side. As she helped position Tracy to start pushing, Amber nodded toward the window.

"Take a look at who has come to see the new arrival," she whispered to Tracy.

"Oh my goodness gracious me," Emma breathed in awe.

"Magnificent," Katie marveled, then helped Tracy turn slightly toward the window.

Along the sill and fluttering in the glass panes were dozens of small, sparkling fairies. Their wings glittered in the light shining out of the room, their smiling faces and cheerful waves bolstering Tracy for the final leg of her journey to motherhood. Tracy's eyes flooded with tears, she knew that while fairies attended births in her dimension, they were never to be seen.

"Why can we see them? I thought they attended births incognito?"

"I think they are here because you are a Protector, Tracy." Tears streamed down Katie's face. "They are here for you because they know Orli can't be."

Those in the bedroom weren't the only ones who had noticed the fairies. Sarat opened the window over the sink in the kitchen to allow the little ones to come inside. After a literal stream entered, their high-pitched voices chattering and laughing, the Land woman leaned out the window.

"They are everywhere," she exclaimed. "There must be thousands of them, all over the Orchards."

"Well I for one feel safer having them around," Zach said, then looked around suddenly. "Hey! Where's Liz?" He'd tried to stay out of her way that day, not certain if they were still fighting or not. Now he realized with a start that he hadn't seen her at all in hours.

"I haven't seen her since Tracy went into labor," Sasha realized.

"Ben either," Sarat said suspiciously, looking around. "Ok, Katie and Amber are inside with Tracy, William and Emma attending. Owen and Steven are here, and we have Sasha, Zach and me. We are definitely missing two Protectors." Her eyes narrowed and she and Sasha exchanged a sudden, almost panicked look.

"No way," Sasha said, but their thoughts were distracted when a sudden scream rent the air, coming from upstairs.

"Oh, man," Zach moaned, turning sheet white, his hands clutching at the table. "This is not good."

"Get over it," Sasha maintained, rolling her eyes expressively. "It's only just begun. Really. Wait until she has the baby. You'll be hearing all kinds of screams then."

"How long has she been pushing?" Steven asked quietly from his seat.

Sarat checked her Beauty and the Beast wristwatch. "About an hour," she said, worry in her voice. "That's a long time, isn't it?"

Steven sighed and looked away, leaving Sasha to answer the question.

"It's getting long, but it can take awhile," she said finally.

Upstairs, inside the bedroom, Katie and Amber kept up a steady stream of encouragement with William occasionally giving directions to the women. Emma took Tracy's hand, motioning for Amber to brace the woman from behind.

"Go ahead and push again, Tracy," Emma said, "Let's see this gorgeous child of yours."

"Can't," Tracy gasped. "Too hard. Hurts."

"You can and will," Emma replied firmly.

"No, no," Tracy moaned, her head falling back against Amber's shoulder. "You don't understand. Hurt…black."

"You're seeing black around the edges?" Amber asked sharply, glancing over at Katie as Tracy nodded weakly.

"It's to be expected," Katie said soothingly, looking at Emma and William. "The stress is bringing out the Too'ki in her," she explained softly. "Where the hell is Liz? I need her to interpret Tracy's aura!"

"She's not here," Amber said firmly, giving Katie a single silencing look when the Oracle appeared ready to rant about the absence.

"We need to get this child born," William said grimly, turning his most intense gaze on Tracy. "Listen to me, Tracy. Listen to me now. You need to focus and to push. Push hard."

"I can't do it!" Tracy said weakly. "I don't want to go back there, I can't go back there!"

"You need to do this," Katie said softly, ignoring Tracy as she continued to shake her head in dismay. "Do it for us, do it for your child."

"No, no, you don't understand," Tracy sobbed.

"I do understand, but you need to do this for your baby," Katie said, desperate as Tracy continued to shake her head.

"I can't, Katie. I can't! You don't know what you are asking me to do. I can't do it! Not even for the baby!"

"Then do it for me."

Tracy's head whipped to the doorway. Orli was standing there, Ben right behind him, grinning from ear to ear.

"Orli?" Tracy whispered, her face shocked. Katie did a double take herself, convinced she was hallucinating.

"It's about time," Amber grumbled, looking at Ben closely. "No sickness?"

"None," the Sea Dimension man replied gratefully. "Thanks for that."

Orli approached the bed, his face a vista of wonderment. "You have never looked more beautiful than right at this moment," he vowed to his wife, pushing a strand of hair from her face.

Tracy laughed through a contraction, turning her cheek into his palm. "You are such a liar."

"Hello, there. I'm William," said the doctor brightly. "Now if you don't mind, I'd like to get this child delivered before it comes out speaking full sentences!"

Ben started to withdraw from the room, but William barked at him over his shoulder. "Ben, get over here and help Amber hold Tracy's legs in position. Katie, you and Orli support Tracy's shoulders and Emma, get ready to help me catch."

"Uh, no, I really shouldn't be in here," Ben said nervously, edging for the door.

"Benjamin Harm! Get your blond ass over here and help me birth this baby!" Tracy bellowed. Ben gave a start and then shuffled to the bed, clearly miserable about being in the room, giving the fairies that were clustered on top of every surface a curious look.

"Ah, there's the Cricket we know and love," Katie murmured to Amber, who bit her lip, which kept some of the laughter inside.

Ben and Amber got into place, with Orli whispering to Tracy while Katie just watched the two of them, tears in her eyes. She'd never seen the two of them together before, and it was somewhat overwhelming to be able to witness this remarkable Interdimensional love firsthand.

"Ok, Tracy, now is the time. This is it. One more good push and I think we'll have ourselves a new little Protector." William said encouragingly.

Tracy nodded and, gritting her teeth, bore down. Katie gasped at the strength with which the woman clutched her hand. Orli appeared oblivious to the painful grip, his sharply planed face alight with excitement and anticipation.

"Here we go," Emma cried out as the child slid into the world. All around the room, the little fairies began to dance and sing, their voices rising to the ceiling like crystal bells, sparkling and shining with every note.

"Congratulations, Orli and Tracy. You have a girl," William announced, placing the baby on the new mother's chest. Expertly clamping the umbilical cord, he turned to Orli. "Would you like to cut the cord?"

"It's tradition here," Katie said gently as the man hesitated. Orli then nodded and took the scissors, cutting the cord.

"Let's get her cleaned up," William said gently, taking the baby to the bassinet that had been prepared. While the midwife took care of delivering the afterbirth and cleaning up Tracy, the doctor gave the child a quick assessment as he wiped her down, putting a soft pink cap on her downy head and wrapping her in the soft aqua colored blanket Ben had brought back from the Sea Dimension.

Fairies perched on the doctor's shoulders and along the edge of the bassinet, watching as they oohed and ahhed over the new arrival. Katie and Ben had also withdrawn from the bed to give the new parents a measure of privacy.

"I don't know how this happened, and I don't care," Tracy was saying to Orli, tracing the planes of his face with trembling fingertips. "But I've never been so glad to see anyone in my entire life."

"I love you," Orli whispered with fervent conviction, lowering his forehead to touch his wife's. "This moment, I will never forget."

"I will always remember," she promised in return, smiling through her tears.

~ 2 4 ~

▼

THE NEW GENERATION

"Does everything look all right with the baby? With Tracy?" Katie asked William in an undertone, Ben hovering anxiously just behind them.

"The babe looks fine, just fine," William replied, scooping up the tiny bundle. He deposited the child in Katie's arms and pushed her gently toward the bed. "As does her mother. Go on, Oracle. Give the happy couple their bundle of joy."

Katie looked down at the small face, the eyes scrunched and wet from the vitamin drops that had been placed in them by the doctor. She walked over to the bed.

"I think you've been waiting for someone," Katie said as she placed the child in Tracy's waiting and eager arms. She put a hand on Tracy's cheek, the other on Orli's. One was so dear to her heart, the other such a familiar stranger, yet no less beloved. "May whatever blessings come your way be only happy ones."

"Oh, Orli, she's beautiful," Tracy breathed, her words barely discernable through her tears.

"Does she have a name?" Ben asked from behind Katie, his hands gently squeezing the Oracle's shoulders.

Orli looked up from the child who, despite her few minutes in the world, already possessed his sharply defined, arching dark brows. "We decided on

Katherine, after the Oracle who brought us together," he replied, his dark brown eyes gazing at Katie, who tried to blink back her tears unsuccessfully. "Thank you, Katie, for all you have done for me and my wife. We would be honored if you would lend our daughter your name."

"Oh, my," Katie found that she was helpless to respond more coherently.

"I think we'll call her Kat for short," Tracy stated firmly.

The fairies in the room rose into the air, beginning to fly in circles around the room. It was an intricate weaving of color and form, allowing all the fairies inside and outside the house and orchard the chance to see the child. It took a long time but finally, the last fairy, the familiar colors of their very own Amber, bowed over the child and then exited the room, continuing their dance of joy and song of welcome as the fairies rose into the dawn and scattered to the winds.

"Amazing," Ben breathed from his place next to Katie. "Let's go tell the others downstairs."

"Yes Ben, let's go downstairs." Katie arched an eyebrow, glancing meaningfully in Orli's direction. "You have some explaining to do!"

They descended the stairs to find a row of expectant faces looking up at them.

"It's a girl!" Katie announced as she paused a few steps up. A cheer rose from the group.

"We figured everything was all right when the fairies started dancing and singing," Sasha commented with a grin. Then she spied Ben behind Katie and her eyes narrowed, taking a deep breath of his still Land-tinged clothes. "Where the hell have you been, Harmster?"

"Where is Liz?" Zach demanded, his hands clenched on his hips.

Ben managed to look guilty and sheepish at the same time. "I can explain—"

"Olli's here," Katie interrupted him, unable to contain her excitement.

"*What*!" Sarat cried out, leaping to her feet. "How the hell did you manage that one?"

"It's a brief switch. Orli came to the World so he could be with Tracy and…" His gaze skittered toward Zach.

"Liz is in the Land?" Zach completed, his eyes becoming dark and stormy. "Are you insane? She was almost killed last time she was there."

"Why Liz?" Sarat wondered in a small voice.

"She wanted to go." Ben spoke softly. "I hope I can explain. She wanted to meet with the Seer and Sweetie, to find out what happens next with her status as the Heir Apparent. But no one is to know," he rushed to say, "the

Prince, Seer, Liz and Sweetie are the only ones who know about this in the Land."

"But I still don't understand how that explains Orli being here," Sarat maintained.

Ben sighed. "Amber arranged it all with Daniel," he admitted, "so I'm a little fuzzy on some of the details. But she went to him and basically demanded that Orli be allowed to come here, since Tracy couldn't go to him, for the birth of his child. From what I gather, they had quite an argument about it. Finally, Daniel agreed but only for a brief period of time and only if one of us went to the Land to even the balance. It couldn't be me, because I was needed for the exchange through the Tree. Anyway, Liz overheard Amber and I discussing it one day—we were trying to figure out how to talk with you about choosing who to go—but she said she wanted to go, and needed it to be a secret."

"But you came back in less than a day," Steven pointed out. "Why didn't you get the Travel sickness? I thought that was a built in protection to prevent you guys from popping in and out at will over there."

"Again, I have to thank Amber and Daniel for that," Ben admitted. "Daniel lifted the ban. I went, got to the Mountain Village as soon as possible, grabbed Orli and handed Liz over to the Seer then hightailed it back here. It still took the better part of the day, though. I was afraid Orli would miss the big event, but thankfully…I got him here, snuck him in the front way and up the stairs, just in time for the birth…" Ben trailed off. It was clear he was exhausted.

"Well, I for one am glad that Daniel relented and let Orli come. I just wish Liz didn't have to go and be there in his place," Sarat maintained.

Ben looked at Zach miserably, saying with heartfelt emotion, "I'm sorry, man. Liz didn't want you to worry about her, so she didn't want to tell you. But she did ask me to give you this letter," he dug it out of his pocket and handed it over to Zach, who snatched it from him angrily.

An awkward silence fell over the room as everyone tried to figure out what to say next. Katie, striving to bring back some of the joy of the day, stated firmly, "Orli was able to get here to see the birth of his child. We need to focus on that happy event, and the joy that this new baby brings."

"I agree," Sasha said staunchly, although she did put her arm around Zach's waist in silent support of him.

"The fairies were amazing," Sarat exclaimed, picking up on the topic gratefully.

They spent several minutes talking about the strange phenomena as well as the choice in names for the baby, gathering around the table once again. Gradually, Zach relaxed, although Katie noticed that every once in a while he would pat the pocket the letter was in, as if checking to make sure it was still there. He barely ate anything, even though Katie tried to tempt him with all his favorites.

William appeared at the bottom of the stairs, his crystal blue eyes crinkled at the sight of the happy people clustered in the kitchen. Behind him, Orli held back, looking slightly overwhelmed by the site of the merry Protectors, not to mention his first glimpse at the modern World his wife called home. When the refrigerator started to hum, Katie saw him flinch with surprise.

Katie waved them both over. "William, how is Tracy?"

The doctor came into the room and crossed to his wife, kissing her on the top of her dark head as he slid one arm around her. "Mother and child are doing fine. They're both getting some well deserved sleep, so I brought Orli down for some sustenance and introductions."

Katie put her hand in Orli's, drawing him into the room. "I didn't get a chance to formally welcome you upstairs," she said with a slight laugh, "but welcome to the World Dimension, Orli." A chorus of greetings rose from the table.

Sarat raced over and hugged her old friend tightly. Happy to see a familiar face, the Mountain Villager gave her a fierce hug then held her at arm's length, marveling at her attire. "You look so different," he said softly, "but so very happy!"

"I'm happy for you!" she crowed, "You're a daddy now, Orli!" Sarat turned and started pointing at people around the table. "You met Katie, and of course you know Ben—he's in the major doghouse now with Zach over Liz staying in the Land—and then that is Owen, my husband, then Steve, Katie's husband—doesn't he look just like the Prince?—let's see… next is Sasha, who you met briefly when she was in the Land, and of course you know her husband William by now. Last we have Zach, of course."

Orli embraced Zach heartily. "It is so good to see you all, and meet the rest of you," Orli said, his hand over his heart. "I am simply amazed to be here in the World. I never expected such a thing was possible. To be here for the birth of my child," his voice choked up slightly as he stumbled over the word, but he recovered nicely, "means so much to me. To have experienced this miracle is something I can hardly put into words. And your support of Tracy, the help, love, and care you gave her during her pregnancy…I can never repay that. I will forever be in your debt."

To Katie's surprise, it was Zach who spoke up. "Tracy is one of us," he told Orli with absolute sincerity shining from those award-wining eyes. "We will always be there for her, and for Kat," the former actor smiled over the name.

The back door slammed opened and Amber stumbled in, her bright red hair slightly disheveled and her eyes suspiciously bright. "Woohoo! We got ourselves a girl!" the fairy yelled as she weaved her way into the room. Spying Orli, she gave a huge grin.

"Damn, you're pretty!" Amber said as she crossed over to him, tripping over her own feet and literally falling into his arms. "Whoops!"

Orli, displaying the quick response he was famous for, caught the woman, and then looked helplessly at the others.

Sasha pulled out a chair from the table and with the help of Zach, Orli poured the clearly intoxicated fairy into the seat. "Amber, have you been drinking fairy wine?" Zach demanded, catching a familiar scent of honeysuckle wafting up from the woman.

"You betcha! Oh, such pretty boys we have in our group." Amber patted his butt fondly, causing Zach to chuckle and remove her hand gently.

"I have no desire to have Daniel on my back," Zach told her firmly. Orli and Ben took cautious steps away from the intoxicated fairy.

"What was up with the fairies?" Katie gestured at the window. "Why were they here? Protection against Evil?"

"Oh that!" Amber waved her hand, blowing a piece of hair from her face. "Whenever a child is born, at least one fairy is in attendance. A fairy from that dimension, anyway. They will hang around until a name is given to the child. A name has an awfully powerful amount of protection, yessiree."

"Well, I'd say we had more than one fairy," Katie pointed out, clearly amused by Amber's state.

The fairy nodded enthusiastically. "Oh, the row that happened over who was going to attend this birth!" she exclaimed, tossing up her hands and knocking over a mug on the table, which was thankfully empty. Steven caught it and set it on the counter. "Every fairy from three dimensions wanted in on this one."

"Three dimensions?" Sasha repeated, confused.

"World, Land, Too'ki," Amber recited. "A few from the Sea wanted in as well, since some of them are more than half convinced that Ben is really the father," she rolled her eyes dramatically at that thought. "As if! Orli and Anja would have his ass if that were the case!"

Ben shifted uncomfortably in his chair, grimacing as Orli shot him a good-natured look.

"So we had to open it up to whoever wanted to come and join the party," Amber finished, tossing up her hands. "And what a party it was, right? Haven't partied like that since Ghandi was born." She slumped back in her chair, grinning foolishly at the memory.

"You need to go sleep this off," Katie said firmly. "Sasha, would you and Sarat see to Amber?"

Turning to Ben and Orli, Katie asked if there was any news about Claire and her Quest. It was clear that they had not had a chance to find out much in their mad dash to and from the Land. After ascertaining that the Meadows Region was still under attack, with the ferocity of the storms increasing in both strength and duration, Katie sighed, rubbing her eyes. She was suddenly weary, tired beyond belief. She should be able to kick back, relax, and celebrate the birth of little Kat, but instead she had to continue to worry about an eighteen year old Protector lost in the wilds of the Meadows Region, fighting a life and death battle against Evil.

~ 2 5 ~

▼

CHARTS AND MEASURES

Claire hung back along the edge of the large tent that the Prince occupied, one hand worrying the chain and bead around her neck. A table had been set up in the middle of the space, and it was covered with a large, detailed map of the Meadows. Clustered around the table were Maxt, the Prince, Ganth, several of the men Ganth had sent into the Meadows Region, and a few wizards who had map skills. They were busy charting out where the storms had passed, using the debris paths ascertain where the storms originated. Since the departure of Sweetie and the Seer the previous night, most of the attention had been on assimilating the data they knew about the storms, trying to make some sense of the situation so an appropriate course of action could be formulated for their upcoming hike into the Meadows.

Claire listened intently, unable to see the map clearly from her place across the room. However, as long as the others were present, she couldn't really go pushing up to the table. While the guardsmen from Ganth's camp would not mind, those from the Prince's entourage were clueless about her identity. For now, she was relegated to the shadows.

Finally, the men were done and the wizards glided from the room, their robes whispering. Counselors of the Prince spoke with him a few moments before departing as well. Ganth sent the guardsmen out to get some food and rest. As soon as the tent closed behind them, Ganth gestured for Claire to come forward, his hand rested on the back of her waist as they made room for her at the table. Maxt noticed the touch and raised eyebrows at the Prince, who returned the gesture.

"Clearly, we have an open patch, where there are no storms, roughly here." Maxt pointed to an area toward the center of the Meadows, on the Marshes side of the region.

"So, that is where we need to go," the Prince remarked, slanting a look in Maxt's direction. "How long will it take to get there?"

"If we leave before the sun comes up, I would guess a day or so, depending on the pace we are allowed to keep," Maxt gave a significant look in Claire's direction.

"I have not found it necessary to modify our hikes to accommodate Claire in any fashion," Ganth replied easily. He also seemed to realize his arm was still around her and snatched it back.

Claire gave him a sidelong glance. Was that a blush creeping up his neck? She bit her lip to keep from smiling. This flirting business was rather fun. The Prince winked at her playfully, as if he read her mind.

"So that settles it. We will each take five men from our contingents, plus Claire and the Prince. We will leave the wizards behind for now, they will only slow us down considerably. With the Seer and Sweetie gone, I feel safe taking a smaller number into the Meadows. It is still dangerous to be in the Meadow's interior, after all." Maxt looked supremely happy.

"Why did the Seer and Sweetie go?" Claire couldn't help but ask.

Maxt and the Prince exchanged a long look. Maxt shrugged one shoulder and the Prince mimicked the gesture. "I think it has something to do with Tracy giving birth," the ruler finally stated.

Claire perked up. "Really? Tracy's having the baby? Excellent! Emma and Harry will be so happy!" The men looked at her with amazement. Claire was actually acting and looking like the girl she was for a moment, and the transformation was remarkable.

She seemed to become aware of their regard and subsided, resting her hands on the flat of her butt and slumping slightly. She was instantly back to being Jones, the quiet and intense Barracks boy.

"Remarkable," the Prince breathed. Maxt nodded his agreement.

"Have you heard anything about Jay?" Claire was desperate to get the attention off of herself.

The Prince frowned. "No. We know he was in Convergence, that he left, and then...nothing. No word from any of the settlements in the Meadows or nearby Mountains."

"What about the Marshes? Could he be in there?"

"Claire, you saw the Marshes Region," Ganth reminded her. "We do not build settlements in that region."

"Oh." Claire chewed her bottom lip. An image of Emma and Harry swam before her eyes, their expressions full of concern.

"We will continue to look for him," Maxt assured her. "Perhaps our journey into the Meadows will garner more information."

Silence fell over the room for a long moment.

"I'm going to go make sure your gear is ready to go tomorrow morning, Ganth," Claire said finally, stepping back from the table.

"That is not necessary."

Claire waved his concern away. "It's my job, remember? Can't let the Prince's entourage think I'm slacking off, now can I?" Giving the Prince and Maxt a wave, she darted from the tent.

⌒   ⌒   ⌒

Silence fell over the tent as the men measured one another in the way that men do.

Maxt spoke first. "Tread carefully. Tread very carefully with this."

Ganth looked Maxt squarely in the eye. "I understand. I hear what you are saying, and I know to do the right thing."

Maxt considered him for a long moment, and then nodded once. "Then you are dismissed to ready your men for tomorrow."

The Prince waited until Ganth had left the tent before rounding on Maxt. "Will he be honorable in this matter? It is clear he is attracted to our Claire."

"When, precisely, did she become *our* Claire?"

"The second she showed up in my Land with her bruised looking eyes and weary soul that is older than her years," the Prince declared thoughtfully. "She is changing, Maxt. Changing for the better. I do not want Ganth to jeopardize her growth. She is realizing her potential, her power, and her place in life. We need to protect that at all costs."

"Agreed, but I would stake my life and reputation on Ganth's ability to read and know his boundaries. He would never harm Claire. I am confident of that fact."

Unaware that his honor was being discussed and dissected, Ganth walked through the camp, his sharp blue eyes taking in the differences in the area from the morning to the evening. There was a lot more talking going on as the two Barracks—Capital City and Forest—merged to discuss the happenings in the Meadows and caught up with one another. In addition, the Prince traveled with several advisors, wizards, and other people, which accounted for the laughter drifting across the camp.

The campfire area was hopping, with the kitchen help from both the Prince and the Forest Barracks working to feed the larger crowd. Ganth stopped to give his men some basic instructions, informing the ones who would be going with him the next day to be ready to go first thing in the morning.

Finally, he was ready to go to his sleeping quarters. Outside, he paused a moment to collect his thoughts and school his features into a deliberately bland expression. Taking a deep breath, he entered the tent.

Claire was repacking her backpack, some of her belongings still strewn on the floor. "Almost done," she said brightly, putting some of her toiletries in the Tupperware container so they did not jostle about while walking.

Ganth crossed over to his cot and sat down, his forearms resting on his thighs, watching her. She was humming a song under her breath as she tied up her pack. Then she looked over at him, her hands stilling.

"What is it? Are Maxt and the Prince going to try and make me stay behind? Because I won't stand for it, Ganth. I won't." Her lips compressed to a mulish line.

"No, that is not it. You are going to the Meadows Region. It is, after all, why you are here, correct?"

"So what's going on? I can tell you're worried about something." Claire moved closer to him and put one hand on his leg, kneeling by the cot.

His hand covered hers. "This is what worries me." His eyes locked on their hands, his large and tanned, hers looking delicate by comparison.

"Oh." They were silent for a long while, and then Claire ventured forth into the void. "I think, and this is only my opinion, but I think that you and I both know the true score here. I'm from the World Dimension and you're from the Land. We know that even if there's an attraction between us, eventually I have to go back to the World. And I can't believe I'm going to say this, but I'm too young to have a huge relationship, to have *the* relationship, you know what I mean?"

Ganth nodded. "I know what you mean. I know that the difference in our ages is a factor as well. From what I understand of the World Dimension, our time goes faster. So every day you are in the Land, I would be getting older than you. Eventually, that would lead to problems."

"So, I'm not the love of your life, and you aren't mine." Claire held up her free hand when he would have instinctively protested. "I'm not saying we aren't attracted to each other. Hell, I'd jump your bones in a heartbeat if I didn't know it would make you feel more guilty than it would be worth." She smiled at him. "But you're the first guy I'd willingly say that about, Ganth. And that means a great deal to me."

"I have no idea what this bone jumping is all about, but I will assume it is a good thing."

"From what I hear, very good," Claire responded with a laugh. She turned her hand over in his so that their fingers intertwined. "I'm comfortable with you, Ganth. I like you, even. Strange how I can trust someone with so much after such a short period of time."

"Agreed." Ganth brought their joined hands up so he could brush a kiss across the back of her hand. "I just find I am full of regrets."

"Hmmm…" Claire tilted her head to one side and considered him evenly. "I think I'd like to kiss you, Ganth. Does that alarm you? Scare you?"

"Alarm? No. Scare? No. Fascinate? Yes." Ganth laughed, then snaked his other hand around her neck and pulled her up to meet his lips.

~   ~   ~

It was a hungry kiss, a wanting kiss, a kiss that said they both wanted it to be so much more but knew that it would not happen. Claire felt, for the first time in her life, the sensation of losing herself in the arms of a man, not caring about anything but the moment right then, right now.

When she came up for air, her cheeks flushed, Claire smiled at Ganth, whose eyes were half lidded and shining a positively sizzling blue fire. "I think I can handle being in lust with you," she told him, tracing his jaw line with her fingers. "Definitely, I can." Twining her arms around his neck, Claire rose up on her knees again and kissed him deeply.

Finally, Ganth gathered her arms from his neck and pulled back, a slight tremor in his voice. "That, I think, is enough. I am only human, after all."

Claire grinned at him. "You need more necking practice," she told him cheekishly. "Back in the World Dimension, folks can kiss all night long. Massive make out parties."

Ganth narrowed his eyes at her. "And how many of these parties have you attended, Claire?"

"None," she replied, feeling cheerful and carefree. She pulled back to her own side of the tent, pondering that sensation. What an odd, wonderful feeling. Giggling, she added, "I feel like the cat who ate the canary."

"What do cats have to do with this?"

"It's an expression." Claire laughed at his expression, the confusion warring with lust that played over his face like wind over the Meadow's grass. Shucking off her pants and reaching under her top to pull off her wraps, she continued. "Meaning I'm very content and happy. If you knew anything about me in the World Dimension, you'd know how very rare it is for me to feel this way." She tossed the wrap over her pack and stretched her arms overhead, taking in a deep breath. "Damn, that feels good."

Ganth's eyes were wide open, and he looked like he was in pain. "Looks good too," he managed in a roughly strangled voice before bolting up from the bed. "I am going for a swim." He suddenly scooped up a towel and headed for the door.

Claire tried not to giggle as she heard him mutter something about hoping the water was cold, very cold. She snuggled down into her bed and for once, drifted right off to sleep, thinking that trust was indeed a wonderful thing.

When Ganth shook her awake the next morning, Claire scrambled from the bed, eager to get going. It was still dark and the coals from the brazier had died down overnight, so the two of them kept bumping into one another. Claire was sleepy and the wraps for her chest were not cooperating as she fumbled to get them around her underneath the cover of the shirt. Ganth, who she figured had the night vision of an owl, pushed aside her hands.

Pulling the shirt up to her shoulders, he told Claire to hold it there. She'd already made the first few passes around her chest with the cloth, so Claire shrugged, figuring he couldn't really see anything anyway, and they'd certainly gotten past the point where such things should matter anyway.

He made quick work of the wraps, reaching around her body to grab and pull them tightly. Finally, he tucked the end into the top of her chest, stepping back to view the results.

"Tis a shame, Claire," he said with amusement. "Tis a crime to hide those."

Claire tugged down her shirt, giving him a mock growl. "It's not like you could see anything of them in the dark."

She could barely see his eyebrows waggle suggestively. "I have seen enough of them to know it is a shame to hide 'em," he replied staunchly. He picked up Claire's pack and handed it to her, scooping up his own as well.

The small group heading into the Region assembled by the Edge. Ganth's group consisted of himself, Claire, Telcor, Newmar and Avar, a fun loving man who gave Claire a quick wink. Maxt's group was introduced, with the names being listed as Fedal, Dentz, Santag and Joaren. Claire's eyes narrowed at the last name; she recalled from the books the Seer had given her regarding the Protectors that Joaren had accompanied Ben on his quest and was the brother of Lukus, the ex-guardsman who had died during Sasha's quest. Lukus had also been the counterpart to Sasha's Worlder husband, William. He was a tall man, younger than Ganth and Maxt, with brown hair and pale blue eyes that were indeed reminiscent of William's, if Claire remembered correctly. He caught Claire looking at him and gave her a forthright stare in return. Claire blinked and looked away.

Lukus had been swayed by Evil before he died. Claire wondered what, if any, kind of relationship the two had prior to Lukus' death. He bore watching.

They set off into the Meadows Region before the sun had even graced the horizon of the ocean. Every other guardsman carried a torch to help light the way. Claire walked in the middle of the pack, having stationed herself right behind Joaren—who she wanted to keep an eye on—and in front of Newmar. She did not have a torch but both Newmar and Joaren carried one.

Maxt set a brutal pace, practically jogging over the grassy plains. Claire was grateful she had taken the time to lighten her pack the night before as her lungs quickly began to burn. She was less appreciative of Ganth's binding abilities as her chest heaved to suck in enough oxygen. It was like being in the New York City Marathon wearing a freaking corset. Soon it was all she could do to concentrate on running and breathing.

Gradually, the sun rose behind them, casting long shadows over the plains. Claire barely noticed the passing Meadows Region landscape. When she did, it was to register the destruction left behind from the many storms that had hit the area.

Late in the morning, they stopped to eat. Claire collapsed, exhausted, only eating when Newmar urged her under his breath. She ate lethargically, watching as Ganth and Maxt walked up the next hill, deep in discussion. Claire was disgusted that neither man, damn their hides, was even breathing heavy.

"It gets easier," Joaren commented suddenly, drawing her attention. She gave him a distrustful look, causing the man to raise his eyebrows. "Begging your pardon, what did I do to you?" His tone half joking, half not.

"I do not know you."

"I am a member of the Prince's Guard," Joaren commented icily. "Generally, that is enough to warrant common respect and courtesy."

A blush started creeping up her neck. "You are right. I am new to the Guard and its ways. Forgive me if I offended you." But don't think I'm not going to keep an eye on you, she warned him silently as Joaren appeared to take her apology at face value.

They continued on their way, resuming the punishing pace of the morning. Now, as the sun arched overhead, the heat added to Claire's discomfort. To her consternation, Newmar and Joaren had switched places, and now the guardsman she mistrusted the most was directly behind her.

She kept her eyes glued to Newmar's back and willed herself to keep up. When Maxt finally called a halt, late in the day, for their dinner break, Claire sat down where she stood, breathing heavily. A shadow fell over her.

"I will eat in a minute, Newmar," she said, without bothering to look up.

Joaren hunkered down next to her, offering her a water skein. "You need to drink. And you need to go and loosen the bindings around your chest so you can breathe easier."

His words worked better than any cool down shower would have. Claire was instantly bathed in a cold sweat. She stared at him while her mind went completely, totally blank.

His light blue eyes were full of nothing but concern. "I have no idea why you are hiding who you are and what you are, and I assume your Barracks Leader is aware that you are a girl. But if you want to keep up for the night portion of the hike, you need to loosen those bindings."

"Night portion?" Claire squeaked, then shook her head. "I do not know what you are talking about with the whole bindings and girl thing."

Joaren gave her a disbelieving look and corresponding snort. "I have been running behind you for hours. You have the hips of a girl, and, like the rest of us, you took off your vest when you got hot. Your shirt plastered to your back with the sweat. I could clearly see the bindings, Jones. I am not stupid. I kept close to your back so no one else could see. But I am telling you, you are going to keel over if you do not loosen them up so you can take a deep breath."

"Why would you help me if you think I am deceiving people?" It seemed like a, well, Evil thing to do, in Claire's opinion.

"Ganth and Maxt appear to trust you. So does Sweetie. So, shall I trust you."

"You were Lukus' brother," Claire blurted without thinking. "So, I don't know if I can trust you."

- 2 6 -

▼

Racing the Storm

Joaren's crystal blue eyes widened then narrowed dangerously. "You *are* a Worlder." It was not a question. Claire found herself nodding slowly. "I thought as much from the speech patterns, but...I understand now. Hiding from someone Evil, I take it?" Claire again nodded, figuring the gig was up anyway.

"A man from Ben's dimension is following me." Claire watched his reaction carefully. She considered herself to be very good at reading people, and his reaction was one of dismay. Maybe she should give him the benefit of the doubt. Everyone else trusted him, after all. "We think he is working with Evil."

Joaren looked out over the horizon for a long moment. Then he shook his head, his blue eyes full of compassion. "That must be killing Ben. To find someone of his dimension, then discover he is with Evil. Ben will hate that with every breath he takes."

Claire felt herself softening somewhat toward the man. It was clear he knew Ben, and his concern was genuine. Yet she was reluctant to trust him fully, especially since he knew her secret. The man's blue eyes fastened on her again.

"Seriously, Jones, loosen the bindings." Joaren tone was matter of fact as he stood back up. "I have been on many, many hikes with Maxt. He is going to set an even faster pace once the sun sets and it cools off. Trust me on this."

Claire nodded grudgingly. She rose and walked away from the others, up and over the next hill. Once out of site of the men, she dropped to her knees and hurriedly reached under her shirt to make adjustments to the wraps. Yet no matter how hard she tried, it was impossible for her to get them loose enough to breath without showing off her bust line.

"Damn it, damn it, damn it!" Claire muttered under her breath as she frantically tried to finish the job before someone came looking for her. Finally she compromised by leaving the wrappings looser but putting her hot vest back on.

The line of the vest did mask the unmistakable curve of her breasts to some degree. She'd be hot, but she'd be concealed. And able to breathe, Claire inhaled deeply. The air was scented with rain, fresh and cleansing to her battered and bruised lungs.

Rain.

Shit.

Claire looked to the horizon then pelted back over the hill. She skidded to a halt in front of the Prince, Maxt and Ganth, who were talking together in low voices.

"Storm's coming," Claire gasped out, pointing over the hill. "Big one, looks like rain and wind. I didn't see a tornado, but you never know…"

The last words were spoken to the backs of the men as they raced up the hill. The guardsmen with them followed, Claire huffing along after them, feeling much better for having loosened her wraps. At the top of the hill, everyone stopped and gawked at the spectacle. Above them, the sky remained the same impossible blue as always. Ahead, the horizon was a mass of bluish black rolling clouds. As they watched in fascinated horror, lightening forked down out of the clouds, scorching the earth below. The winds on the ground were tossing the trees and grass about, almost flattening them with gusts of gale force bursts. The width of the storm was huge, disappearing on either side of them. There was no way they could outrun it by going around the monster. Whatever was making the storms was obviously getting better at producing them, Claire thought absently as she watched a small tree uprooted by a vicious gust of wind.

Claire looked around wildly. They were out in the open. Since they would not be able to outrun the storm, which was fast approaching, they'd have to ride out the storm somehow. Even now, the sky was darkening as it approached.

Maxt turned to the men, his gaze resting briefly on Claire. The wind and rain and hail howled furiously, creating a racket that made it difficult to hear one another speak. "We will have to take cover the best we can," he yelled over the approaching storm. "Lay on your packs, but if the wind takes a pack, let it. Nothing is more important than your safety!"

They found a small hollow half way down the hill, where a ledge had been formed. It was only about two feet deep, but it was better than nothing. The men wedged themselves in, backs against the hill and their packs under their legs. Claire felt particularly squished as both Ganth and Maxt practically overlapped their huge shoulders over her body. The Prince of the Land hunkered down next to Maxt.

Ganth looked over his shoulder at Claire, his blue gaze intent on hers. He crossed his arms over his chest, and under the cover of his sheltering arm, reached for her hand and held it tightly in his. His gaze returned to the front, but he gently squeezed her hand.

Maxt watched the sky. It changed from blue to gray to black with almost the same kind of suddenness that one experienced when crossing over a Region's end. "Here it comes," Maxt called out to the men, who, along with Claire, braced themselves.

The wind kicked down the hill like a live wire, whipping into their recessed hiding place with a vengeance. Claire's hair flew around, getting in her eyes and making it difficult to see what was happening with any kind of clarity. Plus, the amount of grit and dirt in the air didn't make it very appealing to have her eyes open anyway.

Then the hail started pelting them. Golf ball sized and hard as hell. Claire flinched when one nailed her leg right above where her boot ended, feeling like a bullet had gone through her leg. *That's gonna leave a mark.* The area stung and throbbed. One large piece of hail bounced up and caught Maxt in the temple, leaving a streak of blood trickling down his face. Wiggling, Claire ripped a piece of material from the end of her chest wrapping and pressed it to the cut, earning her a grateful glance from the man.

The rain started coming down in sheets, the wind driving it almost sideways. Luckily, the wind was blowing toward the Beaches Region, which meant it wasn't directed at their faces. Yet they were quickly getting drenched. The rain fell like sharp needles, stinging their skin as it hit them.

A large, uprooted tree came barreling down the hill at one point, knocking a few of the men out of their place along the hillside. They scrambled to get back in place, the wind tugging at their bodies and threatening to suck them away. Claire gave a halting sigh of relief when they all were back in their place along the ledge. The entire ground shook as if a herd of elephants raced over it.

When the lightening started to strike, Claire felt terror hit her in the stomach as surely as a bolt of the wicked stuff sparking in the sky. Wind, rain and hail she could tolerate and get through, but the random bursts of electricity bolting down out of the heavens were just too unpredictable, too deadly for her. The acrid smell of the strikes burned her nose. One hit directly in front of them, the white hot flash burning into her retinas so that when she closed her eyes, Claire could still see the imprint of the streak against her eyelids.

She could barely see anything now, the wind and rain combined with the frequent lightening strikes created a tableau of nature's ferocity at its absolute worst. Her feet were numb from the cold and wet rain, her face seemed like it had been rubbed raw. Her knee throbbed to beat the band, and her hand clutched Ganth's frantically. With every gust of the wind or slap of rain, Ganth and Maxt were alternatively shoved and pulled from Claire's body.

It was impossible to tell if the storm lasted an hour or six. The rain continued to pelt down, alternating with hail and vicious bolts of lightening. Claire closed her eyes and leaned her forehead against Ganth's shoulder, wishing it would just be over. Her mind rang from the noise and the wind and the rain. She could barely think, let alone analyze what was happening.

With the same suddenness with which it all started, the storm ended. Overhead, the black clouds continued to roll inexorably toward the Beaches and overhead, a veil of stars was revealed as the clouds passed by.

For several long moments, all that could be heard was the dripping of rain water from various plants and people, along with the harsh breathing of the men huddled in the shadow of the hill.

Maxt heaved a deep breath and hauled himself to his feet, Ganth close behind him. Claire barely remembered to let his hand go before he stood up. The two guardsmen leaders went up and down the row, checking on the men and making sure everyone was all right. Several men were bleeding from various cuts and bruises caused by the hail or flying debris, but luckily no one was seriously hurt.

Claire was reluctant to try and stand just yet. Her muscles shook as if she had just run a hard sprint and her knee throbbed painfully. She wasn't at all sure she would be able to make it to her feet.

"You all right there, Jones?" Joaren asked as he stood up from his spot a few feet from her. Claire nodded and rubbed her hand over her knee. There was a knot the size of a golf ball below her kneecap. Just touching it made shards of pain lance through her system. Damn.

Claire pushed herself off the ground and gingerly tested the leg. It was sore, but bore her weight. That was a good sign. She noticed Ganth watching her, and she gave him a sunny smile and a thumbs up. There was no way she was going to give him any kind of excuse to leave her behind. She'd keep up.

She had to. Claire reached down and grabbed her pack, slinging it over her shoulder.

"The rain is going to make the grass wet and slippery," Maxt called out to the men. "Watch your step and keep up." He gave Claire an inscrutable look and leaned over to speak into Joaren's ear. The man nodded and took his place in line behind Claire. They set off over the hill.

The grass proved as treacherous as Maxt had predicted. The men slipped and fell and continued to push forward at a rapid pace. Claire's knee ached and it was positively agony to go downhill. She sucked it up and kept going. Once or twice she started to slide but Joaren was always right there, catching her under her arm or grabbing the back of her vest to help her along. She was actually grateful to the man, even if she didn't fully trust him yet.

"What did Maxt tell you right before we took off?" Claire asked him once, as he caught her right before she took a nose dive down the side of a rather steep hill.

"To keep an eye on you, make sure your hurt leg does not give out on you. Unlike you, Maxt trusts me." Joaren's voice radiated his amusement. "He also knows that Ganth cannot break tradition of bringing up the rear of the expedition to attend you."

"I don't need an eye kept on me."

Joaren's eyebrow rose. "I would say you do, given that you are refusing to admit you have a bad leg there, Jones." He laughed as Claire growled at him in disgust.

It was late, probably after midnight, before Maxt finally called a halt. He leaned down and felt the grass. "It is dry." Moving his hand a foot over, he pulled it up and looked at it. "Wet here."

"This is where the storm started," Ganth deduced, noting the grass and how it was waving gently in the night breeze more inland, and laid flat in the storm's path.

"That is what I would guess." Maxt stood. "Right. We will camp here, and start looking over the area in the morning. My recommendation is to lay out your pallets on the dry side of the grass." He assigned a few men to be the lookout and then gestured to the rest to bed down.

The men laid out their blankets and rolled into them, with hardly a word spoken. The hike and the storm had exhausted them. Ganth made sure his pallet was close to Claire, who was huddled under her blankets, trying not to shiver in her damp clothes. She was also trying her best to ignore the sharp ache in her shin. The lump seemed to have assumed iceberg proportions, throbbing in time with her heartbeat.

"Jones?" came Ganth's low voice.

"Yeah?"

"Is your leg all right?"

"No."

He was quiet for a long moment. "Can you continue?"

"Yes."

"Are you lying to me?"

"Probably."

Ganth chuckled. "I will look at it in the morning. We will decide then."

Claire nodded, even though he probably could not see her in the darkness. She didn't dare speak, because tears of pain were streaking down her face, and she didn't want him to hear her crying.

She thought she'd been successful until Ganth gave a deep sigh and inched his pallet closer and turned his back to Claire, allowing her to shelter behind his bulk, one hand reaching behind him to give her shoulder a squeeze.

Claire got as close to his warm body as she dared. Gradually, the chills racing through her body stopped, and she was able to drift into an uncomfortable sleep. Every shift of her body sent pain through her leg, but she managed to doze for the rest of the long night.

As dawn streaked the eastern sky, Claire sat up in her pallet, bleary and exhausted. The other men were still sleeping, including Ganth, save for the two men who were prowling the perimeter of the camp. Even the indomitable Maxt was propped against a large rock, his chin on his chest as he slept sitting up.

Claire struggled out of her damp blankets, moving sluggishly and painfully. Every joint in her body seemed to ache in the cool morning air. She pulled up her pant leg to get a look at the bruise on her upper shin. The area was so swollen she was almost unable to get the material over her knee to look at the area.

She winced as the wound came into view. It was the vicious purply-yellow that only the worst kind of bruises seemed to attain. Dead center in the bruise was a raised, red knot, roughly the size of her palm. The entire area was swollen and tender to the touch, and her knee appeared to be affected as well. This was not good.

To her left, she heard someone moan and glanced in that direction. Joaren was asleep on his pallet, his face drawn in pain. Thinking that was weird—Joaren hadn't hurt himself in the storm—she turned in his direction.

Joaren shifted in his sleep, restless and covered in sweat. Suspecting a fever, Claire reached out to feel his forehead. It was damp but cool. Under her hand, Joaren's skin writhed and twitched with his discomfort. Suddenly his crystal blue eyes opened and his gaze bored into Claire's, but she doubted he recognized her.

"Safe. She has to be safe!"

"I'm sure she is," soothed Claire automatically. The man's utter despair was heart wrenching to witness, his eyes still seeing the dream he was trapped within. "You need to wake up, Joaren. Come on, wake up."

With a shudder, Joaren surged up, his breath sucking in deeply. He looked at Claire, bewildered. "What is happening to me?"

His whisper was full of such pain. Claire couldn't help but respond to the sincerity. "What was it, Joaren? A dream?"

"The likes of which I have never experienced…it was dreadful. Frightening. Confusing. But…she is safe now. She is healing."

"Who is she?"

"I do not know."

Claire gazed at him. "Dude, you gotta talk to the Seer or Prince about this. What if Evil is trying to manipulate you in your dreams?"

Again, Joaren shuddered, his entire body wracked by the motion. "I have spoken to both. They are aware, and the Seer does not feel I am touched by Evil. But…the dreams are very vivid. No matter. I have had them my whole life. They are usually a comfort to me, but today? Not much is comforting at the moment." He gave Claire a wan smile and rose to his feet, walking briskly toward the hill for some privacy.

Claire shifted and winced at the resulting jolt to her knee. Falling ass first into the muddy ground, she growled low in her throat. To her disgust, Ganth chose that moment to appear behind her. He peered over her shoulder at the leg. "What is that word you like to spout when something is not good? Oh yes–shit. That looks like shit, Jones."

"Feels that way too," Claire admitted, trying to work the pant leg back over the wound.

Ganth stayed her hand. "Let me make a poultice to help the swelling, or we will be carrying you by mid morning."

Claire nodded and worked on rolling up her blankets while Ganth pulled several small vials from his backpack. He explained to her that since no wizards—the traditional medical personnel of the Land since the Healer line went extinct—were assigned to the Barracks on a regular basis, he had long ago learned some herbal remedies to assist his men. He mixed some herbs in a small basin, adding a few drops of oil from another vial. Then he put the paste on Claire's leg.

It felt icy and warm at the same time, the smell as soothing as the feel of the poultice on her skin. Ganth took a bandana out of his pack and wrapped it snuggly around Claire's leg, then helped her work her pants over the bandage. By the time he finished, the rest of the group had started waking up and breakfast rations were passed around.

~ 27 ~

▼

TRACKING THE BEAST

After breakfast, the men spread out in a horizontal line, putting roughly ten feet between them. The plan was to have the men march across the area of the Meadows, looking for anything out of the ordinary. Claire took her place in line, resolutely ignoring her aching leg. She wasn't surprised when Joaren stationed himself to one side of her and Ganth showed up on the other. She grinned wryly and rolled her eyes. Her personal bodyguards.

"Keep a sharp eye out for anything strange or different," Maxt yelled down the line, where he was standing near the Prince. "If you see something you feel we need to look at more closely, give a whistle or a shout and Ganth or myself will come over immediately. Am I understood?" At the resounding affirmative, Maxt gestured for them to get moving.

Claire's eyes swept the ground in front of her. All she could see was green grass, some dirt, gray rocks and a scattering of wildflowers. Every so often, a jeweled grasshopper or butterfly would explode from the greenery, startled by the tromping boots of the guardsmen. She saw nothing that looked like a machine or instrument. Nothing but the ordinary flora and fauna of the Meadows Region. At least they weren't racing over the plains. Claire was honestly afraid her leg would not handle that kind of strain.

Periodically, a shout or whistle rent the air. Everyone stopped where they were standing and watched as Maxt or Ganth, along with the Prince, strode over to the man who had called out. Claire felt herself holding her breath, watching intently. Inevitably, the man investigating rose, shaking his head. Claire's shoulders would slump and then they would go back to marching along slowly, scanning the area.

They reached the opposite side of the storm-free area around midday. In front of them, the vista showed clear signs of storm damage racing toward the Mountains, which loomed in the distance.

After a quick break during which they ate more rations, Claire sat on a rock, rubbing her leg absently. The throb had subsided to a dull ache, but the muscles around the area were definitely strained. Joaren sat nearby, his eyes scanning the horizon.

Ganth came over to them, his hands on his hips. "We are going to move closer to the Marshes, and walk back across the area, cover another swatch. You doing all right, there, Jones?" he asked Claire point blank.

Claire's hand dropped to her side. "Doing fine, sir." When Ganth looked askance at Joaren, who nodded slowly, Claire smacked the rock she sat on in frustration. "Excuse me, sir, but I answered the question. You don't need to verify with Joaren."

Ganth tilted his head at her, giving Claire a look that clearly said he did not buy her answers when it came to her physical condition. Claire barely resisted the urge to stick her tongue out at him. Barely.

They moved down into place and at a word from Maxt, started back across the area. The trek back was similar to the one before. More green grass, brown dirt, gray rocks, brilliantly colored flowers.

Halfway across, there came a shout from one of the men, but instead of pointing down, he was pointing at the sky. Claire jerked her head around, expecting to see another storm. Nothing was visible but the brilliantly blue sky. Then she squinted.

A dark spot was in the sky. It was getting larger and larger. She glanced around, and noticed that while Maxt did not look happy, the sight in the sky didn't alarm him. Claire shaded her eyes with one hand, and realized why Maxt had the frown on his face.

It was the Griffin. Obviously, the Seer and Sweetie had finished whatever it was that needed to be done and had returned to help in the search. The creature spiraled down slowly, then landed with a gentle thwomp near Maxt.

The Seer slid off the beast, giving it a fond pat on the neck. Then she reached up and plucked Sweetie off the Griffin's back, allowing the child to also say goodbye, which she did by flinging her arms around the creature's neck.

Claire was close enough to see Maxt's thunderous expression. Clearly he did not want the Seer or her charge in the interior of the Meadows Region. After the storm yesterday, Claire couldn't blame him. Sweetie would never be able to handle that kind of adverse condition.

The Seer greeted Maxt with a light kiss on the cheek, seemingly oblivious to his displeasure. Sweetie launched herself at the large man, and his face softened somewhat as she hugged him tightly around the neck. The Seer and the Prince immediately launched into a deep conversation.

Soon the little child wiggled from Maxt's arms and raced across the Meadows to Claire's side. Her face held an expression that Claire could not place. Then she realized it was anxiousness.

"Not nice place," Sweetie announced, sticking her finger in her mouth as she halted in front of Claire. "You fix it. You fix it now."

"I'm tryin', Sweetie, I'm tryin'," Claire muttered, shoving her hair back from her face.

"Hurt?" Sweetie asked, pointing a wet finger at Claire's leg.

"A little."

"Not supposed ta be here," said the little girl.

"I know. It's a dangerous place. But it's where we need to be at the moment."

Maxt gave another yell and motioned for the men to come in. They did, straggling closer until they were all gathered around the Captain and the Griffin.

"I have asked the Griffin if he would consent to taking me up so I can look over the area from the sky," Maxt told them all. "And he has agreed. Maybe something will be more evident from that angle. I want you all to stay here, and keep together. Ganth, you are in charge until I return. Joaren, you are my second. Keep watch."

Ganth nodded, knowing that by that statement, Maxt was also transferring the care and well being of both the Seer and Sweetie. Joaren also nodded.

Maxt got on the Griffin with the ease and familiarity of many a mounting. His lips were compressed and thin, and when the Griffin gathered himself to launch into the sky, the man's face blanched to a pure white.

"He doesn't like heights much, does he?" Claire murmured to Sweetie, who shook her head with the kind of bemused sarcasm that only a the very young can manage with finesse.

The men milled about, sitting on rocks and softly talking to one another. Claire joined the Prince, Joaren and Ganth by the Seer, still holding Sweetie. The Seer was telling Joaren and the Prince about the birth of Tracy's child, and this was a story that Claire very much wanted to hear. Sweetie kept pulling at her arm, but Claire resisted, wanting to know more about the baby and how Orli had traveled to the World Dimension and all. It was fascinating. It was also a relief to see the Seer acting so comfortably around Joaren, which solidified his trustworthiness once and for all.

The guardsman listened intently from his perch on a rock, asking questions of the Seer about the birth and health of the mother and daughter. He was also intensely interested in the exchange of Orli and Liz for a day. Claire had to bite her tongue several times to keep from asking questions, for there were far too many men from Maxt's contingent around.

Sweetie gave her hand another, rather vicious tug. It nearly knocked Claire off balance. "Sweetie, knock it off," Claire said to her. "You can't keep pulling on me like that, my leg hurts too much." As she spoke, she looked down at the little girl in exasperation. The expression raced from her face as Claire glimpsed the child's face. It was full of horror and fright.

Claire knelt by the child. "Sweetie, what is it?" The Seer also paused in her conversation with Joaren, looking over at the child with a quizzical expression.

Sweetie was staring at Joaren, her blue eyes wide with terror. "That's Joaren," Claire said softly. "You know him, right?" Some of her earlier doubts came rising up in her like lava.

Then Sweetie nodded, but her eyes were glued to Joaren. Claire looked at him. He was just sitting there on a brown rock, his face puzzled and confused, but certainly harmless enough. Claire turned back to Sweetie, then a thought struck her head like a missile and she found herself wheeling toward the guardsman again.

Joaren was sitting on a brown rock. Rock. Brown.

Brown?

In her trek across the Region, and back again, Claire had never seen a brown rock in the Meadows. Gray, sure, tons of shades of gray. But not one, single, solitary brown rock.

"Get up *now*," Claire barked at Joaren.

He stared at her, dumbfounded. Claire growled deep in her throat and rushed him, knocking him off the rock. They rolled several yards away from his perch with the force of her tackle. The other guardsmen stopped all activity, becoming alert.

"What the hell is wrong with you?" Ganth said to Claire, picking her up by the back of her vest and setting her on her feet again as Claire winced and hopped, having banged her hurt shin pretty badly in the tackle. "That was an unprovoked attack, Cl–Jones!"

"The rock, the rock, the rock," Claire chanted.

"What are you talking about? There are rocks everywhere," the Prince said, gesturing around him in an exasperated fashion.

"Not brown ones," Claire said, pointing at the large rock that had been Joaren's seat. Ganth stilled, his blue gaze narrowing on the rock in question. The Prince also focused on the rock with an intent look, his hands immediately starting to glow a soft white color.

"What the…" he crept closer to the rock, Claire right behind him.

"It is too smooth to be a natural rock," the Seer observed from one side of Ganth.

"And the wrong color," Claire agreed from the other side of him.

"Bad turtle," Sweetie declared succinctly, hanging onto Ganth's leg.

"Turtle?" The Seer turned her puzzled gaze to Sweetie, and then smacked her forehead. "Darn my obstinate hide! You've been talking about turtles for weeks, and I just assumed it was a real turtle. You meant this one, didn't you Sweetie?"

"Yep, yep, yep," Sweetie chanted. "Bad turtle." She poked at the thing with one finger then looked at Claire. "You fix it."

Ganth suddenly seemed to realize that he had Claire, Sweetie and the Seer practically on top of the thing that could be causing the destruction in the Meadows. He pulled them all away quickly, and ordered the men to stand back. He and the Prince, however, remained close to the rock, which made Claire heave a huffy sigh, one that Sweetie imitated with perfect clarity.

Ganth put his fingers to his lips and gave a sharp whistle. An answering sound was heard from the direction of the Griffin and within moments the creature was gliding in for a landing.

Maxt slid off the back of the Griffin, planting his feet on the earth with a heartfelt sigh. Ganth strode up to him and soon the two were walking toward the brown rock. Claire squared her shoulders and followed. She'd found the thing—well, with Sweetie's help—and it was her purpose in being in the Land, after all.

"Jones, back off." This came from Maxt, and Claire stubbornly shook her head.

"My quest." Squatting down next to the rock, ignoring the pain in her leg at the move, Claire peered at the thing's surface. Over her head, Ganth and Maxt exchanged annoyed looks, but the Prince merely grinned.

"We do not know if it is safe," Ganth protested, and Claire shot him a quelling look.

"Of course it's not safe," Claire said with surprisingly good humor. "But that isn't the point, is it? I need to know what to do. I have to get close to it eventually."

"Maybe finding it was all you were supposed to do," Maxt pointed out. Claire frowned as she perused the brown rock's surface. Was the Captain of the Guard correct? Had she done all she was supposed to do?

The Seer spoke before Claire could marshal her thoughts. "Claire, look at the little tree over to the right. The one next to the clump of purple flowers. Does it look like a Land Tree to you?"

"No, not at all."

"Then your job here is not done." The Seer gave the men a glare that dared them to continue their argument.

"Go ahead and look, Jones," the Prince said finally, quelling any further arguments.

Ganth and Maxt gave up trying to convince the Seer or Claire to back away from the rock, and they all continued to examine it. Now that she had a chance to see it up close, Claire realized that the surface of the rock was extremely smooth—too smooth to be considered natural. It appeared to have been in the ground for a while, given the amount of growth around the base of the thing. She could not see any way that this stupid thing could be wreaking the havoc that it did on the Land.

Suddenly, the Seer pulled on Claire's arm and pointed. They all watched as a small round hole appeared in the top of the rock, opening to the size of a quarter. A puff of dense air escaped the hole, drifting up to the sky. As they watched, the puff coalesced and started to grow, spreading into clouds the higher it got. Within a ten-minute period of time, the puff had become a gigantic thunderhead, steaming toward the Mountains Region.

"Is it some sort of machine?" the Seer wondered aloud. "It doesn't look like one, granted, but…" She eyed the storm dubiously.

"I thought complex machines didn't work in the Land." Claire tapped her lips with her finger as she circled the rock.

"We should flip it over," Ganth suggested. He and Maxt tried to pry it out of the dirt, but the thing was either too heavy or too anchored for them to budge it. They also tried their swords, working the points under the edge of the rock to try and lever it over. It became quickly apparent that their swords would snap in two before the heavy thing moved.

Claire and the Seer exchanged one look as the men were trying their sword routine, and they started searching for longer, heavy poles to use. They found a few long branches, but the pieced proved too flimsy. A few of the men jogged at a fast clip to the storm tossed region and came back with a few sturdy poles, taken from trees uprooted by the winds.

While they were gone, the others started clearing the area around the rock, rolling boulders and stones away, clearing the grass and flowers from the site to attain better access. Ganth and Maxt dug a trench around the base of the rock, trying to ascertain if it was buried in the ground. As they dug down several inches, they were happy to discover it was a solitary rock and not part of the landscape's bedrock.

Next, the men pushed the sturdy branches under the edge of the rock. When the poles were placed under the rock, using another boulder to lever it down, it took four men to lift the rock and topple it to one side.

The bottom part of the rock was as smooth as the upper curved side. The bottom side, as it became exposed, proved to be flat as a board. Claire could not understand how the rock had stayed so anchored to the ground with such a glassy smooth surface.

Claire got her nose right to the surface of the rock, peering at it closely. She heard a gurgling noise coming faintly from the inside of the rock. Tilting her head she considered the options.

"I don't think it's a machine," she said finally. "I think Sweetie is right. I think it's a turtle of some sort. An animal. Creature. Thingy. Turtle."

"A turtle that spits out storms?" Maxt's furrowed brow conveyed his skepticism of the assessment.

The Seer tapped her cheek with one finger. "In a way, it makes sense. Evil knows a machine won't work, so he finds a creature that will do massive amounts of damage and transports it to our dimension."

"It seems like a long shot," Ganth admitted.

"Regardless if it is a machine or a creature, I say we destroy it," Maxt declared, drawing his sword.

"Oh, I don't think that will…" Claire's voice died off as Maxt attacked what she now considered to be a creature, trying to cleave it in two with his sword.

The first blow of the blade had the sword bouncing off the shell, the force causing it to fly from Maxt's hand and end up yards away, buried to its hilt in the Meadow's soil.

"Congratulations, you just successfully slew a daffodil," Claire said to Maxt, who scowled at her.

"Crack it open with rocks?" Ganth suggested, although his voice was not very confident. Maxt shook his head.

"I doubt it will work, but give it a try," he said to the Barracks Leader.

The shell proved too hard to break with the tools they had at hand. They tried swords, knives, poles and other rocks, all to no avail.

Fire was the next suggestion. They piled twigs and grass around the turtle, careful to keep a cleared area to avoid a wild fire in the Region. When the fire was laid, the thing shuddered and gave an eerie moan. To Claire, that confirmed that it was alive. She almost felt sorry for it until she remembered the devastation of the Meadows Barracks. Even Godzilla got shot down by the Japanese Air Force at the end of the movie, so she had to harden her heart.

When the fire died down, the shell was still intact. There weren't even any scorch marks on the creature.

"Now what?" the Seer asked, holding her nose. The only tangible result of the fire was that the turtle had released a horrible fishy stench.

"Let me try," the Prince suggested. When the power orb he sent hurtling at the turtle's shell bounced back, nearly taking off Newmar's head, it was apparent that even an Oracle's power could not penetrate this creature.

"What else could we do to it?" Maxt wondered aloud. "We just do not have the technology to kill it."

"That thing smells worse than the Marshes," Ganth said, waving his hand in front of his face.

Marshes. Something clicked inside Claire's brain. She stared at him, a smile covering her face.

"That's it!" she screeched, and threw herself at him, covering his face with happy kisses. "You are brilliant and don't even know it!"

~ 28 ~

▼

QUICKLY, QUICKLY!

Ganth managed to grab Claire's arms and pulled her from him forcibly. He noticed that several of Maxt's men were staring at him, rather horrified. Shocked mutters were racing through the Capital City crowd, while Ganth's men smothered smiles and stifled chuckles.

"She is a girl," he told Maxt's men rather harshly. Claire ignored him, racing for her pack. She grabbed it and went for the Griffin, ducking past the Prince and Maxt, who were barking questions at her a mile a minute.

"Excuse me, Mr. Griffin. Can you get me to the Marshes?" Claire asked the beast. "You know, as quickly as possible?" The huge orange eye of the creature assessed her, and then nodded slowly. Claire scrambled on board, clutching the lion's fur at the ruff of its neck, sinking her fingers into where the fur changed over to the feathers of its eagle head. She felt the Griffin gathering itself and braced for the leap into the sky.

Within seconds, she was high over the Meadows, heading for the grayish green fog of the Marshes. At the Edge of the Marsh, the Griffin landed on the Meadows side. Claire slid off and raced for the Region's Edge. She turned her pack upside down and impatiently waited for everything to topple out.

"Aha!" She snatched up the Tupperware container that Emma had loaded her cookies in. "Damn, I hope this works." She dumped out the toiletries she'd placed inside. Flipping off the lid, she eyed the large container. Hopefully it would be big enough.

"The Seer said to use what those who love me gave me," Claire said to herself, staring at the tub and licking her lips nervously. "Emma is the only one I know who would care enough about me to send me with cookies, so this container must be the key to my being here."

Standing, Claire took a deep breath. Now that she was here, she wasn't exactly sure how to proceed. She walked to the Edge of the Region and knelt by the murky water.

"Quicksilver is attracted by living flesh," Claire whispered aloud. "Alrighty then." She held the tub firmly in her right hand and plunged her left hand into the water.

The water felt strangely thick, almost as if there were particles suspended in the liquid. It was warm and rather, well, squishy, if Claire had to label it. She waited, watching the shallows for the telltale gleam of silver.

They came silently, streaming toward her hand. Claire kept her eyes on the deathly strings, her heart ratcheting up a notch in fear and anticipation. Keeping her hand steady was difficult given how much she was shaking.

When the Quicksilver had gotten within a few inches of her hand, Claire pulled her hand out of the water and scooped some of the creatures into the Tupperware with the other. She misjudged, though, and missed most of the strands, capturing only a few in her plastic container, but it was enough for her to do some tests on the deadly material.

Claire was careful to keep her fingers out of the basin of the bowl. She put the bowl on the grass and watched the Quicksilver to see what would happen to it when in captivity. The few pieces she had caught milled about in the bottom of the Tupperware, banging against the sides as if it was unaware it was contained.

Claire was satisfied that the stuff would not try and climb out the side of the bowl.

She carefully carried it back to the Edge of the swamp and tipped the Quicksilver back into the murky water. She needed more than just a couple of strands to get rid of that turtle thing.

It took three more tries but finally, Claire was able to get a good tub full of swarming silvery strands. She hoped it would be enough. She snapped the lid on the tub carefully—she did not want that deadly mess dumping all over her and the Griffin mid flight—and approached the Griffin. The beast had watched her endeavors from several feet away, sitting on its haunches and tilting its bird like head with almost human like curiosity.

When she got close to the Griffin, the beast tossed its head, backing up from her. Clearly, it did not relish the thought of having Quicksilver anywhere near it. It was fairly prancing on its feet in nervousness.

"Please, I need to get this back to the turtle," Claire pleaded. "I promise, it won't get out. Tupperware is made to be a solid seal, after all." She showed the beast the bowl and its lid tightly on, even tilting it upside down to prove that the lid would not come off during flight.

The Griffin reached out and poked at the bowl, its beak thunking the plastic with a solid sound. Seemingly satisfied with his exploration, the beast turned to the side so that Claire could climb aboard.

It was difficult flying over the Meadows while holding onto the Griffin and the tub. Claire was reluctant to hug the plastic container to her body or rest it against the Griffin. The thought of what it contained was rather horrifying. Yet, she managed to keep her grip. As the Griffin spiraled down toward the group of people clustered by the weather turtle, a distortion some twenty feet from where they stood caught her attention.

"Wait!" she shrieked into the wind whistling by, simultaneously pulling up on the Griffin's feathers. The beast hissed at her but complied, beating its wings to achieve some height.

It was difficult to focus when sitting on a beast moving through the air, but Claire managed to find the spot that seemed strange. Using her knees to guide the Griffin—she'd learned her lesson about pulling on his feathers—Claire circled the spot.

Yeah, something was not right about that area. The wind rippled the grass around the spot, but within that perfect circle, not a single blade moved. The space seemed duller, somehow, than the surroundings, less bright, less vibrant. No doubt about it, there was something weird with that section of the Meadows Region.

Finally she allowed the Griffin to land. She slid from the beast and leaned against him a moment while her legs got used to being on solid ground. Firming her grip on the Tupperware, she headed for the group by the weather turtle.

"Where did you go?" Ganth demanded, striding up to Claire and standing in front of her, blocking her path.

"You cannot just leave willy-nilly and not explain," Maxt agreed, glowering at her.

Claire held out the Tupperware container in her hands. "I've got Quicksilver in here," she declared. She noticed with grim satisfaction that her statement had the men, and the rest of their party, taking an involuntary step or two back. "It kills all living things, right?"

There was a cautious nod from the group, all eyes still fastened on the bowl in her hands, as if they were afraid it might explode and rain down silver death on them all.

"That turtle thing is alive. The Quicksilver may be able to kill it." Anticipation had her cheeks stained with bright color. She started to walk past the men, eager to get on with it. "At the very least, it should encase it so that the turtle can't fart anymore storms."

"Quicksilver…" The Seer's eyes were assessing. "It could work."

"There's something else," Claire said, setting the Tupperware on the ground, causing the contents to slosh and froth. "Come with me."

She led the way to the area of the Meadows that had seemed different and paused. "Do you see it?"

"See what?" asked Ganth.

She gestured with her hand. "This seems off to me. Don't you see it? There's like, well, a bubble here. Something different."

The Prince stepped forward, his glowing hands extended. "Yes. I do see it, now that Claire has pointed it out. Lady?"

The Seer joined him, her head cocked to one side. "Yes. Yes it is there. I sense…oh my goodness." She turned to the others, her eyes zeroing in on Claire. "It's Jay. He's in there."

"Well, get him out!" Claire rushed forward, only to find herself hauled back by Joaren, who looped an arm around her waist and held her fast.

"You do not know what kind of magic is at work here," the guardsman stated.

"Let her go," said Ganth mildly. Joaren arched an eyebrow his direction, then complied.

Realizing the man was correct and rushing toward some unknown entity was not the wisest thing to do, Claire approached the area cautiously. Reaching out her hand, she felt a vibration in the air. The sensation was tingling, slightly unpleasant but not painful. She pressed harder, but could not penetrate the barrier.

"Come on, Jay, are you in there?" she whispered, spreading her fingers wide.

With a shimmer the illusion fell and there he was. Jay, Wizard and Protector of the Land, huddled in a small bubble, barely wide enough for him to stretch his arms. He was staring right at her, which made Claire screech and pinwheel backwards, right into Maxt, who caught her, set her on her feet and steadied her in mere seconds. Heart pounding, Claire approached the bubble with the Seer and Prince, their trio of guardsmen taking up station behind them.

"Are you all right?" The Seer spoke loudly.

Jay instantly nodded, proving to them all that the man could hear them. He spoke, but no one on the outside of the bubble could hear his words. When they communicated that, Jay grimaced. His beard was out of control, his hair standing up on end as if he'd run his hand through it for days. Proving her right, Jay reached up and scrubbed a hand over his head, making the pouf of it stand up even more. He patted his stomach.

"Hungry?" guessed the Prince.

Jay nodded, his smile wide underneath his beard. He made the universal sign that he was ok. Claire had to smile at the incongruous picture of the man in wizarding robes giving the circled finger/thumb sign.

Jay turned those piercing blue eyes on her. Claire's smile faltered. He knew her as his parent's clerk. How would he feel about seeing her here, in this adopted Land? Did he know—as the others didn't—that she was not worthy of this place, that her history labeled her as damaged goods?

Jay pulled out his Protector necklace, the red and gold glinting. Claire flinched, figuring he was showing her what she'd never have. Then Jay put his hand over the necklace and bowed to her as best he could in his confined space. Straightening, he winked at her and gave her the thumbs up and gestured at the turtle.

"Yes. Claire has a plan. She brought Quicksilver to cover it with." The Seer laughed at Jay's enthusiastic response as he clapped his approval. "But first we need to see if we can release you from this prison."

They circled the bubble, and suddenly the Seer pointed.

"Look!" She traced a line toward the turtle. "The power is connected to the turtle. I can see the pulse of it …"

"Do I try and sever it?" asked the Prince, already hefting a power orb in one hand.

"No," said the Seer, Maxt and Ganth at the same time. The Prince paused, arching an eyebrow.

"We don't know how that thing will react to your power. It bounced off the turtle without harm," pointed out the Seer. Inside the bubble, Jay was also shaking his head and pointing at his belt of potions, then at the ground around him. Leaning closer, the group could see scorch marks on the earth, as well as on Jay's robes.

"Magic must bounce off the bubble," mused Maxt.

"Built in defenses."

"Yes, Claire. I would say that is correct." Maxt put his finger to his chin, considering.

"If the turtle is supplying the power, then we should encase it with the Quicksilver. Kill the beast and the power will be stopped through natural means." Claire scuffed her toe on the grass as everyone stared at her. "Makes sense to me, anyway. Let me get the Tupperware."

"Wait. You are not going to be the one to do it," Maxt declared, his mind finally catching up and realizing that Claire meant to dump the container on the weather turtle right then and there.

"Of course I am," Claire countered sweetly, scooping up the Tupperware and continuing on her way to the turtle.

"No you are not," Ganth stated, reaching for her arm, then stopping as he realized that if he jerked on her body at all, it might upset the container in her hands.

"One of us should do it." The Prince started to reach for the container, and immediately the Quicksilver inside began to churn, beating against the plastic in a frenzy. Claire quickly pulled it out of his reach. The Prince pulled back and Claire gave him a grim smile.

"I don't think they like Oracles."

"Then let Maxt or Ganth," he told Claire, who shook her head stubbornly, holding up her hand when the men vehemently protested her refusal.

"There's a reason I need to do this." She waited until everyone quieted down. "This kind of bowl has a special seal at the top. I've been opening these things my entire life. But I can guarantee you that the first time you try to open one of these things, you are going to splash the contents all over yourself. Do you really want that to happen?"

There was dead silence. The Seer smiled slightly, Sweetie pressed to her side, her bright blue eyes encouraging Claire. It was nice to see the females had faith in her abilities to conquer the weather turtle.

"No more comments? Excellent. Let me get this over with, I don't know how long the Quicksilver will survive outside the Marshes." Claire walked toward the shell, not even noticing her limp as she continued to favor her leg. The rest of the people pulled back several more feet.

Claire stopped and considered how to do what needed to be done. Finally she knelt down by the Tupperware and carefully eased off the lid, taking every precaution to keep the contents from splashing over the rim of the bowl.

When she peeled off the lid, she could see the gleaming Quicksilver. There was almost a sigh of relief from the crowd as the lid was finally tossed to one side. Eying the turtle, she swallowed, hoping that she had brought enough of the stuff to cover the turtle.

"Only one way to find out for sure." She got to her feet and picked up the open tub, standing slowly and carefully.

Stretching her arm out as far as possible, Claire got ready to bolt and then tipped the contents of the tub over the top of the turtle.

The Quicksilver streamed down toward the shell. It spread over the top like icing over a cake, dripping over the sides to the Meadows ground with nary a splash or spilled drop. It seemed to seep under the turtle as well. Claire finished pouring the organism over the turtle and stepped back quickly as the stuff continued to spread and cover the entire surface of the creature.

Within seconds, the weather turtle was completely covered by a thin shield of silver. It gave a shudder and hitched several times, then was still.

Everyone held their breath. The silvery surface hardened and solidified. Now, instead of a brown rock, they had a silvery boulder, perfectly smooth. It looked like nothing more than a huge, foil-covered piece of candy smack dab in the middle of the Meadows.

The air around Jay wavered and appeared to solidify into particles of dust, which fell to the ground in a gentle puff. Jay fell to his knees, gulping in the air.

Instantly he was surrounded, but he quickly waved them off. "Just need…to breathe…fresh air…"

Within moments he was recovered and sitting on a rock several yards from the silver-covered turtle.

"At least we know the creature is dead," said the Seer, helping Jay take a long drink from a wine skein. "What happened to you, Jay? How did it capture you like that?"

"I left Convergence shortly after the blizzard struck," said Jay, gratefully accepting a hunk of bread and cheese from Joaren. "I followed the path of the storms the best I could, I was fortunate enough to see the turtle loose one into the winds. So I sent out a pigeon then tried to work some magic on the beast. First powder I tossed had me encased in that bubble. I barely had a moment to give some sort of shout out before I was unable to penetrate the damned thing. And there I sat, helpless, watching the beast beget storm after storm after storm…"

Jay's voice trailed off and he munched on some bread.

"You tried to escape," ventured the Seer, one finger lightly touching a scorch mark on his robing.

"Tried and failed," said Jay. "So have you caught the man yet?"

Everyone halted. When Maxt finally spoke, his voice was harsh.

"What man?"

"The tall one, with the blond hair? Looks freakishly like Ben? I tell you the first time I saw him, I thought it *was* Ben. But clearly, not." Jay looked around at them. "Wait a minute. You guys don't know anything about that man, do you?"

The Seer filled him in on what little they did know, then asked if Jay could explain what he knew.

"He came two or three times, to check on the turtle. He knew I was here immediately. Laughed at me, called me the Protector-in-a-bubble. Said it was a shame he couldn't release me, since that would necessitate killing his pet, but once the purpose was served, he'd come for me, and take me to his master." Jay swallowed and looked at the horizon a moment, then turned to Maxt. "May I send a pigeon to the Capital City? Let Tona know I am all right?"

"Already done, my friend," said Joaren, clapping Jay on the shoulder. The wizard grunted.

"I'd hate for her to worry about me."

"She will be relieved to know you are safe," said the Seer, patting his arm.

Jay swallowed the cheese he was eating and then stood up, stretching his arms high over his head. "Feels good to do this," he proclaimed, then without warning, turned and swept Claire into his arms. "Good to see you, Claire Jones!"

Disconcerted to be twirled in the grass like a movie star, Claire pushed away from him. Slumping her shoulders she scowled at the ground. "Good to see you, too."

"Yeah, you like me," he replied, slugging her shoulder lightly. "You know you do."

He slung his arm around her shoulders and turned back to the Prince and Seer, discussing the past few weeks. Claire felt flushed by his casual embrace; it was beyond the norm for her to be standing there with someone—especially someone she knew was engaged—who had his arm around her. Even now his thumb was rubbing her shoulder in a casual way. Claire kept her head ducked, but glanced at Ganth from under the cover of her bangs. He was chatting with Maxt and Joaren over by the silver-encased weather turtle. He looked her way now and then but didn't seem to find anything wrong with Jay's casual embrace.

"This makes you uncomfortable, doesn't it?"

Jay's voice, whispered into her ear, had Claire shrinking into herself. "A little."

"Come walk with me."

Jay took her hand and led her into the fragrant grasses of the Meadows. When they were far enough away for the wizard's liking, he simply sank to the ground. "Pull up a patch of grass, Claire."

Claire lowered herself to the ground, sitting cross legged opposite Jay. His face was open and honest, his eyes twinkling in the sunlight. "You're a bit overwhelmed by all this, aren't you?"

"Yeah." When he didn't speak, simply stared at her, she continued into the silence, "Well, I'm not your normal Protector type, you know? I can't help but think that it was all...I dunno..."

"A mistake?"

"Yeah," she repeated, miserable. "I think that shout out you gave was to the Protectors, and because I happened to be standing by the Tree at the time..."

Jay shook his head. "You are here because the Land chose you to come. Was it in response to my call? Maybe. Was it because you are a Protector of the Land? Definitely. Maybe you came too early, maybe you came too late. The important thing is that you came here, and you kicked some serious ass." He leaned closer, covering her hand with his. "Don't minimize what you did here, Claire. You figured out how to disable that creature. You saved lives."

"I did." Claire sat with Jay in the sunshine and allowed that to sink it. Damn, it was a good sensation, this notion that she'd done well for the people of the Land.

"May I ask a question? One that has nothing to do with the Land or Protectors?" When Claire nodded, Jay continued, "How are my parents? I mean really, how are they? They write me letters, and I hear from the Protectors but...I just need to know."

Claire swallowed. She understood what Jay was asking her. He wanted to know that his sacrifice, his decision to stay in the Land, hadn't harmed the people who loved him the most. Claire thought about it; she didn't want to minimize his question with a flip answer. Jay waited patiently, his eyes steady on her.

"I would say they are well. Healthy and happy," started Claire slowly, then gaining speed. "I mean, they aren't pining for you or anything. I'm not going to say that Emma doesn't cry on occasion—" Jay grimaced at that, "—but it is a good kind of cry. The I-miss-you-but-I-know-it's-for-the-best kind of cry. And the Protectors, they love your parents. They really look after them, and take care of them, and make sure that they know what's happening here in the Land. I mean, without terrifying them or anything. They're good, Jay. Extremely proud of you, and doing good."

Jay let out his breath in a long gush, nodding. "Good. That's...good." He stood up and held out his hand to Claire. "Let's go back and see what's next on the menu." As they strolled back to the turtle, Jay glanced at Claire.

"So...Ganth?"

She slugged him in the arm, hard.

Back at the turtle, they found Maxt assigning men to stay behind to watch the creature. After assigning the men to the task, he turned toward Claire, who was again standing with the Prince and Seer, Sweetie and Ganth, still holding hands with Jay. "I guess its time for you to go, then," he told her with real regret, "now that your quest is completed."

"Is there a Land Tree anywhere?" asked Claire. The Seer pointed. "That one."

Claire glanced at the scrawny little bush. "I don't see it in gold and red. I wonder if that means it didn't work? Is the turtle still alive, do you think?"

The Seer tilted her head to one side, and then looked at Sweetie, who was now cavorting over the Meadows, picking flowers and talking to herself. "Sweetie seems much more relaxed now," she observed, and then called out to the little girl. "What is happening with the weather turtle, Sweetie?" she asked when the small Seer had scampered over.

"All gone," Sweetie declared immediately. "No more farts or burps. 'Cept by Maxt." Then she dashed off, chasing a purple and gold butterfly.

"Well, then, that sums that up," the Seer laughed. "No more farts or burps."

"We will keep watch, just the same." The edges of Maxt's lips were twitching to keep from laughing aloud.

"I guess I'm along for the ride a little while longer, then," Claire said slowly. What else was she supposed to do? Expected to do?

The Prince, sensing Claire's uneasiness, put his hand on her shoulder. "I would not worry. Perhaps all the recent Travel back and forth has put things out of line for a moment. When the Land and World are ready, the switch will be made."

Claire nodded, and then cast a sideways glance in Ganth's direction. Who was she to argue, after all? More time in the Land meant more time with Ganth. And with Sweetie, the Seer, Maxt and the Prince. What wasn't to like about that?

After watching the turtle for an entire day, which proved to be dead as a doornail and did not burp or fart anything, the group decided to head back to the Beaches, leaving three men behind to keep watch on the turtle and report any strange activity by carrier pigeon. The group did not rush things, taking their time. Maxt did not want to push it with the Seer and Sweetie tagging along with them, and Jay was still recovering from his time in the bubble. Ganth sent ahead one of his men, telling him to explain what happened to the camps so there was no worry about their delay.

For Claire, the two-day trek was a joy. She was with people whom she enjoyed and was able to shed the Jones persona completely. In her comfortable jeans and t-shirts, she was Claire, able to laugh and joke and tease the men more, especially Ganth. She and Sweetie wove daisy chains for the men, giggling as they adorned the manly men with the delicate flower rings.

As for Ganth, well, Claire discovered the joys of hiding behind the hills and kissing him into recklessness. At night, by the campfire, no one looked askance at them when Ganth pulled Claire close next to him, his arm around her shoulders. On the second day, he held her hand for long periods of time, simply enjoying being in her company. It was, to Claire, a glorious experience, one that she would have written about in a journal if she were the kind of girl who kept such a diary. So she concentrated on just enjoying her time in the Land now that danger had passed.

~ 2 9 ~

▼

THE SEED ONCE PLANTED

Orli came down the back stairs of the Orchard House, moving quietly and quickly. When he came into the kitchen, he found it dark and empty, save for Amber, who sat in a chair drinking a cup of tea. The fairy looked great, and given her highly intoxicated state earlier in the day, Orli found that to be remarkable. He hesitated on the bottom stair.

Amber noticed him anyway, and gave him a sunny smile. "Come on in." She waved him forward. "You're up late."

"I do not have much time here," Orli said, and then felt stupid, since of course Amber knew that already. "And my internal clock is confused anyway. I do not know if it is day or night back home, to be honest."

"Hmmmm." Amber took a sip, her gray eyes fastened on him over the rim of her tea mug. "Sit down, have some tea."

Orli folded himself into a chair, staring around him. It was all so amazing, this World Dimension. He'd seen a box that showed moving pictures, a machine that washed dishes automatically, even a wagon that needed no ox to pull it. Fascinating stuff, really.

"You've had a busy day," Amber observed, as if reading his mind. "There is so much to see in the World, and you've barely scratched the surface."

Orli nodded then gave a wry grin, ducking his head. "Nothing compares to Kat, though."

"Babies are indeed the most marvelous and amazing of all the creatures," Amber agreed, and then shocked him by adding, "I was the fairy present at your birth in the Land, you know."

"Really?" Orli's dark eyebrows rose dramatically.

Amber nodded. "A glorious birth it was, too. I've often wondered if you were touched by fate that day, given my strong ties to the World Dimension. Wondered if those ties affected you somehow to make the choices you did, to come to this place in your life." Amber was thoughtful as she stared out the darkened kitchen window.

"I would be glad for that if it were true," Orli replied honestly. "I would not want my life to be any different. I feel a contentment deep in my being."

"Despite the separations?"

"Despite everything."

"She'll be able to travel to the Land, you know."

"Kat?" Orli's eyes lit up.

"Yes. She has ties to both dimensions, so she has that capability. When Tracy visits, so can your daughter."

"Thank you. I had wondered about that, and worried, and was afraid to ask. I am grateful that I will get to be a part of her life. I am blessed."

"You won't say that when you hit the teenage years, I'm afraid," Amber said, laughter sparking her eyes.

They were silent for a long while, each drinking their tea. Then Amber leaned forward. "Would you do something for me, Orli?" Her gaze intense.

"Anything."

Amber reached into her shirt pocket and withdrew an oblong object. It was roughly the size of her thumb, and was glowing like a pearl. The opaque surface was luminescent in a soft, peaceful sort of way. She handed it to Orli, who held out his hand to accept it.

The rock—or whatever it was—felt smooth and cool to the touch, but there was an odd pulsing feeling emanating from deep within its core. Orli looked up at Amber with questioning brown eyes.

"What is it?" he asked her, turning it over in his hand.

"That, Orli, is my last fairy clutch. A seed, as it were." Amber laughed as Orli flinched, almost dropping the seed in the process. "It's fairly indestructible. I daresay you could sit on it and it would not be the worse for wear."

"What am I to do with it?"

"Take it back with you. Plant it deep in the soil as close to the Cave of Souls as you can, but not in the Mountain Village valley. No one must see you do this act, nor can you tell anyone I have given you this seed."

"Why me?" Orli asked her. "Surely Ben would have been more than willing to do this for you, and he has closer ties to you than me." Orli felt the deed sounded almost, well, intimate. Planting a seed that would grow into a fairy clutch was beyond anything Orli could ken.

Amber shook her head vehemently. "It has to Travel to the Land with someone from the Land. As a Land fairy, it has to be that way. And the way I look at it, what are the chances of me getting someone else from the Land here? So you are my hope, Orli. If you agree to do this, that is."

"Of course I agree." He tucked the seed egg into his pocket. "I am honored to be of service to the fairy guild."

"So pretty," Amber sighed, and then laughed merrily at his somewhat discomforted expression. "Oh, don't worry. I'm way too old for you," she said with barely suppressed laughter.

From upstairs came the sound of a newborn crying. Orli drained his mug and put it on the table, standing. "That is my call," he told Amber, heading for the stairs. He sighed. "I only have a few more hours."

"Then make the most of them, Orli dearest. Go be with your wife and child," Amber replied and the man nodded, continuing up the stairs.

Amber leaned her chin on her hand, watching his tall, lean form ascend the stairs. Halfway up, he turned around to see the fairy sitting at the table, tears rolling down her face. He almost came back down but she waved him up. "Happy tears," she assured Orli.

Later in the night, he sat in the darkness of the room and watched his wife nurse their child, Amber walked in and put her hand on Orli's shoulder. "It's time."

Ben and Katie accompanied Orli on his trek to the Tree. As they approached the spot, they spied the solitary form of Zach, waiting beneath the boughs of the Tree. He clutched the letter from Liz in one hand.

Katie turned to Orli, smiling at him. "I'm so glad to have seen you again. We barely talked when I was in the Mountain Village, I know, but you seem so familiar to me. I hope I haven't acted too forward with you, but you seem like one of us."

Orli enfolded the smaller woman in a warm hug. "The feeling is likewise, Katie. I feel as though I know you as well. And seeing you again, well, it just makes everything so clear to me. How loving and caring you are, how much you look after your Protectors. They are lucky to have you."

"Tracy and Kat are just as lucky to have you," Katie declared, giving his waist a firm squeeze before releasing him.

Ben and Orli exchanged the traditional Land handshake, forearm to forearm, then Ben muttered "Ah, hell," and hugged Orli fiercely.

Zach repeated the gesture, and the embrace, thumping Orli on the back hard enough to make his eyes water.

"It was good to see you, man. We'll take care of Tracy and the baby. I promise."

"I have no doubt." Orli hesitated, finally looking Zach squarely in the eye. "I know that you are upset with Liz, and I do not presume to understand all of what is happening between the two of you. Yet, I will tell you this, do not deny love because of pride. It is never worth it in the end."

"Sound advice," Zach said evenly, but Orli could not tell in the gloom of the night if his expression was one of irritation or acceptance.

Orli gave a salute and turned to the Tree. He walked up to it and placed his hand on the trunk. It took a few seconds, but then, slowly, he started to collapse upon himself until he was gone with a small *snick*.

Zach watched Orli disappear and waited for Liz's familiar, lean form to appear. Several minutes passed while he waited, every muscle taut.

Katie sighed. "I wonder how long do we have to wait until Liz comes home?"

"I really don't know," replied the Sea Dimension man with a philosophical shrug.

Katie glanced Zach's way. "Why don't we leave, then. That way Zach can greet Liz on his own."

Zach gave her a grateful look. Ben tilted his head at Zach. "I'd tell you to remember that all Protectors are under our care," he said in a somewhat stiff voice, "but I know that your love for Liz will outweigh your irritation in the end."

Hard pressed to keep sarcasm from flavoring his words, Zach glowered at his friends. "I'm so glad you're all concerned for Liz. But do you think you can spare some consideration for me as well?"

Katie put her arm around his waist, leaning her head against his arm. "You'll do the right thing. For both of you. We'll be here to support your decision, whichever way it goes." Then she and Ben melted into the night.

Zach prowled around the base of the Tree, his jaw tightly clenched. He glanced at the paper in his hand, but he knew the contents of the short letter by heart.

Dearest, beloved Zach. I don't have much time, but I must ask your indulgence as I go to the Land to speak with the Seer. I know you don't think such things are necessary, but I cannot ask you to share your life with me if I'm going to be ripped from your side to do my duty in the Land. When I return, I want us to talk, seriously talk and discuss the situation. It's my hope we can find a way to compromise and agree, because I want nothing more in life than to be with you, at your side, as your wife.

I am forever yours,

Liz

Zach was anxious to see Liz again, to learn what had happened with the Seer of the Land. The anger he felt at Liz's leaving without telling him warred with concern for her safety. The two emotions swirled in his stomach, creating a pit of fire that threatened to set his heart ablaze.

As he paced, his eyes on the ground, he felt the air around him shimmer and coalesce, then felt a sense of pure peace descending over him, drenching the heat of his distress. He closed his eyes in silent benediction and then turned to face Liz, who was standing before him, dressed in her usual flowing dress, an uncertain look on her serene face.

"You smell like the Land," Zach blurted without thinking, making her smile.

"I guess I do." She sighed. "It was nice going on my own terms and returning on my own terms. I think I really needed to do that, Zach."

"Are things settled?" he asked her intently, his gold-sparked gaze piercing her.

"Settled enough to satisfy me. The Seer feels that Sweetie is strong enough, smart enough and quick enough to handle being a Seer should the need arise. Of course, if it happens within the next few years, the child may need some help, but the Seer feels that between me visiting occasionally and the Prince's guidance, a full time replacement would not be necessary."

The tension continued to drain from him, his shoulders relaxing inch by inch. "So, you are no longer her Heir Apparent?"

"Actually, I still am," Liz said softly, pausing before rushing on. "I told the Seer that if it would take the pressure off Sweetie, keep her out of the target zone, so to speak, I would be glad to be known as her Heir Apparent. I have all of you guys protecting me, after all. Sweetie is still a child and therefore more vulnerable. So, for everyone else, including the Protectors at this time, I'm still to be considered the Heir Apparent."

Zach mulled over her words, turning them over in his mind, examining them from every angle. It was, he decided, no different than the decision he would have made had he been in Liz's shoes. "I'd expect no less from you, Liz. Protecting Sweetie is important to all of us."

They were quiet for a long time. Liz brushed at the floor of the orchard, not looking at him as she strived for a casual tone of voice. "What about us, Zach? Are we settled? Or are we done?"

"Done?" Zach's brow furrowed. "I could never be done with you, Liz. It would not be physically or emotionally possible for me to be done with you, to be honest."

Liz gave him a tremulous smile. "It's just that…you were giving everything you are to me, with an open heart and future. I couldn't do the same in return because a part of me belongs to the Land, and that part could go there at any moment. It didn't seem fair to base our lives together on the premise that something, anything, is more important than the two of us." She ran a hand over her eyes, and Zach could see that hand was shaking violently with emotion.

He stepped closer to Liz, tilting her face up to look at his. "Hey," he said softly, "I know about the Land. It's a part of me as well. I went into this relationship with my eyes open with full knowledge that you could be sent to the Land in an instant. Part of the reason I fell in love with you is because I know you would answer that call in a heartbeat and give them your everything. Don't ever try to make it into an issue of whether you love the Land or me more. I'm a big boy. I can see the big picture here. I love you for all that you are, including the Land. If you love me, then you love the part of me that will always and forever dwell in the Meadows Region and with Sweetie."

He shrugged one large shoulder eloquently. "It's a part of both of us, Liz. It just hurt that you couldn't be honest with me about going back."

"I knew you'd be upset. I wanted to be able to come to you with some answers about my future." She reached up and brushed a lock of hair from his eyes, searching them with her own. "You need to know something, Zach. I had a vision once. Of me leaving the World Dimension."

"When did you have this vision?"

"The winter before your quest."

"You were leaving the World?"

"Yes, and I had a wedding band on. That scared me terribly. It still does. But if I am Heir Apparent only until Sweetie is of age…I can handle that kind of separation."

"So can I. Listen, baby. You and I both know the future is constantly in motion. We can't be sure what you saw will ever come to pass. Nothing is sure in the future of a Protector but Evil and the Land." Zach laughed, then turned serious. He put his hand over her Protector necklace. "This is about the Land, and our status there. It's important to us in ways that most people could never comprehend, not in this lifetime." He reached into his jeans pocket and pulled out a ring with a diamond on it so large that Liz couldn't help but ogle it. She watched, dumbfounded and unresisting as he put it on her ring finger.

"This…" Zach said, closing his fingers around the hand he'd just put the ring on and pulling it close to his heart. "This is about us. No one can tell me that we aren't meant to be together, whether it be in the Land or here, or apart for some period of time."

Liz reached up and kissed him, long and lovingly. Then she nestled against his chest and closed her eyes. "It's perfect that it happened here, Zach. Beneath this Tree. On this day."

"This is the way it was meant to happen," Zach agreed, breathing in the clean, clear scent of the Land from her hair.

~ 30 ~

▼

EVIL TIDES

Claire stalked Ganth around the jousting circle, the pole held loosely in her hands before her. Ganth had stripped to the waist a few moments earlier, and she was trying hard not to be distracted by all that tan, male flesh. He was wearing her gold and red bead around his neck, and she couldn't help but notice that his hair was almost the same color as the deep red of the enameled bead. Weren't redheads supposed to be prone to sunburns? She had to react quickly to whack the pole that was arching toward her head.

"Pay attention," Ganth told her in a teasing voice. Claire narrowed her eyes at him. He'd stripped to distract her. *Two could play at that game.*

"Time out," Claire called, and set her pole down. Casually, she reached for the hem of her loose ivory shirt, pulling it over her head and tying the sleeves around her waist in a leisurely fashion. Underneath, she was wearing a white tank top over her Worlder bra. She knew she'd hit her mark when Ganth's eyes glazed over at the sight, and he wasn't looking at her pretty new golden and ruby Protector necklace as it lay against the white material. When the Prince had given her the necklace, she'd given the one her mother wore to Ganth. It had seemed the right thing to do.

Claire picked up her jousting pole, making sure her profile was on full display for the man. When she faced him again, the look of pure lust on his face was worth it. Then his expression cleared, and he gave her an assessing glare that told her he was onto her trick.

"You are a cruel, cruel woman." Ganth shook his head, his eyes never leaving her form.

"Any advantage I can get," Claire tossed the pole up and down in one hand.

They engaged again, the poles clacking and whacking as they whirled and pivoted. Claire could tell that Ganth was holding back and it infuriated her to no end. She pressed forward, intent on giving him a real run for his money. He parried easily, but was beginning to breathe harder.

Good.

Ganth pivoted, and as he passed by her, reached out and tugged on the shirt tied around her waist. The material loosened and the ocean breeze tore it from her waist.

"No fair!" Claire protested, brandishing her pole at Ganth, but her voice was full of laughter. "That wasn't nice at all!"

"Better get your shirt." Ganth nearly doubled over with laughter of his own.

Claire scowled at him, then jogged down the beach, where her shirt was dancing on the sand. She planted one end of her pole on the sand and then bent over to scoop up the shirt. As she did, all sound around her ceased, as if a window had been closed on the world. She could no longer hear the men in the practice area, or the sound of laughter from the camp, not even the sound of the wind as it snapped through the tents and flags.

Also gone were all the smells. She couldn't smell the smoke of the campfires or even the brine of the salt laden breeze. Claire stood slowly, all the hairs on her forearms rising in sudden fear.

Standing before her, the heels of his feet kissed by the incoming surf, was a tall blond man. He wore his hair in a long queue trailing down his back. His eyes reflected the color of the sea behind him, and his bare feet were very long and narrow. This close, he looked like he might be older than Ben Harm, but who knew how the Sea Dimension people aged, anyway?

Claire swallowed and looked back toward Ganth.

It seemed the entire camp stood about twenty yards away, behind some kind of clear barrier. Ganth stood next to the Prince, Maxt and the Seer, who watched the two inside the bubble intently. Jay was already working some incantation, his hands a blur by his belt as he unhooked and poured ingredients into a vial suspended in midair.

She knew his efforts would be futile. She was in the same kind of bubble that had encased Jay back by the weather turtle, and until the power was turned off, she was stuck in here with…him.

Claire looked back at the man and swallowed. This was going to be up to her, at least in the short run. The man walked toward her, a smile on his handsome face. Claire brought her jousting stick up in front of her in a reflexive motion, ready to defend herself.

The man stopped, holding out his hands in front of him. "Easy there, Little John," he told her with a grin. "I've been waiting for a chance to talk with you."

"What's with the cone of silence?" Claire asked him suspiciously.

"Well, I couldn't very well go strolling into camp and sit down by you at dinnertime." The man's toothpaste ad smile didn't fool Claire one bit. "This way, we have some uninterrupted quality time. Just you and me."

"Why? I cannot imagine that we have anything to say to one another. In any dimension."

"I was rather impressed with your dispatching of the weather turtle," the Sea Dimension man said, ignoring her statement. "Very ingenious of you, using Quicksilver. I had not thought of that kind of attack when I brought the pet from my world here."

"The weather turtle was from the Sea Dimension?" Claire blurted, incredulous.

The Sea Dimension man nodded thoughtfully, rubbing his bare chin. "They're all over the oceans of my home. When they emit the gas, in my world it floats harmlessly away. Well, some people thought they might assist with the tides, but I never agreed with that assessment. Imagine my surprise when it had such a different reaction here. You never know what will happen when you take a creature from its indigenous locale."

"So, the weather turtle wasn't a planned attack? It was an experiment?" Claire's eyebrows rose almost to her hairline.

"I have a question for you," he said, displaying that bad habit of ignoring her questions in favor of his own. "How on earth did you hide those glorious beauties from the people of this Land? Are they really that stupid?"

He was staring with frank and open appreciation at her chest. Claire fought to keep from trying to cover herself up. The asshole was just trying to mess with her, she knew that in her core. It wasn't like she hadn't met his type of bully before in the foster care system. He just wanted to throw her off guard, to make her feel uneasy. No way.

They were silent for a long moment, until the man shrugged. "Well, I am glad to see you are not binding them down any longer, Claire. Your ampleness is rather appealing in a basic fashion. Your workout regime here has made your waist so much more tiny in comparison. Yes. You are doing well, I can see that."

"Somehow, I doubt you came out here to discuss my choice in bras or work out," Claire told him in a forthright tone. "So why don't you just get on with it."

"Your temper is your downfall. And your greatest strength. We've had our eye on you for a long time Claire. A very long time."

"We?" A frisson of cold sliced through her stomach.

"My brethren and I, of course. We had quite a battle to see who would be the one to recruit you. Lucky me."

"Why?"

"We have our own kind of Seers, you know," the man said confidently. "We have forecast the future and have seen your two destinies clearly."

"Two destinies," Claire repeated, somewhat dumbly.

"In one, you go back to the World, where you eek out a meager living, becoming more and more bitter with each passing year. It's a life, but it is a dull, meaningless life, Claire. You deserve so much more than a life of loneliness and hand-to-mouth existing."

He was watching Claire intently, reading her expression. What he saw on her face had him shaking his head. "Claire, Claire. Did you honestly think that the Protectors will want to take care of a sullen, rebellious teenager? Someone like you? Be honest with yourself, Claire. You know the score. They'll leave you behind because you do not fit in their white bread world of Protectordom. You weren't even supposed to travel to the Land, surely you know that!"

Claire heard a peculiar buzzing in her brain. He was right to some extent. What did she have in common with the other Protectors? They were older, wiser, and well…normal. She was the solitary freak of the group. And Sweetie herself had said over and over that she wasn't supposed to be in the Land. In her heart of hearts, Claire knew she hadn't been destined to be a Protector. No matter what Jay had told her, she was not the norm when it came to Quests. And now this man was proving her inner most held secret true.

"You don't think I'm a real Protector." Her voice low, barely heard even in the vacuum of their bubble.

The man smiled, one side of his mouth curling up in a crooked, appealing grin. "You know you aren't. I brought you here. I made it happen."

"The ferrets?" The pieces of the puzzle were there, floating in space in front of her, and Claire struggled to put them together in a cohesive way.

"Mine."

"So you pushed me at the Protectors in the hopes of what? I'd lead you to them?" Fear made sweat drip down her back. She'd never forgive herself if she'd brought Evil to the doorsteps of the Orchard.

The man scuffed at the sand with his toes. "No. No, that was not the intent."

"But I never would have gone to them, never would have come here, if not for those animals attacking me."

"A miscalculation on our part. We had no idea that you were so close to those damned people. How did that get overlooked?" For a brief moment, there was a crack in the man's armor, a glimpse of the frustration simmering under his suave surface. It was gone so quickly that Claire wondered if she'd imagined it. One hand slashed in front of him. "No matter. You are here, and I adjusted. And here we are, as we were meant to be."

"What would have happened back in the World Dimension, with the ferrets, if I hadn't escaped them? What was your plan for me?"

"They were to hold you there until I arrived."

"Stupid. If you'd come alone, without the furry vanguard, I may have listened to you. But those beasts were out to harm me, I could tell."

"Only because they scented the Protectors upon your soul. Very intuitive creatures, my ferret friends. They have been bred, so to speak, to abhor anything to do with the Land, and any who help her. It was an unfortunate matter of instinct overtaking good sense."

A tapping noise came from the side. Both the man and Claire glanced over to see Jay diligently moving his hand over the outside of the bubble, a blue glow emanating from his palm.

"Yeah, I don't think so," sneered the Sea Dimension man. He threw his hand out, as if tossing something at Jay. Instantly the Protector was flung across the beach, bowling over several guardsmen who were watching, a flume of sand marking his path. Claire took several steps forward, tamping down the cry in her throat. With relief she watched Jay gain his feet, brushing off Joaren's help. With an angry twitch of his hands the wizard set his robes aright and returned to the bubble's side. The Sea Dimension shook a finger at the Protector as if chiding a naughty child.

"Leave him alone!"

He turned to her, amusement sparking his aqua eyes. "Such fierceness. Ah, I have such hope for you, Claire. Such hope. Such plans. You will come with me, of course, and take your place. This little side trip to the Land will be forgotten."

"No, I won't go with you like some stupid dog at your beck and call. I belong with them now. I'm a Protector of the Land."

"Nonsense. You aren't a part of them. You know you can only rely on yourself. You've known that for years." The man circled around her, continuing to speak in a low, reasonable, pleasant voice. Claire felt immobile, the jousting pole held lightly in her hands. "You are meant to be alone in the

World Dimension, Claire. This little bit of freedom, togetherness, feeling of being a part of the group, it is transient. It won't last when you are banished from the Land. You know that. It's one of the reasons why you haven't fought staying here, haven't questioned why you are not being sent home."

His words, damn it, had a ring of truth that crashed over her like a wave, bringing all her doubts and fears to the forefront. Claire hadn't been pressing to go home. She relished every second here in the Land. She was accepted by the guardsmen. She was afraid if she went back to the World now, it would all be gone. She'd be alone again, condemned to live her life hoping Emma told her something about the Protectors, to offer her some crumb of information. No. She'd cut those ties as ruthlessly as possible. Why suffer? She'd have to move far, far away.

The Sea Dimension man had stopped talking and watched her closely, minutely even. Claire could not meet his eyes.

"You said there was another path. The one you want me to take with you. If I go with you, what is in that other future?" Her voice was not even her own, it seemed.

He smiled. "If you come with me, work with me, then you have a future of being a part of a big picture, of doing things that matter. You would never, ever be alone, Claire."

"You want me to work for you. Work for Evil. Why do you think I would do that?"

He shrugged. "Look at your past. Look at your soul. You have such capacity for emotion." He ignored her snort of disbelief. "You may act like the sullen teenager, but you have depths, Claire. Given the right stimulus, you could be brimming with anger and temper and passion. You are on the very verge of greatness, Claire." He was behind her, leaning into her, whispering into her ear.

"You're one of us, Claire. And deep down inside, you know it."

Oh, God, what if what he said was true? Tears began to brim in her eyes, and she dashed them away with one hand. "No. That's not the way I have to be."

"It's the way you are," he insisted, his honeyed words winding through her brain. "It's who you are. You've had to fight your entire life, and it is your nature. Fight and get ahead before others can drag you down." The heat from his body radiated into her, and his hand on her hip was a caressing motion of comfort. "Don't think you can elevate yourself from the depths, Claire. This is where you are meant to be. With us. Not with them. Not with the shiny people of the universe. You know it."

Claire reached up to wipe another tear from her cheek, and her hand brushed against the Protector necklace dangling from its chain. Her fist closed around it like a lifeline. Her eyes sought Jay's outside the bubble. He, too, was clenching his pendant as if in solidarity. His eyes never wavered from hers, a source of strength. A source of will. "I'm a Protector of the Land," she whispered, almost desperate.

"You are Claire. Destiny is calling you. Which way will you go?" he asked softly. So softly.

Suddenly, Claire understood. The puzzle pieces fit together and the entire picture was laid before her, in all its horror and glory. Her eyes fixated on the horizon, she said dully, "So, I wasn't here to get rid of the weather turtle. That was just a bit of Interdimensional serendipity. This is why I'm here. This choice. It should have been in another Dimension of your choosing, not here, am I right? The ferret attack was so you could get me away from the World, and this was just all a happenstance you could turn to your benefit. This choice is the reason I Traveled."

"This choice. Your choice." He agreed easily.

"Choose Evil or a life alone in the World. Not much of a future for 'ole Claire, is there?" She gave a half laugh. "Not that there ever was much of a future for me before, either." She looked at the man sharply. "What are the plans for me, if I were to join you?"

"Ah. You shall be the mother of a master race, Claire Jones. The queen of my new world, my new people. Together, we can make it happen, and the master will reward us amply." He smiled at her. "You have to have noticed how children flock to you. It's a gift. We would only amplify that ability. Combine that natural maternalness with your fierce warrior nature and…it will be amazing, Claire. That I promise you."

"But…" She was incapable of forming a coherent thought.

"You are on the precipice, Claire, of a great and bright new world. Your essence brought you here, brought you to this now. This choice, this decision, it will give you all that you desire, all that you want. You shall never be alone again."

She uncurled her fist to look at the necklace, gleaming ruby and golden in her hand. She looked over at the Seer, who was gazing at Claire with compassion and unswerving strength.

Emotions careened through her, around her, like a pack of kittens worrying a ball of yarn. Images of the Protectors, the guardsmen, Sweetie and the Seer and Jay. Maxt. Ganth. Everyone and everything that had impacted her life in the past few weeks. And then Harry and Emma, their faces full of worry and care. She tightened her fingers around the pendant, so that the edges of it cut into her palm, leaving a tangible mark of her inner struggle.

"I'm not alone," she said with surprising power. "I'm a Protector of the Land. I will never, ever be alone again."

He narrowed his gaze at her, his words coming as fast as bullets. "So you choose the namby, pamby world of the Protectors, who will turn their backs on you within a few months, and then forget all about you, just like your father did so many years ago. And your stepfather. No one has *ever* stuck by you, Claire. You have an aura of Evil potential about you that is undeniable. The Protectors will leave you high and dry. Mark my words."

"They won't," Claire declared, her confidence restoring with every word. "They would never do that to me."

"Then you are wasting your life. Wasting it on a future that is so disgustingly bleak that you will never ever have what you have right now."

"If it means the Land is safe from people like you, then so be it."

"So, there is another path for us to take, another turn in the road," the Sea Dimension man said in a harsh tone, flinging out one hand. From outside the bubble, a jousting stick flew over the heads of the people watching avidly. As it passed through the barrier he'd erected, a shower of sparks had people scrambling out of the way. The stick landed in his hands. He twirled it expertly.

"Now, why would you waste time fighting little old me if by choosing to go back to the World, I will eventually be an unimportant bystander in the ways of the dimensional wars?" Claire asked him innocently. Then a dark eyebrow arched over her mossy green eyes. "Or is there another future you have not told me about. One that worries you and your buddies back at the Evil farm?"

He said nothing, simply rotated the pole while staring at her steadily. Without warning, he attacked. Claire brought her pole up to meet his with a sudden crack, twisting her bar under his to try and wrest it out of his hands. He twisted back, going the opposite direction, wrenching her wrists. Claire pivoted and danced out of the way, smacking his next blows with ease.

"I detest the rules that force me to handle this in a way that is not conducive to my many skills," said the man, as if almost bored with the process.

They continued to work around the bubble, Claire blocking him and attacking alternatively. He was good, she had to give him that. He knew what he was doing with the jousting pole. But he wasn't as good as Ganth or as Telcor. She'd been taught by the best. Her confidence growing, she watched him for his weaknesses and when she felt she had his technique nailed, started aggressively pushing him back across the sand.

Over and over she whaled at him, her blows becoming harder and harder, faster and faster, more and more deadly. The man stumbled and fell to one knee, then looked at her. To Claire's amazement, he gave her a brilliant smile.

"So blood thirsty. Ready to move in for the kill. You are closer to me than you realize, Claire. You are one blow away from becoming *just like me.*"

Claire was breathing heavily, and her eyes were wild with rage. She stared at him, aghast. He was right. She was ready to bash him across the head. She allowed the pole to lower.

"I choose the Land," she said clearly and distinctly. "I revoke anything Evil that is in my heart and soul. I know I'll have to fight it every day of my life, but I won't let it win."

"Then I'll have to kill you."

The words penetrated Claire's brain slowly. He arched the jousting pole around, catching Claire behind the legs. She fell with a thud, skidding several yards in the sand, her injured knee sending a spasm of pain through her. Spitting out sand, she panted in frustration as he continued to speak.

"You see, Claire, if I let you live after that pretty little declaration, made here in the Land itself, you would go on to become a key player in the whole Good vs. Evil issue here in the Interdimensional Void." His voice was pleasant, which was so odd, given he was going to kill her.

Directly in front of Claire, on the other side of the bubble, was Sweetie, who was watching her with concern and confusion in her innocent blue eyes. Good God, why didn't the Seer get the child out of there? What good could come from Sweetie seeing Claire get her brains bashed in by some Evil dude from the Sea Dimension?

"Of course, I can always incapacitate you and take you to other realms. Yes. We can still have our plan go forward. You don't have to be willing to be in our stable. Certainly others take that route, and Ibith does have success with his girls… yes. That is a good plan. I can't wait for us to get closer, Claire. The role you are to play in Evil's plans…it will be delicious. I've been practicing, you see, practicing and perfecting. I've had some failure along the way but now…now I am ready for my next step."

"What step is that?"

"You will bear the next generation of Evil, Claire."

"No." Horror clawed at her insides.

"Yes. Already the wheels are in motion. A stable is being readied. You will be one of my chosen, one of my favored. I shall have to tutor you in the ways of pleasing a man, of course. I doubt that red-haired oaf has taught you anything of use."

"I'll never be with you," she snarled.

"Time will tell, Claire."

Claire heard a whoosh of air and barely rolled to one side in time to miss the pole as it buried into the sand with the force of his blow. She followed through with the roll, coming to her feet. The Sea Dimension man advanced again. Directly behind him stood Ganth, who was watching, both hands on his hips, his face full of impotent rage. Directly in front of him, just inside the bubble, Claire's eye fell on a sparkle of gold and red.

Her eyes widened. It was a Tree. A tiny little Tree. She whipped her gaze to her opponent, but he seemed oblivious to the Tree. Swallowing heavily, Claire started to circle closer to where the Tree stood.

A little closer. Just a little closer.

With a roar, the Sea Dimension man charged Claire. She waited until he was mere feet away, then, putting all her considerable strength, stepped to the side and used the jousting pole like a baseball bat, swinging down and through, connecting squarely with the man's mid section. It connected with his stomach with a jarring thud, knocking the pole from her hand. Claire didn't care. She raced toward the Tree.

The Sea Dimension man flung his pole at Claire as she passed. It hit her squarely in the sore spot on her leg, where the hail had bruised her so severely days earlier. For the second time, Claire skidded through the sand. When she lifted her head, she was inches from the Tree.

Claire looked up at Ganth. "Goodbye," Claire mouthed to him. His eyes widened and he nodded slowly, putting one hand on the bubble.

Claire reached out and grabbed the Tree. Right before it sucked her in, she looked to see the Sea Dimension man racing for the ocean. He dove cleanly into the water, making his escape, just as Claire was pulled into the Void.

~ Epilogue ~

▼

Zach came out to the porch in the early morning to find Claire standing at the railing, looking out over the Orchards. One hand pulling on her Protector necklace, toying with the pendant that shone a dull silver in the morning light.

They'd let Claire be since her return from the Land a few days ago. Left her alone, but always kept someone nearby. They did not want Claire to think she was on her own. Abandoned. Berift.

"Morning, sugar."

"Morning, Zach," Claire said over her shoulder. They were quiet for a long time. Then, she sighed. "Was it this hard for you? Adjusting to being back in the World Dimension, I mean?"

"Kind of. But I had a lot of physical healing to get through. Being almost blown up had its down sides for the return to the World. And honestly, Liz was here. That made it easier for me."

Claire had not talked willingly about her feelings on returning in such an abrupt fashion since the first night she had come back, spilling her tale of turtles, Sea Dimension men and choices. She knew the others wanted more information but quite honestly, didn't have the ability to give it to them. There had been enough witnesses on the beach who would send them the story. Claire looked back over the courtyard. "You were lucky," she whispered. "To have found her, I mean. Liz. Very lucky."

Zach walked up behind Claire and slipped his arms around her waist, leaning his chin on her head. To her credit, the girl didn't flinch or try and pull away. Zach had a feeling the old Claire would have had him flat on his back with a bloody nose by now. The new Claire simply leaned against him, grateful. "Nothing is easy in this world," he told her softly. "All you can do is hope that you make the right choices and hook up with the right friends."

"The right friends. I don't think I have any problems there, do I?"

The screen door opened with a bang, and Liz walked out onto the porch. "Horning in on my guy?" She joked with Claire, who rolled her eyes at the taller woman.

"Yeah, he's chucking you over for me and all my obvious glamour and charm," she joked right back. Liz stared at her for a moment, then laughed merrily, smacking Claire on the shoulder smartly. Zach reached out and grabbed Liz's hair, tugging a curl playfully.

"I wasn't supposed to go to the Land." The words blurted out before she could stop them. "I was meant to go with Evil. He said I was like them. That I didn't belong here. Part of me wonders if what he said was true."

Liz and Zach were quiet for several long moments. Claire was glad for it; she appreciated they were thinking about her words, considering them, rather than spouting off some sort of platitude meant to comfort her.

"Here's what I think," said Liz finally, leaning against the railing of the porch. "Sure, you could have been seduced by Evil. We all could have been seduced by Evil at some point in our lives. The fact is, you weren't. You chose to help the Land. You chose to make a difference."

"You chose not to go with the Sea Dimension guy when he tried to jack you off the beach." Zach touched his nose and then pointed the finger at her. "That doesn't seem like the actions of someone Evil, does it?"

"No. But…"

"But nothing." Liz interrupted her firmly. "You were called. You went. You did what needed to be done. And now you are here. You were given the chance to go with Evil and you didn't. That's all that matters in the end."

"You sound so sure of yourselves." Claire's hands dug into her back pockets. "I wish I could be. I just have this feeling that I'm not done with the situation…"

"None of us are," said Zach, reaching over to link hands with Liz.

The Seer continued his line of thought. "I could get called back to the Land at any moment. You didn't have a counterpart in the Land, at least not that we know of. Who knows? You may still have another adventure to tackle with the Land."

"One that includes interaction with a certain tall, red-headed guardsman?" Zach's voice sounded oh-so-innocent.

Claire blushed to the roots of his hair. "Yeah, well. I'm too young for that kind of romance."

"Then let it rest for now," agreed Liz. "And let your life unfold. There are repercussions for all the choices we make. Time will tell if you made the right one. Although I'm certain you did."

From the guest house several yards away came the blaring sound of Euro-tech music. "Ah, Ben is up." Zach stepped back, rubbing his hands together lightly. "This ought to be good."

"What have you done?" This came from Katie, who slipped out onto the porch, cradling a cup of tea.

"Just listen," Zach advised with a waggle of his eyebrows.

The music suddenly segued into a fast paced swing dance beat. "That's more like it," Zach said, pulling Liz out to the courtyard and starting an impromptu dance party. A bellow of rage came from the guest house as Ben tried unsuccessfully to turn the music off.

A window crashed open upstairs and Claire could hear Sarat yelling out to Zach to wait for her to get dressed, which had Zach leering at the window, giving a low wolf whistle.

Steven came out, stretching, Sasha and William following him. The couple was arguing over something silly, but as they walked off the porch, the doctor twirled her in time to the dance music. Sasha gave William a resounding kiss that had everyone applauding.

Ben came charging out of his house, his face set in mutinous lines. "Not now, Harm, I'm dancing," Zach yelled at him casually.

"When is it my turn?" Amber called out from over by the barn. Zach reached out with his other hand and was soon twirling both women around the yard while Ben scolded him like a schoolboy.

From upstairs came a newborn cry, followed by Tracy's yell out the window for everyone to keep it down. Nobody listened.

Claire took it all in with a wide grin on her face. "Yeah, I made the right choice," she said to nobody in particular.

-THE END-